DESPERATE FLIGHT

Sophie stirred, puzzled by her unfamiliar surroundings. Then she remembered. Her clothes were damp and she felt heavy, useless, and frightened. She turned her head to discover William was watching her.

"You are very beautiful when you sleep," he remarked, leaning over to kiss her, and grimaced with pain.

"It's all right," he said at her alarm. He held up his blistered hands for her inspection. "The real problem is these."

Sophie exclaimed in horror and, with tears running down her cheeks, cradled his poor raw hands in her own. What could they do? Here they were, trapped in a barn, without food, with little money and forged papers. If it all went wrong, what then? She shuddered and buried her face in her hands.

"Listen to me." William spoke with an angry determination she had never heard before. "I have known you many things, weak, foolish, unfair even, but never a coward. Never! Remember Héloïse and how she smiled at us as she was taken. Why are you weakening on me now? It angers me."

"Angers you?" she flared up at him. "Have I ever let you down?"

"That's better," he said unexpectedly. "I only wanted to make you angry."

Sophie glared at him. Then her rage subsided. All at once, she saw the truth in what he said.

"Courage, my lady wife," he said. "All is not over yet."

DAUGHTERS OF THE STORM

ELIZABETH BUCHAN

BANTAM BOOKS
NEW YORK · TORONTO · LONDON · SYDNEY · AUCKLAND

DAUGHTERS OF THE STORM

A Bantam Book / published by arrangement with
Macmillan London Ltd.

PRINTING HISTORY
Macmillan edition published 1988
Bantam edition / May 1990

ISBN 0-553-28448-7

Published simultaneously in the United States and Canada

PRINTED IN THE UNITED STATES OF AMERICA

O   0 9 8 7 6 5 4 3 2 1

For Benjie
With love

ACKNOWLEDGEMENTS

Anyone who wishes to read about the French Revolution could do no better than to turn to Christopher Hibbert's clear and accessible book, *The French Revolution* (Allen Lane, 1980; Penguin Books, 1982). I should like to acknowledge my debt to the author.

Similarly, Olivier Blanc's *Last Letters: Prisons and Prisoners of the French Revolution* (André Deutsch, 1987) yielded fascinating information on money in the French Revolution. I would also like to recommend the works of G. Lenôtre whose lovingly detailed studies on revolutionary Paris gave me so much pleasure and inspiration: in particular *La Captivité et la mort de Marie Antoinette* (Librairie Académique, Perrin et Cie, 1907), *Paris in the Revolution* (Hutchinson, 1925), *The Tribunal of Terror* (Heinemann, 1909), *The Guillotine and Its Servants* (Hutchinson, 1929). Among many other publications that I read and enjoyed, four proved invaluable: *A Diary of the French Revolution* by Gouverneur Morris (Houghton Mifflin Company, 1939), *Guide de la Révolution Française: Les lieux, les monuments, les musées, les hommes* (Éditions Horay, 1986), *Paris in 1789-94: Farewell Letters of Victims of the Guillotine* by John Goldworth Alger (George Allen, 1902) and *The French Revolution* by J. M. Thompson (Basil Blackwell, 1943).

In addition, I should like to thank John Haycraft for his expert advice, Caroline Sheldon for her steadfastness, Carole Suddaby for her typing and Fanny Blake whose inspired editing made it all possible.

CONTENTS

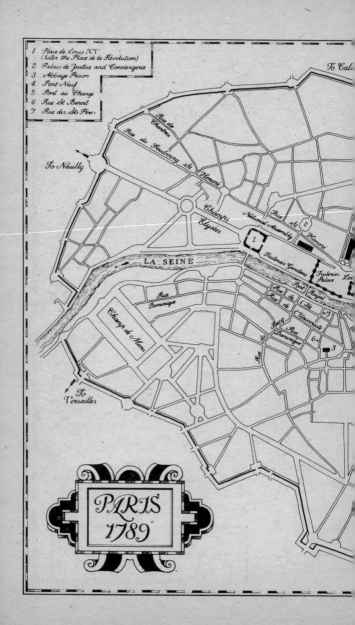

1 Place de Louis XV
   (later the Place de la Révolution)
2 Palais de Justice and Conciergerie
3 Abbaye Prison
4 Pont Neuf
5 Pont au Change
6 Rue St. Benoit
7 Rue des Sts. Pères

To Neuilly

To Calais

Rue de Chartres

Rue du Faubourg St. Honoré

Champs Elysées

National Assembly

Rue St. Honoré

LA SEINE

Tuileries Gardens

Tuileries Palace

Rue Dominique

Pont Royal

Rue de l'Ile

Rue de l'Université

Champ de Mars

Rue du Faubg St.

Rue Dominique

To Versailles

PARIS
1789

Calais, November 1793

The sea, driven by its own turbulent demons, lashed at the coastline. It whipped up great walls of spray and dashed the flotsam held in its watery grasp against the breakwater. The small boats had made for land, huddling for protection inside the harbour walls, and out in the Channel the bigger boats trapped in the weather grimly rode out the storm. On land the wind matched the waves in its anger, sending scudderings of dried leaves whirling into piles and tossing them up in clusters like migrating birds. The trees shook, groaning and protesting at their violent treatment, and the black skies parted now and again to let through the moon's fretful ray. There hadn't been a storm like it for years.

Sophie stood by the casement window of the inn and looked out over the sea. Every so often, as the spasms grew more insistent, her hands tightened on her swollen belly. It seemed to her that the water was full of blood and that its noise was the moaning of prisoners. Their cries would not let her rest. They were branded into her memory just as the pains seemed to be tearing deeper into her body.

'It was too much,' she murmured. 'Too much of everything. Blood. Death. Fear. Wasted hope . . .'

Down below a door banged and she knew it was her husband with the midwife. She turned with difficulty, using her arm to support herself against the wall, and tried to walk over to the bed. She shuddered as she brushed against one of the many cobwebs that festooned the room, and at the sight of the bed with its soiled sheets. She did not want to lie on it, but she knew she must.

Sophie gasped as the pain ripped her body in two. She forced herself to take a step forward and the process took an age. Still gasping, she heaved her ungainly bulk on to the sheets, swung her legs up and lay back with a sigh. The unaccustomed

3

sensations washed over her and she sank on to the pillows, allowing them to take her where they wanted.

Downstairs in the kitchen all was frantic activity. Two kitchen maids staggered into the room with a basket of wood. It was already tropically hot but they piled more logs on to the fire and the flame leapt up under the cauldrons of water which were suspended on the cast-iron spit.

Her husband watched as the midwife divested herself of her dripping outer clothes.

'Hurry,' he said tersely.

The midwife nodded as she rubbed herself dry. The cook stood by anxiously.

'*Mon Dieu*, what a night for a birth,' she said, going to the cupboard where she pulled out a large white apron. 'You will need this,' she said, tying it around the midwife's waist.

Upstairs the bedroom was quiet. Sophie imagined for a moment that she was back in Paris, and she was sure she could smell chocolate made hot and thick as she liked it. She could hear the clop-clop of wooden sabots in the street outside. Then the pain closed in again, tugging unmercifully at her flesh, and her vision dimmed into a long, dark tunnel where she was at one end and her body at another.

She heard a moan, forced out of some unbearable torment, and was surprised to realise that the sound came from her. What is happening? she wondered. Then she remembered. She was having her baby and it was coming too early. She had tried to stop it, but it had been no use. She raised her head from the filthy pillow and saw a figure bending over a basin pouring something from a jug. She felt the heat of the fire and turned her head to the side. Someone was bending over her with a cloth to wipe her sweating face. She sensed who it was.

'Hush,' said her husband, his voice hoarse with strain. 'Hush now. It won't be long.'

Sophie made a gigantic effort. 'Am I . . .?' she whispered. 'Is it all right?'

'It is well,' said the midwife, placing a hand on her stomach. 'You must be patient.'

Sophie moved restlessly. 'Patient. . . . With this?' She fell back, and tried to find a place to hide, away from a strange half-world peopled with whispering memories and ghosts.

'It is time to examine her,' the midwife said, and her husband helped to lift Sophie higher on to the pillows. He stroked back her long, tangled hair and made a clumsy effort to braid it. Sophie brushed his hand away with a low cry. The midwife rolled up Sophie's linen shift and her swollen body leapt into

4

relief. The white thighs were streaked with blood and the distended belly contracted visibly.

'It's coming,' said the midwife. 'Lift her up.'

He went to raise her up and eased his shoulders between Sophie and the bed.

This is what it is like to die, thought Sophie, her head hanging down on to her breast. But I haven't said my prayers.

'Dear God . . .,' she began, but a roaring in her ears and a burning, splitting sensation blotted out conscious thought. She was back in Paris again, to a time when death smelt in the hot sun and the noise of marching feet rent the peace of the nights, and the thud of falling heads sounded into the breathless silence of watching crowds. Somewhere among it all was Héloïse, but she didn't know where. She strained to find her but Héloïse eluded her, and Sophie couldn't remember what had happened.

The baby was not coming as quickly as it should.

'Turn her on her side,' the midwife said quietly.

He obeyed, shifting Sophie's heavy body awkwardly. A log on the fire broke in half with a crack and the flames spurted higher, sending a shadow flickering up the wall.

'Try to push,' said the midwife.

'I can't,' Sophie gasped. 'I can't. Oh, but I can't . . . I can't . . .'

The midwife's hands darted between her legs and cupped gently at the tiny head emerging between them.

'It's almost here,' she said reassuringly. 'Easy.'

With a slither the baby arrived and Sophie subsided into the arms that held her. Her husband laid her down and went to look as the small body was lifted clear.

'A boy,' said the midwife. 'Madame, a boy.'

Sophie's exhausted face registered puzzlement for a moment and then puckered as the pain gripped her again. She screamed. And then screamed again. The pain was coming back when it should have finished. There was to be no mercy after all. Why? What had happened?

'There's another,' cried the midwife. 'Quick.'

Sophie's husband took the baby from the midwife and cradled it in his arms where it cried the desolate cry of the new-born. With infinite care, the midwife helped an even smaller, more delicate baby into the world and placed it on the bed. Its downy pink limbs jerked spasmodically. Sophie stretched out an arm with an effort, and her fingers brushed at its head. The midwife bent to cut the cord and then wrapped the baby in a shawl.

'There, little girl,' she crooned. 'It is over.'

She laid it in the cradle which stood waiting and reached for its twin, arranging them so they lay together like tiny effigies.

Sensing each other, brother and sister closed their eyes and lay still.

Sophie was dimly aware of the midwife's hands busying themselves with the afterbirth. The peace was overwhelming and a cocoon of contentment settled around her, cutting out the sights and sounds of the room. It wrapped her in its embrace, pressing her down into a haven where nothing could touch her. She closed her eyes. Small sparks of light filtered between her eyelashes, twisting and turning like petals in a breeze. How strange, she thought, it's like apple blossom. It's like High Mullions all those years ago . . . when she was another person in another time. The petals heaped gently on to her face, pushing her back, back, back . . .

PART ONE
The Rising Storm
May–October
1789

Chapter 1

Sophie, May 1789

'Sophie Maria,' admonished her governess. 'I must beg you to adjust your skirts. It is not seemly.'

Sophie looked down in some surprise. She had been thinking about other things – the beautiful spring weather, the way the apple blossom was tinged with pink, and of the scents that came with spring. Light, tangy scents that held infinite promise of sun-warmed days and drowsy nights when the warmth closed around you and lulled you to sleep. It seemed such a long time since she had felt like this, for the winter had been hard and everyone, including the animals, had suffered from its iron grip. Now it was intoxicating to be out in the fresh, sunny air and to dream of summer.

She brushed her skirts down over her ankles and settled herself more comfortably on the rug. Miss Edgeworth and she had come to an arrangement. A geography lesson would be so much better out of doors, Sophie had reasoned, so much more appropriate than in the small, darkly panelled schoolroom where they spent so much of their time.

Miss Edgeworth had agreed, as Sophie knew she would. Miss Edgeworth always welcomed a change in the routine and, goodness knows, there was little enough excitement in her life. Not that Miss Edgeworth complained. She knew her duty and her place: but she had not always been so resigned. Once there had beat a tiny pulse of hope and excitement in her breast. It had been quickly stilled. Poverty and her consequent lack of expectations had seen to that, but Miss Edgeworth remembered what it felt like to be eighteen and so she had given in to Sophie's eager request, knowing that her excellent employers trusted her judgement.

Miss Edgeworth sniffed gently. Indeed, the Luttrells, Sir Brinsley and his French wife, Lady Aimée, were unusual, in her experience, in the latitude they permitted their governess over

9

matters concerning their beloved only daughter. Miss Edgeworth had no intention of betraying that trust; neither did she have occasion for regret in taking up the post, for in Sophie she found a willing pupil who if anything had to be dissuaded sometimes from spending too much time with her nose in a book or from scribbling for hours in her journal. Yes, Miss Edgeworth reflected for the thousandth time as she arranged her primers under one of the trees in the orchard, I have been fortunate in Sophie, who is as sweet-tempered as she is lovely. But in Miss Edgeworth's real opinion, it was the seriousness that underlay Sophie's youthful high spirits, the suggestion that here was a mind capable of feeling and compassion, that gave Sophie a special quality. Rather disloyally, Miss Edgeworth regretted that Sophie was destined to spend her life at High Mullions as a dutiful wife and mother, although she did not doubt that Sophie would be perfectly content.

Luckily for Miss Edgeworth, the subject of her speculations could not see into her governess's incurably romantic heart, for she would have been both puzzled and offended if she had. Sophie was very happy with her lot and far too innocent to question it. The only child of adoring parents, cherished, cosseted and endowed with a loving temperament that evoked love in return, she had passed through an unclouded childhood and grown into a model daughter whose only faults were a tendency to flare up when provoked and an occasional bout of stubbornness.

'Have you seen my cousin?' she was asking Miss Edgeworth. 'He promised to take me riding.'

Miss Edgeworth had indeed seen Ned Luttrell and, if she was not mistaken, he had been making his way towards Wainwright's cottage in which dwelt Wainwright's daughter, a remarkably pretty girl of some seventeen summers. Ned had taken to visiting it quite often. It was a predictable development, but one, since she knew of Sophie's feelings for Ned, that needed to be handled carefully on her part.

'It is time to continue our lesson,' she replied, avoiding a direct answer. 'Where was I?'

'In France,' replied Sophie, diverted, the name causing a frisson to go through her.

'Ah, yes. In France.'

Sophie twisted a lock of fair hair round her fingers, a habit she had when she was thinking. France! A place of mysterious sophistication and allure which she would soon be experiencing for herself. For as long as she could remember, the Luttrells had promised that she could make a prolonged visit, and now that

Sophie was eighteen the arrangements had finally been made. A year would be spent being launched into French society by her cousins and nearest relatives, the de Guinots, who were of the bluest blood. They were also rich, powerful and close to the king. Spending time with them, Lady Luttrell had often insisted, would be the very best way of acquiring the polish that Sophie lacked at the moment.

'Don't I please you as I am?' Sophie had once asked wistfully. Lady Luttrell had looked at her daughter and then grown serious.

'Of course, *ma fille*, you please me more that you can possibly guess. But I have a duty to prepare you for life, and your father and I agree that a little knowledge of the world would be a good thing. Once that is accomplished, you may return to marry.'

Sophie watched Miss Edgeworth fumble in her basket for a handkerchief and a little smile hovered round the corners of her lips. There had never been any question of whom she would marry. She would marry Ned, her adored second cousin who had been brought up by the Luttrells after both his parents had succumbed to smallpox. As eldest surviving male descendant of his generation, Ned would inherit High Mullions. Lady Aimée's inability to provide her husband with a son had seen to that. It was a cross that the Luttrells bore with dignity, even if they determined in their quiet way to ensure that the house with its rolling, fertile land would remain in their branch of the family. Happily, it was possible. Of course, if Ned had proved unsuitable the Luttrells would not have dreamt of sacrificing their daughter. But Ned was more than suitable. Three years older than Sophie, he was possessed of dashing good looks and a charm which could cajole even the most censorious dowager into smiling. If his education sat lightly on him, he was also strongly opinioned but good-humoured too and had all the makings of an excellent squire and landlord. Brought up in the shadow of this god-like being, Sophie was easy prey, and in her eyes Ned could do no wrong. The Luttrells told themselves that it would all work out perfectly. Safely netted in her loving family circle with her dreams confined to the limited world around her, Sophie was entirely happy with the future that had been mapped out for her. And if Ned had any objections to the arrangement, he never voiced them.

'Have you ever been to France, Miss Edgeworth?' she asked, wrenching her thoughts away from Ned.

'Once,' replied Miss Edgeworth unexpectedly, blowing her nose with a decided snort. 'I travelled around the country with my father. He was an agriculturalist, you know, and I

11

accompanied him to help transcribe his notes. I have never forgotten it,' she finished, and there was a wistful note in her quiet voice.

'Did you?' said Sophie, sitting up. 'What's Paris like?'

'Crowded and very noisy. It's a beautiful city even so. Very dangerous to walk in and everybody who can travels by carriage or fiacre, so it is difficult to stop and admire the architecture. I am very interested in architecture.'

Miss Edgeworth spoke absently, the memory of a promising young French architect whom she had once met and failed to excite ever green in her thin, unloved breast. 'The streets are so narrow that I was sometimes in fear of my life. The hostelries are expensive, dirty and full of vermin. But the area you will be staying in is distinguished by some fine houses. And', she added drily, 'I don't expect you will be walking anywhere.'

But Sophie was not listening. She had seen Ned coming towards them from the house. Her heart leapt and she sprang to her feet and waved.

'Sit down, Miss Luttrell, if you please,' commanded Miss Edgeworth.

Sophie obeyed reluctantly and once again arranged her disobedient skirts. Ned appeared at the gate which led into the orchard and vaulted over it. Sophie bit her lip. He was so very handsome in the short green coat that he favoured, despite the fact that his light brown hair was tied anyhow into a black ribbon and a lock had fallen over his forehead. He was wearing a pair of well-worn top-boots and carried his flat-topped hat in his hand. Ned never gave any care to his appearance but somehow it did not matter. His clothes always seemed to sit easily on him, their disarray only accentuating his long-limbed good looks.

'The two handmaidens of spring, I see,' he called out good-naturedly as he walked towards them.

Miss Edgeworth blushed despite herself and Sophie raised a radiant face.

'You have come to take me riding after all,' she said.

Ned pressed the corners of his mouth down into a mock grimace.

'Good heavens. I had quite forgotten,' he said ruefully, tugging at his cravat which was half-undone. 'In fact, I've arranged . . .'

Sophie's face fell.

'Now, don't take on, puss,' he said. 'If you insist I will take you riding as I said, but I came to tell you that I shall be escorting you both to Paris and staying over for a while. Your father has finally persuaded me. Does that please you?'

Sophie whirled to her feet and threw her arms around him.

'Indeed it does,' she said, the words tumbling out in her excitement. 'I can't think of anything I would like better.'

Ned disentangled himself.

'Careful,' he said. 'You are in danger of strangling me.'

Sophie released him at once and some of the joy died out of her face. She knew that he had not meant to, but Ned's protest had made her impulsiveness appear awkward and childish.

'Miss Edgeworth,' said Ned, consulting a gold half-hunter watch from which dangled two fashionably heavy fobs, 'I will take my cousin riding now. I am sure Lady Luttrell will excuse Miss Luttrell the rest of the lesson.'

There was no mistaking the note of command in his voice. Miss Edgeworth hesitated, torn between insisting that he wait and the tempting vision of having some time to herself. Indulgence won.

'An hour only, then, sir, if you please,' she contented herself by saying. She retrieved some sewing out of her basket and made every sign of getting on with it, but as soon as Sophie and Ned were safely out of sight, she allowed it to drop and sank back with a sigh.

'Will you stay long in Paris?' asked Sophie, scrambling after Ned as fast as her dress would permit, delighted to have him to herself.

'For a while,' he replied, amused by her transparent excitement.

'But we will have some time together? You will escort me to balls and take me riding and perhaps we can arrange to see some of the sights?'

Sophie's voice betrayed her nervousness at the prospect of being left entirely alone in Paris.

'Of course.' Ned spoke with a trace of regret. 'That is why I agreed to your father's request to accompany you. But I don't care for the notion of being away for too long. Something might go amiss. In fact, Sophie, I don't mind telling you I took a little convincing. All that worry and fuss, and I don't over-fancy the notion of foreign food.'

'Ned!' Sophie exclaimed. 'Surely you don't mean that. Doesn't the thought of all those strange and wonderful places entice you a little? High Mullions will be all right. After all, Papa has managed it all his life.'

'Not particularly,' he said, laughing at her. 'This jaunt will seriously disrupt my summer. I don't really see the need for it and I have a perfectly good social life here. Miss Edgeworth and our Frenchie cousins will look after you. You will buy a new wardrobe, acquire some admirers and start spouting the lingo all the time instead of half the time. In short, you will thoroughly enjoy yourself. As for me, I don't see the point of acting like a damned monkey at some French ball or other when I am needed to oversee the crops.'

Ned was only telling her half the truth. A tempting vision of Margaret Wainwright's black hair and rounded breasts occupied the other half.

Sophie coloured.

'I will never permit admirers,' she said hotly. 'Never. And . . . I . . . I am surprised you are not more anxious to take me to Paris.'

Ned paused. They were standing on the path that led up through the garden towards the south aspect of the house.

'Sophie. I don't think you quite understand. Looking after High Mullions is a serious business and, as you know, your dear papa isn't exactly receptive to the improvements I have proposed. Not that I am not devoted to him,' he added hastily.

Touched by this confidence, Sophie nodded. She quite understood, or thought that she did, the unspoken undercurrent of tension that flowed between the older and younger man. It worried her sometimes, for she did not care to think of her beloved father being displaced. It was true that Ned took care not to appear too impatient or tactless with regard to Sir Brinsley who, after all, had offered Ned a home and seen to his wants, but she knew that Ned often felt very constricted by his more conservative uncle. Still, if Sophie was honest, she understood Ned's feelings – Sir Brinsley was not always willing to try out new ideas and it was only natural that the two should fall out from time to time.

'Perhaps you are right,' she said thoughtfully.

Ned flicked at her chin with a careless finger. 'Of course I am, pusskin,' he said, kindly enough, but Sophie was miserably conscious that his attention had wandered away from her. 'You must trust my judgement,' he added. 'Now, go and get changed before I change my mind.'

Twenty minutes later, Sophie gave a critical glance in the mirror to reassure herself. Cased in the tight crimson broadcloth of her riding habit, she was as slim and as supple as ever. Pushing the skirt round with one booted foot, she stood in profile to make sure the line of her habit followed her figure. It did, to perfection. Not a wrinkle or a bulge marred the outline of her body and only the tumbling muslin of her jabot broke its symmetry, its snowy folds and intricate knot adding a teasing sumptuousness to the severity of the costume. Sophie was reasonably satisfied. She gave one last tug to her skirt, arranged her hat at a jaunty angle and picked up her whip.

The sun felt unseasonably hot as the small party, composed of Ned, Sophie and Bragge the groom, set off up the hill towards the ridge at the top, and even the disapproving face that Bragge habitually wore wasn't enough to dampen their spirits. The trees were thick with their new leaves and the apple blossom was sending its petals down in a thick rain. They caught in Sophie's hat and jabot and she brushed them carelessly away. The ill-made road wound up a steep hill, past the outlying cottages of the estate, and as they mounted upwards Sophie twisted in the saddle to look back at her home. Mellow and beautiful, High Mullions sat securely on its slight incline, its lawns rolling up to the windows, and the pink-red brick wall that bordered its gardens glimmered in the distance. All was well.

At the crest of the hill, they swung left towards Bluebell Wood and vied with each other to see who could catch the first sight of the famous carpet of blue. Overhead, a cuckoo sounded and the soft whirr of a bird's wings flurried as they passed and then settled again. A slight breeze sprang up, cooling the air, but even so the shade was refreshing. They picked their way in single file along the track between the trees and emerged on to high ground which gave them a view of the river plain in the distance. Sophie was content. There was nothing she liked better than to ride out into the country – the country that she considered her territory. The late spring was quickening all that she saw, and the woods and fields were stirring with new life and colour.

'I'm going to pull down Henchard's cottage,' said Ned, waving his whip in the direction of a small brick building, 'and enlarge the field.'

'You're not?' countered Sophie quickly. 'Where will Henchard go?'

'He can rent the spare cottage over by Wakehurst's mill.'

'But that is five miles from here and Henchard is too ill to be taken from his home. You can't mean it, Ned?' Sophie, who knew the Henchard family well and often visited them, contradicted him without thinking.

'Nonsense, Sophie. He will have to do as he is told,' said Ned decisively. 'I am not ill-treating him. The Wakehurst cottage is in much better condition, you know.'

'But, Ned, you don't understand. The cottage is his home. He is comfortable there. You can imagine what he will feel.'

'Don't be foolish, Sophie. My plans will suit him well enough in the end.'

Ned smiled to take the sting out of his words. Sophie stared at him, anguished at the thought of the old man being chased from the only home he had ever known and perplexed that Ned didn't understand. But as she looked at him, the realisation dawned, as it did with increasing frequency, that there was nothing to prevent Ned doing exactly as he pleased. Ned was going to be master at High Mullions and her place was to obey him, not to dictate. She pricked her horse onwards, an uncharacteristic bitterness rising in her for the accident of her sex.

Ned regarded her from behind with a quizzical expression. He was fond of Sophie, of course, and fully intended to make her a good husband, but he found her whims and impulses irritating at times. He was very happy to leave the running of the house, even the accounts, to his wife, and he would make an effort not to interfere with the children, but the estate was his domain and she should learn to accept it.

'Don't poker up, Sophie,' he called out. 'You must leave these decisions to me.'

She glanced back at him.

'You are wrong to do this,' was all she said.

At her wrathful expression, Ned burst out laughing and spurred his horse. 'You'll get wrinkles if you frown,' he said infuriatingly. 'How about a gallop?'

For an answer, Sophie leant over her mare and touched her sides. Her mount leapt forward to the accompanying thud of Ned's horse's hoofs.

'Faster,' she breathed, 'faster.'

She flashed past the line of trees to her right, the mare skimming over the turf, her well-trained feet avoiding the rabbit holes. Suddenly it was important to Sophie that she won this race. She gritted her teeth and made a mental calculation as to how far Ned was behind her. If she kept to the middle of the path, which was thickly wooded on either side, he would find it difficult to pass her. Sophie was not averse to using cunning and she edged her horse further into the centre of the track.

'To the oak tree at the end,' she shouted. 'I will beat you by a head.'

'No, you won't, by God,' Ned answered, and spurred his horse with a raucous yell.

Sophie concentrated on her horse and the deceptively smooth lie of the ground in front, all other considerations dissipating in the wild rush of air that beat at her cheeks and the powerful stride of the animal beneath the saddle. She swerved past a fallen tree, put up a hand to secure her hat and was nearly unseated.

16

Her mare, however, did not let her down and, with Sophie using every ounce of skill she possessed, the distance between the two horses lengthened, until at last she reined in, flushed and triumphant, under the tree. Ned thundered up.

'Well ridden,' he called. 'I'll say this for you, Sophie, there is none to beat you in the saddle.'

Considerably more in charity with her cousin, and restored to her customary good humour, Sophie allowed Ned to lead her blown mare and the long-suffering Bragge along the track and down into a small valley where they wound alongside the stream towards High Mullions.

Once back in the stable yard, Sophie let the reins go slack and waited for Ned to lift her down. As she did so, she saw the figure of Margaret Wainwright slip into the yard where she stood staring at the party and giggling when Ned's reins became tangled in his whip. Sophie liked Margaret, so she gave a friendly wave and slid down into Ned's waiting arms.

'Goodness, Ned, how flushed you are,' she said.

Sophie often thought of that ride during the months that followed – and caught her breath at the memory of a time when she had been uncomplicated, ignorant, foolish and young.

After an early dinner (the Luttrells kept country hours), she sat with her mother in the drawing room which overlooked the lawn. The long windows trapped every trace of late-afternoon sun and warmed the room. Sophie was drowsy from her ride but made an effort to get out her sewing and concentrate on a pile of white work that needed repair. They had dined well and the men were still at the table, occupied by a bottle of port that required careful attention.

Lady Luttrell had chosen her moment carefully.

'Sophie . . .'

Her charmingly accented English caught Sophie's ear for the thousandth time. Lady Luttrell would never speak English well, despite having lived in England for nearly twenty years. Nor did she wish to. And since Sir Brinsley spoke excellent French, Lady Luttrell's less than perfect grasp of her adoptive language had posed no bar to a successful marriage.

'About your cousins in France, *ma chère*. I think we should discuss them a little.'

Sophie laid down her needlework, always glad of an opportunity to do so.

'I am all attention, *Maman*.'

'*Naturellement*, you do not know them well, apart from what I have told you. I, too, have lost touch a little, although my sister,

17

your *tante*, Marguerite and I correspond regularly. Perhaps one day, I might . . . after all . . .'

Lady Luttrell's voice trailed into silence and Sophie, ever quick to sense her mother's moods, knew she was longing for her country.

'Tell me more, *Maman*,' she said to divert her.

'In France, things are ordered differently,' Lady Luttrell continued after a moment. 'Daughters, *par exemple*, are not free to say and do as they please, as is more the custom over here, a custom that your father and I approve of, and we have always allowed you to speak your mind within reason. But you will have to watch your tongue *un peu* and take care to observe how your cousins, Cécile and Héloïse, behave and try to copy them. I don't want you to feel too restrained, but I want you to be a credit for us.'

'*To* us,' Sophie interposed from force of long habit.

Her mother frowned at her. 'To us,' she repeated with dignity and switched into French. 'What was I saying? Ah, yes, your aunt Marguerite is strict in her views.'

'What is she like, *Maman*?' Sophie tossed aside her ill-treated sewing and settled herself more comfortably. Lady Luttrell reflected for a moment.

'She was the beauty of us two. So beautiful that men would stop and stare openly. I used to be quite jealous of her until I married, and then I knew that I had more than enough to be content.' Lady Luttrell smiled, a tender, disarming smile. 'The de Guinots', she continued, 'have many estates, a beautiful house in Paris and the apartments in Versailles. I hope you will visit La Joyeuse, their château near Paris. I thought it a most exquisite place.'

'But my cousins, what of them?' asked Sophie.

'I know as much as you do, *chérie*. I have seen them once, that time your aunt brought them to us here.'

Sophie had a distant memory of two rather proper young girls who refused to climb trees. Her chief recollection was one of exasperation.

'You must remember', said Lady Luttrell gently, 'that you are an ambassador for our – your – country and what you say or do will reflect on us in a noticeable way.'

'Yes, *Maman*,' said Sophie obediently, rising in a soft frou-frou of muslin and going over to the window. She sighed.

'Does anything trouble you, *ma fille*?' asked her mother.

Sophie turned and went to sit down beside her on the comfortable sofa over which Lady Luttrell had flung some pretty striped calico as a cover. She fingered it restlessly.

'No . . . nothing,' she said. 'But we have been so happy as a family, have we not?'

'Yes. Yes, we have. We have been blessed.'

Sophie thought for a moment.

'And I shall marry Ned.'

'That is our dearest wish.'

Sophie gazed past her mother, the low shafts of the dying sun tipping cheeks flushed with health and exercise. Her grey, thickly lashed eyes opened wide and in their depths lay a troubled expression which alarmed her mother.

'Sophie. You do wish to marry Ned?'

Sophie shook her head to banish a doubt that had crept, unwanted, into her mind. Why had Margaret Wainwright been at the stables when they came back from their ride? And was she imagining it, or had Ned given Margaret a little nod which she had thought nothing of at the time?

'Sophie,' repeated her mother. 'You are happy about Ned?'

Sophie looked at her and tried to think clearly. Was it possible that Ned was conducting an intrigue with Margaret? No – she was being fanciful.

'I wish for nothing more,' she said at last.

'You are sure?'

She smiled to reassure her mother. 'Yes,' she said, and meant it.

'Then, why do you look like that?'

'I was thinking,' said Sophie slowly, fumbling for some sort of answer. 'I shall change, shall I not, over a year? I wish to visit France very much, but it won't be the same when I return. I shall be different and I hope it won't spoil our happiness.'

Satisfied that Sophie was only expressing the normal doubts of a young girl about to embark on society, Lady Luttrell caressed Sophie's abundant fair hair and tugged at a small curl at the nape of her neck.

'It is in the nature of things,' she said. 'You must not be afraid. *Reste tranquille, ma fille*, your father and I are quite sure that you will not let us down either in France or when you return.'

Comforted by Lady Luttrell's soothing words, Sophie let her cheek drop on to her mother's hand where it rested for a long moment.

Sophie was so sleepy that she decided to retire early that night and, after bidding her parents good night, she let herself into the hall to collect her candle. The dark had closed in and she stopped by the wall table to light the candle before mounting the stairs to her room. She was attending to the wick, which needed trimming, and was surprised to see the figure of Ned appear at the top of the stairs. He was dressed in his overcoat and gave a start when her candle flared into the gloom.

'Sophie. I didn't expect . . .'

'Are you going out, Ned?' she asked, cupping her hand to steady the flame, hoping that he would stay to talk to her.

'For a while.'

'At this hour?'

'Curiosity did for the cat, dearest Sophie.'

Ned was teasing, but it was clear to Sophie that he did not wish to discuss the subject.

'Of course,' she said hastily. 'I didn't mean to pry.'

'Good,' he said, pulling the cuffs of his coat down over his wrists. 'You must be tired, puss. You gave me a good ride, you know. Sleep well.'

He patted her hand, set his hat on his head, dropped a kiss on to the top of her hair and swaggered away down the corridor.

Sophie stared after his departing figure and a desolate feeling opened in the pit of her stomach. It was so intense that she was forced to grasp the banister for support until it passed. She began to mount the stairs and failed to silence the voice that whispered in her head what she knew now to be true. Ned was going to meet Margaret Wainwright.

She pushed open the door of her room and set down the candle beside the mirror on her dressing table. Its reflection danced up the silvered glass, mocking her. She gazed into the mirror and ran her fingers across her cheek. Surely she was not so ugly? She dropped her head into her hands. Jealousy was not something Sophie had experienced before, but now it flamed unchecked through her and her heart felt as heavy as lead. Ned didn't love her. He preferred a black-haired, brown-skinned, unlettered girl, and it hurt so much she could not bear it.

After a while, the first shock of her discovery receded a little and she was able to sit up and look round the room, surprised to find that nothing had changed. Her innate good sense began to reassert itself. Of course Ned had been diverted, and she could not blame him. She had had so little opportunity to be with him these last six months, so much time had been taken up with lessons and with the business of preparing for France, that he had failed to see that she had grown up. She could hardly blame him for seeking company elsewhere. But they would be together during the journey and in Paris where she could enjoy his undivided attention, and then things would be different. Sophie took a deep breath. She must be sensible and forgive and forget this incident and never allow it to trouble her again. It would be difficult to do so, but do it she must, and with good grace.

Heartened by her reflections, Sophie undressed. She threw a shawl over her night-robe and moved the candle to a table by the window. She sat down, unlocked the drawer and drew out a bundle of papers and arranged them in a pile. Then she removed the porcelain cover from the ink-stand to reveal an ink-pot and sand dredger underneath. Her quill was already trimmed and she regarded it thoughtfully before dipping it into the ink.

Normally, this was the time that Sophie loved best. Alone and unhindered, she could indulge in what had become a secret passion. It was something she never talked about and hoped that nobody would ever discover because what she wrote was too private to be revealed.

Sophie could not remember when exactly she had begun to scribble her thoughts down on paper, but hardly a day passed when she did not manage to find time to cover a sheet or so in her neat handwriting. Sometimes she was content merely to record the day's events, at other times she tried to assuage a jumble of feelings that unaccountably gripped her and left her puzzled and exhausted, and page after page would be scored out in despair when her pen failed to match her thoughts. Sometimes she turned to her small supply of books for inspiration – *Robinson Crusoe*, and the daring philosophy of Rousseau's *La Nouvelle Héloïse* – but in the end her need to express herself drove her to try once again.

Tonight was different. Drawing the paper towards her, Sophie traced with her pen the words:

On Being a Wife.
To Obey My Husband in All Things . . .
To . . .

Ned's image filled the room. Her pen faltered and she swallowed back a treacherous lump in her throat. He was so very dear to her. How could he have . . .? But no matter. Together they would rule over High Mullions and it would be a place where peace and plenty reigned, and the estate would flourish under their dual care.

Her pen travelled over the page and her dreams went spinning into the future. Lady Edward Luttrell, Lady Edward Luttrell, Lady Edward Luttrell. Sophie wrote it over and over again, and scrawled a determined black line under each word.

21

PARIS, July 13th–14th, 1789

Change was in the air. It had been there for decades, forced underground by the royal police. It had lain, quiescent, but simmering, waiting for a signal. Few had dared to acknowledge it – that was to court exile or imprisonment. But now, throughout France, something had finally forced its way to the surface: a sense of expectation, of frustration and outrage. There it was, a small flame, burning at the bottom of a pyre, fuelled by the hunger and despair of a country organised to favour a few and to forget the rest.

It was unpredictable and heady, this feeling, and the newly elected representatives of the Third Estate of the Estates-General – meeting for the first time in a hundred and fifty years – who had made their way to Versailles in May 1789 were not immune to its seduction.

Summoned by a reluctant king to help him make some sense of the financial crisis that threatened to swamp the country, the representatives were hastily billeted on the hapless inhabitants of the town, bringing with them a flavour of provincial France and a medley of strange accents. Crowding into the already packed corridors of the great palace of Versailles, many of them ill at ease in the glittering, sophisticated throng, they debated and plotted with the fervour of those who considered themselves men of the hour. Many of them could ill afford the time spent away from their land and homes, and longed for the comfort of familiar food and surroundings, but all of them, increasingly bitter at their political impotence, considered they had a duty to perform. And no amount of well-calculated snubs from their ecclesiastical or aristocratic superiors was going to deflect them from the business of making the voice of the Third Estate heard.

'We are given hope,' declaimed Mirabeau, the fiery, ugly, eloquent noble who had crossed the floor to join the Third Estate. 'We are given hope that we are beginning the history of man.'

And in the days of political confusion that followed when the Estates-General was reborn in the guise of the National Assembly, and during the years after when France erupted, many of them remembered those words . . .

22

Mirabeau's words had filtered down Paris's network of streets, inflaming emotions already at fever pitch. Men thumped their fists on tables in dens and drinking houses and held forth on the horrifying price of corn and the ever-present threat of a foreign army invading the capital. They harangued each other over the antics of the spendthrift bitch of a queen, the corruptions of the ministers, the sufferings of the people, and every so often they went on the rampage, to the terror of their neighbours.

In the most fashionable area of the city, the crowds gathered regularly in the gardens of the Palais Royal, fanning out between the lines of the trees and tinkling fountains, jostling and gossiping. The press was often thickest round the cafés and there were many who listened to a young lawyer holding forth on the night of July 13th, 1789, from a table at the Café Foy. There was no trace now in his speech of the painful stammer which customarily afflicted him as he called to the people to take their destiny into their own hands.

'To the Bastille,' he cried. 'Patriots take action.'

The crowd cheered and yelled its approval while the orator tossed his long, curly hair out of his eyes and his yellowish complexion took on a pink flush of excitement. Desmoulins reached beneath his coat and, with a dramatic flourish, drew out two pistols.

'I will never fall alive into the hands of the police,' he thundered. 'They are watching us, citizens. Aux armes, mes amis.'

Eager hands helped him down from the table, and while he adjusted the green cockade in his hat – emblem of hope and liberty – his listeners cheered him to the echo and surged into the streets. Within a few hours the assault on the Bastille had begun.

Chapter 2

Marie-Victoire, July 1789

Marie-Victoire rubbed her sweating forehead with her free arm. The other held a length of lace that she was ironing clamped on to a bench. Beside her a growing pile of freshly pressed nightgowns and undergarments was stacked on a table, and another, even larger bundle lay as yet unpressed in the basket at her feet.

She sighed. It would take an hour or more, at least, to finish her work and she was hot and tired, and longed to escape and walk in the fields before throwing herself on to her attic bed. The heat in the kitchens was bad today. It spread like a thick covering through the rooms, normally so cool and dim, and sent tempers soaring and food to spoil. Through the door she could see the maids heaving pans and dishes around the big kitchen, and hear Claude's petulant tones as he laboured to create yet another new dish to please his masters.

She lifted the flat-iron off the board and tested it with a wetted finger. It was too cold. Wearily she made her way towards the great range, removed the second flat-iron that was heating, put the first in its place and returned to her task. She ironed swiftly, for she had a real talent for this kind of work and did it with artistry and grace. Anything that came under Marie-Victoire's deft fingers underwent a sea-change: crumpled bits of linen turned into shirts, lace took on a new life and the most complicated pleats and goffered edges fell effortlessly into place. Mademoiselle Héloïse, the youngest de Guinot, often remarked on this gift and encouraged Marie-Victoire to try her hand at dress-making, and she was proving an apt pupil. Madame Cécile, Héloïse's married sister, had declared that only Marie-Victoire might attend to her clothes whenever she resided at La Joyeuse. As a consequence, Marie-Victoire was kept busy through the daylight hours and often well into the night, for their demands were heavy. But she was thankful to have such a role to fulfil. It gave her a sense of purpose and helped to dull her grief for her mother, Marie, who had died the previous year, leaving her quite alone.

Out of the corner of her eye, she saw a familiar figure creeping through the kitchen towards the drying room.

'What are you doing here?' she asked. 'You should be with the horses.'

'Looking for you, of course,' replied Jacques Maillard.

The odours of the stable which he brought with him warred with the clean, starchy smell of her ironing. Marie-Victoire sighed again. Jacques was becoming a nuisance and she wished he would leave her alone.

'Go away,' she said crossly, banging down the iron and wiping her wet hands on her apron. 'I have too much to do. Mademoiselle Héloïse is expecting visitors from England and I want to have everything of Mademoiselle Héloïse's in order before they arrive.'

'Come for a walk,' he said. 'I want to ask you something.'

'Can't you ask me here?'

Jacques' chin took on an obstinate set and his black eyes burned with a look that was becoming all too familiar to Marie-Victoire. Obviously, another bee had settled in his bonnet. Normally, she was content to listen to what he had to say – and Jacques was becoming increasingly vociferous in his views, for he nourished ideas well above his station as a de Guinot stable-lad. But today she felt too tired. Besides, she wanted to think her own thoughts, alone in the soft quiet of the evening.

'Go away,' she said again. 'Another time, Jacques.'

He frowned and made as if to speak, but then thought better of it. Marie-Victoire went on ironing.

'Look,' he said at last. 'I've got some bread and sausage. We could eat it together.'

He held up a cloth-wrapped package. Marie-Victoire softened. Jacques looked so eager to please her and it was a small request.

'All right,' she said slowly. 'If I have time I will come and fetch you from the stables. But I won't promise anything.'

Jacques' frown disappeared.

'Good,' he said. 'Don't forget. I shall be waiting.'

She watched his tall, almost emaciated form disappear out of the kitchen. When, finally, she stacked the last chemise into the basket and went to lay the ironing on the racks to air, the evening was well advanced. The frenzy in the kitchen had reached a peak, for tonight the de Guinots were holding a card party to be followed by a late supper. Nothing too elaborate, for they were still in mourning for the marquis' mother, the Maréchale de

25

Guinot, who had died a couple of months previously, but it was enough to keep Claude at a pitch of hysteria.

Marie-Victoire hovered at the kitchen door. Perhaps, after all, she could give Jacques the slip and pretend that she had gone straight to bed, or even that she had been required to attend the marquise. The idea was too tempting to resist and with the ease of long practice, born from years of playing truant from her mother, she melted into the shadow thrown by the kitchen wing, skirted the yard and struck out towards the fields that lay to the north of the château. Within minutes she had reached her favourite meadow, and stood leaning on the gate that led into the vineyard.

The peace enfolded her in its embrace and Marie-Victoire felt her body soften and relax with relief. She rubbed the back of her neck where it ached, and hitched her skirts higher to enjoy the air playing around her ankles. Her head throbbed and she pressed her fingers into the soft spot at her temples.

After a minute or two, she looked up and stood gazing down the valley. I shall miss this, she thought, and tried to imagine for the thousandth time what Paris would be like. It was so far away, twenty-five miles at least, an unknown place filled with noise and unaccustomed ways. Still, she was lucky to get the opportunity to see it and she had better make the most of it.

Unlike Jacques, Marie-Victoire had no illusions as to her place. Even if she had, Marie would have quickly dunned them out of her. Marie-Victoire was expected to serve the de Guinots, thankful for employment and a roof over her head. As such she was sure of a regular supply of cast-off clothes and a kind word now and then which Mademoiselle Héloïse, at least, would be sure to give her. That, and a place on one of the estates if she got too old or too ill to work any longer. It sounded well enough and Marie-Victoire realised that her position was infinitely better than many she knew.

A hand slid round her waist and she jumped.

'Thinking of me?' said a voice from behind.

'Oh, it's you,' said Marie-Victoire with a giggle. 'You surprised me.'

'I meant to,' said Jacques Maillard darkly. 'I have been watching you for some time. Why did you not come as you promised?'

Marie-Victoire shrugged at the tone of his voice. She had heard it often and knew it was best to ignore it.

'Because . . .,' she said flatly.

So Jacques was in one of his moods! She felt too weary to humour him. It was one of the many things he demanded of her. Sometimes I feel I know him so well, she thought, and yet

26

increasingly I don't understand him at all. In fact, there are times when he almost frightens me. She kept her eyes firmly ahead, waiting for a torrent of invective and resolved to keep her temper.

The son of the chief groom at La Joyeuse, Jacques had known Marie-Victoire all his life and from the beginning had claimed her for his own property. As grubby children, they had played in the fields and claimed the stables as their private territory. Neither of them had paid much attention to the others of their age because they had found each other's company more than sufficient, and there were often pitched battles between them and hostile gangs.

'Who cares about them?' Jacques would say, scrubbing his bloodied fists into his eyes. 'They are sheep.' And he would be even angrier if the more moderate Marie-Victoire showed signs of conciliation.

As he grew older, he became more vehement. He had never liked La Joyeuse or the de Guinots, whom he saw as enemies to be fought with lies and guile, and he would spend hours describing to Marie-Victoire how he would escape.

'We are different,' he told her. 'We are going to do something with our lives. I am going to take you away from here.' His arm would sweep out in a gesture that dismissed the estate. 'We shall not be lackeys for ever.'

Sensibly, Marie-Victoire would point out that they needed money to go, and neither of them possessed more than a couple of sous, nor were they likely to do so. But she would admire his courage in saying these things, and sympathised with the hunger for independence that lay behind the bluster.

It was for Jacques' sake that she taught herself to read, huddled against the stable wall where in winter the lanterns swung on iron brackets and the light danced on the strange signs in front of her, and in summer the sun's rays warmed her face and made her sleepy. She learned quicker than Jacques, who was too impatient to be a good pupil, and it was Marie-Victoire who guided his hand down the text, listened to his halting syllables and urged him to try just one more time. Jacques was better at arguing, though, Marie-Victoire had to concede, if reluctantly. Once Jacques got hold of an idea – and his ideas were becoming more and more wild – he worried it like a dog with a bone. Then he would flood Marie-Victoire with a stream of words, leaving her to despair of ever being able to make him understand her point of view. She would throw a handful of hay over him instead, or chase him round the yard, which invariably ended with Marie-Victoire being caught and tickled.

Strangely enough, Jacques was the only one who had understood what she had felt when Marie died. No one else at La Joyeuse had bothered much; they were too busy with their own concerns to waste time on the bereft girl. But Jacques, who had grown up without parents – his mother had died in childbirth and his father treated him with the roughest indifference amounting to total neglect – had gone out of his way to let Marie-Victoire know that he mourned her too. For that she was grateful, and it helped to check her growing unease whenever she thought about him.

Jacques had changed lately. Always greedy for her time, he now demanded that she spend every free moment with him. He would stare at her in a way that she didn't understand and had come to hate, his narrow shoulders hunched and defensive. Sometimes he leaned over her and his breath played on her skin. His cunning, unshaven face began to invade her dreams, and she woke sweating and anxious to avoid him.

'What were you thinking of?' Jacques asked, edging closer to her.

'Nothing much.'

'You were,' he said. 'I can see it on your face. What was it? Tell me.'

'It was nothing,' she said again.

'Tell me. I demand it.'

Marie-Victoire sighed.

'I was thinking of Paris if you must know.'

Jacques drew out the knife he always wore in his belt and began to whittle at a piece of wood. The blade scraped sharply against the green wood and he peeled back the bark to reveal the pulpy core that lay underneath. Marie-Victoire reached over to take the knife from him and pointed it playfully at his breast.

'Careful,' he said. 'You might injure me.'

She gave it back.

'I don't want you to go,' he said eventually.

'Don't be silly, Jacques. I must go. I want to go. You should be pleased that I shall see more of the world. It's what you always said I should do.'

Jacques' neck mottled a painful red. 'Your place is with me,' he announced.

Marie-Victoire looked up at him in genuine astonishment.

Jacques' stomach contracted at the sight of her heart-shaped face framed by light brown hair curling damply round her cap. Marie-Victoire was not beautiful and her small body would probably grow sturdy with age, but her gold-tipped eyelashes and bright cornflower eyes were lovely, and she exuded a freshness that stirred his pulses.

'I mean it,' he said. He cleaned the knife blade on his sleeve. 'I want you for myself. We could run away to Paris and live cheaply. I'll find work.'

He sensed rather than saw her recoil.

'I see,' he said sullenly. 'You don't want me. You would rather spend your life with those *cochons*, running about emptying their slops from morning to night or darning their chemises or whatever you do. What will you have at the end of it? Nothing.'

'I will have my work and a place in the house for as long as I am useful. It counts for much in my eyes,' she replied, shrinking away from him.

'Don't make me laugh,' said Jacques savagely. 'They'll suck you dry and fling you out with the night-soil, like they do everyone round here. Look around you, Marie-Victoire! People like us don't count. We die early, and worn out. Have you been to the village lately? Obviously not, or you wouldn't be talking like this.'

There was enough truth in what he said to make Marie-Victoire pause.

'I shall see you often enough when I return,' she said.

'No, you won't. I've made up my mind. That is what I wanted to talk to you about.'

He flung the words out into the evening air and waited for a reply.

'I never promised you anything, Jacques.'

Marie-Victoire spoke sadly because she did not like to see Jacques hurt; nevertheless, like an animal sensing danger, she wanted to run for home.

'I did not think I had to. Is it not plain what I feel?'

'What is it, then, that you want?' she asked. But she knew very well.

For an answer, he pulled her towards him, ignoring her protests. Marie-Victoire's small, work-roughened hands beat at his chest.

'Stop it, Jacques. I am too tired to be teased.'

But Jacques, intoxicated by the smell of her body, bent his head and buried his lips in the nape of her neck.

'You shan't leave me,' he muttered thickly into the curve of her shoulder, tasting the warm skin with his tongue.

Marie-Victoire struggled harder. Suddenly, she was very afraid. The stranger who was showering her with kisses in places she had never been kissed before had nothing to do with the boy with whom she had gone fishing on summer evenings, or pelted with snowballs on winter afternoons when the low-slung sun sent its weak rays over a whitened land. She twisted frantically in his grasp.

'Stop it,' she managed to say. The panic in her voice succeeded in arresting the hands that had found their way under her dress.

'Don't be stupid, Marie-Victoire,' Jacques said, his eyes narrowing. 'You want me really.'

Marie-Victoire disentangled herself and backed away.

'No. No. NO. I don't.' There was no mistaking her fear. 'Leave me alone, Jacques.'

For a moment he was disconcerted and she seized her advantage. She turned and stumbled up the path towards La Joyeuse. Jacques stared after her and bent to pick up his knife. He turned it slowly in his hands and then, with a sharp blow, drove it deep into the barrel of the gate, where it stuck, quivering. He began to run.

When she heard him behind her, Marie-Victoire's pace quickened. The long grass whipped at her legs, her heart pounded and her breath came in sobbing gasps. He was too fast for her, she knew that, but fear lent her speed and she skimmed through a line of trees by the side of the meadow.

She stumbled on a tuft of grass.

'Marie-Victoire,' shouted Jacques. He lunged forward and caught at her skirts, and with one quick movement felled her to the ground. The earth rose up to meet her with a sickening thud. In an instant, he was on her, blind with passion. Marie-Victoire lay beneath him, feeling his body hard against hers, its familiar contours now changed into something quite alien.

'Don't do this,' she begged, her mouth crushed against his shoulder, but he did not, nor did he want to, hear her. His knee forced its way past her twisted legs and jerked into the softest part of her. She screamed with terror but her scream echoed uselessly among the trees and disappeared. No one heard.

Jacques pinioned her with one arm. With the other, he forced her skirts up to her waist and found the places he was seeking.

'You will be mine,' he whispered. 'I will make you wish you had never heard of Héloïse de Guinot. They have taken you from me, but they shouldn't have done. You were not theirs to take.'

She wrenched her head away from those magnetic eyes and struggled harder. But it was no use. Jacques fumbled at the laces of his breeches and she felt him thrust between her legs. He ripped into her and her neck arched in anguish.

It was all over in a minute. No sooner had he invaded her shrinking flesh than he jerked, groaned and lay still, his face buried on her breast. Marie-Victoire lay motionless, except for her fingers which scrabbled at the grass beneath her body. Never again will I be able to enjoy the smell of hay, she thought, or the sight of scarlet poppies in the grass. They are tainted now with the smell of lust and the memory of an unwanted body on mine. She felt the pain that comes with violation, a pain that invaded the spirit as well as the body, and she knew, as she lay there with the wetness between her thighs drying in the hot air, that she hated Jacques Maillard. Hated him for his animal weakness and for his betrayal of their childhood loyalties, and would do so for as long as she lived.

Presently, Jacques rolled over on to his side and lay without saying anything, his arms huddled over his head. Free at last, Marie-Victoire inched her way to her feet and tried to staunch the blood that ran down her legs, but found herself unequal to the task. Her bruised flesh protesting at each step, she began to walk away, holding her torn bodice together as best she could. Jacques moaned.

'Marie-Victoire, forgive me,' he muttered into the ground. 'I never meant this.'

She paused.

'I will never forgive you,' she said bitterly, without looking at him.

'Have you no pity?'

'Had *you*?' she replied.

He raised his head and tears mingled with the dirt smeared on his face. Marie-Victoire did not bother to pick up her cap, which lay crushed in a patch of flattened grass, nor did she give him a backward glance.

'Marie-Victoire.'

Jacques' piteous voice floated up at her for the last time. Marie-Victoire gritted her teeth and concentrated on the interminable way home.

At the entrance to the stable yard, her knees gave way and she clung to the gate-post, surprised out of her trance by the sight that greeted her. Instead of the quiet evening routine of grooms settling horses, the yard was alive with activity. In the middle stood a foam-flecked horse, its rider nowhere to be seen. The stable-boys fussed round it with hay and water, and a group of de Guinot servants were talking agitatedly. No one noticed the small, crumpled figure that stood swaying by the gate. They were too busy discussing the news from Paris.

Apparently, a huge mob had marched through the city to the old Parisian fortress prison of the Bastille and, after a day of fighting, had succeeded in storming it. They had killed the governor and released the prisoners who lurked in its gloomy cells. There were seven in all. One of the de Guinot agents had ridden, hot-foot, to inform the marquis.

Chapter 3

Jacques, July 1789

The beating had been a harsh one and it had been administered by his own father. From the moment Héloïse had discovered Marie-Victoire in a faint outside her door and had demanded to know what had happened, Jacques' punishment had been unavoidable.

'Filthy pig,' his father had said, raising the whip high. 'Couldn't you have chosen a sensible wench, not a pampered favourite?'

Since Jacques' father was notorious for his indiscriminate lusts, the question was a formality.

'Like father, like son,' Jacques ground out between bitten lips.

'Stupid bastard,' said his father, bringing the whip down. 'Stick to the village next time. They throw their skirts up without fuss and, if you pay them, so much the better.'

The whip lashed on to his back, tearing it into ribbons, and with each blow something was driven out of him, never to return. When at last Jacques staggered to his feet, all traces of the boy had gone and in his place stood someone infinitely more dangerous.

'Fuck off,' said his father indifferently. 'Mind you don't put a foot wrong again. I don't want trouble.' He laughed coarsely. 'It ain't your feet that's the problem.'

Jacques clung to the lintel of the stable door and waited for the first agony to subside. Then, moving like an old man, he reeled inside and flung himself on to a pile of hay.

It took two days for his wounds to scab over and two more days for Jacques to make up his mind. Most of the time, he lay fighting the pain while the vermin made free with his open wounds. Occasionally he fetched up at the kitchens for food, but the maids kept out of his way, repelled by the expression on his face and by his stinking, blood-matted clothes. His father left him alone.

Marie-Victoire was ill, they said, confined to her bed in the attic, and she certainly wasn't going to see Jacques. Mademoiselle de Guinot had forbidden it. Would Marie-Victoire spare a thought for him? he wondered bitterly. Did she understand that he cursed himself for the fool that he was? Had she heard his despairing cry as she fled from him? In his heart of hearts, Jacques knew that she had, and that hurt him worst of all.

When night fell he was fully clothed with his knife tucked into his belt. He eased himself upward, trying not to bend to avoid splitting his wounds, and made his way towards the kitchen wing. Once there, he shuffled into a stone passage that led between the larder and the still-room down to a small room at the end. He took out his knife and prised open the lock in the wooden door, a trick learnt long ago, and let himself in. A pile of candle-ends lay on the shelf. He picked up one and sniffed at it. It was made of the best imported myrtle wax and gave off a delicate smell. Jacques knew that the de Guinots never stinted themselves over candles, and La Joyeuse often blazed with them even if relatively unimportant visitors were expected. He rolled it thoughtfully between his fingers. Candle-ends of such quality were in great demand and he smiled to think of the chief footman's anger when he discovered that his source of extra income had been raided.

He stuffed as many as he could into a sack he had brought with him, tucked it awkwardly under his arm and retraced his steps. Outside the kitchen he hesitated, and then slipped through the door. A basket of loaves lay on the sideboard and he slid two into his sack. He turned to go and, as he did so, caught sight of a pile of silver teaspoons waiting to be cleaned. He pocketed three of them.

The dogs, who knew him well, were quiet as he hobbled silently through the yard towards the back gates. It was easy. Jacques knew every stick and stone of La Joyeuse and if he hadn't been so hampered by his back he would have made swift progress. But his spirit sang with exhilaration at what he was doing. Safe in the woods at last, he flung himself down on his stomach and gave himself up to his dreams of revenge.

He could never go back. His pride would never allow it, not even if it meant starving. No longer would he, Jacques Maillard, act as a lackey to the family he hated, and no longer would they have power over his destiny. He would find his own way and take a chance. Better death in the gutter than a life of servitude. Jacques had talked often to the carriers who came from the city to collect produce, and they had told him a thing or two. Now he intended to make use of their advice. He'd find a way of surviving somehow.

He beat his fists into the summer-dry earth.

'I'll kill them. I'll kill them,' he vowed and raised his face to the sky. There was no answer from the trees that hid him or from the light wind that dried the sweat on his body. Jacques was alone.

A week later he joined the traffic that flowed along the road towards the northern entrance to Paris and a good-natured waggoner gave him a lift for the last part of the way. Swaying with the movement of the cart, his face transparent with suffering, Jacques clutched his sack and watched the country slip away. Deep inside him beat a pulse that grew stronger and stronger with each jolt, a certain knowledge that one day he would repay the de Guinots and claim back Marie-Victoire. Meanwhile, he would devote himself to making it possible. He didn't care how.

The smell of the city assaulted him as he passed the *barrière* gates. Once inside the walls, he struggled to his feet, thanked his kind benefactor and stood gazing at the close-knit houses and filthy roads. Then, following some primitive instinct, he disappeared riverwards, slipping into the tide of human flotsam that flowed down the streets and vanished into the vast pool of dispossessed humanity that washed ceaselessly through the capital.

Chapter 4

Héloïse, August 1789

Héloïse awoke abruptly. She lay on the lace-edged pillows and gazed up at the silk swags adorning the bed, listening to the early-morning sounds. Outside, the yellow stone of the Hôtel de Guinot ripened into a deeper colour as the sun rose higher in the sky and the dawn birdsong faded. Her hands clutched the sheets, then lay motionless, and she closed her eyes hoping that the blackness would quieten her beating heart and hold her safe for a few moments longer.

Today two things were going to happen. She would be introduced to Sophie Luttrell, her cousin, and she would be betrothed.

A familiar sense of dread washed over her.

'Remember, your duty is to us,' she heard her mother, the Marquise de Guinot, admonish in her repressive manner.

'But, my dear child, this marriage will further our interests greatly. In fact it is due partly to Monsieur le Comte de Choissy that I have been able to take up this post as minister. You must be reasonable.' Her father was less cold but equally implacable on the subject.

Reasonable! Héloïse's shoulders tensed. Was it fair that she was about to be sacrificed to her family's ambition? Even if it wasn't, she knew that it was unavoidable. The de Guinot family conducted themselves with assurance, ignored the wishes of everyone except themselves and had grown used to being close to the seat of power. Personal feelings did not enter into the intricate business of dynastic marriages and Héloïse was a fool to imagine that they did. Both foolish and impractical. There was a scratch on the door and Marie-Victoire entered. Héloïse could escape awakening no longer.

By ten o'clock she was dressed in a charming half-morning toilette of lavender silk over a white satin petticoat, which was laced at the back and drawn in tight at the waist with a fringed silk sash. At half-past ten precisely the hairdresser bustled in, clutching the instruments of his trade in one hand while he swept a profound bow with the other. Close behind him minced the perfumier and the glove-maker, and Héloïse was forced to endure their chatter while they busied themselves about her. Héloïse could have caught some interesting tit-bits if she had wanted, but their high-pitched voices and stifled giggles jarred on her nerves and she tried not to listen.

The sound of a coach arriving outside made her start and the hairdresser clucked disapprovingly. His hands darted around Héloïse's carefully coiffed hair as he tucked a final ostrich plume into her diamond aigrette, and coaxed a curl to lie just so. Then, with a flourish, he removed the sheet that covered Héloïse's shoulders and entreated mademoiselle to gaze at herself in the mirror.

Pale and wooden, her face stared back and Héloïse made an inarticulate noise. Worried by her mistress's pallor, Marie-Victoire hastened to shoo the protesting coterie out of the room. When, at last, she had closed the door on them, she went over to Héloïse.

'There, mademoiselle, they have gone. Let me get you some wine.'

Héloïse bent her head and Marie-Victoire saw that the tears were running unchecked down her cheeks and splashing on to her gown. She hesitated, and then she sank to her knees and took one of Héloïse's hands in her own. Her gesture was so unexpected that Héloïse did not respond for a moment. Sensing her surprise, Marie-Victoire withdrew her hands but remained kneeling.

'Mademoiselle, can I do something?'

Héloïse shook her head. Her maid was scarcely the person to help her. But the sight of Marie-Victoire's anxious and sympathetic face brought on a fresh storm of tears.

Héloïse was aware of a pair of arms stealing round her as, heedless of custom, Marie-Victoire drew her close and held her against her shoulder. The reassurance of another giving comfort penetrated through her misery and had the effect of calming Héloïse. Gradually her sobs quietened. Marie-Victoire got to her feet and left the room. Presently she reappeared with a tray. She poured some wine into a glass and gave it to Héloïse, who accepted it gratefully.

'Thank you,' she said. 'This will not happen again.' She cradled the glass between her hands. 'It is only . . .'

'Would you like to tell me, mademoiselle? It might help.'

Héloïse set down her glass and searched on her dressing table for her handkerchief. 'I have told no one of this,' she said, conscious that Marie-Victoire was not the right person to unburden herself to, but enormously relieved at being able to do so, 'but you remember the day my grandmother died at La Joyeuse?'

Marie-Victoire nodded. 'Very well.'

'I had gone into the garden. It is a favourite spot of mine . . .'

She remembered as if it were yesterday that day in June at La Joyeuse, picking her way through the walled kitchen garden fragrant with gillyflowers and growing herbs. Inside the house her grandmother, the maréchale, lay dying and the de Guinots were clustered in the death-chamber, surrounded by candles and stifled by the choking smell of hot wax.

She had stood for a long time gazing at the house and its surrounding lands. It was a satisfying vista of well-tended meadows and woods set off by a series of formal flowerbeds that swept up to the house in an orderly fashion – the maréchale had not permitted the Parisian rage for anything English to invade her domain. There was an air of neatness at La Joyeuse: the cattle in the field were sleek, the crops sturdy and the fields well managed. Only in the village, straggling further down the valley, did a contrast intrude. Here the cottages, pock-marked by damp and decay, opened their dark interiors on to pitifully small patches of garden and the children who played in the mud and dirt were thin and sore-encrusted. The flies swarmed everywhere: over the middens, into the houses and on to the prematurely old faces of their inhabitants.

Héloïse had not always been happy at La Joyeuse, but it was dear to her and she looked affectionately at its tall, classically pure outline that rose to the sky. Her bitterest regret was that one day she would leave it in order to marry. Still, she would inherit a very pretty house near Neuilly from her grandmother and she looked forward to making that a place of retreat.

Héloïse rose to her feet. It was time to go. If she was not careful she would be missed and her mother would reprimand her. She lingered for a moment longer by a large stone urn placed at the end of an avenue of rare rose-bushes. The early blooms frothed in a riot of scent and colour, mingling with the buds in delicious variations of pink, white and red, and she smiled with pleasure.

The stranger who wandered into the garden, crushing some petals between his fingers as he went, noted the picture Héloïse made with approval. In her black dress, trimmed with a wide ribbon sash, and with her hair swept up to reveal a long neck set off by a necklace of pearls, she made a charming picture. Oblivious of his presence, she bent to snap off a dead flower and he saw that she was endowed with a face that showed great promise. Waiting beneath its youth and vulnerability was a woman who had as yet to grow into her beauty, but his long experience of women told him that maturity would make that beauty exquisite.

Héloïse turned to retrace her steps and, as she did so, she caught sight of the onlooker and stopped. What was he doing, standing there so confidently, almost as if he had the right? She stood rooted by surprise, taking in his well-cut coat, his extravagant lace cravat and the look of amused arrogance that sat on features which, but for the lines of dissipation and a curious discontent, would have been extraordinarily good-looking. It was a cruel visage, which revealed that this man knew too much to be at ease with the world or with himself. At that moment Héloïse sensed that here was someone used to having his own way. She shivered, but recalled her manners and stepped forward to enquire if she could be of any help. The stranger bowed at her greeting.

'Beautiful gardens and beautiful women always go together,' he said, and bent to pick a particularly fine rose which he presented to Héloïse with a flourish. She accepted it with nerveless fingers.

'No,' he rebuked her. 'You must not treat such a fine specimen in such a cavalier fashion,' and leaning over he retrieved the flower and tucked it into her sash.

Héloïse wondered if she was dreaming, for his hands lingered over her body in an intimate and repulsive manner almost as if he owned her. He took his time and adjusted the bloom to the angle that set it off best. She took a step backwards.

'Monsieur, I would prefer it if you would desist,' she said coldly.

He seemed not to heed her. 'That's better,' he remarked. 'Although on reflection it is not the precise colour I would have chosen to compliment your complexion.'

Héloïse drew herself up.

'I think, monsieur, whoever you are, that you had better take your leave. Your presence is not welcome.'

There was no mistaking the anger in her voice. The stranger laughed and Héloïse saw that her anger only added to his enjoyment.

'Spirit *and* beauty,' he said softly, and before she knew what was happening he had drawn her to him.

'How strange,' he said, and his eyes were unfathomably cold. 'You remind me of my mother. She was a remarkably beautiful woman.'

Héloïse was left with the impression of white skin and a

pungent musky smell before she wrenched her face away, so angry she could not speak.

'Let me go,' she ordered. 'My father, Monsieur le Marquis, will hear of this.'

'Your father, my dear, would approve. I speak with the highest authority.'

He bent his face to hers and kissed her so ruthlessly that it was impossible for her to prevent it. Her hands flailed at her sides while his mouth crawled over hers with an expertise that betrayed extensive practice until, at last, he released her.

'Delightful,' he said, in the same soft voice. 'Quite delightful. Fresh, young and innocent.' But his expression belied his words.

'You should not have done that,' Héloïse managed to say and, raising her hand, she tried to wipe away the imprint of his mouth on hers. 'I presume you are a visitor here,' she said eventually. 'But you have betrayed a trust and I shall not forget it.'

She tore at the rose in her sash, now crushed beyond recall, and threw it to the ground where it lay between them. Then, to the sound of the stranger's mocking laughter, she turned on her heel and walked away, praying that her trembling knees would bear her. Once out of sight, she pressed her hands to her hot cheeks, gathered up her skirts and fled, heedless of onlookers, towards the privacy of her room.

'So you will understand how I felt', she said to Marie-Victoire, still hearing the stranger's laughter reverberating in her ears, 'when I discovered him to be the man my parents had chosen for me to marry.'

Marie-Victoire remained very still, then she bent to adjust one of Héloïse's stockings.

'I do understand, mademoiselle. Very well,' she said, drawing it up the tender flesh of Héloïse's thigh.

The stocking correctly in place, Marie-Victoire rose to her feet and went over to the walnut armoire that held Héloïse's clothes and retied the embroidered ribbons that held them in tidy piles. Then she tucked some rose-petals into the folds and closed the doors.

'What would you do if you were me?'

It was an odd question for Héloïse to ask, but it slipped out before she could prevent it.

Marie-Victoire thought before replying.

'They say . . .'

Héloïse smiled wryly. Of course, the servants always knew everything first.

'They say that Monsieur le Comte de Choissy is rich, that he keeps two mistresses and his first wife died of a broken heart.'

'That does not surprise me.'

Marie-Victoire turned to face Héloïse. 'But it has always been so, has it not, mademoiselle? You must marry and take your place in society. These are things you must do. You are not free to choose . . . as I am,' she added almost to herself.

Héloïse looked hard at her maid, impressed by Marie-Victoire's directness and good sense. She got up and went over to the girl.

'Marie-Victoire, will you remain with me in Paris?' she asked. 'I know it would mean leaving La Joyeuse for good, but we shall visit it often. I can arrange it with Madame la Marquise, and I would like it very much.'

Marie-Victoire hesitated, but only for a moment. La Joyeuse was too full of unwanted memories for her to wish to go back.

'Of course, mademoiselle. It is as my mother would have wished. I shall do my best to serve you well.'

Half an hour later, they were summoned downstairs. Marie-Victoire whisked the hare's-foot over Héloïse's face for the last time while impossible thoughts of flight winged through Héloïse's mind, whispering to her that it would be so easy to plead illness, or to faint. Anything! Then sanity intervened and her pride resurrected itself. After all, she was a de Guinot and cowardice was not one of her failings. She held out her hand for her fan and walked out of the room.

Outside the closed double doors of the salon there was a rise and fall of voices. The doors opened and the marquise stood framed in the doorway. She had taken trouble today and her jewels sparkled on a magnificent silk dress embroidered with a black and white feather pattern, worn over an underskirt of white satin sewn with spangles and gold thread. Her normally severe countenance wore a smile.

'Come, daughter,' she said and held out her hand.

Héloïse did not move.

'Chut,' said the marquise, her smile vanishing and her face hardening. 'You are not about to disgrace us, Héloïse, I hope. Remember your father and I have looked very carefully into the financial arrangements of this marriage and they suit us. You will be rich and your position will be as it should.' She furled her fan and tapped Héloïse sharply on her shoulder. 'Remember also,' she added in an undertone. 'If you and Monsieur le Comte do not suit, then you can choose to live apart. Nobody will expect you to be in each other's company all of the time.'

Under the pretext of arranging Héloïse's sash, Marie-Victoire gave Héloïse the tiniest push and Héloïse gathered her courage to begin the long walk down the salon filled with onlookers, at whose furthest end were grouped her father, the notary, the de Choissy party and what must be her two English visitors who had arrived late the night before.

'What beautiful hair,' she heard someone say.

An eternity later, having negotiated the slippery parquet de Versailles in her high-heeled shoes, Héloïse stood in front of her future husband. She raised her eyes. The face from the garden greeted her gaze, its dissipated lines etched harshly in the morning light, the thin lips registering amusement.

De Choissy looked deep into the troubled face of his young and reluctant bride. The situation was exactly as he had predicted and the fact that Héloïse was obviously unwilling did not displease him. Rather it mixed a certain piquancy into the situation, and de Choissy was not averse to having his jaded senses teased into life. Héloïse sank into a curtsy, and de Choissy stepped forward and extended an arm clad in olive-green stripes to help her up.

'*Enchanté, mademoiselle,*' he said, and then, in a voice meant only for her: 'Or should I say Madame la Comtesse?'

Héloïse's gloved hand shook slightly in his, and it took all of her self-control to bite back the reply. 'Not yet.'

'How pleasant to meet you properly,' he said in the same muted tone. Héloïse took back her hand.

'If Monsieur le Comte is referring to a certain incident at La Joyeuse, then I shall do my best to forget it and trust that it will not be repeated.'

De Choissy had the grace to lower his eyes, but Héloïse knew that he was laughing at her and it stiffened her resolve to speak as little with him as she dared.

She turned to her father, who gave the signal for the notary to commence proceedings. The formalities were brief, the contract having been signed the day before and the settlements already negotiated. Afterwards Héloïse moved into the receiving line beside her fiancé and the doors of the saloon were thrown open to admit more guests. She nodded and smiled, and submitted to being kissed on both cheeks. But all the time she felt as if a thin gauze separated her from the world. Out of the corner of her eye she saw Sophie was besieged by the older generation of de Guinots and hoped that her cousin would not be too embarrassed by their scrutiny.

The guests moved on in well-trained lines. The gossip today, she gathered, was of rents and of her cousin Narbonne's wish to mortgage a house in Paris in order to pay his debts. The de Guinots were always interested in the subject of rent, and in

41

politics, and just now her father was particularly in demand. Not only had he been summoned to Versailles to attend the recently convened Estates-General but he also enjoyed a superior knowledge of the English taxation system, a topic currently under hot debate, for a formidable body of French opinion considered it the only model to solve the French financial crisis.

How can they, she thought in despairing, when my heart is breaking?

'*Bonjour, ma fille.*' A well-known voice broke into her thoughts.

Héloïse returned the greeting of her favourite great-uncle and relaxed a little. Uncle Albert could always make her laugh. He once told Héloïse that he had been bored stupid in his youth by the constant hectoring of his relations and in consequence he had resolved never to inflict his views on his own descendants. Albert leant forward to kiss her cheek and squeezed her hand.

'Remember,' he whispered in her ear. 'You are dead for a very long time. You must enjoy yourself and use this marriage to your advantage.'

Héloïse felt better and she managed a genuine smile in return.

De Choissy was at her elbow.

'Come, you have nothing to drink,' he said, steering her over to the sideboard arranged under a fine still-life by Desportes. It was laid with a deep blue Sèvres porcelain dinner service picked out in gold stars and with heavy crystal glasses. At its centre stood a salt-cellar made by Cellini at the height of his fame. Héloïse nodded to Galante, the black servant, to pour her some wine and sipped at it while de Choissy accepted another. She murmured her thanks through dry lips, hardly conscious of what she was saying. De Choissy gave a short laugh. Really, the child was so pretty that he almost felt sorry for her.

'Perhaps the crush is too much for you, mademoiselle? Certainly this is not the best time to become properly acquainted. But there is time. Plenty of time. I want you to know that I look forward to our union.'

His words succeeded in piercing her shell. Fear and dislike flooded through her in waves. She struggled for composure, determined not to be outfaced by him.

'Tell me about your family,' she said with an effort. 'I am not yet well acquainted with your circumstances.'

De Choissy's face registered approval.

'Well done, my dear,' he said unexpectedly. 'You will not be surprised to learn that on account of my vast age – I am nearly forty – I don't have many close relations left.'

He proceeded to give her a cleverly articulated sketch of the de Choissys. Héloïse listened, intrigued despite herself by the intelligence that lay behind the throwaway remarks. It seemed inconceivable to her not to be surrounded by a large and inquisitive family, and she wondered vaguely if it might be an advantage.

'Come,' said de Choissy at last, judging his effect on her to a nicety. 'I will make a start and introduce you to my sisters.'

He led her forward. 'This is my eldest sister, Madame de Roix,' he announced.

Héloïse found herself being looked up and down by a bored woman of some forty years who, for all her fashionable dress and deportment, could not hide the fact that she was ageing.

'I do not like you,' said Héloïse to herself as the older woman's gaze wandered pointedly over her figure with barely concealed envy.

'And this', continued de Choissy, 'is Madame la Duchesse de Fleury, my youngest sister. Adèle, I shall count on you to be kind to my bride.'

Héloïse curtseyed to a ravishingly dressed and very pretty blonde whose face expressed concern and interest.

'I knew she would be bewitching,' cried Adèle, who had been waiting for the introduction. 'And she is, Hervé. You are extremely fortunate. I shall look forward to my new sister.'

Héloïse dipped a curtsy. No one could fail to respond to Adèle, as her many lovers and friends had so often exasperatedly concluded. Wild, carefree and, unlike her brother and sister, affectionate, she scattered love and money in equal quantities but accompanied her many sins and omissions with such charming contriteness that few remained angry with her for long.

De Choissy stood back, well satisfied that, in an unusual display of consideration for his bride, he had insisted that Adèle be present today. She had not been at all willing, being far more concerned with attending some rout or other at Versailles with her latest lover. But when her brother commanded attendance, she knew better than to protest. Adèle was also pleased with what she saw, not the least because Héloïse's dowry was more than respectable, which meant she might, after all, be able to cajole de Choissy into loosening his purse strings.

'I wish to talk to you,' she murmured, thinking of a particularly fine pair of diamond earrings that had taken her fancy.

'No,' said de Choissy before Adèle could embark on her crusade. 'Definitely not.'

Adèle sighed. Hervé was so tight-fisted when it came to his sisters, and had declared more than once that the honour of paying their bills rested with their husbands.

'Eh bien,' she said, accepting the inevitable, and turned back

43

to Héloïse. The girl has real possibilities, she thought to herself, and I like her looks.

'Welcome to our family,' she said.

'Your parents,' asked Héloïse politely. 'Have they been dead long?'

Adèle paused. 'Goodness, yes. My father of over-indulgence and my mother . . .' She paused again and lowered her voice. 'Our mother abandoned us for her lover when we were very young. It caused a great scandal at the time. Hervé went after her and was found wandering on the road two days later. He was well beaten and locked up for a week for a punishment. I don't think he ever forgave her. Of course, being the eldest, he loved her the best. I can't remember her at all.' Adèle changed the subject. 'When will you be married?' she asked, mentally rearranging her wardrobe, a process that tended to involve a complete refurbishment.

Héloïse furled her fan. 'In the New Year,' she replied, and tried to make her tone as light as possible.

'And will you be taking up a position in the queen's household?'

'That will be settled later.'

Héloïse had been well instructed by the marquise. The matter had yet to be finally decided because the queen was reluctant to take on a new bride who might, at any minute, find herself pregnant and thus unfit for the tiring duties required of her.

'But I am to be presented after my marriage,' she added.

Madame de Roix yawned. Her back teeth were quite rotten.

'So *ennuyant*, mademoiselle,' she commented, in a lazy drawl reminiscent of her brother's, shutting her mouth quickly. 'I am afraid you will find it very tedious.'

Adèle suppressed a smile. Her sister was displaying just the right touch of boredom, so fashionable just now, over the subject of Versailles.

Héloïse had no further private conversation with de Choissy. A musical interlude followed during which a string quartet executed some pieces by a composer called Mozart. What they lacked in real feeling they made up for in expertise, and the guests appeared pleased. An elaborate dinner occupied the rest of the afternoon. Héloïse forced herself to eat a small portion of quenelles, for which their cook was famed, and was relieved to find that it made her feel better. Plate in hand, she circulated among her guests and managed to give a good account of herself. The marquise rustled over to Héloïse.

'You are doing well, daughter. I am pleased.'

This was praise indeed from the stern marquise. Héloïse placed her plate on a convenient table and dropped her a little curtsy.

'If you say so, *ma mère*.'

The marquise considered her daughter. Héloïse was behaving just as she should.

'Rise, Madame la Comtesse de Choissy,' she said, with a great deal of satisfaction, and arranged her skirts in a billowing arc around her. 'Now go and talk to your cousin.'

Héloïse dropped a second curtsy and went to find Sophie in the smaller saloon. She stood looking in, a slim, correct and elegant figure, and Sophie, rising to greet her from a chair where she had flung herself, was momentarily a little unnerved.

For her part, Héloïse was treated to a vision of glowing, golden beauty which bore only the faintest traces of travel fatigue. Taller and bigger-boned than her cousin, Sophie exuded an aura of health and high spirits. Her white gown, trimmed with a silver strip, set off to advantage her luxuriant hair, and the cunning (if slightly fussy) arrangements of ribbon and lace indicated that she knew how to dress with taste.

The two girls surveyed each other, neither of them quite sure what to say. Then Sophie gave her warm smile.

'I did not expect you to be so beautiful,' she said disarmingly.

'Nor I you,' replied Héloïse, and held out her hand.

Sophie took it and they looked again at each other. Both of them liked what they saw. Héloïse dropped into one of the chairs and patted the other one invitingly.

'Are you rested after your journey?' she asked.

'Indeed yes.' Sophie tried not to think of the flea bites that still marked her body, the legacy of one of the dirty and uncomfortable inns that they had stayed in on their route from Calais.

'Your cousin, Monsieur Luttrell?'

'He has gone to fetch me some wine and will be here directly.'

'*Bien*,' said Héloïse. 'I am glad of the opportunity to meet you alone. I have thought so much about you.'

The last was not true, for Héloïse had been entirely preoccupied by her own affairs, but she thought it proper to express the sentiment.

'And I of you.' Sophie spoke in rapid French.

Héloïse countered in English. 'I am sure we will be the greatest of friends.'

'Who speaks better?' asked Sophie. 'Me in French or you in English?'

'Why, yourself, of course,' replied Héloïse politely.

'I think perhaps I do,' said Sophie because it was the truth, but pointed out. 'You do not have the advantage of an English mother.'

'*C'est vrai.*' Héloïse stretched out her hand on which reposed the de Choissy emerald and diamond ring.

Emeralds are bad luck! The thought flashed through Sophie's head before she could stop herself.

'I am so tired,' Héloïse said wearily. 'Why don't you tell me about my uncle and aunt?'

Sophie complied and began to describe the Luttrells and High Mullions, speaking with such warmth and affection of her parents that Héloïse was seized by envy. She could never imagine feeling for her family in the way that Sophie so obviously felt for hers. Something of her thoughts must have shown in her face, for Sophie paused and then stopped.

'But your marriage, cousin, are you content? I have quite forgotten to offer you my felicitations.'

Héloïse hesitated. She felt it was important that she was honest with her cousin.

'Yes and no,' she admitted. 'Naturally, I like the idea of marrying someone so distinguished as Monsieur le Comte, and I know what is expected of me. But I wish . . . I wish I had been at liberty to choose someone who was more congenial.'

Sophie, who had been somewhat awed by the magnificence of the de Guinot ceremonial, was aware of the tension in the young woman beside her and her sympathy was aroused.

'Are you frightened of him?' she asked, privately considering that it was barbaric to force her cousin into a marriage she did not welcome.

'I think I am, a little,' replied Héloïse. 'I had not considered it in that light and I will never admit it to him. He is so much older, and so cold and uncaring.'

For the thousandth time she rubbed her hand across her lips to eradicate the memory of de Choissy's kiss.

'Can you not acquaint your parents with your feelings?' cried Sophie.

'No. It is not possible,' Héloïse replied. 'My wishes do not carry any importance. It is my duty to do as they ask.'

Sophie dropped her gaze to her lap.

'But do you not have a duty to yourself . . .?'

Her sentence trailed away. Sophie did not yet know Héloïse well enough to continue such a dangerous subject. Héloïse shrugged.

'But what of you, Miss Luttrell?'

Sophie gave a little flutter of her eyelashes. 'Well . . .,' she began.

The entrance of Ned bearing two glasses of wine put a stop to any further intimacies and Héloïse rose to greet him. Ned put the wine down and swept her a magnificent bow.

'You are even more beautiful close to,' he said, and kissed her hand with a flourish.

Sophie subsided happily into her chair. She had been a little worried by this meeting, for the journey to France had not been without incident and Ned had occasionally been a trifle short-tempered. Héloïse was smiling up at Ned who was melting visibly under the impact of her dark eyes.

'I hope you will stay with us for a while, Monsieur Luttrell,' she said. 'We would take it unkindly if you did not. Madame, *ma mère*, has arranged that we shall enjoy ourselves,' she added to tempt him. 'In fact, our engagements are such that we shall be quite worn out by the end of the season.'

'Then, you can rely on me,' Ned said gallantly.

Héloïse inclined her head. 'I would take it personally, Monsieur Luttrell, if I could not,' she said, enjoying the look of pure admiration that he sent her.

Sophie stood up and laid a hand on Ned's arm.

'I have so much to learn, cousin, and I wish to consult you on all manner of things, beginning with wardrobe.'

'Ah, but that is arranged,' Héloïse said mysteriously. 'Wait and see.'

'Mademoiselle de Guinot.' Ned was now serious. 'I have heard that there has been trouble in the city.'

Héloïse nodded, not wishing to alarm her guests. 'Yes. Some of the poorer elements marched on one of our prisons, the Bastille, and took it. It is a very old place and there were hardly any prisoners left, but the crowd took it into their head that it was worth "liberating". The authorities have it well in hand.'

'Why?' asked Sophie her curiosity aroused.

'There has been much talk of change lately – in France, you know, we like to debate politics. There are some people, who do not have the right to do so, who wish to participate in the government of the country. This time, they went too far.'

'And what is your opinion, Mademoiselle de Guinot?' asked Ned, forcing her to look at him.

'It is simple,' Héloïse replied. 'The king rules by divine consent and what he sees fit to do we must follow. There can be no debate about that. *C'est tout*.'

She moved towards the door.

'I must see to my guests, but I am so glad that you have come,' she said, and meant it. She left them together, Sophie still clasping Ned's arm. Ned's appreciative gaze followed her through the door.

At last, de Choissy came to make his farewells.

'I look forward to visiting you frequently in Paris and at Versailles,' he informed his betrothed. He reached out his long, thin fingers to kiss her hand and she knew he was goading her.

'You cannot avoid me,' he said, 'so you must learn to bear with me.'

She swallowed. 'As God is my witness,' she said slowly. 'I never wished for this, but I will do what is required of me.'

De Choissy stood quite still. 'I believe I am growing quite fond of you already,' he said, and watched her eyes widen in disbelief. He raised his eye-glass. 'There are many things you do not understand, *ma belle*, but I shall enjoy teaching you. Who knows? Perhaps you will be the saving of me. You possess both beauty and innocence, and they are rare commodities in my life.'

His eye-glass fell back on his breast and she stepped backwards, desperate to get away from his strange, almost satanic presence.

'I shall not detain you any longer, mademoiselle. I can see you wish me to take my leave.'

Then he was gone, leaving the imprint of his lips burning on the blue-veined skin of her hand.

Chapter 5

William, August 1789

William Jones cursed under his breath. Like everything he did, his swearing was fluent and efficient. The porter, who hastened to step forward at the sight of a well-to-do passenger, stopped in his tracks and listened with admiration. But since William was swearing in English the finer points, regretfully, were lost on him. Nevertheless, the porter conceded, here was a milord indeed worthy of his services, and he redoubled his efforts to engage William's attention.

William directed him to search through the pile of luggage that lay heaped in the middle of the square that was the diligence's final stop after the long journey from Calais.

'A green portfolio, with a large lock wrought in silver,' he said. 'It's missing. I had it in my hand a minute since, but I laid it down to search through my other bag and I fear someone has picked it up in error.'

His French was halting and unpractised, but grammatical enough. The porter signalled his understanding, squared his shoulders and proceeded to knock passengers and fellow porters flying as he waded into the fray. Minutes later, he emerged triumphant, holding the missing portfolio.

William took it gratefully and sat down on his trunk to check its contents, ignoring the reproachful looks directed at him by the unfortunates who had suffered at the porter's elbows. Thank God! The papers were intact. It would have been disastrous if they had fallen into the wrong hands.

William reread the letter bearing General Washington's signature which confirmed that he was seconded on a special mission for three years, and that his brief was to report back to the general on all that he considered politically or economically interesting in France. Then he slipped the letter back into the pocket concealed behind the lining where it joined a list of contacts, letter-drops and useful addresses that he was under orders to destroy if he considered it necessary. He had spent much of the sea voyage memorising the addresses and perfecting his grasp of the cipher in which he was to write his reports. He was almost ready to destroy the incriminating list but had decided that it was wiser to wait until he was more fully established in Paris.

William had never intended to be a spy – for that is what he had agreed to become – and was still getting used to the idea. He had not been surprised at the summons to Washington's home outside Williamsburg shortly after the great man's inauguration as president, because Mr Jones senior was married to Washington's second cousin and therefore entitled to petition his illustrious connection on behalf of his promising only son. But he had been surprised by the nature of the position offered. It did not take William long to make up his mind. This was a good opportunity which would lead to further advancement, and William was ambitious. If he had a flicker of squeamishness as to the morality of the role, William dismissed it as being necessary in the service of his country.

'Not', the general had inflected sternly at the interview, 'that we have any malign purpose in mind, Mr Jones. In fact, we look upon France with the warmest of feelings, but my agents inform me that a large pot is about to boil over there. I need not point out that the growth of any republican movement is of particular interest. You will write to me at regular intervals and account to me for your expenses, but to all intents and purposes you are a Mr William Jones from Williamsburg, Virginia, on a mission to sell land to possible settlers.'

William grimaced at his narrow escape and wondered how the general would rate him if he had seen him commit such a primary blunder as leaving his papers unguarded. It did not bear thinking of. He picked up his hat, settled it firmly on his head and pulled down the sleeves of his new coat. Made by an English tailor recently arrived in America, it was of light blue cloth, unlined except for the tails, and sported a turn-down collar, under which masterpiece he wore a double-breasted waistcoat of sprigged satin. William gave it an extra pat, fully satisfied with his appearance: neat, ordered and yet the cut of his tailoring betraying a certain dash. He looked round for a fiacre, ordered his luggage to be taken up and climbed inside.

The day was cloudy, but even so the fluid Gothic lines of the numerous churches and the yellow and grey stone houses lining the thoroughfares made a deep impression on him, used as he was to square red-brick buildings and white-painted wood. Here was a city that had a long ancient history, and for a visitor from the New World such as William it promised rewards. He looked forward to sampling its pleasures. Now all he had to do was carry out his mission, and although he did not underestimate the skill he would need or the sacrifices that he might be called on to make, or, indeed, the dangers, William was confident in his own powers. There was just a trace of complacency on his features as he sat back on the squabs of the fiacre.

At the Hôtel de Richelieu the American envoy, Gouverneur Morris, was waiting to welcome him. Gregarious, clever, of easy address and possessed of only one leg, which made him the target of many a soft-hearted lady, he moved in the highest of circles, and he was more than happy to put his savoir faire at William's disposal. Without enquiring too deeply, Mr Morris indicated that he understood William's needs.

'I have arranged for you to meet several of my acquaintances, among them Monsieur le Comte de Choissy, who seems particularly anxious to discuss business with you. If you play your cards right, you might be asked to stay at the Hôtel de Choissy – his hospitality is famous. You can, of course, remain here as long as you wish but I must point out that my apartments are limited in size.'

Mr Morris paused delicately.

'I will not impose on you any longer than necessary,' William reassured him.

'Meanwhile,' continued Mr Morris, 'I believe you will have need of a room in which to conduct your business.' He handed William a key and added enigmatically, 'I think this is suitable for your needs.'

This is the beginning of a double life, thought William as he alighted from a cab several days later. He was in the Marais quarter of Paris and it was growing dark. He had chosen the hour deliberately, but the gloom added to his problems of finding his way. The Marais was an area well suited to the clandestine: an unknown territory of narrow winding streets and swarming populace, of houses with secrets exits, of unexpected short cuts, dangerous-looking alleys and unalleviated darkness, for few, if any, lanterns were slung on ropes across the streets. It was here that his game of pretence and counter-pretence would be fought, using subterfuge, intrigue and his cool, reasoning intelligence.

William struck eastwards along the street. At the Place Royale he turned right and followed the delapidated stone arcade that ran around the square. Even in the bad light William could see that it had once been magnificent, but now there was an emptiness hovering over the decaying pavilions that struck a chill in him. Mr Morris had told him that once it had been

51

the centre of fashionable Paris where the nobility had come to entertain and be entertained in hired rooms. Outside number 7 he stopped, pushed open the main door, which yielded with a creak, and let himself into the vestibule. He scrabbled in his pocket for a tinder, lit a taper and ascended the staircase. Halfway up, he halted and his heart beat erratically with fright. He thought he had heard the whisper of voices and the scuffle of feet and for a moment he imagined that the house was peopled with painted and bejewelled shades from long ago. Then he smiled at his own fancifulness. It was only the rats running for cover at the sound of his footsteps.

Nevertheless, his hand shook a little as he fitted his key into the lock of the room that opened off the first landing. He stood safeguarding his light until his eyes adjusted and the acrid odour of decay had receded, and discovered he was standing in a huge reception room whose windows overlooked the garden in the square's centre. Even after the summer the chill was intense. William saw at once that the room was far too large for his needs and he walked down it towards a pair of double doors at one end.

These gave off on to a much smaller room, which he noted with satisfaction held a fireplace. He inspected the room thoroughly, testing the walls with his hands, where he encountered patches of damp and peeling plaster. It would do, he decided. When he was settled in he would arrange for some furniture to be brought and order some cupboards to be made, into which he would build a secret compartment.

William smoothed back his hair with a nervous gesture. The Place Royale would be the place where he received his agents, kept his reports and worked on his documents – a world away from the other William Jones who had an entrée into the best French society and intended to make use of it. If he was careful and prudent, his secrets would be safe, and there was no reason at all why anyone should ever suspect the persona of Mr William Jones, land agent. William foresaw no problem at all.

Chapter 6

The Cousins, September 1789

'Ned, you are being ridiculous.' Sophie almost stamped her foot in frustration. 'There can be no possible harm in it. Either you or Miss Edgeworth can chaperon me.'

'I don't approve of it. Why don't you go on one of your infernal sight-seeing trips with Miss Edgeworth instead? The marquise has put the cabriolet at your disposal.'

Ned spoke from the depths of a chair where he was perusing a broadsheet. His tone was lazy, but Sophie knew that he meant what he said.

'But it's so important that we take an interest.'

'Is it? I can't think why.'

Sophie was trying to persuade Ned to take her to listen to the debates in the National Assembly at Versailles, and Ned would have none of it.

'Ned, you don't understand.'

Ned gave a short laugh. 'If you mean by "understand" that I should allow you to become infected with political nonsense which is none of your business, then I don't.'

He peered harder at his paper.

'Good God. Some of the things they print about Her Majesty are quite outrageous. I think the authorities should put a stop to it.'

'May I see?' asked Sophie.

She went to take the broadsheet from him, but Ned folded it up and shook his head.

'Ned! Will you stop treating me like a child?'

'I will when you grow up and behave sensibly.'

'But I have grown up. Look at me.'

Ned flicked her a glance.

'And, anyway,' continued Sophie, determined not to give in. 'I can hardly be corrupted in one afternoon.' She softened her tone. 'Please let me see the broadsheet,' she begged.

Ned gave in and tossed her the offending publication.

'The French are all hot air,' he pronounced. 'Give me the quiet English countryside any day.'

Sophie made no comment. Ned's views had apparently not prevented him from throwing himself with gusto into their social engagements, which left very little time for private conversation. But when they did meet, he displayed this new tendency to be overly concerned with keeping a check on her movements.

Héloïse entered the room. Ned sat up.

'Mademoiselle Héloïse, I need you. Will you please explain to Sophie that she cannot be seen in the National Assembly?'

'Certainly she cannot,' said Héloïse at once. 'We have far too much to do.'

Ned got up and swept her a bow. 'You are both beautiful and wise. I knew I could rely on you,' he said in a tone that made Sophie turn away.

Héloïse laughed. Ned was so transparent and so English.

'She cannot go because Madame, *ma mère*, requires her. But when we visit Versailles in October I shall take her into the visitors' gallery. All the best people are to be found there. So you won't object, will you, dear Monsieur Luttrell?'

Without further ado, she bore Sophie away to their boudoir where, under the marquise's sharp scrutiny, no less a personage than Mademoiselle Bertin, the queen's dressmaker, was waiting to record Sophie's measurements in her black book and to explain her ideas for the transformation of the English 'Meez's' wardrobe. Sophie soon discovered that backs were being cut narrower, that dresses were now made in one piece and that sleeves were tighter. She emerged, dazed, a couple of hours later, having ordered a white muslin robe embroidered with chain stitch, a pink silk afternoon gown embellished with narrow green and silver stripes, a lace ball-gown, a riding habit, shoes, gloves, stockings and a daring cloak of black silk gauze woven in serpentine stripes.

Héloïse returned the kiss that Sophie, delighted that her toilettes would soon rival the best in Paris, bestowed on her cheek. The two cousins smiled at each other, well pleased with their growing intimacy. Not only did the Luttrells provide Héloïse with a perfect excuse for pushing all thoughts of her marriage to the back of her mind, but she had come to love Sophie and to trust her – not a thing that Héloïse did easily. For her part, Sophie had seen through the façade of the elegant Mademoiselle de Guinot and her compassion went out to the girl starved of affection that lay beneath.

'Now for tonight,' said Héloïse conspiratorially.

Sophie glanced at the card on the mantelpiece. They were going to Adèle de Fleury's ball that evening, an event which promised to be the most sought-after in the calender. Adèle was famed for her exclusive gatherings where no expense was spared. 'Ladies will wear white,' read the legend on her gold-edged invitation. Sophie and Héloïse had spent some time discussing this dictate and they had decided on a daring course of action. Hervé de Choissy had also promised to attend. He had been away from Paris on a visit since the betrothal and, naturally, Sophie was curious to meet him properly.

Paris had never seemed so extravagant or so glittering as it did that September. In the salons and eating houses, in the burgeoning political clubs and market-places, and down in the twisting alleys, the heat of a late summer fanned the atmosphere to fever pitch. The talk everywhere was of a new age; the mood, except amongst the poor, was of pleasure. Seated in the de Guinot coach on the way to the ball, Sophie gazed at the sights and sounds of fashionable Paris preparing to amuse itself, and felt the memory of High Mullions grow dim. I belong here, she thought with surprise, her country-tutored eyes ravished yet again by the beauty of the city.

Adèle's house was situated in the west of Paris, but for tonight she had prevailed on her dearest friend (whose husband was also Adèle's lover) to lend her house in St Germain. Resplendent in their evening attire, the marquis and marquise ascended the flambeaux-lit steps, Héloïse and Sophie behind them. Héloïse had become very quiet and Sophie did not press her to talk. She smoothed her robe into place with satisfaction: both of them, she considered, were looking their best, and she was looking forward to the reception their costumes would undoubtedly provoke.

The cousins were dressed in identical ball-gowns of soft blue crêpe. In their hair, coiffed by Léonard, the court hairdresser (procured after an enormous inducement), nodded blue ostrich feathers of an exact match. Tied with blue ribbons, their fans dangled from wrists which were sheathed in blue kid, and, in a final touch, they carried bouquets of blue forget-me-nots and white marguerites. The material frothed around Sophie's feet, on which she wore a pair of shoes adorned with diamond buckles, given to her by Héloïse as a present. Thus attired, Sophie felt interesting, very daring and ready to face the world.

She felt Héloïse tremble as they mounted the staircase, and tucked her arm into hers.

'Thank you, but I am all right,' Héloïse murmured gratefully, but a line on her normally smooth forehead indicated that she was suffering from nerves. Or from the prospect of meeting Monsieur le Comte.

'*Courage, chérie,*' she whispered back.

They waited at the top while the de Guinots went ahead, and Sophie looked through to the scene inside the long reception room and caught her breath.

Everywhere candles of the whitest wax blazed. Their flames painted the walls and mirrors with a mysterious brilliance, and left pools of shadow in between. Moving through these islands of light were the guests; and, like painted butterflies, they eddied from gossiping knot to another, calling out greetings and beckoning to their friends. Each face had assumed a different mask. Frivolous pleasure-seekers, predatory fortune-hunters and speculators; faces hungry for love and avid for power, faces of spoiled innocence and corrupted expectations – together they represented the tapestry of human vanity. The colours worn by the men shimmered as Sophie watched and the whites of the women blended into shades of cream, magnolia and the palest of white musk rose. Waves of scent and wax rose into the air with the deeper odour of hot bodies, hair grease and perfumed pastilles chewed against mephitic breath.

All of a sudden, Sophie felt nauseated. She swayed and fumbled for her handkerchief.

'Cousin.' Héloïse was beside her. 'Sophie, what is it? Are you ill?'

Sophie raised her head and tried to smile. For a moment, amounting to no more than a split second, she had had an impression that she was watching a crowd of ghosts.

'You must sit down,' said Héloïse firmly. 'Here, lean on me.'

Ignoring the ripple of surprise that greeted their non-conformist attire, she pushed her way inside and ushered Sophie to a chair. She sat down beside her.

'What is it, Sophie?' she asked. 'Tell me.'

Sophie shook her head.

'My mind is playing tricks. I think my excitement got the better of me. It is nothing. See.' She held out her hands, which were perfectly steady.' 'I am quite well now.'

Sophie pressed her handkerchief embroidered with blue flowers to her lips and tried to smile. After a minute, she began to feel better. This, she told herself, was the result of indulging in too much rich food, and she had better take care. These practical reflections, which reminded her of Miss Edgeworth, had the effect of quite restoring her spirits. She flashed a smile at Héloïse.

'Where is Ned?'

Héloïse pointed with her finger. 'I am afraid Monsieur Luttrell has not noticed us,' she said.

Lounging very much at his ease in a corner, Ned was entertaining a circle of beauties with some of his anecdotes. There was a great deal of laughter, much fluttering of fans and shrugging of powdered shoulders. He was far too occupied to notice their arrival. Sophie tried not to feel disappointed.

'I see Adèle coming towards us,' said Héloïse. 'We must prepare ourselves for her scolding.'

Sophie liked Adèle – who could fail to? And for some reason, known only to Adèle's volatile mind, she had chosen to champion Sophie. Sophie, seduced by Adèle's warmth and fascinated by the mingled wisdom and selfishness with which she conducted her life, had proved a ready victim. So it was with real pleasure that she made room for Adèle to join them.

'Pouf,' said Adèle, who had abandoned a posse of disappointed cavaliers with patently insincere excuses. 'Why do men always want to make love to you when you want to talk about something sensible for a change?'

'Perhaps', Héloïse said shrewdly, 'it is because you wish them to.'

Adèle regarded her for a moment and then turned to Sophie with a shrug.

'Your cousin is so clever,' she remarked. 'And now I shall exact my revenge on you two for ignoring my command to dress in white by ordering you to sit here and talk to me.'

'For five minutes, perhaps,' said Sophie, who had been watching Adèle's recklessly abandoned swain. Adèle chose to ignore her.

'Ah! There is de la Fourgères,' she said inconsequentially, and shuddered. 'Another time, perhaps, I shall introduce you, but he has such a bad case of head lice tonight. They are crawling quite openly. He really should speak to his hairdresser.'

'Who is that lady over there?' asked Sophie. She gestured towards a woman dressed in red satin. Adèle's face hardened.

'Oh,' she said, in freezing tones. 'De Genlis. Definitely not comme il faut, for all that she had the highest entrée. She is stuffed with republican ideas and I have recently quarrelled with her.'

Sophie scrutinised Madame de Genlis with interest. The mistress of the notorious Duc d'Orléans, or Philippe Égalité as he liked to be known, her weekly dinners and advanced educational ideas had made her notorious.

'It was very, very clever, and not at all well done of you, to dress in blue,' continued Adèle. 'Everyone is talking about you both and I am mortified because you cast me quite into the shade.'

Adèle plucked at the sleeves of her extremely expensive gown, which was of white silk trimmed with Mechlin lace and silver spangles, on to which tiny seed pearls had been sewn. She was hardly a figure in need of consolation, and she glowed with beauty and high spirits, knowing her ball was the success she had planned it to be.

Sophie inclined her head. 'My cousin and I knew that we could not compete with you on your own terms, madame. The situation was desperate, you will agree.'

Adèle trilled with laughter. 'Flatterer. I almost forgive you. But we will see how you stand up to the censure of my dear brother, who is even now coming to seek us out. Hervé, come here at once.'

There was no doubt that in full evening dress Hervé de Choissy was a notable sight. Clad in coat and breeches of blue and black spotted silk embroidered with satin stitch, set off by a white silk waistcoat, he had chosen to powder his hair, anchoring it back with a black ribbon. Concealed among the folds of his coat was a small dress sword, and into his lace cravat he had set a diamond pin. His aquiline face was alive with sardonic amusement. Why, he is superb, thought Sophie.

'You must be patient, Adèle,' said de Choissy. 'My first duty is to greet my bride-to-be.'

He carried Héloïse's hand to his lips and allowed them to linger as if he was calculating just how far he could go. Héloïse removed her hand and her eyes narrowed. She had decided that, whatever her aversion to de Choissy, she was not going to be bullied by him.

'On the contrary,' she said. 'I think the first introductions should go to my cousin.'

'Touché.' De Choissy registered the hit and turned to his sister. 'Mademoiselle de Guinot has reminded me of my manners.'

Adèle performed the introductions and Sophie gave him her hand. She smiled easily up at him.

'Very beautiful and very English,' he said.

'Not entirely, Monsieur le Comte,' she reminded him. 'I am half-French.'

'So you are,' he agreed. 'Then, you will enjoy many things about our country. Now it is my turn to make the presentations.'

He beckoned over the crush to a man standing by himself.

'Permit me to make known to you Mr William Jones from America. Mr Jones is here to sell land to anyone who wishes to take up the challenge, and I have persuaded him to make the

Hôtel de Choissy his home for the present. Mr Jones, Madame la Duchesse de Fleury, Mademoiselle de Guinot and Miss Luttrell from England.'

Sophie had the impression of white-blond hair and a contrasting pair of very dark eyebrows set in a thin face. Mr Jones was dressed neatly in a suit of green silk twill with silver buttons and stood at least six feet tall, and there was something about him that was quite different from anyone she had met before. A flush burned on her cheek and she raised her fan to hide it, both intrigued and excited. William saw a beautiful wide forehead and large grey eyes and his own signalled appreciation. Miss Luttrell was a striking figure.

Adèle's chatter restored Sophie's wits. She pulled herself together and made her greetings. William addressed himself politely to Héloïse, but as soon as he was at liberty to do so he turned his attention to Sophie. De Choissy claimed an unwilling Héloïse, and Adèle moved off to rejoin her abandoned swain.

'Shall we sit down?'

William steered Sophie towards a convenient sofa in the smaller of the reception rooms, and they sat down.

'How long are you planning to be in Paris?' he asked.

'At least a year,' she replied. 'I feel already that it is my second home. Of course I miss England and my parents, but less than I had imagined.'

Soon they were talking quite freely, and Sophie began to feel at ease with William. He enquired as to where she lived and she furnished him with some details. He, in turn, told her about his home in America and the reason for his visit. Sophie was interested.

'You mean anyone can buy land in America?'

'They can and they do. It is possible to make an excellent life in my country – if you don't mind hard work. We have plantation up-river and a town house in Williamsburg, and there is plenty of room for settlers.'

'When did your family arrive?'

'My grandparents left England after a series of misfortunes and they have never looked back. The land in Virginia is fertile, the tobacco luxuriant and our hams are famed throughout the nation.'

'So you are a quarter English?'

William's drawl became more pronounced. 'I like to think of myself as wholly American, Miss Luttrell.'

Although he was proud of his English heritage, William's loyalties centred entirely on his Americanness.

'Nevertheless, we have something in common,' said Sophie

and gave him one of her ravishing smiles. William determined there and then that he would make it his business to call on Miss Luttrell every day.

'Have you been following events in France?' he asked, in order to collect his thoughts. 'You may have been worried by the trouble at the Bastille.'

'No, indeed. I am under the best protection, you know, and sufficiently in tune with what is happening to rather approve.'

'Are you, Miss Luttrell? How very interesting. I admire that in you. It is so unusual to meet . . . What I mean is . . .' William did not wish to be rude and finished, 'On what do you base your observations?'

'On reading – I have been making use of my uncle's library and I have set myself a course to read through the winter – and by listening. It is not so hard to use one's wits, Mr Jones. I am sure you use yours.'

William permitted himself a wry reflection on just how important his wits were. 'So you wish to see the king divested of his power?'

'Dear me, no,' said Sophie, pleased that someone at last was interested in her opinions. 'I would wish only that he rule with a parliament, like the system we have.'

William said nothing. Sophie frowned.

'Mr Jones, forgive me, but you appear concerned. Is there something you know that we do not?'

'No,' he answered. 'Except to say that events, once set in train, have a habit of gathering speed and turning into something quite different. I have a feeling that France will be no exception to the rule.'

Sophie was not quite sure what the intriguing Mr Jones was driving at, but his words made her uneasy. William watched the pulse at the fusion of her collar-bone and neck and wished that he could touch the satin skin.

'I wonder if you will be proved correct, Mr Jones,' was all she said.

'Sophie.'

A voice intruded into their conversation. Sophie glanced up with a start. She had been so absorbed by Mr Jones that she had quite forgotten about Ned. He was leaning against the wall, watching them and taking a pinch of snuff.

'Do introduce me, cousin,' he said.

William and Sophie got to their feet. The two men were of similar height and build. They sized each other up.

'Ned, this is Mr Jones from Virginia in America. He has been telling me all about his country.'

'So I see,' said Ned, making the briefest of bows.

Sophie stared at him. It was so unlike Ned to sound hostile.

'Mr Jones is staying in Paris with Monsieur le Comte. Is that not fortunate?' she said quickly.

'Very,' said Ned.

'Oh, but I shall be travelling for the next few months. I plan to winter in the South and perhaps journey on into northern Spain for a while,' said William, for the first time regretting the fact. 'I have some business there.'

'Perhaps we shall see you when you return?'

Sophie sounded a little depressed, and Ned was quick to notice it.

'If we are still in Paris, Sophie. We have not yet finalised our plans. Otherwise we would be delighted.'

'Yes, but . . .'

Ned cut in on her.

'It was very good of you to look after my cousin, Mr Jones, when there must be so many others you wish to talk to, but if you will permit me, it is time I claimed her back.'

William took the hint. He bowed, and Sophie could have sworn he was frowning.

'I fear I have been monopolising Miss Luttrell,' he said politely, not at all pleased at his dismissal. 'Perhaps we can further our acquaintance another time.'

He looked straight into her eyes as he spoke, and was rewarded by the response that leapt involuntarily into hers. Ned made no further comment.

Deciding that he did not like Ned Luttrell one bit, William took his leave and went to join the circle around de Choissy. They were discussing the unprecedented events that had taken place in the National Assembly one hot August night.

'It was unbelievable,' declared the Chevalier de Bergère, who had been present on the occasion when, in a fit of collective madness, the nobility of France stood up and renounced their feudal rights and privileges.

'That is all very well,' said de Choissy to his audience, 'but have you considered the consequences?'

'Meaning, Monsieur le Comte?' asked William, trying to work out exactly what relationship Ned Luttrell bore to the interesting Miss Luttrell.

'Our revenues, my poor fool, our revenues,' replied his host. 'I, for one, shall lose my moneys from the toll of the Dordogne and from the properties on the Loire.'

'What you mean, my dear Hervé,' said an exquisite young man with a yawn, 'is that you will have to restrict yourself to

61

drinking the ordinary wine of the region instead of laying up a great store of vintage grape in that famous cellar of yours. Or perhaps', he added maliciously, 'you will have to curtail the spending of your future comtesse.'

De Choissy glanced in the direction of Héloïse. She was fending off imminent abduction to the card table by some gallants who wished to avail themselves of Mademoiselle de Guinot's famous luck. Always painfully sensitive to his presence, Héloïse met his look. Then she dropped her gaze and allowed herself to be led towards the green and white card room which had been decorated with banks of foliage tied in white ribbon. De Choissy raised an eyebrow.

'You may be right, my dear François,' he said thinly, dismissing the subject. 'Now, Mr Jones,' he continued, tapping William on the arm, 'let us discuss your forthcoming visit to Versailles before we rejoin the ladies.'

They moved away.

Ned unhooked Sophie's fan from her wrist and spread it open.

'Who is he exactly?' he asked, examining the pretty pastoral scene depicted on it with studied interest. Sophie dipped a curtsy to a very grand lady in silk brocade and sat down again on the sofa.

'I know little more than you do,' she said. 'Mr Jones is staying with Monsieur le Comte. I found him very interesting,' she added with a hint of mischief.

Ned shut her fan with a snap. 'Is he?' he said lightly. 'Well, you certainly made it obvious. I have been watching you for the past twenty minutes. You must have a care to your reputation, puss.'

'*Tiens!*' Sophie was bewildered. 'What do you mean, Ned?'

'I am sure my aunt will have warned you against flirting with strangers,' he replied.

Sophie relieved him of her fan. 'Would you rather I flirted with someone I know?' she asked.

'Don't be tedious, Sophie.' Ned's face darkened. Sophie had rarely spoken to him in such a tone and he did not care for it. 'It is merely that you must be careful.'

She was silent. She recognised the expression that had sprung for a second into his face. She recognised it because back at High Mullions she, too, had experienced just such a feeling of possessiveness and understood a little of its nature. But there the comparison was at an end, for Sophie's emotions were honestly based. Ned's were not.

He laced his fingers into her blue-gloved hand. 'Remember,

you belong to me,' he reminded her, 'and you have the Luttrell name to uphold.'

'I have never heard you talk in such a manner before,' Sophie said, by now thoroughly upset. 'I did not think it mattered to you very much what I did. In fact, so attentive have you been to cousin Héloïse and to the others that I have been forced to conclude . . .'

Sophie fanned herself vigorously and to her horror felt tears pricking behind her eyes. She was tired and it was late and much of the pleasure had gone out of the evening.

'There you are wrong,' he replied. 'I mind very much. You were foolish to think otherwise.'

Sophie gazed at her lap and slowly disengaged her hand from Ned's.

'I see. You may talk to whom you wish. What I mean is, you may visit Margaret Wainwright but I must be circumspect,' she finished in a rush.

'What do you mean?' asked Ned. He was angry. 'I forbid you to say any more.'

'But it is true, isn't it, Ned?'

He neither confirmed nor denied her accusation.

'You must not pry, Sophie.'

'No,' she said miserably, 'I promised myself that I would not.'

'That is very wise of you, puss,' he said, softening, and again she caught the fleeting echo of a stronger emotion. 'Now will you do as I say and take the greatest care?'

He bent towards her and his shadow fell across her face.

'You are growing rather pretty, Miss Luttrell,' he teased her, 'and I must look after you.'

Sophie closed her eyes. Ned was saying the things to her that she had wished so many times for him to say. Through her lashes she saw the room imprinted like an etching on her mind, smelt the musk from a hundred bodies and tasted the wine she had drunk on her tongue – sensations that would be now forever woven into a memory of her longing for something, for someone. For Ned. She turned, and Ned, who could never resist the sight of a female face tilted temptingly towards him, bent to kiss her. His lips pressed firm and dry against hers and she put up a hand to his shoulder. Ned leaned back with a smile.

Sophie spread her fan out to a quarter of its width. The vignette revealed on the painted silk showed a charming little shepherdess frolicking with her lover. She was looking over her shoulder while her swain held out his hand to guide her over a stile. Sophie spread the fan out to half its width. The sheep browsed peacefully on radiant fields and the sky shone with a clear blue. She spread it to its furthest extent and the scene changed abruptly. Lurking in the trees was the figure of another man, and it was he towards whom the shepherdess was extending her invitation.

'There's Héloïse,' she said, to cover her confusion, for Ned had never attempted such intimacies before and Sophie had never received a kiss such as the one he had just given her. Ned got to his feet at once, and went to engage Héloïse in conversation. He left Sophie to gaze after him in some perplexity. At that precise moment her overwhelming emotion was one of disappointment and she could not understand why.

PARIS, October 4th, 1789

In September 1789 the National Assembly in Versailles declared that all men 'are born and remain free and equal in rights'.

Nevertheless, many of the nobles who had so recklessly stood up in the chamber to renounce their feudal dues regretted it when they reflected in the sober light of morning, and the king quite simply refused to countenance any measures that encroached on his authority or position.

The country seethed with rumours and the economic crisis was forcing hundreds of vagabonds on to the roads. Violence stalked through the rural villages and towns as roaming cadres of bandits swept through the countryside, fuelling the unease. People came to talk of the time of the Grande Peur, when every stranger was regarded with suspicion and men took turns to stand guard over their fields. In Normandy, Hainault, Alsace, Franche-Comté and the Soane valley armed peasants attacked and despoiled the houses of their seigneurs and the rumours flew thick and fast that France was under attack from invading armies.

In Paris the struggle for existence continued. As a result of a drought which made it impossible for millers to grind their corn, bread was expensive and difficult to obtain. Bread queues became a familiar sight. They were neither quiet nor peaceful, and bakers, often in fear of their lives, requested guards to be posted outside their shops. The queues were fertile hunting grounds for agents provocateurs who slipped from quarter to quarter stirring the waters of revolution. 'We must march on Versailles and bring back the king to the capital where he belongs. Only then will we have bread,' they said.

On October 1st a dinner was given in the opera house for the officers of the Flanders Regiment newly arrived at Versailles. Both the king and the queen, holding the dauphin in her arms, appeared in their box, and, it was said, the red and blue cockade was trampled underfoot. News of the royal banquet appeared in the Courrier on October 3rd. Unrest flamed into open rebellion.

On the morning of October 5th crowds of women began to gather in the centre of Paris, desperate for food. While the tocsin rang out above *the clamour, they stood and shouted for action. Fishwives jostled with prostitutes, market-women rubbed shoulders with neatly clad bourgeoises, gauze-workers with seamstresses, the sick with the healthy, the old with the young in an unruly tide that swept down from the Faubourg St Antoine to the headquarters of the Parisian municipal authorities, the Hôtel de Ville.*

The tocsin clanged on, sending out its clarion note of defiance. By the time the Hôtel de Ville had been plundered for arms, its cannon seized and its guards persuaded to join the march, the rabble army was over 6,000 strong.

Through Paris they surged, sweeping up anybody who lay in their path and calling to their brothers and sisters to accompany them. The streets filled with the echoes of their hoarse cries . . . 'To Versailles. To Versailles . . .'

Chapter 7

Versailles, October 5th, 1789

The recent elevation of the marquis to minister of supplies required his constant presence around the king. It was, therefore, sensible that the de Guinots removed themselves to Versailles where the marquise could organise a series of weekly dinners and maintain a firm supervision of petitioners and contacts. The move had been arranged for the first week of October. Marie-Victoire was kept busy sorting linen and supervising Sophie and Héloïse's wardrobe, and checking and rechecking chests, bags and bandboxes for which she was responsible. By the time the marquise was handed into the first of the two waiting coaches and her maid and secretary disposed beside her, Marie-Victoire was quite exhausted.

There had been no time to think too much about Jacques during the last few months, nor did she wish to. She knew that he had fled from La Joyeuse as he had threatened after his beating, and had apparently stolen some silver teaspoons. She knew, too, that that fact alone would ensure that he never returned, because he would like as not be hanged for the crime. Luckily for Marie-Victoire, there had been no complications from the rape, although in contrast to the purple bruises on her body, which had eventually faded, the memory would remain with her always.

Marie-Victoire placed a leather dressing case beside Héloïse and Sophie and climbed into the second coach. There were just the three of them. Ned Luttrell had chosen to ride by another route, declaring that he needed the fresh air. Miss Edgeworth was to remain at the Hôtel de Guinot, the marquise having informed her that the apartments in Versailles were too small to accommodate extra persons. Miss Edgeworth, it was clear, had no option but to incline her head in graceful submission, which, being Miss Edgeworth, she did.

The coach eased its way through the stone gateway and out

into the street. Marie-Victoire settled back on the blue leather seat and stared out of the window, anxious to see as much as possible. The driver skirted the wall of the house and stopped to allow a cart that was slewed back across the road to right itself. Suddenly Marie-Victoire pressed back into her seat and her hand flew to her mouth. Surely it could not be? She steeled herself to look again at a tall man talking to a woman in the street. There was something about the set of his thin shoulders that reminded her forcibly of the one person she did not wish to see . . .

The coach jerked forward. The man looked up from his conversation and Marie-Victoire gave a little hiss of relief. He was nothing like Jacques. It was only her imagination playing tricks, but as the rhythmic clack of horses' hoofs steadied into a trot a little refrain played through her mind. I hate him. I hate him. And then Marie-Victoire felt ashamed, fumbled in the folds of her skirt for her rosary and sent up a silent prayer, unsure of whether she was praying for Jacques or herself. She looked out on the parade of street life unfolding before her. There were porters negotiating in the middle of the road, housewives prodding at fruit and vegetables and rouged street gallants pushing their way through the bodies with outstretched canes. In several of the squares they passed the daily markets were in full swing. Marie-Victoire caught glimpses of bird-sellers hawking their pathetic wares, quacks offering every nostrum under the sun, jugglers, dentists, dog-gelders, and even a pickpocket sliding through the scrum. There were wine booths on every corner, rows of lime trees, dingy hotels, stonemasons' yards, ruined churches and slums seething with prostitutes, beggars and children so ragged and thin that they did not appear human at all. Marie-Victoire saw it all and was humbled, and hoped that one day her failure of charity regarding Jacques would turn into forgiveness.

Settled into her side of the coach, Sophie could see much the same as Marie-Victoire, but her mind was elsewhere. For some reason, her thoughts kept returning time and time again to the night of Adèle's ball, but, like a tongue unable to leave off exploring an aching tooth, the memory brought no relief, only an unexplained desire to burst into tears. Sophie was bewildered by her mood and could offer no explanation for it. She stared even harder out of the window as if to obtain enlightenment from outside. The coach slowed down at a crossroads and two little girls ran out to watch. They were so thin that the bones stuck out from their sore-encrusted bodies and their matted hair hung from oozing and partly bald scalps. Sophie jerked back into the present. Her heart twisted by pity and horror, she fumbled in her travelling case for a coin which she flung out of the window, and then looked away in real distress, suddenly hating her fine muslin and fluttering ribbons, when the children dived for it like wild animals.

Héloïse leant over and shut the window with a snap.

'I hope they don't suffer for your kindness,' she said gently. 'Someone bigger than they are might take it from them by force.'

Sophie's face registered such revulsion that Héloïse hastened to point out a particularly fine church in order to divert her. Sophie's kind heart was one of the many things she loved in her cousin. By comparison, her own often felt barren and empty. Perhaps it needed to be, she reflected. Héloïse had not been encouraged to love many people in her life; and the future that faced her was very different from Sophie's. To feel too much as the wife of Monsieur le Comte de Choissy was to invite additional unhappiness. The luxury of softer emotions was something, Héloïse had decided, she must leave to others.

The coach rolled on, containing the three women deep in their private thoughts, and Paris was left behind. Once on the Versailles road there were no other vehicles to speak of and they made good progress. The coachman whipped up his horses.

Hoping to banish the spectre of Jacques, Marie-Victoire closed her eyes and opened them again abruptly when the coach swerved violently to the left throwing her on top of Sophie, who yelped as Marie-Victoire's elbow dug into her side. The coach swayed, appeared to skid and then swung to a halt, tilted at a precarious angle. Marie-Victoire managed to extricate herself from Sophie with some difficulty.

'Are you hurt?' she asked.

Sophie shook her head and rubbed her side.

'Are *you*?' she enquired of Héloïse.

Shaken, but in one piece, Héloïse confirmed that she was alive.

The coachman appeared at the window in a considerable state of agitation and managed to prise open the door. Héloïse gathered up the skirts of her blue travelling dress and descended gingerly.

'Careful,' she warned.

They surveyed the scene. At this point, the roadside was heavily wooded and the overhead branches made a canopy which permitted only a little daylight to filter through. A huge branch lay across the road, and the coach's left-hand wheels lay entrenched in a deep rut by the side of the road as a result of trying to avoid it. It was obvious even to an untrained observer that it was going to take a great deal of skill and effort to right it. The coachman's mate was endeavouring to calm the horses, and failing. The coachman himself was almost incoherent and spluttering apologies. Héloïse hastened to reassure him that she did not consider it his fault, but could he apply himself to remedying the situation?

The coachman clapped his hat on his head and went to shout at his mate.

Héloïse shrugged her shoulders and sighed.

'*Alors*,' she said, and raised her eyes heavenwards.

Sophie grinned and went to stand by the horses' heads while Héloïse supervised the removal of the branch, which took a considerable time. In the end Marie-Victoire offered her assistance. Sophie talked quietly to the horses and tried to ignore the ache in her ribs.

'Now for the coach,' Héloïse called out. 'You had better stand back.'

Sophie and Marie-Victoire withdrew to a prudent distance. The coachman shouted an order, his mate leapt to the horses' heads and the horses strained in the shafts. The coach swayed, groaned and moved forward an inch or so.

'Again,' ordered Héloïse.

The wheels juddered and spun, sending out little spurts of dirt and dust, but remained obstinately trapped. Deciding that there was nothing else for it, Sophie, thankful there was nobody to witness her hoydenish behaviour, hitched up her skirt as far as she dared and went to stand behind the coach.

'You will have to help me, Marie-Victoire,' she called over her shoulder.

'*Attention*,' warned Héloïse. 'It could be dangerous.'

Sophie spread her hands up against the bodywork and the two girls pushed until their breath failed.

'It's no good,' Sophie panted at last. 'We need help.'

The coachman subsided visibly and then made a gigantic effort to be positive.

'If mademoiselle is prepared to wait,' he addressed Héloïse, 'I will walk to the next village and get help.'

'Mademoiselle has no other option,' said Héloïse, torn between laughter and exasperation. She was not exactly frightened at being left almost unguarded on the lone stretch of road, but the prospect was a little worrying. She looked around to see if there was any possible form of help in sight. As she did so, she caught her foot in the hem of her skirt, staggered and fell heavily.

'Héloïse!'

Sophie ran to help her. Héloïse struggled into a sitting position and allowed Sophie to slip an arm around her shoulders. Her hair had tumbled loose and cascaded down her back and she was white with shock, but she managed a crooked smile.

'This is becoming ridiculous,' she said when she had got her breath.

Sophie helped her to her feet and led her towards the bank where she sat her down on a large stone. Héloïse clung to her for a minute.

'What a sight I must look,' she said shakily.

'A damsel in distress,' said Sophie in an attempt at lightness, and searched in her pocket for a handkerchief with which she wiped Héloïse's face and hands. 'You should fall more often, cousin, you look quite delightful.' She glanced down the road. 'What is more,' she continued, 'like all good damsels in the stories we are about to be rescued. There is someone coming.'

Héloïse straightened up and began frantically to arrange her hair.

'Help me, Sophie,' she implored as a party of eight to ten riders trotted towards them.

'Soldiers,' breathed Marie-Victoire, impressed by their red epaulettes and white coats.

The soldiers swung to a halt.

'Can we be of assistance?' enquired a courteous voice.

One finger still twisted into her hair, Héloïse raised her eyes. Mounted on a huge chestnut stallion was a grenadier officer from the Versailles National Guard.

'Indeed, if you would, monsieur,' she said gratefully. 'I am Héloïse de Guinot . . .'

'Mademoiselle de Guinot,' said the officer. 'Of course, I should have recognised the arms on your coach. I am acquainted with some of your family . . . but are you all right?'

He swung down off his horse and came towards her, a tall, well-made man whose uniform set his figure off to advantage. He swept off his plumed hat and revealed a head of thick dark hair and a very handsome face, tanned from summer exercises. He seemed completely in command of the situation.

'My name is Louis d'Épinon. You must permit me to help you,' he said with a bow.

Sophie observed that he had an obstinate chin, offset by a generously proportioned mouth and a practised address. In all, he was a very dashing saviour to call on for help.

'Thank you,' said Héloïse, vastly relieved.

She encountered a pair of lapis-lazuli blue eyes, eyes Héloïse knew in a flash could hold tenderness and humour; and, without warning, a quiver of electricity shot through her.

71

'I am sorry you have had this distressing experience,' said Louis, 'but I am sure we can sort it out very quickly.'

'It was nothing,' replied Héloïse, her spirits rising. 'I knew it would not be long before we obtained assistance.'

'Still, I would not like to have thought of you remaining alone for long, mademoiselle,' said Louis, who had noticed that she had the most beautifully shaped head. 'It can be dangerous, and there are worrying reports of rioting in some of the villages.'

'Yes, indeed.' Héloïse was warm in her appreciation. 'Miss Luttrell and I cannot thank you enough.'

Louis issued some orders. Six of his men dismounted and the lieutenant rode to the front of the coach to take charge, thus obliterating completely what remained of the coachman's professional pride. It took a couple of minutes to ease the coach back on to the road with the minimum of fuss and there was only a minute scratch on the bodywork to show for its mishap.

Louis proffered his arm to Héloïse. She hesitated.

'Monsieur le Capitaine, Miss Luttrell and I are both so grateful. I know my father, Monsieur le Marquis, will wish to thank you in person. Perhaps you would be good enough to call on us at Versailles?'

Louis bowed, and again a current cut through the air between them. Héloïse began to feel a little light-headed, and she was suddenly intensely aware of the colour of Louis' uniform, the feel of fresh air on her face, and of a sensation that all things were possible. Then common sense intervened.

How foolish I am, she thought. There were other things to face first, and she had been acquainted with Monsieur d'Épinon for less than twenty minutes. She gave herself a mental shake and accepted his arm. The moment passed. Louis handed her into the coach.

'We were on reconnaissance,' he remarked conversationally, shooting a professional glance down the road, 'and I had been warned of possible trouble in this area, so I decided with my men to take a look. I think you should continue your journey immediately, Mademoiselle de Guinot. My men will escort you – if you agree.'

The offer was accepted.

'Remind me', Héloïse said to Sophie as she sank thankfully back into the seat, 'never to permit that idiot of a coachman to drive us again.'

'Poor man,' said Sophie. 'He was so upset. You must forgive him.'

'I don't feel like it,' said Héloïse, 'but for your sake, Sophie, and only for your sake, I will.'

*

Nearer to the town of Versailles the road opened up into a well-paved, tree-lined avenue over which large oil lamps were suspended. They swayed in the light breeze that had sprung up, and the road stretched out smooth and apparently trouble-free. In a very short space of time they reached the outskirts, and Sophie exclaimed with delight at the elegant stone houses and streets that opened off the avenue.

Louis had given orders for his men to deploy themselves in front as well as behind the de Guinot coach which allowed him to trot beside it, from which position he had an unimpeded view of Héloïse's profile. She sat very still inside and he wondered briefly what she was thinking, but his thoughts were soon diverted. He was worried by the situation that was developing. A new National Guard for Versailles had recently been formed, to which he had been seconded to supervise the recruits, but it was under the command of a man renowned for his arrogance. Monsieur le Comte d'Estaing would certainly not notice if the ranks were being infiltrated by men infected by some of the insurrectionary ideas being hawked in the capital, which, as Louis had discovered, they were. Louis had never taxed himself before about such matters – there had been no cause for concern. But recent events in the National Assembly had been worrying, the fall of the Bastille ominous, and his sixth sense convinced him that trouble was brewing.

He knew himself to be a good officer: brave, meticulous and caring of his men, something of a rarity at a time when a commission meant nothing so much as a pleasant sinecure. But he and the more thoughtful of his brother officers were beginning to wonder if all the good intentions in the world would be enough if the king, God forbid, found himself in a position where he was forced to defend himself from his own subjects.

Louis had always nourished ambitions for the army, and, as a second son, he had been destined for it. That or the Church. Since the latter failed to appeal, his father had made an effort to ensure that his son had joined an acceptable regiment. Louis had been grateful. The life suited him and it also allowed him, as he had hoped, to be in direct proximity to the court and its social life. He pricked his horse into a faster trot and smiled to himself. At thirty he was still unmarried and his elder brother, who had succeeded on the death of his father to a flourishing family estate, urged him constantly to do so. Louis usually fobbed off the idea with a shrug of his elegantly (and very expensively) clad shoulder. He left such matters to his brother. After all, the responsibility of continuing the family's name was his, not Louis'. Besides, the thought of maintaining a household and a nursery bored Louis and it was very costly to keep a wife. Louis' allowance, although adequate, was not princely, nor was his pay, and anyway his time was taken up by certain other ladies. Like Jeanne.

Delicious Jeanne, who took her pleasures so deftly – and so ruthlessly. Or Thérèse, who wound her auburn hair around his neck while she parted her white thighs and drew his hand down between them. Or Violette, still a little wary but all the more delicious for that, who insisted on making love surrounded by a blaze of candles. They were cultivated, assured and sophisticated married ladies, all of them, who knew how to play the game according to the rules, and Louis liked it so.

The road curved to the right, and once more Louis was presented with a view of Héloïse's profile. All thoughts of Jeanne, Thérèse and Violette faded. Beautiful, vulnerable, untouched: the words that described her slid into Louis' mind before he was aware they were there. He knew without prior knowledge that Héloïse was all of those things, and that she was ripe for someone to awaken her. A shiver of desire caught at the back of his throat, and with it came the temptation. 'It could be me.'

The sight of the pink and gold palace of Versailles at the end of the Avenue de Paris restored Louis to the present. The Marquis and Marquise de Guinot had, no doubt, made their plans for their daughter, and he was a fool to contemplate such a liaison on the strength of one chance meeting – yet. If Mademoiselle de Guinot were to be married, then, and only then, after she had done her duty and produced an heir, would it be time to launch a campaign to make her his mistress. He would have to be patient.

A lieutenant was waiting for Louis as the entourage swept into the Place d'Armes and halted in front of the palace gates.

'Sir, the reports from Paris require your urgent attention,' he informed Louis curtly.

'Trouble?'

'Yes, sir.'

Louis dismounted. 'Escort Mademoiselle de Guinot and her party to their apartments and then return to me.'

After what was necessarily the briefest of goodbyes, Louis led his horse towards the stables, leaving Héloïse, Sophie and Marie-Victoire to follow the lieutenant through the wrought-iron gates and up the gently inclining courtyard of the Cour des Ministres, where they turned left and disappeared into the wing assigned for the use of the king's ministers.

His headquarters smelt of sweat and leather, and there was

74

an unusual stir of activity. One of Louis' fellow officers looked up at his entrance and waved a dispatch in front of his nose.

'You had better read this,' he said. 'Paris is in an uproar and a mass of fishwives are marching on Versailles.'

'You're not serious?' said Louis, taking it from him.

'The agents have only just managed to pass this through. The Parisians have been massing in the streets since dawn and many of the roads are blocked. Apparently, Monsieur le Duc d'Orléans has been whipping up support in the bread queues against the king and inciting the mob to march on Versailles. It *sounds* ridiculous, but we had better take steps to deal with it.'

Louis frowned. 'What of the Paris National Guard? Where are they?'

The officer tapped the paper with his finger. 'Who knows? The first report suggests that they are not much in evidence. They are under the command of Général Lafayette, of course, but where he is I cannot tell you.'

'And there is no other support?'

'It seems not.'

Louis adjusted his sword belt. 'We must assemble the detachments. Will you see to it while I get something to eat?'

It was afternoon by the time Louis returned to the Place d'Armes and the palace was quiet. The king had been out hunting since the early morning, and the queen, who was supervising the gardener at the Petit Trianon, had given orders not to be disturbed. Many of the courtiers were either making visits in the town or riding and walking in the grounds. Louis gazed up at the familiar buildings – the older palace with its cast-iron roof decorations and elaborate stonework built around the inner marble court, the calm spaciousness of the two courts that opened beneath it and the elongated lines of the royal chapel to the right – and it seemed impossible to him that they could be under threat. So thinking, he walked towards the Avenue de Paris, and was stopped in his tracks.

Someone was galloping at full speed towards the palace, shouting and waving his hat. The rider grew closer and Louis took a step back. It was the Duc de Maillé. Louis raised his hand in greeting. But the duke never slackened his pace, and swerved to avoid Louis.

'Paris is marching on us with guns,' he shouted, and then, bending double over the saddle, he passed in a flurry of clattering hoofbeats that stilled abruptly when he flung himself from his mount and disappeared towards the royal apartments. Louis stared after him and it took a second or two for his brain to clear. He began to run towards the stables opposite the gates, seized the nearest horse from a surprised groom and flung himself across the saddle.

The Hôtel des Menus Plaisirs lay further down the Avenue de Paris to the right, just past the Hôtel du Grand Maître. Louis set spur to his horse. It was imperative that he warn the Assembly, which was in session, of what was happening. But when he eventually burst through the door he was informed that the Assembly could not be disturbed. Furious at this unexpected obstacle, Louis decided to waste no more time. He left urgent messages with instructions to convey them to the president of the Assembly as soon as possible, turned on his heel and remounted his horse.

Back in the Place d'Armes, he issued the call to arms and sent messengers scurrying to all corners of the palace and into the town. His men took up their formations just as the first scout ran in and gasped out his story of how a huge mob of women had walked the twelve miles from Paris to Versailles, intent on bringing the king back to the capital. Worse, the scout reported, the Paris National Guard had also decided to join the uprising and was following behind with guns and cannon.

'What is that man Lafayette thinking of? He should have been able to prevent this,' snapped Louis, more to himself than to anybody.

'He is with them,' the scout reported, 'and sends word that he has them under control.'

'Can we trust him?' asked Louis unguardedly. He narrowed his eyes and added in an undertone, 'I think the général cares more for his own glory than to protect the king.'

The scout stood to attention. It was not his business to comment.

'Did no one think to close the Sèvres bridge,' demanded Louis, 'and prevent their crossing?'

The scout shook his head and Louis dismissed him.

It was quite clear to Louis that Versailles was under serious attack, and he acted swiftly. He sent word to the commanding officer of the Flanders Regiment with a request for his men to join him. He ordered the horses to be saddled and yet another messenger was dispatched to summon the remainder of the King's Swiss Guards a few miles to the north-east at Courbevoie. As he worked, Louis rejected first one plan then another: the king should be advised to leave; the queen must return from the Trianon; the royal children, at least, should be taken to some place of safety. And all the time he was conscious of a growing sense of unreality. This could not be happening. It should not be happening. Something had gone very wrong.

The Place d'Armes was now alive with men and rang to the sound of cornets and shouted orders. Inside the Cour Royale the Swiss Regiment ran to take up their positions under the chapel arch and, for the first time since the days of Louis XIV, the great black iron gates of the château swung shut with a clang. Despite his preoccupation, Louis managed to spare a thought for Héloïse and toyed with the idea of sending a messenger to the de Guinot apartments, advising them to leave Versailles by another route, but thought better of it. Then he forgot all about her.

Like many others in the palace, the de Guinot party was unaware of any impending crisis. Having retired briefly to their rooms to refresh themselves – and Sophie was astonished to see how small and cramped the rooms were – they had met up with Ned and embarked at once on a walking party in the grounds, the marquise having already departed on some engagement of her own.

It had been a very pleasant afternoon despite the damp weather which had curtailed the expedition a little, but Sophie was so eager to see the palace and to explore the delights of its fabled terraces, flowerbeds and statues that she did not mind. The gardens were as awe-inspiring as reports had made out and quite impossible to see in their entirety in one short afternoon. Sophie looked forward to many more such outings, both walking and riding. She was particularly impressed by the vista of the lake, which stretched out for miles into the distance, and exclaimed over the impressiveness of the fountains. She and Ned rambled up the avenue of lime trees that led towards the Trianon and vied with each other as to the respective merits of the statues.

Ned was in a very good humour. His ride had given him some exercise and he felt better for it. He had also managed to capture Héloïse for five minutes and had made her laugh at one of his jokes. Actually, the palace didn't stir any special feelings in him, he rather preferred the sight of a well-managed English estate, but he was perfectly content to stand chatting with Sophie while they looked up at the palace from the terrace steps. The air was growing chill and he took her arm to lead her back to the apartments.

'How perfect it is,' exclaimed Sophie as she ascended the huge stone steps. 'It is so beautiful and so peaceful.'

She paused to regain her breath, and her gaze swept over the landscape which was tinted with autumnal reds and oranges, and down to the figures who moved in and out of trees and along the lake.

It reminded her of nothing so much as a painting. A beautiful oil, wrought with the rich strokes of a master – an elegant and perfect composition, frozen for ever in time.

Chapter 8

Revolution, October 5th–6th, 1789

In the Place d'Armes the minutes ticked by, stringing out taut nerves. The men shifted in their places occasionally, their leather boots squeaking and their muskets scraping at the coarse cloth of their coats.

And still nothing happened.

Towards half-past three the king and his suite galloped back from hunting at full tilt. Those who were nearest to him set up a cheer – '*Vive le roi!*' – but the king's face registered no emotion at all and, instead of acknowledging the support, the monarch rode past without a gesture.

And still nothing happened.

By now the rain that had threatened all day began to fall and soaked the watchers. Louis strained his eyes down the avenue. Perhaps, after all, the rain might deter the marchers and they would return to Paris. Suddenly, through the wet mist, he saw a stumbling figure. Then another. And another.

'Quiet,' he ordered, as an apprehensive ripple broke out among his men. Gradually the avenue filled up, the shapes blurred at first, then merging into a mass that surged closer and closer towards the palace.

'*Dieu*, it is true,' muttered a keen-sighted man next to Louis, 'they are women.'

There they were, a motley crowd which heaved and jostled like a stormy sea. The faces were still too far away for Louis to make out properly, but their intent was quite obvious. Onwards down the avenue they came, their cries becoming clearer with every step.

'*Le roi.*'

'Bread.'

'To Paris with the king.'

'Where is Mirabeau, our little father?'

Level with the Assembly at the Hôtel des Menus Plaisirs, the leaders turned and led the mob up towards the entrance. They beat back the terrified, protesting guard and a pistol shot rang out. The doorman fell, clutching at his arm. The women swirled round the bright gout of red that gushed from his wound on to the ground and forced their way inside. Louis learnt later that they had poured into the silent Assembly chamber, climbed on to the benches and shouted obscenities. The prettiest among them had sat herself on Mirabeau's lap and kissed him.

An hour passed and for the watchers at the palace gates every second was unbearably long, every minute an eternity – the lull, if they had but known it, before the storm that would echo through the world . . .

Tired of their sport in the Assembly, the women regrouped and swarmed down the road towards the Place d'Armes. Louis could see them properly now. Some were dressed in the gaily striped toilettes of the well-to-do. Others were poorly but respectably dressed, their tuckered muslins and linen aprons clinging to their sodden figures. Others were in rags. Here and there an extra-large outline loomed out of the rain and Louis stiffened. These surely were not women? They were men, dressed as women. He tightened his grip on his sword.

Exhausted and cold, the figures lurched forward, and he saw that many of them had babies clutched to their half-naked breasts, and their wails threaded through the furore.

'They're drunk,' said Louis grimly to his sergeant.

God in Heaven, how was he supposed to fire on a rabble of drunken women? What had driven them to do this? Orléans' agents must have been more effective in spreading their anti-royalist lies than he supposed – or was it a collective madness born out of true hunger and desperation? Whatever is happening, he thought, is much bigger than I understand. He summoned his lieutenant.

'You are to go to His Majesty,' he ordered, 'and inform him that we recommend that Their Highnesses repair to Rambouillet. I cannot vouch for their safety if they remain here.'

Watching from their apartment window on the second floor of the ministry building, Héloïse and Sophie watched Louis' messenger cross the Cour des Ministres and pass through the connecting iron grille into the Cour Royale. Héloïse was so shocked she could hardly speak.

'What do they want?' asked Sophie through dry lips.

'To take the king to Paris,' reported Ned, who had been listening out of the window.

'But this is monstrous,' cried Héloïse. 'The king is not theirs to command.'

'We must leave,' said Ned, looking worried. 'If we order a carriage now there must be some way out of the palace. Mademoiselle de Guinot, you will know.'

'But we can't leave,' said Sophie. 'How could we commandeer a carriage at the moment?'

'It is my duty to look after you,' Ned persisted. 'And I think this looks dangerous.'

'No, we cannot go,' Héloïse said in a strange voice. 'It would not be right.'

Ned made an impatient sound and Sophie laid her hand on his arm. She knew that his worry was for her and not for himself. Héloïse resumed her vigil. By now the women had reached the Place d'Armes and were facing the soldiers. Somewhere among them was Louis d'Épinon and she was frightened for him, but beneath that lay another fear, one she could not have explained if asked, a fear that the seemingly safe foundations of her life were crumbling.

Darkness came quickly that evening and blotted out the landscape. The palace buildings changed into indistinct shadowy blocks and only the torches, hissing in the rain, threw light enough to illuminate a soldier or the softer shapes of swirling skirts. The noise was incessant, and every now and again a scuffle broke out as a woman goaded a soldier. Louis was kept busy calling his men to order, many of whom, as he had suspected, showed an alarming tendency to sympathise with the women. The king had sent an answer in reply to his message saying that he was grateful for Monsieur le Capitaine's advice but he would remain at Versailles for the present. Louis had heard no more since then. He suppressed his anger as he barked out yet another order to his sergeant.

'Get them in line. What do they think they are doing?'

The sergeant met his look. 'It is difficult, sir. They are not used to facing their own people,' he said.

'Well, they had better get used to it. Fast,' Louis said and turned on his heel.

In the de Guinot apartments, Ned tried once more to persuade Héloïse.

'At least let us try to find Monsieur le Marquis,' he said.

To this Héloïse agreed, and they filed down the stairs and let themselves into the Cour des Ministres. Outside, the undulating ranks of the soldiers glistened with rain. To their right the gates loomed up into a black sky and beyond them were the lines of packed faces and spluttering torches. At a stroke, the palace had been transformed into an alien place that bore no resemblance to its ornate, superior majesty of the day. Héloïse spoke to the

81

soldier standing guard at the entrance to the Cour Royale. He stood back to let them pass. No one else challenged them, and within minutes they were climbing a deserted staircase and walking through a series of magnificent rooms towards the Hall of Mirrors.

Sophie gasped as she entered, for it was an imposing sight. Only a few of the thirty-two silver chandeliers had been lit, but there was still enough light to observe the famous mirrors and the silver tubs planted with flowers and orange trees. Huge Savonnerie carpets lay on the floor, and the walls and cornices were elaborately gilded, a reminder of the craftsmanship that the kings of France could command. Sophie had never before seen anything like it.

Despite the courtiers, who stood huddled in knots, there was a curious hush and an almost palpable tension in the hall. The groups spoke in whispers and the servants were rushing in every direction with orders to pack, to unpack and to pack again. Héloïse searched the room for either of her parents.

'Stay here,' she told the Luttrells, 'and I will try to find out what is happening.'

'I will come with you.' Ned placed his hand under Héloïse's elbow to support her.

They pushed their way towards the Oeil-de-Boeuf and managed to gain entrance. The famous false window after which the room was named looked serenely down on the confusion as advisers and ministers hurried to and from the inner sanctum of the king's bedchamber, which opened off it. The marquis was there, talking to his aides, but she managed to catch his eye. He detached himself, frowning and preoccupied.

'Can you tell us what is happening?' asked Héloïse.

The marquis lowered his voice and spoke rapidly.

'We have been trying to persuade His Majesty to leave, or, at least, Her Majesty. But neither of them will agree. It's probably too late anyway because it would be impossible to get at the carriages. The last time somebody tried, the insurgents cut the traces.' He took out his snuff box and inhaled a pinch. 'His Majesty has received a deputation from the women and he has talked to them. They have professed themselves satisfied and I think he has persuaded them to return to Paris. If he has, the crisis is over.'

'Thank God, sir,' Ned said with feeling.

'Try to find your mother and see that she is comfortable,' the marquis addressed his daughter.

One of his aides tapped him on the arm.

'Monsieur, there is news. Lafayette is coming. He has been

persuaded to accompany the Paris National Guard. They are apparently under control, but, monsieur, they are bringing cannon.'

There was a rising hysteria in the aide's voice. The marquis' face tightened.

'Then, the crisis is not over,' he said angrily. 'God alone knows what they want – and I feel sure that not even Lafayette can control them.' He placed a hand on Héloïse's shoulder. 'I know I can rely on you, daughter, and you, Monsieur Luttrell, to do what is best. I am needed here.'

Héloïse curtsied as he left them.

They found Sophie sitting wearily on the floor, propped up against the wall. Many of the other courtiers, careless of protocol, had done the same, chairs and footstools being in short supply. Ned and Héloïse rejoined her. They sat in almost total silence as the hours ticked by.

'At least we are not outside,' commented Sophie.

'I should have insisted that we left earlier,' said Ned, suppressing his anger. 'I shall not forgive myself if either of you is harmed.'

'You forget that we are guarded by our soldiers,' said Héloïse with a hint of reproof.

Ned fell silent and contented himself with looking around the hall, which he considered far too ostentatious for his simpler tastes. Sophie watched some candles burn lower and lower and traced a pattern in the flames, wondering just how much danger they were in. Surely the famous Général Lafayette would be able to keep the National Guardsmen in check?

It was past midnight when Général Lafayette eventually walked into the Hall of Mirrors and made for the Oeil-de-Boeuf. He moved stiffly, racked with exhaustion and splattered with mud. The crowd parted to let him through. He looked neither to the right nor to the left, affecting not to notice the uneasy courtiers who watched his every move. Would he save the palace from invasion? Could he?

In the Oeil-de-Boeuf, the door to the king's bedchamber opened and onlookers were granted an interesting glimpse into the room. A selection of the king's ministers stood clustered around the sovereign, while the king, his wig tumbling in disorder down his neck, peered at them short-sightedly. A hush fell. The general went down on one knee.

'Sire, I have come to die in your service,' he said dramatically.

The king motioned him to rise and Lafayette entered the bedchamber. The door closed.

Héloïse looked up at this point and saw the marquise pushing

83

her way through to her. She was walking with difficulty. Héloïse jumped to her feet.

'Madame, *ma mère*, what has happened?'

The marquise shuddered.

'That unspeakable rabble,' she said. 'I was calling on your cousin in the town and when I tried to return they surrounded the coach and would not let it pass. I was thrown against the side.' She held up her arm, on which a purple bruise was forming. 'I managed to get in through the gardens eventually, and I have been resting in Madame d'Hénin's apartments.'

'You should not have risked coming back,' Héloïse reproved her, quite forgetting her customary deference to her mother. 'It was too dangerous.'

The marquise's drained features still held their hauteur as she looked at her daughter.

'My place is with your father.'

Héloïse led her back to the Luttrells and somehow they managed to beg a stool for the marquise, who slumped down and closed her eyes with a sigh and permitted Héloïse to inspect her arm. Sophie made her way over to one of the great windows which overlooked the gardens and peered through the panes. The rain swept down outside, but she could just make out the silhouettes of the soldiers who had been ordered to bivouac for the night behind the palace.

In the Place d'Armes on the other side of the palace, the rain trickled over the bottles which littered the ground and hissed into the enormous campfires which had been lit to roast a couple of horses killed in a skirmish. The smell of their roasting flesh mixed with the odour of damp clothes and vomit. Bodies lay drunkenly on the wet ground and the women who had remained at Versailles and who were still upright amused themselves by offering wine-laden kisses and coarse invitations to Lafayette's guardsmen, with varying success. The town of Versailles lay silent and terrified. Accustomed only to devoting themselves to pleasure and frivolity, its occupants listened with mounting horror and incomprehension to the bands of armed Parisians who roamed the empty streets in search of plunder.

Sophie could see none of this, but she could sense it and her fear sharpened.

'Miss Luttrell.'

Jerked out of her reverie, Sophie took a moment to recognise who addressed her.

William smiled.

'We meet again,' he said.

Sophie's hand fluttered to her throat and tugged at her pearl pendant so hard that it was in danger of destruction. She was absurdly glad to see Mr Jones.

'Can I be of help?' he enquired.

Sophie's mind cleared and she held out her hand. William's clasp was firm and reassuring.

'I did not expect my first visit to Versailles to be so eventful,' he said conversationally as she led him towards the marquise. 'But I am glad I have found you.'

Héloïse was ministering to her mother, who was close to fainting. The marquise was ashen and she held her injured arm awkwardly on her lap. Sophie lifted up her skirts and tried discreetly to rip a strip of her petticoat, but failed. Then, blushing for her immodesty, she tugged at the muslin fichu that covered her breast.

'Here,' she said, 'use this as a sling.'

Héloïse accepted it gratefully. Sophie's neck and shoulders were left enticingly bare but there was no help for it. Ned took one look and his face changed, but he said nothing. William busied himself with helping Héloïse fashion a makeshift sling and offered his own handkerchief so that she could wipe the marquise's damp forehead. Ned got to his feet.

'I shall go and find out if there is any news,' he said and began to thread his way towards the Oeil-de-Boeuf. He returned within minutes.

'The king has given orders that we retire to our apartments. Général Lafayette has assured him that the situation is under control. The soldiers will make camp for the night.'

It was past two o'clock when the small group re-entered the de Guinot apartments, where they were met at the door by a frightened Marie-Victoire who had sat for hours cowering in the empty rooms. Ned and William supported the marquise inside and Marie-Victoire hastened to help her on to a bed. Héloïse made sure her mother was as comfortable as possible and went to join the others in the tiny saloon, where they fell on the wine and fruit that had been intended as a refreshment for the previous day. Héloïse insisted that Marie-Victoire took a glass as well, and the girl sipped at it while Ned and William sketched out a plan of action.

It was decided that the two men should take it in turns to keep watch. Héloïse and Sophie were to get as much sleep as they could for the rest of the short night. Héloïse half-protested, but her tiredness made her objections uncertain and she allowed herself to be persuaded. Still fully dressed, she and Sophie flung themselves down on to the bed in the second bedroom.

But, tired as she was, sleep eluded Héloïse, and she tossed and turned, her nerves stretched to screaming point. At last, towards dawn, she sank into a stupefied doze, only to be tormented by dreams where mobs of women tore at her clothes, singing raucous songs as they did so. Somewhere among them was Louis d'Épinon but she was powerless to call out to him. Instead, she felt the lips of Hervé de Choissy close down on hers with cruel insistence . . . 'You remind me so much of my mother,' she heard him whisper quite clearly.

The sound of running feet and shouting under the window jerked her awake. She sat up instantly, threw back the coverlet and ran to look outside. It was dawn: a grey, cold dawn that loured uneasily over the palace and tipped the roofscapes with a damp mist. Héloïse tugged open the window and looked out. Her eyes widened in horror. Surging below her room from the Cour des Princes into the Cour des Ministres were the Parisians. They were armed with sabres and pikes and at their head was a huge, savage-looking man brandishing an axe.

'Oh my God,' she breathed. 'How have they got in?'

A shot rang out from a window opposite and a young man at the front of the invaders sank to the ground with a scream of pain. Roaring with anger, their leader launched himself at one of the surprised soldiers guarding the entrance to the Cour des Princes and, with a stroke that smashed through his neck, decapitated him on the spot. Within seconds, his companion had suffered a similar fate. The mob formed a circle round the bodies and shouted for the 'Austrian whore', promising to tear out her heart and fry her liver.

Héloïse swung round and ran to the bed.

'Sophie, get up,' she shouted.

Sophie stirred reluctantly. 'What is it?' she murmured, still drugged with sleep.

'Go and alert the others. We're under attack.'

Sophie swung her legs over the side of the bed and vanished. The mob continued to stream through a side entrance which had been left carelessly unlocked towards the entrance which led to the queen's staircase. There, egged on by the leader, it forced its way through the doors and up the marble staircase to the guardroom situated at the top.

Louis had spent a sleepless night in the Place d'Armes, staring out into the darkness towards the Parisians ranged only a few yards distant. His men slept where they stood, although many of them had gone to seek shelter wherever they could find it. At four o'clock a message had arrived requesting him to return to the palace in order to inspect the arrangements inside. Reluctantly he had handed over to a junior officer and, pulling his greatcoat tighter around his body, he had slipped through the gates. He had just completed his final inspection of the Queen's Guard and was conferring with the sergeant on duty when the noise below made him glance up. He was dog-tired and felt stupid from lack of sleep, and it took a moment for him to understand that the noise was the sound of many feet. Then, in a flash, he understood.

He groaned and ran at top speed back towards the queen's bedchamber, and beat frantically on the door.

'Awaken Her Majesty,' he shouted. 'Save the queen. They're going to attack her.'

Then he turned, drew his sword and stood with his back to the door. One of the guards ran to join him and they waited together – a moment imprinted for ever on Louis' memory.

A multitude of thoughts chased through him. Regret for his short life and the things he had never done. There was triumph in the fact of his dying in the execution of his duty, and there was the feel of the blood quickening in his ears as he strained to make his courage surmount his fear. He saw them coming towards him – pikes and staves outstretched, their faces set in hatred – and was conscious of an overpowering distaste. In the moment or two it took for the unequally matched sides to lock in battle, Louis knew that he was ready to die.

An axe crashed into the guard beside him and the man fell without a sound, his blood pumping on to the marble floor. One of the attackers slipped in the wetness and Louis had the satisfaction of driving his sword deep into his body. The blade crunched on bone. He pulled it out and the smell pricked at his nostrils. He lifted his sword, ready to thrust again, praying that the queen had had time to escape, when his head exploded into a million stars. Without a murmur, Louis slid into blackness.

His body sprawled across the floor, blocking the entrance to the bedroom, and with an oath one of the attackers kicked it into the window niche. They began to beat down the door. A big raddled woman who brought up the rear stopped to crack a coarse joke at Louis' expense. Nobody paid any attention and, casting a furtive look around her, she thrust her hands into his jacket and ferreted about with the indifference of a butcher preparing meat. Finding nothing of interest, she spat wetly on to the floor and tugged at the silver buttons on Louis' uniform. After a struggle they yielded and the beldame pocketed them. For good measure, she wrenched off the black ribbon that confined Louis' hair and stuffed it down her bodice. Then, propelled by some hideous urge, she dragged Louis' unconscious body back through the guardroom, his blood smearing the floor, until she reached the top of the stairs. She stood panting for a moment and, with a shriek, she kicked at him hard and watched with satisfaction as Louis rolled to the bottom, where he lay still.

Minutes later, Marie-Victoire slipped in through the entrance near to where Louis lay, sobbing with fright. Despite Héloïse's protests, she had insisted that it should be she who went to see what was happening, arguing that nobody would notice her in the mêlée. Marie-Victoire was regretting her boldness and had almost turned back in the courtyard at the sight of a bearded man, surrounded by cheering women, in the act of beheading a wounded soldier. Sickened beyond measure, she had shrunk back against a wall, realising too late that her clean white apron would probably betray her, and watched horrified as the last tendon was severed and the bloody mass fixed to a pike. Waving his trophy on high, the man led his group towards Marie-Victoire and, without stopping to think, she darted into the nearest door – anything to escape the sight of the dead mouth twisted into its snarl of agony.

At the foot of the stairs, she looked up. Chairs and statues lay on their sides, the paintings had been slashed and pike marks disfigured the wooden doors. She mounted the steps to the point where the staircase turned and then lost her nerve and ran back down again, in her haste tripping over the body that lay at the bottom. She sprang back and made as if to leave, and then her pity got the better of her.

She bent down and at once recognised Louis, despite the wound that disfigured his forehead. Marie-Victoire dropped to her knees and felt for his pulse. His hand was very cold. Fearing the worst, she listened for his heart and was rewarded by the sound of a few sluggish breaths. Seizing him by the ankles, she managed to pull him into a niche opposite the stairs and then ran as fast as she could back the way she had come.

She burst into the apartments and stood breathless and incoherent. Héloïse leapt to her feet and pushed her down into a chair.

'What is it?'

Marie-Victoire fought for control. 'It is terrible,' she said, dashing her hand over her eyes. 'They are killing everywhere. Monsieur le Capitaine d'Épinon is lying badly hurt out there. He needs help.'

'Who?' said Ned.

'Oh, no!' Héloïse gave a little cry. 'I must do something.' She appealed to Ned. 'Monsieur Luttrell, will you help me?'

'Of course, Mademoiselle Héloïse,' said Ned at once.

88

Sophie hastened to explain to Ned who he was. Ned turned to Marie-Victoire.

'Tell me exactly where.'

Marie-Victoire told him and Ned looked at William, their antipathy for the moment forgotten.

'We will both go,' he declared.

Sophie took a juddering breath. William was already removing his coat and rolling up his shirt sleeves.

'Of course,' he said quietly.

The two men stood framed in the doorway and Sophie clenched her hands so tight that her nails bit into her palm. Then they were gone.

Time stood still then for all of them. The marquise joined the girls and the four of them sat silently in an oddly similar pose with their hands folded into their laps. The pose, Sophie found herself thinking, that all women assume when waiting . . . waiting . . . waiting.

At the sound of footsteps, Héloïse and Sophie got to their feet. The door swung open, and Ned and William edged in with Louis' body slung between them. His arms were limp and his head nodded with every step. Héloïse took in his bloody countenance and his pallor. She swallowed.

'Please take him to the bedroom,' she said.

William eased Louis on to the bed and Héloïse arranged the pillows under his head and tried to pull the crumpled sheets into some kind of order.

'We had to find a route round the side of the palace,' said Ned in response to Sophie's unasked question. 'It was too dangerous otherwise and there are too many in the courtyard. See for yourself.'

Sophie obediently went back into the saloon and looked out of the window. Underneath her lay chaos. The courtyard was packed with bodies pressed up against the grilles and they spread as far as she could make out to the edge of the inner marble court. The air was thick with demands for the queen to show herself. Sophie averted her eyes and tried to imagine how Marie-Antoinette must feel, knowing that she was the target of so much hatred, and her pity stirred. Thinking that Ned stood there, she felt blindly behind her and, to her surprise, encountered William. Her hand trembled when he took it in his and held it, as if treasuring the contact.

'Sophie.'

Héloïse was calling for her from the next room. Sophie blushed to the roots of her hair, disengaged her hand from William's grasp and went to help.

Inch by careful inch, the two of them peeled off Louis' tight jacket as gently as they could. Héloïse was sweating with the effort not to hurt him, but he moaned once or twice and rolled his head.

'Marie-Victoire.' Héloïse spoke more firmly than she felt. 'Go and see if you can obtain some water.'

Marie-Victoire did as she was asked, angry at herself for the weakness that turned her knees to jelly. She returned almost immediately, carrying a pitcher and a bowl. Héloïse fumbled at her skirts and took off her petticoat, and with Marie-Victoire's help Sophie managed to tear it into uneven strips. She took the bowl and held it while Héloïse dipped the material into the water and sponged gingerly at Louis' wound. The water was soon bright red but, cleansed of the blood that caked his hairline, Louis began to appear more normal. The wound, Héloïse was relieved to see, was less serious than it looked. She had seen worse on the hunting field. Louis moaned again.

How strange, thought Héloïse as she worked, that I should be handling the body of this man in such a way, a man who means nothing to me . . . should mean nothing to me . . . and yet this is one of the most intimate moments that I have ever experienced.

Louis' eyes opened, regarded Héloïse with a direct, unblinking stare and then closed. Héloïse arranged a makeshift bandage around his head, taking care not to cover his eyes, and stretched out her hand to feel his pulse. Suddenly, she felt her hand imprisoned and looked up to see he was looking at her.

'Can you talk?' she enquired softly, laying down his arm.

Louis' lips stretched painfully. 'Yes,' he said with an effort.

'You are in the apartments of my father, Monsieur le Marquis de Guinot. You were found by my maid and brought here.'

Louis grimaced. 'The queen,' he muttered.

'I cannot answer that,' replied Héloïse. 'Can you tell us what happened?'

But Louis had slipped back into unconsciousness.

Sophie returned to the window. The hubbub outside had quietened. Straining out of the casement, she could see that the Parisians had crowded further towards the marble court and they appeared to be watching someone.

'The queen,' she said. 'I think the queen is on the balcony.'

'One must admire her courage,' said William under his breath.

He drew Sophie to one side. 'There is no question that we must remain here for the moment and I think we are reasonably safe. I wanted to tell you, Miss Luttrell, that I think you have been both brave and calm.'

'But so were you, Mr Jones,' she replied. She intercepted a

look from Ned and blushed for the second time that morning.

The sky was lightening. The heavy rain of the previous evening had washed it pale and clean, and the smell of rain-washed stones percolated through the window, bringing with it a welcome freshness to the heavy atmosphere inside. It did nothing to dispel the oppression that hung over them or the feelings of shock and impotence that the new day brought, but at least it was light.

The marquise stirred, winced from the pain in her arm and pressed her good hand to her face. Héloïse bent over to comfort her and was dismayed to notice lines on her mother's face that she had never seen before. Suddenly, the marquise looked all of her forty years.

'Monsieur le Marquis?' she was asking.

Héloïse was assaulted by a sudden fear. It was unlike her mother to be so unfocused.

'He is safe,' she replied.

Sophie went over to the marquise and knelt by her side.

'Don't distress yourself, Aunt Marguerite,' she tried to comfort her. 'We will find him.'

The marquise threw her a weak smile and touched Sophie's hand.

'You are a good girl,' she said approvingly. 'I will write and tell my sister so.'

In the bedroom, Héloïse was relieved to see that Louis was fully conscious and had been watching them through the connecting door. Héloïse returned his scrutiny with a question in her raised eyebrows. Louis smiled. A poor, weak apology of a smile, but recognisable nevertheless.

'How?' he asked.

'You were fortunate,' Héloïse replied, not wishing to over-tax him.

'Yes, I was,' said Louis enigmatically, and so softly that Héloïse had to bend over to hear him. Her heart gave one wild thump and, to hide her confusion, she busied herself with the pillows.

'Look at me,' he begged.

She raised her head.

'You are beautiful,' he told her. 'I just wanted to make sure.'

Héloïse hoped he was not delirious, but when she read his expression she knew him to be in command of his senses.

'Thank you,' she replied.

Louis turned his head.

'Who are they?' he asked.

Héloïse explained, but Louis' attention wandered. His gaze anchored on her face.

91

'Do you always entertain strange gentlemen in your bed?'

'In my bedroom perhaps, as is the custom,' she said. 'But not in my bed. But, monsieur, how can you joke at such a time as this?'

Héloïse could have bitten her tongue out, for his mouth contracted.

'I was forgetting,' he said. 'Tell me what has happened and I must return to my duties.'

He made to rise. Héloïse pushed him back down on to the pillows. Louis reached again for her hand. His own felt hot and dry, and she regarded him with renewed concern.

'Tell me,' he said. 'Their Majesties. Are they safe?'

'If I knew,' replied Héloïse, choosing her words with care, 'I would tell you.'

'*Mon Dieu*,' he exclaimed impatiently. 'What a time to be wounded.'

'You must remain quiet,' ordered Héloïse. 'Or you will harm yourself.'

Louis surprised her by agreeing. She adjusted the bandage and smoothed back his hair. Louis appeared to be dozing. Héloïse eased her weary body upright. She longed to loosen her laces and to wipe away the moisture that trickled down her shoulders under her tight busk. Instead, she wiped her face with the hem of her skirt and began to search in a chest for a comb. Sophie entered the room and Héloïse placed a finger on her lips to indicate that Louis was asleep.

The sound of footsteps in the corridor broke the silence. Instinctively, the two girls moved closer together. The footsteps came nearer. Héloïse and Sophie looked at each other. Each knew what the other was thinking. Héloïse picked up the empty pitcher and Sophie grabbed a spindly chair by the wall. Héloïse remembered thinking, quite irrelevantly, what a painting Sophie would make. Sophie's once elegant gown was now limp and stained, and her fair hair was scraped back anyhow from her face with a borrowed ribbon, but her eyes were full of defiant fire and life.

A movement from the bed made Héloïse swing round. Louis had managed to pull himself upright and was clinging to the bedpost. Sophie went to help him.

'Thank you,' he said gratefully, and tried to tuck his shirt into his breeches.

In the salon, meanwhile, both Ned and William had positioned themselves by the door, ready to spring on intruders. William's stomach tightened and a pulse beat quite clearly on Ned's temple. The door opened slowly. Héloïse grasped at the pitcher. And then dropped it again.

The Marquis de Guinot stood surveying the scene, and beside him was the man Héloïse had done her best to forget. Hervé de Choissy smiled his cruel smile. How typical of him, she thought, noting his immaculate linen and freshly pressed redingote, to look so . . . so *au point*. Observing her expression, de Choissy raised his eye-glass and his smile broadened. He inclined his head towards Héloïse in a private greeting.

'*Ma chère*.'

The marquis greeted his wife, who stretched out her uninjured hand towards him.

Héloïse stared at her father in consternation. She had never seen him looking so dishevelled. The marquis' hair had lost most of its powder and his tail-coat was rumpled beyond recognition; he was obviously exhausted. Marie-Victoire burst into tears in the corner and Héloïse went to lay a comforting hand on her shoulders.

'We shall be returning to Paris,' said the marquis at last. 'The king has decided to give in to the rebels' demands and to take up immediate residence in the Tuileries Palace. The Parisians have promised to return home. Versailles will be abandoned and we shall, of course, accompany the king.'

The marquise slumped back in her seat.

'Where will all this end?' she asked for all of them.

'I wish I could answer that,' replied her husband. 'I cannot feel the king has been wise in his decision, but it is our duty to obey.'

'I shall never forgive them,' the marquise declared. 'They are unforgivable.'

Louis fell back on to the bed and tried to master the weakness that threatened to overwhelm him. In response to the marquis' enquiry, Héloïse hastened to explain who he was. The marquis went over to Louis.

'I owe you thanks for my daughter's safety,' he said. 'When this incident is over, then I hope you will allow me to thank you properly. Meanwhile you must rest and I must return to the king.' There was incomprehension as well as anger in his voice. 'I never thought I would live to see this day,' he finished.

There was nothing any of them felt they could add. Overnight, a precedent had been established, and all of them felt it was too dangerous to try to explain it.

The marquise reasserted some of her authority.

'We must pack,' she said.

The marquis kissed her hand.

'I shall leave it to you, as always,' he said. 'I will send over any of our household I find and I shall order the carriages.'

The noise of departure became audible. Horses' hoofs clattered on the stones and there were sounds of hastily issued orders. Marie-Victoire slipped into the bedroom and began to repack. De Choissy raised a manicured hand.

'Now that you are persuaded that I need not be hit on the head, perhaps I can persuade you to take a glass of wine.'

He went over to the table and poured out the remnants of the wine. Héloïse accepted a glass. 'Drink,' he admonished in an undertone. 'You will have need of it.'

He handed out the rest of the glasses.

'It appears the mob did succeed in invading the queen's bed-chamber,' he informed them. 'Fortunately, Her Majesty managed to escape in time. Later, she went on to the balcony and managed to quieten the rebels. I saw her as I arrived. I had been warned there was trouble, so I took a different route from my usual one.'

His light, carefully modulated tones forced the others to resume a semblance of normality. Héloïse gulped at her wine, torn between hatred and admiration – a hatred she couldn't shake off and a genuine appreciation of his composure.

'Come,' said de Choissy, and slipped his arm possessively around Héloïse's waist, pressing his fingers into the curve between her hip and breast. He led her to the window. 'This is a historic moment, and we should observe it.'

It was a strange sight: a tangled confusion of men and women, of sweating, restless horses and immobilised carriages which stretched towards Paris as far as the eye could see. Framed in the palace windows, the courtiers clad in their silks and satins watched in silence as their king departed to the jeers of his subjects. Their silence said everything, and it said nothing.

When, at last, the procession wound its way down the majestic avenue, the silence deepened. It enfolded the once crowded rooms in its pall, broken only here and there by the echoes of shutters banging into the emptiness.

PART TWO
The Tocsin Sounds
January–September 1792

FRANCE, October 1789–January 1792

The spectacle of the Bourbons virtually imprisoned by their own people sent uneasy shivers through Europe's corridors of power. Where would it end? Which sovereign would be next? Nevertheless, none of the watchers was going to risk going to war to help the tottering French monarchy, except perhaps Sweden, and she was too bankrupt to do more than issue promises. Instead, an army of secret agents were sent by their governments into battle, slipping through the treacherous shallows that lapped the infant revolution and fanning out into the streets, towns and cities where they listened and waited. For what? No one was quite sure.

A trickle, then a stream, of carriages, bearing aristocratic families who were abandoning their estates and incomes, headed towards Mainz and Koblenz. They preferred the dullness of exile to the dangers of a France where the social order was under attack. In the Tuileries Palace the king struggled to retain what shreds of authority remained to him and to work with the National Assembly, while his family settled down to re-create Versailles court life in the musty old palace. Curious to see their sovereigns, the Parisians peered in through the windows and concluded that they were nothing much to look at after all. The king was fat and the queen, whose hair was streaked with grey, had lost much of her beauty.

The National Assembly had followed the king to Paris and was ensconced in the old riding school close to the palace. The more conservative monarchists and constitutionalists sat to the right of the president's rostrum. The more radical and republican members sat to the left. There was fierce rivalry for the leadership of this 'left' party which was composed of many liberal nobles as well as bourgeoise and it was represented by many of the finest minds in France. Encouraged by the good harvest that had finally been garnered, these self-styled 'patriots' set about pushing through their ideas for a France which was both free and equal.

The National Assembly now declared that the king ruled no longer by divine right but merely through the rule of law. It introduced a new constitution for the clergy which aimed to sever the historical ties that bound them to Rome and placed the clergy under the necessity of taking an oath in order to confirm their patriotism. Many of the clergy refused to take the constitutional oath and this increased their unpopularity.

The 'federation' movement grew stronger. 'We shall be free together,' went up the cry, and the provincial authorities, anxious to make their feelings known, urged the king to let their fédérés come to Paris. The king, suspicious of any such spontaneous representation, was persuaded, however, to allow fédérés from provincial National Guards to attend a ceremony of federation in the capital. On July 14th, 1790, the anniversary of the fall of the Bastille, the whole of Paris turned out to celebrate the new France, and monarchists were reassured by the Parisians' enthusiastic reception of the king.

The underlying truth was stark. The king and queen were virtually impotent; they were surrounded by the wrong advisers; and the Revolution was launched on a course that no one could stop. Day by day, republican feeling grew. 'It is easier', mourned Mirabeau, who had cause to regret his earlier support for reform, 'to light the flames than to try to stamp them out.' Not even his powerful charisma could prevent the rising storm.

At Easter, 1791, the king and queen were prevented from leaving Paris for a holiday at St Cloud.

In June, a large yellow berline, outfitted in white Utrecht velvet and taffeta cushions, set off from Paris in the dead of night and lumbered its way towards the frontier, stopping frequently to let its occupants stretch their legs. At Varennes it was halted, and inside was discovered the royal family. In a sweltering heatwave, the berline crawled back to Paris and drew up in front of the brilliantly lit Tuileries. Out of it stepped the dusty, dishevelled and pathetic royal prisoners, never to leave Paris again.

In August, a document, signed by the King of Prussia and the Emperor of Austria, called on fellow monarchs to come to the Bourbons' aid. It achieved nothing and by September the king felt he had no option but to accept the new constitution which had been debated by the Assembly.

In November, a newly elected Assembly, almost totally purged of its former aristocratic members, decreed that all émigrés suspected of conspiring against France should return home. Safe in their headquarters outside France, the king's brothers, the dukes of Artois and Provence, continued to provide a focus for the royalist forces that had begun to mass on the borders.

As the year went by, life continued as normal for the poorer elements. The city had been divided into forty-eight sections, each of which elected three members to the Hôtel de Ville. Each section dealt with poor relief, and maintained a company of the National Guard which mounted guard at the section headquarters and at the barrière. The sections also *organised a committee to search for saltpetre, badly needed for the manufacture of gunpowder. Markets hummed, the price of bread fluctuated and the journeymen, craftsmen and workers confined within Paris's walls struggled, as always, to make ends meet. But in the houses and salons of the rich and fashionable, in the cafés and theatres, in literary gatherings and political clubs, the political debates raged. 'We are all amusing ourselves,' wrote one observer. It became de rigueur for the fashionable to wear Constitution jewellery and Liberty caps decorated with blood-red ribbons.*

Some of the fiercest radicals who had gone to ground to avoid persecution by the still moderately inclined authorities – Marat, for example, who had hidden in the city's sewers – scenting that the tide was turning, began to emerge. On the Left Bank a series of small presses stirred into life and their pamphlets began to flood the city. Meanwhile, the Revolution presented a perfect opportunity for extremists and fanatics to exploit. These men were moving through the streets, constantly on the watch, constantly debating, nourishing their resentments and waiting.

Chapter 1

Pierre, January 1792

Pierre whistled to cheer himself up. It was cold, his horse was slow and his head hurt from the previous night. The tune was infectious and suddenly he grinned, feeling better. Last night had been worth it, and the girl he had finally lain with had been, unlike many he had known, fresh and wholesome. He had paid her with a lapful of walnuts and a bottle of good oil, knowing that nobody would enquire too closely where they had come from.

His horse lengthened its stride. He would be in Paris within a few minutes and back at the Hôtel de Choissy within the hour, where the cook would give him a meal. Pierre made some calculations. He would be the richer by a sack of good white flour and a large ham which were his fee for working as a carrier to and from the de Choissy farm just outside Étampes. Plus the bread and oil that he had quietly helped himself to from the stores. He planned to smuggle them through the *barrière* without paying the dues and to sell them to his good friend in the Rue de la Harpe.

Evading the toll was a game that Pierre often played. Once he had even hidden a sack of beans in a hole in the wall when the guard wasn't looking and had retrieved it later. There was no lack of willing hands to help with the smuggling. No one liked the levies, the women in particular – and women's skirts had their uses quite apart from the pleasure of lifting them.

At the big gates, the guard challenged him. Pierre ground to a halt and began his negotiations. The guard was talkative and friendly. Pierre exerted himself to amuse him with local news and anecdotes and the man quite forgot to look under the driver's seat or into the 'empty' barrel at the back of the cart. They discussed the unsuccessful flight of the king from Paris the previous summer, a juicy titbit about the queen and the price of bread. Pierre handed over some money, cracked a joke and rolled off in the direction of the Rue de l'Université.

If he played his cards right, he would soon have enough money to buy a cart and two horses. After that he would begin his own business. After that he would rent his own house. And after that? Who knew? He was alone in the world, committed to no one, free with his favours and determined to make his way.

Meanwhile there were plenty of girls to amuse him and plenty of contacts to cultivate. There were the meetings he had begun to attend with his friends, ostensibly to discuss politics, but also to drink and to enjoy themselves with the women.

Yes, life was pleasant if you knew how to organise it. Very pleasant indeed.

Chapter 2

Marie-Victoire, February 1792

She picked her way down the street, ducking every now and again to avoid the carriages which bore down on pedestrians with absolutely no regard for life or limb. As she bunched her skirts tightly around her to avoid the inevitable lashing of mud, Marie-Victoire reflected that she would never get used to the dirt and the danger of Parisian streets.

The quiet lanes around La Joyeuse were far away. It was well over two years since she had seen them and she was often homesick. Like many other big houses in France, it had not escaped attack from local peasants. Apparently, the villagers had marched on La Joyeuse one night and destroyed whatever they could lay their hands on. The de Guinots had been both devastated and angry at the news. The marquis had travelled there immediately and returned ashen-faced and grim to report the damage. He had given orders for repairs to the house and garden, but the sacking had affected the family badly. Still, Marie-Victoire thought, with a wry twist of her lips, it hadn't stopped any of them spending money or demanding the best.

Marie-Victoire mourned the old La Joyeuse, even if she experienced a secret thrill at the news of the sacking. Part of her was with those who had taken up their pitchforks and staves that dark night to wreak their anger; part of her remained loyal to the family she served and who fed her. But only part. It must be the influence of Pierre, she thought, or perhaps I am changing anyway.

She turned left into a street that was less than fifteen feet across, and flinched at the stench. At her feet the water, overflowing from a gulley that served as a gutter, washed its foul contents all over the cobbles. Marie-Victoire glanced upwards, but the houses were so closely set together that it was almost impossible to see the sky. It was bitterly cold and her cloak, although serviceable, only just kept her from freezing. She was wearing her best dress, skilfully adapted from a cast-off in Héloïse's wardrobe, and she was pleased by its pale green colour which was so very pretty and so totally impractical. But it set off her hair and her colouring to advantage.

Marie-Victoire had lost weight since she had come to Paris, and much of the healthy glow that comes from country air, but the mirror told her it suited her. Mademoiselle Héloïse was always generous with her lotions, and Marie-Victoire did not hesitate to use them. If they did not actually improve her appearance, they made her feel better.

Mademoiselle Héloïse was very generous to her these days and went out of her way to make her maidservant feel appreciated. She was now Madame la Comtesse de Choissy – and what a wedding that had been. The wedding breakfast had been laid for five hundred and favours distributed to the guests that would have kept several families for weeks. No matter that the new comtesse, dressed in a gown of white crêpe and Brussels lace with a cluster of orange blossoms in her hair, had stood stiff and silent while her groom made polished conversation beside her. Nor that Marie-Victoire had discovered the bride of two hours in her room, crying once again with tears of fear and unhappiness. Nor that Héloïse went out of her way to seek out Marie-Victoire and talk to her of that day at Versailles when they found Louis d'Épinon on the staircase. It didn't take much for Marie-Victoire to fathom the reason, and she puzzled as to why Monsieur d'Épinon had not reappeared on the scene when he, too, was so obviously taken by Héloïse.

Marie-Victoire wrapped her cloak more firmly around her and gave a little shrug of her shoulders. Fond as she was of her mistress (and she was more fond than she cared to admit), her common sense told her that Héloïse was paying the price for the luxury of her position. This was the manner in which people such as the de Guinots conducted themselves, and Héloïse could expect nothing else. Even so, she felt sorry for Héloïse and did all she could to help her.

A sharp wind laced with ice whistled down the street. Although it was only early afternoon, the street was empty. Occasionally, there was a burst of noise from one of the drinking dens that she passed and the sound of raucous laughter. Out of habit, she glanced over her shoulder, half-expecting to see Jacques' thin figure. There was nothing – but she could never rid herself of the feeling that one day he would be there.

'Pierre,' she said, without realising that she spoke out loud, and the anxiety that flooded her whenever she thought of Jacques lifted. Pierre Labourchard. Black-haired, olive-skinned,

103

quick-witted, mercurial Pierre. She was longing to see him, yet afraid to do so. Afraid that the meeting would fall below her expectations or that he would fail to look at her again with that expression that she liked to think was meant only for her.

Marie-Victoire had met him at the Hôtel de Choissy. He had discovered her huddled in the kitchen after attending Héloïse to a ball. She was eating some bread and cheese before dragging herself to bed. It was very late, and she was almost speechless with fatigue. Pierre had arrived earlier and had stopped to eat. He had stood over her, a glass of beer in one hand, and demanded to know who she was. Why hadn't he seen her before? Where was she from? His questions came thick and fast, and before long Marie-Victoire had forgotten her tiredness and was regaling him with the story of her life.

'Can you read?' he asked when she had finished.

'Why, yes,' she replied, surprised.

He had rummaged in his pocket.

'Here,' he said. 'You might like these.'

He thrust a bundle of papers into her hand. Marie-Victoire examined them. Badly printed, the black ink splotching the cheap paper, they were obviously the product of a back-street press. The first was called *L'Ami du peuple* and contained some biting satire on the royal family. Crude, venomous and scurrilous, it held her fascinated. The other, which was entitled *Père Duchesne*, was not so interesting. It was more obvious and very obscene, but the sheer force of its anti-monarchist invective was hard to ignore.

Marie-Victoire had read them again and again, and when she next encountered Pierre she had asked him to explain some things. He had been quick to oblige, and his explanations were clear and precise. His enthusiasm awakened an excitement in Marie-Victoire and gradually she began to understand what Jacques had so often tried to instil in her: that change for the better was possible and she, too, could play a part in it.

I am changing, she thought, and Pierre had much to do with it.

By now she had reached a narrow cul-de-sac, the opposite end of which was taken up by a house which stretched the width of the opening. Even by Parisian standards it was very old and must once have stood surrounded by fields and gardens. Now it sagged with age and its windows stood crookedly on the sills. Some of the casements were rotten and many were stuffed with rags to keep out the cold. A light shone from the top storey and she could hear voices spilling out into the keen air. Skirting a heap of rubbish, she made her way over the cobbles to a nail-studded door and pushed it open.

Upstairs she paused to adjust her dress and to brush away specks of paint that had fallen on to her cloak, before entering the room. She had been here before with Pierre so the sight that greeted her was a familiar one. A table occupied most of the space and it was strewn with bottles and the remnants of a meal. Six or seven men, with as many women, were sitting around it, and it was obvious they had been drinking. Marie-Victoire's heart sank. Drink made their hands wander and their comments sharper.

She saw that Pierre had been drinking too, but he got to his feet and came to greet her. His normally neat neckerchief was loosened and his shirt-tails hung down under his short jacket.

'Welcome, *mon petit chou*,' he said, his beer-laden breath forcing Marie-Victoire to take a step back. 'We are discussing the republic – when it comes.'

His words raised a drunken cheer from his companions.

Marie-Victoire had never seen him quite so flown with drink, but she was reassured by his smile. She shut the door and sat down in the chair that Pierre pulled forward. Someone shoved a pewter mug into her hand. Marie-Victoire took it. Normally she refused wine or beer, but today she was cold and nervous. Why not? she thought, and took an experimental gulp. She gasped as the liquid hit the back of her throat. It burned its way down to the pit of her stomach, and presently a sense of well-being stole over her. She leant over to cut herself a slice of bread. She had not eaten since early that morning and she was hungry.

She took another gulp of beer and concluded that, after all, the assembled company was very friendly. There was nothing wrong in enjoying a drink with friends, and she really did not mind the scuffles that came from the corner as one of the men flipped the skirts of a woman up over her dirt-streaked thighs. Where else were they to take their pleasures?

The afternoon passed in a pleasant haze. Pierre held forth on his theory that Paris should be declared a commune, to be ruled by the people. Marie-Victoire agreed with all he suggested and thought that he put his case very well. A large, unshaven man jumped to his feet after Pierre had finished and advocated that those hoarding food should be strung up in the streets. He was cheered roundly. The door kept opening to admit more people, all of them clutching bottles, and despite the cold the heat grew.

'You know, you are very pretty.'

Pierre broke into Marie-Victoire's thoughts. His hand slid

round her shoulders while the other fondled the curls which had escaped from her cap. She looked down at her lap, anxious that the others should not hear. She need not have worried; no one was taking the least interest in either her or Pierre. She turned to look at him and was gratified to see that he was staring at her with an expression she had not seen before. It dawned on her that he was asking her a question, and a thrill of triumph shot through her breast.

Recklessly, she allowed Pierre to refill her mug, and drank it off. Her head began to feel very muzzy and she jumped when Pierre took her hand.

'*Pardon*. I did not mean to startle you.'

'It was nothing,' she said, and curled her fingers into his.

'There are things I wish to say to you, Marie-Victoire.'

'What?'

'I cannot say them here. They are for your ears only.'

Marie-Victoire trembled, and her cheeks turned a deep pink.

'Let's go,' breathed Pierre.

Obediently, Marie-Victoire looked round for her cloak and shrugged herself back into it. The close atmosphere, the unfamiliar alcohol and her excitement had combined to make her feel slightly queasy, and she was relieved to feel the cold air on her face as they descended the staircase.

At the bottom she leant against the wall for support and waited for Pierre. But instead his arms reached out and pinioned her. His face swooped down, intent and serious, and she stood quite still in the darkness. His lips searched for hers. Her head spinning, Marie-Victoire gave herself up to the moment and savoured the taste of his mouth. It was an experimental kiss. The memory of her rape was too fresh, and the wounds Jacques had inflicted too raw, for her to relax completely.

Pierre's hands fumbled beneath her cloak and caressed her breasts. Marie-Victoire tried to say something, but stopped as waves of pleasure began to wash over her. His lips moved to her neck and he kissed the bare skin, sending strange sensations down her spine. Pierre's knee moved between her legs and he reached to lift up her skirt. For the second time in her life, Marie-Victoire felt a man's fingers move between her legs, only this time they searched so softly and sweetly that she ached for more. She shifted slightly to help him and gasped as he touched her moist flesh.

Suddenly her stomach lurched and her desire fled. She pushed Pierre frantically away. Taken off his guard, he released her at once and she stumbled out through the door and was ignominiously sick on the ground outside. Retching, miserable and numb

106

with the shame of it, she tried to apologise. Pierre held her very close and wiped her mouth with the corner of her cloak.

'You should have told me,' he said, amused at her distress. She was encouraged by his tone to look up.

'It was the beer. I am not used to it,' she explained.

'I can see that,' he replied. 'I should have taken more care of you.'

It was at that moment that Marie-Victoire fell in love with Pierre. Amongst the stink and the refuse of the dirty courtyard, her feelings blazed into life, so shaking her with their arrival that she cried out.

'Pierre.'

And she hid her face in his shoulder, unable to say any more.

Touched by her cry, Pierre kissed her damp head and murmured words of endearment, amazed that he was enjoying comforting Marie-Victoire when only a moment ago he had had every intention of seducing her.

'I'm sorry,' she said at last.

Pierre laughed. 'Don't think about it. It doesn't matter.' He held her very gently and added, 'Nothing matters, Marie-Victoire, except that you come and live with me.'

'Live with you?'

Marie-Victoire was as surprised as Pierre at his suggestion. The words had just slipped out . . . without his thinking.

'Of course.'

He was growing excited by the idea.

'You must leave the Hôtel de Choissy. There are plenty of things we can do to earn a living.'

'But . . .'

'Marie-Victoire! You trust me, don't you?'

Her golden-lashed eyes shone up at him.

'I think with my life,' she said gravely, and knew it to be true.

'Well, then. Now is the time. Think. With all that's happening around us.' He swept out an arm to embrace the city. 'We must take a chance. The old days are over. We are part of the future. We can be free. We can be independent and together.'

She leant against him and, for a moment, allowed herself to dream. What Pierre suggested made sense. It seemed so simple and so right. It was also so final.

'Don't,' she said. 'I must think about it.'

Pierre was a little nonplussed.

'But you *will* think about it,' he urged. He had never made such a suggestion before to any woman, and, used to easy conquests, he was disappointed by her response.

'It would be difficult to leave Madame Héloïse. I owe her much and my family have been with theirs for a long time,' she tried to explain.

'Enough,' said Pierre. He wanted to kiss her again and banish her doubts.

They stood a moment longer and then, hand in hand, they walked back down the cul-de-sac. They were talking so hard that they did not at first see the figure that rose out of the gloom and into their vision.

The man stood in front of them, blocking their way into the street. He was tall and cadaverously thin, and the hunger-shadows under his eyes rendered them large and brilliant in contrast to the drawn cheeks beneath. Dressed in virtual rags, his linen fouled and his shoes in tatters, Jacques Maillard drew enormous satisfaction from Marie-Victoire's anguished sob of horror and alarm when she recognised who it was.

'I've found you at last,' he said unemotionally. 'I promised myself I would.'

'No.'

Marie-Victoire shrank back. Instinctively, Pierre placed an arm around her and held her tightly. His body tensed.

'Who are you?' he demanded.

'Ask the woman,' replied Jacques. 'She will tell you I am an old friend.'

'Get out of our way,' snapped Pierre.

'Not until I have told Marie-Victoire what I have to tell her.'

Marie-Victoire's voice rose. 'Pierre, I don't want to listen. I don't want to listen, I tell you.' She was desperate to make him understand that Jacques meant nothing to her. That she didn't want him, now or ever. Pierre understood the message and attempted to push past Maillard.

'Marie-Victoire,' said Jacques, wearily, for he had not eaten for a day.

Despite herself, Marie-Victoire paused. His voice brought back echoes from the past, and a sharp and sudden nostalgia for her childhood. Perhaps, after all, she owed Jacques something?

'Please wait,' she said to Pierre.

She stood in front of Maillard and clutched at her cloak.

'Where have you been all these months?'

'In Paris,' he said shortly. 'It is easy to disappear. Just as, in the end, it was easy to find you.'

'Are you well?'

He shrugged. 'Well enough.' He thrust his hands into his pockets. 'No, better than that. I like it here. I fit in and my friends suit me. We think alike and we know what we want. We agree that one day the de Guinots and their breed will disappear. It can't be soon enough as far as I am concerned, and then we will take their place. Meanwhile, I live in different places and I make myself useful in the Cordeliers and in the Hôtel de Ville. I am becoming known for my views. "That Maillard," they say. "He will stop at nothing."'

'What is it you want?' Marie-Victoire had heard enough.

'You,' he said simply. 'Come back to me.'

Marie-Victoire could sense Pierre's astonishment and knew that he was bristling. For herself, she was not surprised. Her fears had been proved correct. Jacques had not let her go.

'You have no right to ask that,' she said, nevertheless, with a heavy heart. 'I owe you nothing, nor do I wish to see you. Our friendship is over.'

Maillard gave a short exclamation.

'Marie-Victoire,' he said, with an obvious effort, so softly that Pierre could not hear. 'What I did to you was in madness. I am sorry for it. Truly. Can you not forgive me?'

For a second, she was back lying in the long grass by the vineyard at La Joyeuse, feeling her fingers dig into the earth beneath her. She remembered the long nights when she had been tormented by the memory of what had happened. It was enough. In the dark it was impossible to read the expression on her face, but her voice was cold when she answered.

'I can forgive you, just. But I can never forget.'

Maillard raised his hand to his eyes. It was shaking.

'Enough,' Pierre intervened. 'Whoever you are, you are not wanted. Clear off.'

Maillard lowered his arm and Marie-Victoire sensed the second before he moved what he was about to do. She gave a cry of warning just as Maillard sprang forward. Pierre dodged to the left and Maillard went sprawling on to the cobbles.

Maillard scrambled back to his feet and launched himself once more at Pierre. This time Pierre met him head on. The two men locked together. They swayed backwards and forwards, cursing at each other.

'Leave my woman alone, you son of a bitch.'

'She's *my* woman now.'

'She's mine.'

'Haven't you got the message? Can't you see she doesn't want you?'

Their breath came in pants and their feet slid over the freezing ground.

Shivering with fear, Marie-Victoire watched them. Pierre was thicker and better-fed, but Maillard was maddened by anger and she knew his strength from bitter experience. Maillard's fist connected with Pierre's cheek and the sound of bone on bone cracked like a pistol shot into the air. Pierre staggered and almost fell before renewing his attack. Gradually, he gained the upper hand and forced Maillard back against the wall. Under the impact of his blows, Maillard weakened, until, completely dazed, he ended up clinging for support to an old tethering ring set in the wall.

Pierre hit him viciously one last time and then stepped back.

'That will teach you, you scum,' he said through clenched teeth, and rubbed at the bruise that was already discolouring his cheek.

Fighting his dizziness, Maillard raised his head.

'You will pay for this,' he spat at Pierre, between breaths. 'I will remember you.'

Marie-Victoire tugged at Pierre's arm. 'Come away, he's dangerous.'

Maillard threw a look at her.

'Remember also, Marie-Victoire, that I have twice asked you for mercy and you have refused. I swear that I will be even with you – with you both.'

He let go of the iron ring and slumped on to his knees, his sharp shoulderblades showing clearly through his torn jacket.

'Jacques.'

Swept by sudden pity, Marie-Victoire ran to kneel beside him. He pushed her away, his face distorted by rage, and she recoiled, regretting her impulse. Pierre helped her to her feet.

'Come,' he ordered. 'He's insane.'

She looked down at Maillard. 'You have been stupid and unwise, Jacques,' she said. 'But I will try to forget it. Don't come looking for me again. Goodbye.'

She did not stay to hear his reply, but took Pierre's arm. They walked rapidly towards the street and disappeared into the night.

Half-concealed by the shadows, Maillard swore to himself. Eventually, he pulled himself to his feet and stumbled, painfully, in the direction of his lodgings.

It was only a matter of time, he told himself. It was only a matter of time.

Chapter 3

William, February 1792

As Jacques finally disappeared into the street, a second figure detached himself from a doorway from where he had been watching the drama with interest. He stood for a moment, a tall man nondescriptly dressed in a merino brown suit which had seen better days topped with an old-fashioned tricorn hat.

William shook out the ruffle at his wrist, took a grip on his swordstick and cast a wary glance around him. You could never be too sure. He smiled ruefully, a smile compounded as much of pity as of amusement. He had no wish to spy on such intimate scenes as the one he had just witnessed. His object had been merely to follow Maillard and see what he was up to. Maillard was the sort of man his government wished to know about – an explosive mixture of naïvety and discontent, ripe for political extremism. So far, William had been correct in his assumptions. Maillard had been mixing with radical company whose doctrines were calculated to appeal to a man searching for a cause.

He had been tipped off about Maillard by a contact he had made in the Cordeliers section. Maillard had been throwing his weight around in the section headquarters and not everyone there liked it. He had trailed Maillard, dodging into doorways and freezing on street corners as Maillard, in his turn, tracked Marie-Victoire. William was puzzled as to the connection, then he remembered that his informant had told him that Maillard had once lived on a de Guinot estate.

His professional detachment had been shaken by Maillard's humiliation, and he sympathised with Marie-Victoire's obvious anguish. Poor girl, he reflected, she was so young. He would have liked to warn her that she was embarking on a well-trodden path: a brief flaring of love, inevitable maternity and the gradual extinguishing of passion and energy as the struggle to survive took over. Like many ambitious men, William supposed he would escape such a fate.

111

His fingers were now stiff with cold inside their cloth gloves and his skin felt taut in the icy air. William decided that his investigations could be concluded for the night. He had obtained enough material and, besides, he had an important appointment, a report to draft and an engagement that he wanted to keep. He consulted his watch and began to walk in the direction of the Palais de Justice.

At the gates of the Palais, he watched the torches inside the wrought-iron gates. Behind them, the towers of the Conciergerie prison dimmed into nothingness as the sky blotted them into the winter night. Here and there a few lights shone in the window, otherwise it was lifeless. An uncharacteristic desolation gripped him. William had been away from Paris for well over eighteen months and the atmosphere on returning had been a shock. He had gone south to Toulon to reconnoitre the naval establishments and to complete the line of agents that he had set up through the country. He had fallen seriously ill there of a fever which had left him so weak that he had taken six months to recover. By then, one of the chief agents in the southern network had disappeared, William had never discovered why, and he had been forced to begin all over again. It took time and patience to piece a network together. But now it was done and he had returned the previous week to a very different city from the one he had left. Paris, he now felt, contained an animal force – the product of a pent-up anger and unsatisfied ambitions – and it was terrifying.

A guard emerged by the gates and challenged him. William debated whether to hail a fiacre and decided that the exercise would do him good. He crossed the river and walked north, stopping occasionally to take his bearings, and emerged at the Châtelet. As he passed, a carriage turned into the prison near by. A young woman alighted, sobbing, and was escorted through the doorway. William stared after her thoughtfully. This was not the first arrest he had seen. The question was: were the authorities under Général Lafayette keeping control or were they being ousted by their radical colleagues? William shivered.

An hour later he emerged from the Place Royale and hailed a cab. He had changed his shabby brown suit for a double-breasted striped coat and white breeches, striped stockings and a high, flat-topped hat of the latest design. William was once again Mr Jones from Virginia.

The gardens of the Palais Royal were situated off the Rue St Honoré, and, as befitted one of the most popular venues in Paris, they were full of noise and movement. Lights burned in the booths under the colonnade, and pedestrians, hurrying across the courtyards or ambling in search of diversion, called out greetings. The cafés were enjoying their nightly trade. From the Café de Foy floated strains of *Ninon*, the popular song of the moment, and at number 79 William could hear Desmoulins and his friends reading from their latest political writings. Lurking under the arches and by the fountains were cutpurses, pickpockets and whores. They were waiting for the big houses to disgorge the rich prey who flocked to the Palais Royal on their way to card parties, soirées and the opera. William brushed aside a girl with a sore-encrusted mouth who plucked at his elbow. Gouverneur Morris was right: Paris existed for pleasure.

Tonight, William had no time to enjoy the spectacle. Standing under a convenient light, he consulted a piece of paper. He crossed the gardens, turned into a street of well-maintained houses set back from the road and tapped gently on the door of the largest. It swung open immediately. He was conducted upstairs into a room that appeared to run the width of the house.

William was tired and cold after his walk. He made for the fire, seated himself in a chair and stretched out his hands to the blaze. No expense had been spared in the furnishing of this room, which was decorated with several excellent paintings, draped silk window-hangings and tasteful furniture. But something puzzled him about it that he could not put his finger on. Then it struck him: the room was an unsettling mixture of masculine and feminine, as if the two were doing battle, and the result was disconcerting.

It took him a moment to realise that the connecting doors had opened and he was being carefully scrutinised. William rose hastily and bowed. The gentleman standing there acknowledged the greeting with an inclination of his head and William saw he had a plump and dissipated face, heavily scored by indulgence. It was the visage of a vicious man, but also a weak one, and therefore dangerous.

'You were careful?' Philippe Égalité, Duc d'Orléans, demanded.

'I obeyed your orders to the letter,' replied William.

'Good,' said the duke. 'Are you enjoying your stay in our city?'

'Indeed, Monsieur le Duc, it has become my home.'

A ringed hand waved in the air. 'Which brings me to the point of this meeting. It is, of course, of the utmost confidentiality.'

William bowed his assent.

'I am informed that you are here, shall we say, at the pleasure of your government.'

'I am here, Monsieur le Duc, to sell land.'

The duke stared at him and William caught the suggestion of a shrewd intelligence.

'That is only part of your work. Or am I mistaken?'

The duke poured a glass of wine and offered it to William.

'I rather feel I am not mistaken. You see, I know about agents.'

'Naturally my work requires me to gather a good deal of information,' William commented.

'I see. Tell me, Mr Jones, what is your opinion of the situation? It is always refreshing to hear the views of someone who is not quite so prejudiced – or perhaps not quite so close to events.'

William gave a brief if guarded outline of how he perceived the king's position and the prevailing mood in Paris. The duke listened.

'What you say is accurate,' he finally concurred. His heavy eyelids drooped. 'How does your government feel on the subject of émigrés?'

William was beginning to see why he had been invited to this interview.

'I should say it depends who they are, Monsieur le Duc.'

'If they brought a great deal of money with them, presumably the way in is made easier?'

William nodded. 'I should think, sir, that if anyone of very high rank was to contemplate a new life in my country, then they should inform my government first.'

'Would you be a suitable channel?' The question darted out, rapier quick.

William paused. 'I have no authority to approach my government in any official capacity, but of course it is always of interest to me in my general capacity as an observer to know of these matters.'

'You may tell your government that there are persons of high rank interested in taking refuge in America, particularly if the situation becomes dangerous.'

William caught a hint of panic in the silky tones. The duke had sailed very close to the wind with his so-called egalitarian ideas, but he obviously did not trust his confrères.

'In return,' the duke continued, 'my agent, de Laclos, will be available to help anyone who should so desire to make use of certain information or to make contact with persons of importance.'

William nodded. He understood that if he made the duke's wishes known in the right places, his path in Paris would be smoothed in certain quarters. Not that it would work necessarily to his advantage. To be in the party of Égalité was to ally yourself with dangerous elements. William realised he would have to cover his tracks very carefully.

'Otherwise,' the duke broke into these reflections, 'you will find I am not a sensible person to have ignored.'

'Indeed not,' said William. 'One cannot but be cognisant of the very great influence of Monsieur le Duc.'

'I shall be in England for a time, but I will be in constant touch with my people.'

William had a mental vision of this slippery, power-hungry man throwing out his lures to the English government. He doubted if Mr Pitt would relish the idea of such an inconvenient cuckoo in his nest. William bowed himself out, not a little repelled by what he had seen. Not so much by the duke's betraying his position, but rather by the unappeased ambition that flickered in his eyes.

The Comte de Choissy had insisted that, on his return to Paris, William should take up residence under his roof once again. William had wondered if the count wished to make use of him, and how, but he had accepted gratefully. He had a particular reason for doing so. He sat down in his bedchamber to draft his report. The business of composing and then transliterating his words into cipher demanded total concentration, but he found it soothing – an excellent way of making sense of what he had seen and heard. Often he did not know what he would say until he lifted his quill. Then the sound of his pen scratching over blank paper and the lines of black ink exerted their own discipline.

Jones to Washington

George Washington, Esqr.ParisPhiladelphia28 February, 1792
On the twelfth day of this month the property of all émigrés was declared forfeit. This is a harsh measure designed to inflict maximum hardship on those considered traitors to the country by their act of abandoning France. It leaves persons who have so acted and who now reside in such towns as Mainz, Koblenz and Baden without sources of income. Thus, it is reasoned, they will not be able to spend money on counter-revolutionary activity. In my opinion, however, this makes the likelihood of war more certain as many will feel that they now have nothing to lose.

I have today been approached by a person of high rank as to the possibility of taking up residence in America. This person is close to the royal family. In my opinion they would constitute a danger and an embarrassment and should not be encouraged. I will not name them in case this report gets into the wrong hands. I will enclose it later if you indicate that I should, or if it becomes necessary to take the matter further from here.

As to the city itself, there is no doubt that unrest is growing, fuelled by disruptive elements which are moving around the city. I have today followed one such . . .

His pen moved on, splattering the paper with occasional blots of ink which he sanded off. Once finished, the report would be sealed into oiled cloth and sent through the network of agents to Rouen and on to Le Havre. Failing that, he would send it via a chain of agents who would take it from letter-drop to letter-drop to La Rochelle, where it would be conveyed on to one of the ships waiting to cross the Atlantic.

At last William finished. He stood up, yawned, and rang the bell to summon the valet. Tonight Héloïse was holding a soirée, and most of Paris would be attending, anxious to partake of her first-class food and wines and to lose money in her gaming room.

The valet was efficient and before long William was dressed in a black velvet evening suit with an extremely handsome black and silver waistcoat. He stared at himself thoughtfully in the mirror. Tonight he wished to take special pains with his appearance, and he directed the valet to brush back his fair hair a little more severely from his brow and to tie it with a black ribbon. His faced stared back at him.

Was it a face that Miss Sophie Luttrell remembered? Or would place her faith in? William's reflections were less than cool when it came to this subject. In fact they presented him with an infuriating tangle in which impatience to see her again mixed with an annoyance at wishing to do so. The feelings that he had discovered himself to be nurturing while on his travels and, in particular, on his sickbed had no place in his cool, considered plans. Those calculations had involved returning to America, capturing the hand of Elizabeth Fitzjohn, the biggest matrimonial prize in Virginia, and settling down. But try as he might, the memory of Elizabeth's appeal dimmed beside Sophie's.

As a personable bachelor he had already enjoyed several flirtations and had looked forward to some discreet dalliances in Paris. He had been careful, therefore, to say nothing definite to Elizabeth before he left America. He was glad now that he had not. William was not accustomed to doubting his emotions, nor to deviating from his plans. It unsettled him, and he knew it would be wiser never to see Miss Luttrell again.

He dismissed his valet with a word of thanks and picked up

his handkerchief. He was sorry for the pain he would cause Elizabeth. She would grieve as she gazed over the neat farmland that stretched between her house and his own. William flushed. He did not care to think that she might consider him wanton or irresponsible. No, he did not care for that at all. But she would not be abandoned for long. There would be other suitors only too glad to pay court to the rich and good-looking Elizabeth Fitzjohn.

Meanwhile, there was Sophie and the problem of the protective Mr Luttrell. He had no idea where the situation was leading, only that he had fallen in love with an English girl with a ravishing smile. Could he persuade her? Should he persuade her to love him? William did not know.

Surrounded by a high, statue-studded wall, the Hôtel de Choissy was set well back off the main road. Tonight there was the usual crush of vehicles fighting to gain entrance into the courtyard that evening, but once inside the guests paused to admire the immense staircase before ascending to the first floor where they were greeted by the sound of stringed instruments.

Héloïse had organised everything with her customary efficiency and William stood admiring the scene while he sipped at a glass of champagne. Massed on crystal candelabra where they worked their flattering magic, the candles helped to smooth out complexions and soften harsh outlines. The de Choissys had spared no expense in the construction of their house, and only the finest of materials had been employed. One of Héloïse's first moves as the Comtesse de Choissy had been to call in the decorators, and the freshly applied gilding on the carved panels glistened against the new white paint of the panelling. A huge oval mirror hung over the mantelpiece and a series of smaller mirrors on the walls. On the floor lay the finest Gobelin carpet that William had ever seen – a fantasy of flowers and fruit in the rich, opulent colours that only French craftsmen could create. The windows were draped in white Lyons silk, folded into fashionable pelmets and decorated with tassels and braid that picked up the porcelain blue in the carpet. There were some well-hung paintings: some were obviously de Choissy ancestors who looked down at the company with indifference, while others depicted landscapes and classical fantasies. The whole effect was very French, very sophisticated and very pleasing – and Paris would enjoy speculating on just how much the new countess had cost her husband in refurbishing bills.

Héloïse was receiving her guests with de Choissy beside her. Once again, William was struck by her elegance, but also by the strain that registered at the corners of her mouth and eyes. He responded to her greeting and congratulated her on the room. Héloïse relaxed. Mr Jones was so easy to talk to.

'Yes,' she said. 'I found it very absorbing to work on.'

William was about to reply when a sixth sense told him to look round.

There she was. A glowing vision of beauty. Arranged *à la hérisson*, and lightly powdered, Sophie's hair clustered in large, frizzed waves over her white shoulders. Her dress which was of her favourite green was trimmed with white needle lace and, ably aided and abetted by Mlle Bertin's clever seamstresses, it enhanced her height and slimness. The results told William that here was a woman who understood and enjoyed the value of such attentions. Sophie was no longer a simple country girl from England, and he saw that her beauty had grown. Her expression, too, spoke of a change. Her eyes still shone, but hidden in them was a new subtlety and maturity – and a new seductiveness. Behind her stood Ned. He had filled out and acquired a more fashionable air. He did not look pleased at the encounter. William braced himself.

The Luttrells made their greetings and enquired after his health and travels. William furnished them with a brief outline. Sophie told him a little of her news, mainly that they had both found themselves staying in Paris much longer than originally planned. It was true that Ned had gone back to High Mullions for two months during the summer of 1790 to help Sir Brinsley supervise the harvest and to give Lady Luttrell a first-hand account of her daughter's welfare. But all last year he had remained in Paris with Sophie.

'I could not bear to leave and my parents were happy to let me stay, provided Ned returned to keep me company,' she told him.

William asked after the Marquis and Marquise de Guinot.

'They are in good health,' said Sophie, 'but a little worried by the latest political developments. In fact,' she added with a slight frown, 'I worry sometimes that we are too much of a burden to them.'

'I've been considering that, my dearest Sophie,' said Héloïse, appearing at her elbow. 'And I have decided you must come here and live with me.'

William saw the special look that Sophie gave Héloïse. Truly, these cousins seemed very close, and he understood that loving the one meant loving the other too. Sophie linked her arm in Héloïse's, and for a moment they looked extraordinarily alike. Then Sophie turned to Ned and the likeness shattered.

'Ned, what a clever idea. I think it would suit my uncle and aunt much better.'

Ned took a pinch of snuff.

'Let us discuss it later,' he said. 'But you are very kind,' he added, with a slight bow to Héloïse.

'Of course,' said Héloïse, and moved away to her duties.

'Miss Luttrell.' William launched his carefully considered strategy. 'I know you are interested in political ideas – or you were – and I wonder if you would care to join me at one of the dinners in White's Hotel? It is a gathering held by English and Americans living in Paris to discuss such matters. The invitation, of course, includes Mr Luttrell.'

The two men looked at each other. It was clear that neither had revised his opinion of the other.

'I would be delighted,' said Sophie quickly. So he had not forgotten her after all.

'Thank you,' said Ned firmly. 'But I think not.'

Sophie's smile faded and William felt that the sun had gone in.

'Of course, if you would rather not . . .,' he said, anxious to spare her embarrassment.

'That is correct,' said Ned. 'Miss Luttrell and I prefer not to be associated with anything political. Our position, you see.'

Although politely put, his explanation was provocative. Sophie was annoyed. Up to this moment she and Ned had been getting on so well, and they had been happy. Ned had ceased flirting so blatantly and had taken trouble to squire her on outings and to balls. He had been more careful of her feelings and she had been grateful. Nevertheless, the unquestioning adoration in which she had once held him had vanished. For Sophie was now a grown woman who could see more of the truth. Her tastes had developed, and so, under her self-imposed régime of reading, had her mind. Ned did not follow her in this and she regretted sometimes that she could not talk to him more seriously. Most of the time, however, she was content. If she ever thought of Mr Jones with inexplicable flashes of regret, she suppressed them.

Mr Jones had now returned and, like all women faced with the prospect of two suitors – and William's invitation was a deliberate challenge to Ned – Sophie could not resist the sense of power it gave her. At the same time, she was also constricted by her sense of duty, and by her loyalty. Sophie did not wish to question those. Mr Jones had thrown her into confusion and she was frightened by the sharpness of her pleasure at seeing him again.

Ned went into battle.

119

'I would like a word with you, Mr Jones,' he declared.

William was taken aback.

'Ned!' interjected Sophie.

'Certainly,' said William, collecting his wits. 'Is anything wrong?'

'In private, if you please,' said Ned.

William looked around. The situation was developing quicker than he had supposed. He led the Luttrells into the music room at one end of the saloon. Ned took up a position by the fireplace and William went over to the harpsichord. Sophie sat on a chair and fiddled nervously with the button on her long gloves.

'I thought it best to speak plainly,' said Ned. 'In that way we can avoid any confusion.'

'Yes?' queried William, knowing perfectly well what Ned was talking about.

'Miss Luttrell is in Paris under my protection. When we return to England we will be married. You will quite understand, therefore, that neither of us welcomes your attentions. I am sorry to be so blunt, but I think the situation requires it.'

William's heart sank. Nothing had changed in his absence and it seemed that Sophie was out of reach. At this point, a wise man would have bowed himself out and forgotten the whole episode. But Ned's manner infuriated him. He glanced at Sophie, who was gazing with a fixed look into the fireplace.

'Perhaps the lady herself is the best judge of that,' he replied. He turned to Sophie. 'Are my attentions unwelcome, Miss Luttrell?'

'I . . . what I mean . . . no, of course not,' she replied, quite unable to say either 'yes' or 'no'.

'Sophie!'

Ned was furious. The humour in his face had vanished and his mouth was set in a hard line.

'I think you should make it absolutely clear to Mr Jones that you cannot accept his invitations.'

Stung by his words, and by the unfairness of his demand, Sophie spoke up.

'May I remind you, Ned, that I am not yet married to you?'

There and then, William made up his mind to fight.

Ned's jaw dropped. He had never, ever heard Sophie address him in that way.

'I think you owe an apology to Mr Jones,' she was saying. 'At once.'

She rose to her feet and stood between them. Faced with an intransigent Sophie and with the threat of a rival, Ned lost his temper.

'Certainly not,' he said. 'Mr Jones should leave. Now.'

'Ned,' said Sophie meaningfully. 'If you say one more word, I shall never forgive you. I shall . . .'

Ned gave her an angry look.

'What, Sophie?'

Sophie was silent.

'I see,' said Ned. 'Are you trying to tell me that you *don't* wish to marry me?'

Sophie was hot with guilt and shame. How could Ned expose her like this in front of Mr Jones? She could not believe his behaviour.

'I am surprised at you, Sophie,' Ned said contemptuously. 'I had no idea you were a flirt.'

Sophie felt that she was drowning. Why can't I tell Ned it isn't true? she asked herself. Has all reason deserted me? All she felt at that particular moment for Ned was distaste – for the unpleasant scene they now found themselves in and for his stupidity in provoking it. Fully intending to tell William that, under the circumstances, it would be better if they did not meet again, Sophie raised her eyes and met the American's gaze. The words failed to reach her lips. William dropped his hand on to the harpsichord and played the first few bars of a Mozart aria. Sophie took a deep breath. It was Don Giovanni's unforgettably seductive invitation to Zerlina, which she knew and loved.

'I suggest we rejoin the guests,' she said, with a calm she was far from feeling. 'If you wish to talk to me, Ned, then you may do so later. I think Mr Jones has been treated to quite enough of your rudeness.'

Ned drummed his fingers on the mantelpiece.

'So you will say nothing, Sophie? Can I add dishonesty to the list of your credits? A dishonesty that prevents you from telling Mr Jones that you are contracted to me? Well, I have no wish for a wife that cheats.'

'You forget yourself, Mr Luttrell.'

William had stood enough.

'I have listened while you have insulted me. That is your privilege and I am prepared, for various reasons, to overlook it. But I cannot allow you to insult Miss Luttrell. I suggest you retire to your room and throw a jug of water over your head.'

His words were meant to offend, and they succeeded. For one ice-cold second Sophie thought Ned was going to hit William. She held up her hand to parry the blow. It never came, for some last vestiges of prudence restrained Ned. He pulled himself upright. Sophie hardly recognised the man who glowered down at her.

'I have been thinking for a while that it is time this visit to

121

Paris came to an end,' he said. 'And perhaps now is the moment. If you are determined to stay, which I imagine you are, then I cannot force you. However, my absence will give you time to think over what has happened. I shall inform your parents as to the reasons for leaving you.'

Sophie blanched and William clenched his fists.

'Mr Luttrell,' he spat out between his teeth. 'You are beneath contempt. Not only are you abandoning the lady you profess to love but you are returning to England as a tale-bearer.'

Too late, Ned realised he had made a tactical error. But his pride refused to allow him to retreat.

'At least,' he replied maliciously, 'at least, Mr Jones, I am not a thief.'

He looked towards Sophie, hoping for a reprieve.

'Go, then,' was all she said.

Ned sketched a bow.

'With pleasure, Miss Luttrell. I trust that Madame la Marquise will have better control over you than I have had. But rest assured, I shall be back.' He left the room so quickly that he almost knocked over the figure in the doorway. Ned muttered an excuse and shouldered his way into the saloon, where he stood downing glass after glass of brandy.

Left alone, William raised Sophie's hand to his lips. In a daze, she allowed him to do so.

'Thank you,' he said, 'you have given me hope.'

'Dear me,' said de Choissy from the doorway where he had been listening with interest for some time. 'I had no idea I harboured so much passion under my roof. How unwise of Mr Luttrell to abandon the field.'

'Good God,' expostulated Sophie weakly. 'Did you hear everything?'

'Enough,' replied her host. 'I did not mean to intrude. I came merely to introduce you to a friend of mine. I see that I shall have to exert myself to induce Miss Edgeworth to remain with you in Paris. I hardly think that my wife, who informs me you are coming to live here, will suffice. I shall be away quite a lot in the future on . . . on business, shall we say?'

William pricked up his ears. With what business would Monsieur le Comte be concerned?

'Two young and beautiful women such as yourselves', de Choissy continued, 'will offer so much temptation, don't you think?'

He cast a meaningful look at William.

'Don't rest on your laurels, my friend,' he said. 'The rules of the game change constantly.'

Impulsively, Sophie reached out her hand and touched de Choissy on his satin-clad sleeve.

'Thank you,' she said gratefully. 'You are very good.'

De Choissy covered her hand with his own. He had his own reasons for what he had said, but he had also grown very fond of Sophie. He liked her warmth and the natural wit that lay behind her recently acquired sophistication. Sophie treated him without the slightest trace of coquetry, and he was content to admire her beauty in an abstract way. It allowed them to be friends.

'If I am good to you it is because I am fond of you and you love my wife,' he said enigmatically, leaving Sophie at a loss as to what he meant. 'Meanwhile, I think it would be a good idea if we rejoined the guests.'

It was only later, in the privacy of his room, that William wondered why de Choissy had been quite so emphatic on the point of a chaperon. It took him a little time to realise that the count had really been referring to the countess. It was Héloïse he wished to protect – or to guard.

Chapter 4

Sophie, March 1792

Sophie picked up her hairbrush wearily. It had been a long day, beginning with a musical gathering at Adèle's, followed by a fashionably late dinner, then by a card party and supper, neither of which had been attended by William. Or Ned.

She sighed. Ned had been as good as his word. The day after Héloïse's soirée he had packed his bags and made his excuses. Something to do with the crops and Sir Brinsley requiring him. Héloïse had listened in silence, and de Choissy with a knowing smile. Then Ned had departed without another word to Sophie, only the curtest of nods.

His leaving hurt her more than she had imagined. With him went her past, and the memory of the girl she had once been, and she disliked to think of the distress she had caused Ned. Part of her hated herself for allowing Mr Jones to come between them. Part of her dreaded the letters she knew would come from England chiding her for her behaviour, or, worse, ordering her to return. But the more truthful part of her was more puzzling. Sophie was conscious of the shabbier emotion of relief.

Her gaze wandered around the luxurious bedroom that had been given over to her use in the Hôtel de Choissy. Every small detail bespoke taste and refinement, from the muslin drapes around her bed to the silver-topped bottles that littered the dressing table. Everywhere spoke of Héloïse's thoughtful and loving attention to Sophie's comfort.

Only a little while ago Sophie would have gasped in amazement at so much luxury, but now, like the life that went on in this fascinating, colourful city, she had grown accustomed to it, even to take it for granted. 'Sophie Luttrell,' she said to herself, 'you *are* in danger of becoming spoilt.'

Spoilt? Or was it infatuated with a man she hardly knew? The seriousness of the question did not alter her expression. Her face remained composed and her eyes unclouded.

'Have I changed very much?' she asked herself and, after a moment, went on: 'Undoubtedly so. I cannot fail to have done. From a raw miss to a sophisticated French mademoiselle who has virtually thrown her cap at a complete stranger.'

Now her eyes had altered. Into them sprang a wariness, a shadow of doubt and disgust at herself, and she found she was clutching the edge of the table. As long as she could remember, Ned had been there, a solid bulwark against childish disasters, a comfortable haven to fling herself against when trouble loomed, someone to admire as she grew up. Now that feeling had gone and in its place lurked anger and irritation and regret for its loss.

A knock at the door interrupted her. It opened, and in came Héloïse followed by Marie-Victoire. Sophie straightened her shoulders. Marie-Victoire picked up the brush from the dressing table and began to brush Sophie's hair with her customary soothing strokes. Sophie leant back thankfully. Héloïse settled herself on the stool by the window and prepared to indulge in the late-night conversation which had become a habit with them both.

'I'm exhausted,' Héloïse said with a yawn.

Sophie glanced at her out of the corner of her eye. She was a little worried by her cousin who had grown thinner and more transparent since her marriage. It had not suited Héloïse, this transformation into an established bride, and she seemed anxious and unhappy.

'You did well,' Sophie commented. 'Acting Madame la Comtesse to the manner born.'

Héloïse shrugged. 'I am used to it,' she said. 'It is nothing.'

'Thank you, Marie-Victoire,' Sophie said as the girl finished plaiting her hair and tucked it under a frilled *dormeuse* nightcap. 'I shall not be needing anything more.'

The door closed behind Marie-Victoire with a click, and silence fell.

Héloïse stirred. 'I see Monsieur Jones was absent tonight. Have you sent him away?' she asked curiously. She was intrigued by the quiet, serious young American whose gaze seemed to miss nothing and who was obviously more than a little interested in her cousin.

'No,' said Sophie, 'not exactly.'

'*Tiens*, a "lover's tiff"?'

'Don't be foolish,' said Sophie with unusual asperity. 'He is not my lover.'

'But you like him, *chérie*?'

'Yes, I do,' admitted Sophie with a smile. 'I forgot to tell you he has asked me to accompany him to a dinner at White's Hotel.'

'*Tiens*,' said Héloïse again. 'You will be dining with red-hot republicans.'

'What's wrong with that?' asked Sophie, intending to be provocative.

'Is it not obvious?' said Héloïse, and it was her turn to sound sharp. She was sometimes worried by Sophie's inquisitive liberal sentiments, and anxious to curb them.

'Why don't you come too?' asked Sophie.

'I couldn't,' said Héloïse at once.

'Why ever not? You won't turn into a criminal over dinner.'

Héloïse ignored the joke and spoke, a serious expression on her face. 'Sophie, I beg you to be careful. Listen to me, spies are everywhere. I know. I hear things at the palace.'

Sophie thought for a moment. 'All right. I accept that I must be careful – as you must be too. But I hardly think that one dinner will put me in danger.'

'Oh, Sophie, how . . .'

'How what?'

'How innocent you are,' said Héloïse, between laughter and anger. 'This is France, not a small village in England.'

She got to her feet and stood looking down at her cousin with a great deal of tenderness and just a hint of patronage in her gaze. Sophie shifted uncomfortably. Héloïse suddenly made her feel rash and a little foolish, but all the same it did not alter her decision to accompany William to White's Hotel.

'You must know that the authorities are keeping an eye on anyone with revolutionary tendencies,' said Héloïse, 'with orders to report back to Général Lafayette. Besides,' she continued, 'Hervé would not approve, and you do live under his roof.'

'The Comte de Choissy, whatever else he may be, is a man of the world,' remarked Sophie.

Héloïse bit her lip. 'Yes,' she said, her voice brittle with an emotion that Sophie couldn't quite place. For a moment, she thought it was fear, then it flashed on her that the strange note in Héloïse's voice was hatred. She glanced up in surprise. It was as if a door had opened on to an attic full of strange and unwelcome secrets instead of a pleasant room that she had expected. She swivelled on her seat.

'*Mignonne*, are you very unhappy?'

Héloïse flung herself down by her cousin, crushing her delicate chamber-robe. She hid her face in her hands. With a quick movement, Sophie knelt by her side and took Héloïse into her arms.

'Tell me,' she implored. 'Tell me.'

Héloïse shuddered. Sophie held her tighter and waited.

'I hate him.' The words dragged out of Héloïse as if they burnt her mouth. 'He fills me with such disgust.'

Sophie was silent. She did not feel competent to say anything.

'He is so vile. So smooth and yet so animal. You can't conceive.'

By now Sophie had a pretty accurate idea as to what Héloïse was referring to.

'You mean his attentions . . . His attentions are . . .?'

Héloïse buried her face deeper in Sophie's shoulder and tried to blot out the memories of the nights and the torment that came with them. Nothing and no one had prepared her for the humiliation and the pain, the disgust and the fear. The horror of her wedding night would stay with her for ever.

He had come silently into the room where she had lain washed and scented in her bridal night-gown. The guests had come and gone with their offers of advice and spiced wine. The noise of their easy laughter faded, leaving only her mother to indicate the space which she would occupy in the huge bed. Then she, too, had disappeared without a backward glance.

'I trust you are comfortable,' de Choissy had said, appearing out of nowhere, and she had tensed at the sound of his voice.

Silently, he divested himself of his brocaded chamber-robe, folded it over the stool at the end of the bed, and stood naked in front of her.

Instinctively, Héloïse averted her eyes. De Choissy laughed.

'Madame Timid,' he said, and in one quick movement stripped back the satin cover from Héloïse's shrinking body.

'Take it off,' he commanded.

Héloïse removed her night-robe.

De Choissy's eyes travelled up and down her, as calmly as if he was assessing a brood mare for his stock. Then he lay down beside her. The candles guttered and sent flaring shadows up over the walls.

'Open your legs,' he said. Then, a little later, 'Don't move. Do just as I tell you.' He thrust between her shrinking flesh. The pain made her gasp, and she felt as if he was pressing her through the bed.

'Don't move,' said de Choissy again. 'I don't like it.'

His thrusting became more insistent and pain welled through her body. De Choissy anchored himself more firmly on top of her and caught at her arms, imprisoning them tightly to her sides. Héloïse closed her eyes and clenched her lips together to force back the scream as he gasped his way up and onwards until, shuddering, he collapsed on top of her and buried his face in her shoulder.

After a while, he rolled to one side and got out of bed.

'Thank you, madame wife,' he said, shrugging on his chamber-robe. 'I enjoyed that interlude and I look forward to more. I bid you good night.'

Taking a candle, he shone it full into her face. What he saw appeared to please him, for he smiled, the mockery clear on his face. Then he left, closing the door sharply behind him.

Héloïse lay there, stiff, bruised and aching. Tears trickled down her cheek and spread damply on to the linen sheets. She raised herself to a sitting position and sat clutching her sore thighs. After a while she struggled to her feet. She poured water from the pitcher into a bowl and washed, allowing the water to drip down her face and to run down into the valley between her breasts. Then, as silently as she could, she set the bed to rights, smoothing the satin coverlet back into rigid folds and adjusting the lace-trimmed pillows to precise angles. Then she lay down and gazed into the dark for a very long time.

It was the first of many such visitations, each as horrible as the last. Always, she was forbidden to say anything, or to move, and de Choissy took his pleasure in a way calculated to hurt and humiliate her. . . . But these were things she could never confide to Sophie, or to anyone.

Héloïse got to her feet. 'It's all right, Sophie,' she said. 'I was being stupid for no good reason.'

Sophie frowned. 'I wish you would tell me,' she said. 'I could try to understand.'

'It's not that I don't wish to,' said Héloïse, 'but it is difficult.'

'Could it be anything to do with Monsieur d'Épinon?'

Héloïse coloured violently.

'Héloïse, I am not blind.'

Héloïse looked at her hands. 'No. I suppose that you are not.'

'What is Monsieur d'Épinon to you?'

Héloïse avoided Sophie's gaze. 'Someone I could love,' she whispered, with such sadness that Sophie shivered.

'Héloïse,' she murmured. 'Oh, Héloïse . . .'

'It doesn't matter,' said her cousin. 'I can take him as a lover if I wish. Perhaps I shall. Who knows?'

Sophie dropped on to the bed. 'You could, but is it wise?'

Héloïse shrugged in a very French gesture. 'It is the way,' she replied. She faced Sophie. 'You mustn't worry about me,' she said. 'Our marriages are not for love. It has always been so, you know. We are quite used to making our own arrangements.'

The misery in her voice did not make her words sound very convincing.

'I know all about that,' said Sophie impatiently. 'We are not so *very* different in England. But I am still worried about you. Intrigue does not suit you.'

'It will,' said Héloïse. 'I shall turn into a perfect replica of Adèle de Fleury or that Tallien woman. I shall live a long life filled with lovers and hold the most exciting salon in Paris.' Her voice trailed away.

Sophie thought of her own close-knit family.

'Héloïse,' she said slowly, recalling de Choissy's strange remark the night she had quarrelled with Ned. 'Do you not think . . .?'

'But this is fancy,' cut in Héloïse. 'Louis d'Épinon has never sought me out since that time – since that time at Versailles.'

'Does he have to?' commented Sophie drily. 'It would seem that both of us require a chaperon.'

Sophie dressed with care for dinner at White's Hotel. Nothing too sumptuous, just a simple but exquisitely fashioned muslin dress with a striped silk sash and pearl earrings. Later, at the dinner table, Sophie looked around her and was glad she had been circumspect.

There were a lot of people crushed into the small, rather shabby, dining room, and they had an air of taking themselves seriously. The room had seen better days, but it still bore traces of gold paint on the wainscotting, and the window drapes, which Sophie suspected had once been crimson velvet, still retained their dignity despite a tendency to fray at the edges. The table was laid with a good porcelain service and a roll lay on top of the napkin at each place. The sideboard was laden with food.

Sophie could only partially see Miss Edgeworth, through a huge flower arrangement, but she could hear her conversing in lively, heavily accented French. This was exactly the kind of occasion that suited her governess and Sophie was glad for her. Miss Edgeworth did not live an exciting life and she had been invaluable to Sophie. When, after some hesitation, Sophie had offered an edited version of the reasons for Ned's departure, Miss Edgeworth had actually laughed.

'Dear me,' she had commented. 'How very character-building.'

'What do you mean?' said Sophie, who felt the subject should be taken more seriously.

'Nursing bruised pride in time-honoured fashion will be very good for Ned. You'll see.'

'Miss Edgeworth,' said Sophie, between laughter and tears, 'I knew I could rely on you.'

'Does something amuse you?' asked William, unfolding the napkin and proffering it with a flourish.

'No. Nothing,' she replied hastily, fearing to seem rude. She knew that he had gone to some trouble to arrange the outing. It was very pleasant to talk English again and she was particularly pleased to be introduced to the famous Helen Williams. Sophie had been very curious to meet this lady, a well-known writer and literary hostess, and she was hoping that she would learn something from the encounter, for she had not abandoned her own early ambitions.

Plump, berouged and very fond of her own voice, the poetess was not exactly how Sophie had pictured her. Nevertheless, Miss Williams obviously possessed a kind heart and a great deal of inquisitiveness, which she instantly trained on Sophie. Miss Williams had chatted away, issuing invitations to her 'evening' and promising to send a copy of an interesting pamphlet. She also wanted to know what Sophie thought about the constitution, her opinions of the latest fashions and how she came to be acquainted with Mr Jones. Overwhelmed by this barrage, Sophie was glad to retreat to the table.

'How is your mission progressing?' she asked William.

'Not quite as I hoped,' William said carefully. 'It is difficult selling land that the buyer cannot inspect. However, if I don't do better I may be forced to return home.'

Their eyes locked, and Sophie hastily changed the subject.

'Do you ever write, Mr Jones?'

William was caught off his guard. There was no reason to suspect her question was not as innocent as it sounded. Still, he must be circumspect.

'What sort of things, Miss Luttrell?'

'Essays, poems, anything,' she replied.

'Do you?'

'I would like to write something useful. Perhaps a novel.'

'*Are* novels useful?'

'In a way, yes.'

'To put over some moral point?'

'Exactly.'

William asked for the salt, which he sprinkled over his beef ragout.

'Can you justify eating this beef while others starve?' he asked seriously, suppressing a smile.

'Come. I am not so nonsensical as that. But perhaps I could write something that showed a way for everyone to be able to eat beef,' she replied, equally seriously.

William gave a shout of laughter.

'Miss Luttrell, you are quite enchanting. I have never met another woman like you, and you are, despite everything, very

English. You will be a roaring success in your own country with such a work. The roast beef of England!'

'It would be an honest effort,' she countered indignantly.

'Ah, yes, very honest,' replied William.

'As an honest man, you should approve.'

She was puzzled by the shadow that passed over his face. 'Have I said something to offend you, Mr Jones?'

He turned towards her, and there was something in his expression that was to dog her memory. An uncertainty, an evasiveness that she did not like.

'Will you marry me?' he asked.

Sophie dropped her fork with a clatter. She picked it up and then laid it down again with a shaking hand.

'I do not know you, sir.'

'I know you.'

'I am not free to answer that question.'

'Nor I to ask it, but I am asking it all the same.'

'Then, you have commitments.'

'I do. I had, but they are not insuperable.'

'This is too soon,' she said, knowing she was being illogical.

'On the contrary, Miss Luttrell . . . Sophie, there is no time to lose. My instincts tell me that there will soon be trouble in France. Consider: the king was forced by his nobles to summon the Estates-General. The nobles have now been ousted by an Assembly mainly composed of lawyers and petty officials. Where next? A government by *enragés*? You and I will not be immune to events, and then anything might happen.'

His words filtered through the chatter around her. With a sinking feeling, she realised he might be right.

'But . . .,' she began.

At this point, Sir Edwin Robinson rose to his feet to give a paper he had prepared on the latest debate in the National Assembly. Sophie fixed her gaze on him and tried to think. Sir Edwin droned on. He had augmented his text with heavy classical references which she found hard to follow. I must attend, she thought. I want to understand what is happening. I am, after all, part of it. But her thoughts refused to obey her, and by the time Sir Edwin had finished she could remember nothing of what he had said. She applauded dutifully and hoped that nobody would question her as to the content of the lecture.

'Too exciting, don't you think?' said Miss Williams, her bracelets tinkling on her plump arms as she swept Sophie off for coffee in the salon.

'Is "exciting" the right word?' asked Sophie.

'Indeed so, my dear. The eyes of the world are on Paris. We

131

are forging a new age.' She tapped Sophie on the arm to emphasise her point.

'Are you not worried by the restlessness in some areas of the city?' asked Sophie.

'Paris is always restless, is it not, Mr Jones?'

Helen included William in the conversation with another tap of her fan.

'Dear me, I was forgetting you are a relative newcomer. The price of bread is always rising and if our friends, the deputies from the Gironde, get their way in the Assembly, then it will be quickly put to rights.'

'But they must not be too hasty,' interjected William. 'Each measure must be considered properly.'

Helen shot him a quizzical look. 'The people will know their interests are being taken care of,' she said with finality.

'Will you excuse me?' said William. 'There is someone I must see.'

Helen drew Sophie aside. 'Goodness,' she said in a stage whisper, 'he is in love with you. Have you the slightest *tendresse* for him?'

Sophie shook her head, not sure whether to be amused or not.

'Aha,' said Helen. 'You do.' She linked her arm through Sophie's. 'I feel that we shall be friends, my dear, even if I do have an edge – a very slight edge – in years. Promise me that you will visit me.'

'What are you doing here?' William was speaking in an undertone to the slight man in green who had appeared at his side. 'We agreed never to be seen in public together.'

'You haven't paid me.'

'Last month's accounts were paid in full. May I remind you, Chevalier, that I require results before I open my purse again.'

William was very clipped, but the Chevalier Floyd was not so easily put off.

'I have done what you asked, Mr Jones. I have made a contact at the British Embassy and I have given you the information you require from the port at Brest. Now I want more money.'

William thought rapidly. A slippery customer, the Chevalier Floyd was one of his mistakes and he had suspected more than once that he was acting as a double agent. The man was too greedy. He was also a liability, particularly if he was going to track him down in places like White's Hotel. William decided it was time to get rid of him.

'We will not discuss it here. Come to the Place Royale,' he said.

'But we *will* discuss it here, Mr Jones. That is why I have come. I want a thousand livres – in coin. Otherwise, I shall be embarrassing.'

'Lower your voice, you fool.'

William hustled the chevalier further into a corner.

'By coming here you have reneged on our agreement. I consider our contract is now void and our association ended.'

Fury swept across the chevalier's wily face.

'You will be sorry for this, Mr Jones.'

William's hand shot out and gripped the chevalier's arm.

'You will walk with me to the door,' he said, 'and you will get out of here. Do you understand?'

The chevalier shook himself free. 'Don't bother,' he said. 'I am going. But you will regret this, Mr Jones. I have plenty of friends at the Hôtel de Ville who will be interested to know about you. I might write them a friendly letter.'

He stopped, warned by the expression on William's face, and with a little wave walked towards the door and vanished. William stared after him. He was furious, but not so angry that he could afford to discount the chevalier's threat. He did some mental calculations. The chevalier's credit had run out with the British, which was why William had taken him on. So, it was possible that he would trade information with the French in an effort to drum up new business. By informing on him, however, the chevalier would be forced to reveal some of his own activities which would not go down well. All things considered, it was unlikely the chevalier would carry out his threat. But he couldn't be sure. William would have to move carefully from now on.

'Who was that man?' Sophie asked when he rejoined them. She had been watching William out of the corner of her eye.

'Riff-raff, Miss Luttrell. I told him to go.'

Helen twinkled up at him.

'How observant you are, Mr Jones,' she said archly. 'He did not look at all the type we want here.'

William's gaze did not waver.

'I like observing,' he said and took out his snuff-box. 'It gives me food for my journal.'

'So you do write, Mr Jones,' interposed Sophie.

'Touché, Miss Luttrell,' said William, and bowed.

As she lay in bed that night, Sophie puzzled as to why William had not admitted to keeping a journal. Then she dismissed the subject. There were a thousand reasons why he would not have confessed. Perhaps he considered it too private a matter. Sophie quite understood; she herself cherished, and was comforted by, her own secret attempts at writing.

She slept at last, and in her dream she went back to High Mullions. She was up in the loft searching for her mother's wedding dress which she wanted, one day, to make over for her own. In her dream she could smell the must, and the sharp tang of the apples stored at one end of the attic. A shaft of sun slid through the open window and trapped a hundred thousand motes, and she paused to watch their changing patterns. She turned to the neatly labelled wooden chests and read off their contents. Fans, shoes, chemises. Dresses. She prized open the lid and pushed aside the silver paper. The materials shone up at her – green, blue, peach and white that had aged into yellow. Some of the garments were beautifully embroidered. Others were stiff with brocade. She searched on until she found what she had come for – a sprigged satin of the palest green. She held it up and shook out its folds, and a shower of lavender and rosemary fell around her, releasing a spicy odour. She laughed with the excitement of it, and felt the breeze blow in from the fields, carrying with it the smell of the wild country things that she loved.

She awoke desolate. Turning on to her side, she pressed her face into the pillow and cried.

Chapter 5

Marie-Victoire, April 1792

'Why won't you make up your mind?'

'I have to think,' replied Marie-Victoire.

'No, you don't. You've had plenty of time to think.' Pierre drew her arm into his and gave her hand a playful squeeze. 'Come on, Marie-Victoire, be honest.'

'I will be leaving behind all that I know.'

'But you haven't got much,' he said. 'Think of what you will gain.'

'Yes . . .,' said Marie-Victoire.

They crossed the Pont Royal in silence. Marie-Victoire had been looking forward to their outing in the Tuileries Gardens and Pierre had promised to buy her a meal afterwards in one of the eating houses along the river quai. Marie-Victoire had sat up until late to finish a short red *caraco* jacket, and she was pleased with the result. It matched the tricolour cockade which she had fastened into her cap.

The Tuileries Gardens were crowded with Parisians enjoying the spring air and Marie-Victoire exclaimed with delight at the lights suspended in the trees. A crowd had gathered round some puppeteers, families were picnicking on the benches, there were dogs being taken for a walk, and on the terraces vendors hawked liquorice water and pancakes. Pierre bought one and presented it to Marie-Victoire with a flourish.

'Is it that man who is stopping you?' he asked.

Marie-Victoire almost choked on her mouthful.

'*Attention!* I am eating my pancake. Jacques has something to do with it, yes. I know he won't give up. He always carries out his promises.'

'You must forget him,' said Pierre decisively. 'I will look after you. I promise.'

'Have you got something I can wipe my hands on?'

He proffered his sleeve.

'What happens if we can't get work? I don't want to end up in the streets.'

'You are young and I am strong. We'll get work. You mustn't worry.'

They stopped by the flowerbeds.

'You would stay with me?' she asked eventually.

'Why do you think I am asking you to come? I am not going to promise you the world, Marie-Victoire, nor can I tell what is going to happen. I have never asked a woman to live with me before, and I don't think I will again.'

Pierre started to whistle a tune. He was becoming a little impatient.

'Don't think me foolish, Pierre, but I do worry about Madame Héloïse. She needs me.'

'Not as much as I do. The countess can find another maid.'

'I suppose that's right,' said Marie-Victoire with a tiny sigh.

'Do you know, you are the prettiest girl here,' Pierre announced, changing the subject. '*Do* you love me?'

'Oh, yes.'

'Then, what is stopping you?'

'*Regard*, Pierre!' Marie-Victoire pointed.

A group of National Guardsmen stood on the terrace alongside the palace. One of them carried a pipe and the other a drum. The piper began playing and his companion took up the tune. Soon they attracted quite a crowd.

'Let's go and see,' she cried, dragging Pierre after her. By the time they reached the terrace through the parterres, an impromptu dance had begun. Marie-Victoire stood on tiptoe.

'Come on,' she begged.

Before Pierre could protest they had joined in the dance, a new revolutionary dance called the *carmagnole*.

'*Liberté!*' cried Pierre, who got quickly into the mood. '*Egalité!*' he said, swinging Marie-Victoire off her feet.

'*Fraternité!*' she shouted back at him.

They whirled on, caught up by the music and the joy of being alive.

'I've just thought,' she said, gasping for breath. 'I could keep a shop.'

'What sort?'

'Well, clothes. Stockings, shifts, materials. The things I know about and am good at making.'

'Not a bad idea,' said Pierre. He came to a halt. 'In fact, it is quite a good idea.'

'I could alter dresses and mend clothes . . .'

'Brilliant,' Pierre almost shouted. 'You are quite brilliant,

Marie-Victoire. You see, I can get you everything you need.'

'How?' She was almost too breathless to speak.

'I've got friends all over Paris.'

Pierre grabbed her again and they danced on, flushed with their love, excited by their idea and intoxicated by the dance.

All too soon the piper ended his tune and the drummer packed away his sticks. The dancers were disappointed and begged them to continue, but the guardsmen shook their heads. They were supposed to be manning the bridge and they were late for duty. Marie-Victoire adjusted her jacket and pulled her cockade into a more prominent position.

'Hurray,' she shouted to Pierre. 'I feel wonderful.'

'Have you given me your answer, Marie-Victoire?' he said.

Marie-Victoire took a deep breath.

'Of course I will come, Pierre. The answer is yes.'

'You don't have to shout, Marie-Victoire. The whole world will hear.'

'See if I care.'

'That man won't bother you?'

'You're right, Pierre. Let's forget him.'

'Come on, then, Marie-Victoire, let's go and see if we can spy on the fat king and his queen through the windows.'

Hand in hand, they walked up towards the palace terrace. Marie-Victoire was awash with excitement, knowing at last that her future lay with Pierre. And she knew she would be happy – however could she not be?

Chapter 6

Héloïse, April 1792

The de Choissy coach trotted through the gateway into the Cour des Tuileries and drew up outside the palace with a flourish.

Inside, Hervé de Choissy leant forward to kiss his wife's hand. Still aching from yet another nocturnal encounter, Héloïse permitted him to do so in silence. Only a few more minutes and she would be free of him. De Choissy had announced that he was going on a tour of inspection to his properties in Burgundy. He was sorry, but he did not feel it was quite the right moment for Héloïse to come with him. Héloïse had toyed with the idea of telling him that she had no intention of accompanying him but considered, in the end, that the gesture would have been useless.

De Choissy retained her hand longer than was strictly necessary.

'Will you miss me, *ma chère*?'

'Of course, monsieur,' Héloïse said politely.

De Choissy's expression became serious.

'I want you to take these,' he said, and proffered a packet of documents wrapped in red ribbon.

'What are they?' she asked, as she examined the densely written paper.

'Copies of bank drafts and deeds of transfer for our properties. If you or I, together or separately, need to leave the country, these will provide us with funds in either Germany or Holland and ensure that our properties in France are transferred to our incognitos. You will see that there is a passport made out in the name of Madame Fauconnier. You must use it if necessary.'

Héloïse stared at her husband. 'You *are* planning to leave,' she said accusingly. 'Without consulting me?'

De Choissy gazed out of the window. A pulse beat at his temple. 'I need hardly remind you that you are my wife, and that you will do as I wish.'

'A wife, yes, but not entirely without rights. I have no wish to leave France and, what is more, I do not intend to do so.'

De Choissy's eyes narrowed, and he put out a hand to steady himself as one of the horses strained the harness and rocked the coach.

'Now, why, I wonder? No.' He held up his hand to prevent her replying. 'Spare me your patriotic diatribe. It does not convince me one little bit. In the end, most people prefer to save their skins, and preferably in comfort. You are very blinkered if you don't see which way the wind is blowing. But I am convinced that is not the case. May I remind you, Héloïse, that you have not yet provided me with an heir?'

'Perhaps, monsieur, the fault is not entirely mine?' Héloïse shot the words out without really thinking, and regretted them.

De Choissy's voice went cold.

'You are under an obligation to me, *ma chère*,' he said, 'until you do provide me with an heir, and I will not countenance any evasion of that obligation. I trust that you understand me?'

Héloïse nodded. 'Perfectly,' she said.

De Choissy relaxed. 'Meanwhile,' he said, 'you will oblige me by looking after these papers until I return.'

Héloïse held the packet reflectively between her fingers and then slipped it into her pocket. De Choissy tapped on the coach roof with his cane and the coachman came round to let down the steps. Héloïse made to descend, but de Choissy's arm restrained her.

'No word of farewell, Héloïse?'

She sighed and looked at him, troubled by the implication of his gesture and saddened by the hostility that cloaked her dealings with him. Full of their world-weary secrets, his eyes challenged hers, as if willing her to rebel. She felt all her old repugnance rising. What was the point of her trying to understand someone so complicated and so vicious, and who used her so badly?

'I wish you a safe journey,' was all she said, and alighted into the courtyard without a backward glance. De Choissy remained motionless for a moment longer while he watched her. Then he tapped once more with his cane and the horses moved forward.

The Tuileries Palace was not easy for anyone to find their way around, not even those who knew it well. Situated between the huge Louvre buildings which fronted the river and the Rue St Honoré to the north, the palace was masked on its eastern aspect by a jumble of houses and alleys surrounding the Place du Carrousel which lay directly in front of the palace courtyard. On the west side of the palace a tree-dotted garden ran down to the

Place Louis XV. The entrance was guarded by high terraces and by a swing bridge over the moat. Beyond the Place Louis XV stretched the Champs Élysées. To the north of the gardens, which were skirted by the Terrasse des Feuillants, lay the royal stables, or Manège, which now housed the National Assembly, and beyond that were the ancient religious houses belonging to the Capuchins and Feuillants. A narrow passage leading from the gardens to the Rue St Honoré ran between them. On the south side of the gardens, a breast-high wall ran alongside the river.

Freezing in winter, stifling in summer, rabbit-warrened with passages, entresols and staircases which had been thrown up by the pensioners, artists, actors and soldiers who had infested the building until the summary arrival of the royal family when they were hastily evicted, the palace now housed the court – the king's cupbearer, the officers of the king's roast, the fire attendant, the queen's German baker, doctors, surgeons, apothecaries, officials and functionaries of every description. In short, a whole army of expensive and, to the inquisitive Parisians, useless servants.

Because it knew of no other way, the court did its best to preserve a semblance of normality and to resume its butterfly existence. The corridors echoed to the same gossip as they had done at Versailles, and jockeying for position and intrigue continued unchecked. But now a new element had crept into the atmosphere, an unease that undercut the formalities and subterranean power struggles. The fear that asked, 'What next?' was never publicly voiced, but it was there nevertheless.

And all the time, despite the Assembly's punitive decrees against *émigrés*, the big berlines and coaches, laden with possessions, servants and their aristocratic owners, lumbered down the road towards Brussels or the German border into havens which rapidly became stifling and despairing outposts of France on foreign soil. 'To be an *émigré* or not?' The question was debated with increasing urgency by the dwindling numbers of courtiers who sensed that their privileges were slipping away like so many grains of sand . . .

Héloïse had never considered for one moment that she would join them. Too much of what she loved and cared for lay in Paris. Her world, and her understanding, was French and, besides, she did not care very much at the moment what happened to her, or so she told herself. Raw and wounded as she was by her marriage, her instincts revolted at the thought of flight – and at the thought of abandoning all hope of seeing Louis d'Épinon again.

She also had her duties to consider. The depletion in the ranks of the queen's household had resulted in her promotion to the post of lady-in-waiting much sooner than she had been led to expect, and she was often called from the Hôtel de Choissy to take on extra tours of duty at a moment's notice. Héloïse was glad of it, even though the elaborate rituals and enforced waiting around required a degree of self-discipline and physical fortitude which left her exhausted.

'Do not face Her Majesty with your face in the full light,' one of the older ladies had warned her. 'The queen does not like to be reminded that she is getting older.'

'You may not feel ill,' confirmed another.

'You may not sneeze, blow your nose or adjust your clothing. Do not, above all, faint,' added a third.

The strictures came thick and fast and the dos and don'ts were innumerable. Rushing to find a place in chapel, walking behind the queen in a careful line according to rank, sitting on the lowest and smallest of stools while the king and queen ate, queueing to have one's hair done by Léonard – the formalities were endless and wearisome, but Héloïse, feeling that it was important for the court to continue as it always had, bore them ungrudgingly.

She had been, of course, formally presented to the queen earlier. Robed in a pale straw-coloured silk dress trimmed with rows of blonde lace and wearing the de Choissy waterfall of diamonds at her throat, she had curtsied to the pale, anxious face with its slightly bulging eyes and murmured replies to the polite but uninterested questions put to her in Marie-Antoinette's accented French. The queen was now too careworn and busy with her political intrigues and with the heroic business of rallying her lacklustre husband to care greatly about the welfare of one of her less important ladies. Nevertheless, Héloïse had felt the force of her charm, and her heart had contracted in pity for one who was so beleaguered.

De Choissy had been pleased at her appointment and most insistent that she perform her tasks to the letter.

'I need your eyes and ears, madame,' he said. 'And, of course, I know I can rely on your first loyalty to me.'

His voice dared her to contradict him.

'But of course,' replied Héloïse coolly. She was becoming daily more adept at playing the games with which de Choissy liked to tease her.

'*Bien*,' said her husband. 'Then, I shall expect a full report at frequent intervals.'

Héloïse now realised why. De Choissy was anxious to save his own skin.

Deep in thought, she mounted the staircase, pausing occasionally to permit messengers to overtake her, or to allow ministers to go past on their way to and from meetings. At the top, she stopped in front of her favourite painting, a small, age-darkened portrait of a young woman. Héloïse looked at it often, and marvelled at the skill of the painter who had caught his subject with such subtlety and intuition. The girl in the picture was young, but also hauntingly world-weary and sad, and she never failed to touch a chord in Héloïse.

She was so absorbed that she did not notice a detachment of soldiers push past, or the officer who swung to a halt behind her.

'At last!' said a voice.

Héloïse swung round. Louis d'Épinon was looking down at her.

She was so frail-looking, he thought, but her dark hair hadn't changed. Nor, of course, had the beautiful bones beneath her translucent skin. She was very thin, her bosom only just swelling the low-cut neckline of her muslin gown, her waist hardly filling its folds – and he saw that all trace of gaiety had vanished from her eyes. He remembered her courage and sweetness at Versailles, and a rush of longing swept over her.

Louis ordered his men to continue, and waited until they were out of sight.

'Are you well?' he asked, his composure temporarily deserting him.

'Quite well,' she answered, wishing she had something witty or significant to say – anything to keep him standing there for a moment longer. But Louis had no intention of leaving.

'Madame la Comtesse . . .,' he began.

'Monsieur le Capitaine . . .,' she began.

'Yes,' he said softly.

'I was only going to enquire if you were quite recovered from the injury you received at Versailles. But I see that you have. It has been a long time,' she added, a trifle wistfully.

Louis brushed a hand over his forehead.

'I suffer from headaches occasionally, but nothing insupportable. Of course, my fine scar will be with me for life.'

Héloïse longed to touch his forehead where the mark of his wound still showed faintly pink, and to smooth it under her fingers.

'But I mustn't detain you . . .,' he said.

'I am happy that you do so,' she said, because it was the truth.

'Are you?' he asked abruptly. 'Are you happy to see me?'

Héloïse straightened her thin shoulders.

'Oh, yes,' she said, very simply.

'Can I see you again?' Louis asked. 'I cannot talk to you here.'

Héloïse hesitated. 'Why?' she replied, determined to be sure that her intuition was not deceiving her.

Louis paused. 'You know as well as I,' he said at last.

Héloïse's eyelids snapped down over eyes that were suddenly radiant with light.

'I have to think,' she said. 'There are things . . .'

'Of course,' said Louis, and took a step back. 'But will you meet me all the same?'

Héloïse's fingers closed round the packet in her skirts, but within seconds she had made up her mind.

'I have a box at the opera tomorrow night,' she said. 'Would you care to make up the numbers? It is Piccinni.'

Louis brought his heels smartly together and bowed. 'I would be delighted,' he said. 'Until tomorrow, then.'

Dressed in pale primrose satin over a spangled white satin underskirt with its waist cut fashionably high and its back very narrow, Héloïse took her place in the box the following evening knowing that she looked her best. She wore her favourite diamond aigrette in her hair, offset by three ostrich plumes, and in her ears and on her breast sparkled the de Choissy diamonds.

Sophie was pleased; she had never seen Héloïse look so animated or so carefree. She glanced down at her own gown of palest violet and smoothed her gloves over her arms. Tonight was Héloïse's night and she was happy to take second place. Besides, William had invited himself to supper after the opera and she wanted to sit and listen to the music in pleasurable anticipation, content to let Héloïse and Louis, resplendent in a suit of dark blue silk, enjoy an uninterrupted conversation.

Can I do this? questioned Héloïse as the opening chords struck up and the snuffed candles dimmed the auditorium into intimacy. She knew Louis was watching her and had deliberately arranged his chair so that it was close to hers. Her nerves prickled both elation and warning. Should I let this happen? Never before had the music seemed so sweet or so full of yearning, the harmony so unearthly, or the human voice so beautiful and she found herself transported to an enchanted paradise where she longed to stay. When it was over, Héloïse was left with an aching lump in her throat, unwilling to return to earth.

Her mood did not remain with her for long, and by the time they were seated in one of the fashionable eating houses near the Palais Royal, where William joined them, it had changed to one of elation. Her appetite had quite deserted her, and she only nibbled at her plate of veal seethed in almond milk and toyed with a mouthful of fresh spinach. But the wine, heavy, fruity and tasting of the sun, slipped down and warmed her body.

Louis found he could not keep his eyes off Héloïse and he watched her carefully. Whatever the evening would bring, it was reward enough to hear her laugh with genuine amusement. He suspected that she had very little of that in her life. He kept up a flow of effortless conversation, parrying wit with wit and contributing some well-timed anecdotes, and relaxed himself, glad to be away from the Tuileries and its sad occupants.

Why not? Héloïse thought, when, at the finish of their meal, Louis took her arm to escort her into the gardens of the Palais Royal. I will be so careful. Am I not allowed a little happiness?

They stopped to exchange greetings with an acquaintance of de Choissy's, and a cool voice of reason began again to sound in her head. The acquaintance moved on, not without an appraising glance thrown in Louis' direction. You must not, said the voice. It is madness. Provide de Choissy with an heir first and then think again.

'You have gone very quiet,' commented Louis, handing her through the entrance to the gardens.

But Héloïse, unwilling to share her thoughts, said nothing.

It was easy enough to become lost in the Palais Royal. It was a place meant for assignation, and for secrets, and before long Héloïse and Louis found that they were wandering by themselves among the crowd. They stopped to watch a party of jugglers and to drink a glass of indifferent mulled wine, for the night was a little chilly.

Héloïse shrugged her cloak tighter around her and laughed at a particularly stupid antic.

'I like to see my escorts enjoy themselves,' remarked Louis.

'Your escorts?' said Héloïse quickly, and then paused. 'But, of course, your escorts.'

'Don't look like that, Héloïse,' said Louis, stricken by the expression on her face. 'My . . . escorts are not very important.'

'I have no right to ask such a question,' she said. 'Forgive me.'

'Most men have lovers,' he reminded her, 'and most women.'

'I know,' she replied, and looked up into his face.

With a sudden movement, Louis pulled her back into the shadows and drew her close. Héloïse was so surprised that she did nothing, except to taste, as she had longed to taste, the firmness of his mouth as it descended on hers. It was so very different from de Choissy's. Then, with a little cry, she relaxed against him.

At last, they moved apart.

'I have wished to do that since I first met you,' he said tenderly.

'I am glad.'

'Héloïse, I want you.' Louis was not usually so direct. He liked to spin the game out a little further in order to prolong the enjoyment.

'Why did you not come sooner?'

Louis shrugged. 'It was not the right time,' he said, with the wisdom born of experience in the art of seduction. And then wished he hadn't.

'Time wasted,' she said, and shivered a little.

Louis pressed a finger against her mouth to silence her. They stood face to face, locked together in a moment that all lovers recognise.

He took her hand and kissed the inside of her wrist.

'When? How?'

'Are you not better at these things?' she replied.

Louis laughed with a catch in his throat.

'Yes, I am,' he replied, for the first time in his life a little ashamed to admit it. He moved away from her, conscious that prying eyes might spy them. 'Tomorrow, at four o'clock at the Louvre. Ask for Madame Junot. Everyone knows her. I will arrange it.'

Héloïse nodded, her heart thudding audibly in her ears. 'Tomorrow, then,' she said slowly, more to herself than to Louis.

Héloïse slept badly that night, tossing restlessly from side to side. The party had gone on from the Palais Royal to play cards at Madame Duffand's and she had been badly dipped. Usually her uncanny luck and her skill at cards ensured that she never lost too much. But tonight had been different; and it had much to do with the nearness of the blue-suited figure that stood behind her and steadily consumed a bottle of brandy.

Debts Héloïse knew she could pay, for, whatever else de Choissy might be, he had seen to it that Héloïse retained a generous part of her dowry and, moreover, had settled an allowance on her. Matters of honour were less easy to arrange, and Héloïse knew, as she lay enshrouded by the quiet of her room, that she was about to cross a boundary between innocence and complicity. She thought of the sponge soaked in vinegar that she had obtained from the herbalist. It lay waiting for her to use it, the first of many little deceitful acts and one she prayed would be effective. She could not, in all conscience, ever deliberately foist a child of Louis' on to de Choissy.

The dawn arrived, sending the first ray of light of what promised to be an unseasonably warm day through the shutters. Abandoning all pretence of sleep, Héloïse arose, folded back the shutters and sat by the window, her chin cupped in her hands.

The light grew stronger, throwing out a tantalising hint of spring that promised infinite possibilities. A ray of sun sneaked into the courtyard below, a warm, white light quite different from the harsh summer sun.

As Héloïse watched, the walls of the house grew lighter, turning from dull yellow into pure gold, yielding up the secrets of their corners and elaborate carved doorways. Except for a sleepy maid who stumbled out of the stable block in order to draw water for the household, no one stirred, and the scent of dust, mixed with the perfume of the lilac that bloomed against the south wall, filtered sweet and heavy through the air.

Out in the street, Paris woke into life. The sound of carts coming in from the country loaded with their vegetables, walnuts, oil, dried beans and fresh white cheeses wrapped in vine leaves, mingled with the thump of wooden sabots on the cobbles. Occasionally someone shouted a warning. There were frequent rapid exchanges of greetings and horses blew down their noses in companionable snorts.

Upstairs in the Hôtel de Choissy, the first footsteps clattered on the uncarpeted floors as the servants went about their early-morning tasks. Soon the smell of chocolate and fresh bread wafted through the house and Héloïse's stomach growled in anticipation. She sighed with pleasure at the peaceful scene, and remained thus for a long time.

At half-past three a de Choissy coach picked its way across the Pont Royal and swung east alongside the huge Louvre buildings. The streets were crowded with afternoon traffic – coaches and carts – and on the way she had noticed a surprising number of soldiers. Héloïse wondered if the gossip at the Tuileries was correct and if war, long predicted by those who pretended to be in the know, was imminent.

At the Louvre she alighted and gave detailed instructions to the coachman. She waited for the coach to move on before picking up her skirts and making her way towards one of the doors in the vast façade. She had sometimes paid a call on one of her friends who lived in one of the apartments that honeycombed the building, but she had never before come alone on an assignation such as this. Héloïse wanted to be sure that no gossip would be relayed back to the Rue de l'Université.

One or two passers-by threw a curious look at her veiled figure. Today, she had chosen to wear a pink sprigged muslin and Léonard had swept her hair into deliciously contrived curls on top of which was angled a daring hat trimmed with heron plumes. Sweeping in full, soft folds to her feet and tied with a striped silk sash into a huge bow, her dress hung with just the right degree of artfulness, managing both to conceal and reveal her figure. A beribboned cane completed her outfit. The knowledge that she looked both expensive and elegant helped to steady Héloïse's nerves, but not enough to quiet the fluttering in her breast or to prevent her hands going quite cold inside her kid gloves.

Madame Junot was easily found and Héloïse trod obediently behind her up a carved staircase and into a well-furnished room at one end of which stood a bed hung with fresh white cotton. Madame Junot took a smiling departure and Héloïse almost followed her back down the stairs, so revolted was she with the woman's knowing look.

She sat down in a chair, averting her eyes from the bed, and waited. The minutes ticked from a fine enamelled clock that stood on an equally fine Boule table. Obviously, Madame Junot had taste. But, then, madames who let out their houses often did.

The chair was comfortable and the room pleasantly cool. Héloïse sighed and passed her hand over her forehead where the beginnings of a headache were making themselves felt. She sank lower into her seat, untied her veil, took off her hat and tossed it on to the table beside her. Her eyelids drooped wearily. The clock ticked on with its soothing beat. Imperceptibly, the world darkened and Héloïse sank into an exhausted doze and finally into sleep.

She was roused by the touch of unfamiliar hands lifting her up and placing her gently on the bed. The same hands removed the fichu from her neck. Héloïse sighed and stirred, imagining that she was still deep in her dreams of drowsy darkness. The hands busied themselves with the laces of her dress. Her shoes were removed and her white silk stockings peeled away. Somehow, she was lying in her chemise and then the air was bathing her naked body from head to toe.

Héloïse's eyes fluttered open. It was not a dream. Louis was gazing down on her with an amused and tender expression. He turned to divest himself of his uniform. Héloïse moved drowsily, still not sure if she was waking or dreaming. Louis' hands began to move across her body, lightly at first and then with increasing urgency, and when his mouth swept across hers, Héloïse knew that she was awake.

'*Mignonne*,' Louis whispered. 'Open your eyes, there is nothing to be ashamed of.'

She allowed him to wrap her in his arms and turned her face to meet his kiss. But when he put out an arm to caress one of her thighs, she flinched.

147

Louis raised himself on one elbow and gazed into her face. Héloïse lifted her hand and touched his face in apology.

'What has he done to you?' he asked savagely.

'Nothing that you cannot heal,' she replied.

Surely I am going to die, she thought a little while later. I never dreamed it could be like this.

Later still, when they lay entwined, the sweat cooling their bodies, Louis spoke.

'I should not be here. The king has declared war on Austria.'

Héloïse dragged herself back to the present.

'Poor France.'

Louis kissed a strand of her hair that had fallen across his face.

'This is serious. It might mean the end of the king.'

'Exile or imprisonment?' Héloïse asked dreamily.

'Either.'

Héloïse sat up, and Louis drank in the sight of her slight, pointed breasts and alabaster skin.

'I cannot think of anything very serious at the moment,' she said, 'except that war might take you from me.'

He drew her down to him, assaulted by an emotion that he had rarely felt before. He had come to this tryst much in the spirit he had come to others – curious, stirred and not a little smitten – but the things that had so recently passed between them had shown Louis that this time it was different. So different that he felt that one short afternoon had changed him.

It was not so much Héloïse's beauty and fragility, although both of those things roused in him a deep protectiveness, or even the passion with which she eventually greeted his. It was something other, a mysterious ingredient, a sense of completeness that touched him with the weight of love. Louis had no words to describe the feeling. At this moment, nothing else mattered for him and nothing else existed.

Another hour drifted away and the room echoed to their quiet whispers and absorbed their soft cries of pleasure. All thoughts of de Choissy had fled from Héloïse. She knew only that this was right and perfect, a golden surrender snatched from the humiliation of her marraige.

At last Louis drew away.

'I must go.'

Héloïse disengaged herself from his arms. Louis sat up and swung his legs over the bed. Héloïse smiled to herself as she watched him dress, the secret smile of a woman who rejoices in the intimacy of her love – the careful appraisal of the beloved body, the delighted acknowledgement of a tiny flaw, the never-to-be-forgotten closeness of watching something so ordinary, and so precious, as your lover dressing.

Louis bent over and kissed her eyelids. Héloïse lay back on the tumbled sheets, her dark hair offering a lovely contrast to their whiteness.

'We will meet again soon?' he asked, and she was quick to notice the question in his voice and could not resist the opportunity to tease him.

'Perhaps,' she said languidly, and was enormously pleased to see the frown that sprang across his forehead.

'Perhaps?' he said brusquely. 'Only perhaps?'

For her answer, she reached for his hand and kissed his fingers one by one.

'Need you ask?' she said, and watched the frown clear as if by magic from his face.

Louis kissed her lips lingeringly.

'I will send word,' he said. 'Trust me.'

Then he was gone. Héloïse stretched like a cat in the sun and slid out of bed to wash, aglow with happiness.

De Choissy was absent for longer than he had originally planned. Three weeks went by with no news except for a scrawled missive in which he regretted his enforced absence and promised to return forthwith.

'You don't regret it at all, *ma mie*,' observed Sophie shrewdly when Héloïse read out the letter one morning after breakfast. 'Be honest.'

Héloïse giggled. 'How right you are, dearest Sophie. Every day that my very dear husband is away is another day of freedom.'

She blushed to think just how free they had been. Louis and she had met as often as their duties allowed, and each time Héloïse had returned deeper and deeper in love – wrapped in happiness so fierce that she was sure anyone who cared to could read her secret. Any thoughts of the price she might have to pay were pushed firmly to the back of her mind.

Sophie sat down beside Héloïse on the sofa and cupped her cousin's face in her hands.

'You know,' she said reflectively, looking deep into Héloïse's eyes, 'you have changed these past few weeks. You seem . . . well, more at peace.'

Héloïse tried to avoid Sophie's loving scrutiny. She ached to confide in Sophie, but the caution she had learned in her childhood when secrecy had been her only weapon against prying eyes was too engrained.

'Is it anything to do with Monsieur d'Épinon?' asked Sophie, who had decided to talk directly.

Héloïse drew back. 'You forget I am recently married,' she said, and the dishonesty of her reply sounded hollow even in her ears.

'Héloïse, do me the goodness to treat me as a grown woman,' said Sophie bluntly. 'And as your loving, concerned friend. We have had some conversation on the subject before and I know how things are arranged over here. You are not some housewife determined to protect her reputation.'

'There you are wrong,' replied Héloïse. 'I *am* concerned to protect my reputation.'

Sophie sighed.

'All right,' she said, a little hurt by Héloïse's refusal to trust in her. 'But I know you better than you think.'

At that precise moment, de Choissy entered the room. Booted and spurred, he stood for a moment surveying the charming picture that the two girls made with their morning gowns billowing around them.

'If I were you, my dear,' he greeted his wife, 'I would not wear that colour against the blue of the upholstery if you plan to sit for any length in this room.'

Héloïse stiffened, the familiar sense of dislike tightening her throat. She fought it back and rose to her feet. 'Hervé,' she said nervously. 'I did not expect you yet. Is all well?'

De Choissy tossed his gloves on to the chair and went over to a tray laid with a decanter and glasses.

'No, all is *not* well,' he replied. He poured himself a glass and drank it straight off. 'I am afraid La Tesse has been subjected to the same treatment as La Joyeuse. In fact,' he said softly between clenched teeth, 'the *canaille* have looted the entire house.'

Something like pain crossed his features.

'Thus it is, madame wife, that I shall not be taking you on a wedding tour to visit La Tesse.'

'How dreadful,' cried Sophie impulsively, genuinely grieved for the fate of what was reputedly a beautiful house. 'Was anyone hurt?'

'Only the concierge and his son. Apparently my good Cabouchon chose to fight rather than give in to the demands of the rabble. He might have saved himself the trouble.'

De Choissy drained a second glass and replaced it carefully on the tray.

'I'm sorry,' said Héloïse, and touched his arm in a rare gesture. Her own happiness had made her more sensitive to others' pain, even de Choissy's.

De Choissy allowed her hand to rest on his sleeve and made

no move to disengage himself. Sophie bent her head; she had an unaccountable feeling that she was prying into something she should not.

'No doubt you will mourn the fact that you have less to be mistress over,' said de Choissy. 'In fact, if this continues, marrying me will prove a very poor bargain.'

'Good God,' cried Héloïse sharply. 'What matters is your safety.'

She moved away from her husband and sat down beside Sophie.

'Really, my dear, I never knew you cared so much,' drawled de Choissy, and Sophie wondered why he was so angry. Then she understood. De Choissy was not angry with them but with himself.

'Don't be stupid, monsieur,' said Héloïse icily, picking up her embroidery and jabbing the needle into the canvas.

Strangely enough, de Choissy appeared to approve of her flash of spirit, for he nodded, and then said, in a considerably modified tone, 'Perhaps I am, Héloïse, but you must bear with me, for I cared for La Tesse far more than most things and it gives me acute pain to contemplate its destruction.'

That night he was more violent with Héloïse than he had ever been, and the involuntary cry that burst from her lips at one point only served to invite him to more savage delight.

'Cry, will you, my pretty wife?' he said, grinding his hips deep into her soft flesh.

His fingers probed without mercy. Héloïse bit her lip and stared over his white shoulders into the dark beyond, trying to summon up the shade of Louis to help her endure it. But no comfort came. De Choissy forced open her legs and pressed himself into her. Tears sprang into her eyes.

'I have your body, my sweet,' de Choissy breathed into her ear. 'Now I am searching for your soul, the part of you that you hide from me, my dear, but I know is there.'

In reply, she clenched her teeth and turned her head as far away from his as she could, and waited for him to finish.

He lay, one hand clasped lightly over her breast, his white, finely made body relaxed and heavy and his hair tumbling in disorder over his neck. When Héloïse rose from the bed, reached for a candle and shone it down into the face of her husband and tormentor, she perceived for the first time that he was extraordinarily handsome.

'Monsieur,' she said, finally goaded beyond her endurance, 'I insist that in future you treat me with more respect. I must, it seems, and I will, God help me, accommodate your needs. That

151

is quite clear. But I do have some say in the matter. I will not be treated like an animal. Do I make my meaning plain?'

De Choissy propped himself up on one elbow. Into his eyes shot a gleam of comprehension.

'Rebellion, it would seem, is quite the fashion,' he commented. 'Now what, I wonder, has stirred up this particular one? I do not, in general, take kindly to my wives dictating to me.'

Héloïse held the candle higher. She was, to her surprise, furiously angry.

'I do not care, monsieur, what your poor unfortunate first wife accepted at your hands. I am telling you that *I* am not prepared to accept this treatment.'

With a swift movement, de Choissy was on his knees. One hand wrested the candle from Héloïse. He set it down on the table. With the other he forced her up to the side of the bed.

'Release me, if you please,' said Héloïse icily. 'You have taken your pleasure for tonight.'

His hand bore down on hers and forced her on to the floor by the side of the bed. He muttered something.

'You remind me too much of her.'

'Who?' Héloïse was frozen with loathing. De Choissy reached out to fondle her breast.

'My mother.'

His face was incandescent with anger and with a strange emotion she could not put a name to. Was it pride? Or was it, she wondered with a sinking heart, some sort of love?

'Take your hands off me, monsieur,' she said again and looked him straight in the eye. Under her gaze, his own wavered and his grip slackened.

'Quite a fishwife, I see,' he said, and lay back on the pillows.

Héloïse pressed home her advantage.

'You may come to my chamber whenever you wish,' she said, 'but I insist that you treat me with respect and gentleness. In return, I will perform whatever duties you require of me.'

He was silent, but he pulled her slowly towards him. She resisted, but it was useless. He was far too strong. His hands circled her throat and pressed hard against her windpipe. Héloïse struggled for breath, and when he saw that he was in danger of really hurting her, he recovered himself and relaxed his hold. She swallowed.

'Since you plead so eloquently, Héloïse, I will concede to your request. Remember, it is a bargain. If I ever discover that you have reneged on your side – that you have taken a lover without first providing me with an heir – I cannot answer for what I will do.'

His long fingers teased at her throat in a parody of tenderness.

'Do you hear me?'

So saying, he released her abruptly, and Héloïse staggered back, rubbing at her throat.

'Why do you do this?' she burst out, goaded beyond endurance. 'What have I ever done to deserve this treatment?'

'Why do you ask, madame wife? Do you care?'

'No.'

He smiled bitterly. 'Do you know, I almost mind, Héloïse.'

'How can I care?'

'How can you indeed? Nevertheless, there is something about you that makes me wish that you did. How little we give each other, Madame la Comtesse. Sometimes I think it could be different. How would you feel if I told you I loved you? Or is the name that I gave you sufficient?'

'Enough,' said Héloïse, sickened. 'We have said enough.'

De Choissy became very still.

'So be it,' he said. 'But I will have no cuckoos in my nest, Héloïse.'

She looked away, hating his naked body and cynical face.

'As you wish,' she said at last. 'I have made my point.'

De Choissy smiled, and for a moment she thought she was looking at a madman. But when he spoke it was with his usual urbanity.

'Come,' he said, 'we are beginning to understand one another at last. To celebrate our new understanding, I shall spend the night.'

When she awoke the next morning, Héloïse was alone, and only the rumpled sheets beside her showed that de Choissy had occupied her bed. Marie-Victoire was bending over her, holding a tray. The smell of chocolate was pungent and it made her feel nauseous.

'No, thank you,' she said, waving it away.

Surprised, Marie-Victoire set down the tray on the table and went to draw back the drapes at the window. At her touch, the light flooded over the room, which looked reassuringly normal. Héloïse raised herself on the pillows.

'I think I shall lie for a bit longer,' she said faintly, and she looked so pale that Marie-Victoire hastened to wring out a cloth in lavender Cologne which she pressed on to Héloïse's temples. Héloïse submitted gratefully and lay watching while Marie-Victoire began to set the room in order. Her tasks done, Marie-Victoire came to stand by the bed. Héloïse pushed back the compress.

'Do you wish to talk to me?' she asked.

Marie-Victoire hesitated.

'If you please, madame.'

Héloïse indicated for her to continue.

'If you please,' she said, 'I wish to leave your service.'

Héloïse pulled herself upright with an effort.

'Leave?' she said blankly.

'Yes, madame.'

If she hadn't felt so ill, Héloïse might have been angry. As it was, Marie-Victoire had succeeded in taking her breath away.

'You are serious?'

'I am, madame, very serious.'

'Yes, of course,' said Héloïse quickly, not wishing to give offence. 'This is very sudden. Are you sure it is wise? You see, I feel responsible for your welfare . . . Marie would never . . . what I mean is that I loved your mother and I have grown to love you. In fact, I rely on you to help me . . .'

Héloïse gestured feebly at the luxurious room with its well-appointed fittings and beautiful furniture. Marie-Victoire heard the despondency in her voice and her own heart sank. This interview would be harder than she thought.

'It's what I wish to do, madame,' she said, and tried to harden her heart.

Héloïse recovered herself, ashamed at her weakness. If only she wasn't feeling sick.

'I see,' she said. 'Then, I must ask you.' She felt her way delicately. 'Have you sufficient funds? Or a protector?'

'Both, madame.'

Marie-Victoire did not wish to elaborate further. Nor was she going to furnish Hèloïse with the details of the transactions that had taken place between Pierre and herself and a querulous old man who was renting out a dank room in the Rue des Sts Pères.

'I shall be sorry to leave you, madame,' she said, and the enormity of what she was abandoning struck her anew. The house. Her position. Her life with Héloïse. I must think of Pierre, she said to herself. I must keep thinking of Pierre.

'And I so very, very sorry to lose you,' said Héloïse, and so great was her sadness that she could say no more.

She sat up and swung her legs over the bed, and tried to stand. Marie-Victoire went to help her. Héloïse swayed and pressed her hand to her mouth.

'I can't think what is wrong with me,' she said.

Marie-Victoire's country upbringing asserted itself, and she asked a few pertinent questions, to which Héloïse gave the answers.

'Madame is *enceinte*,' pronounced Marie-Victoire with a smile.

'You think I am pregnant?'

Héloïse thought back over the month. She was sure the child was Louis'. Panic shook her, dousing her initial flare of excitement.

'Oh, Marie-Victoire. You can't think of leaving me now,' she exclaimed.

Marie-Victoire helped Héloïse into her *robe de chambre* and her expression was troubled.

'I am sorry, madame,' she said quietly. 'But my plans are made.'

I need help as I never have before, thought Héloïse, and the one person who can help is going. I can't tell Sophie. It would not be right to burden her with such a secret. It is selfish of Marie-Victoire. No, it isn't. She has the right. But I am not sure that I understand. I will miss her.

I am free, thought Marie-Victoire, but her pleasure was tinged with sadness. I have broken away. There is nothing to stop Pierre and me now. But I hope I go with madame's good will.

Héloïse pressed a handkerchief hard against her lips. Marie-Victoire watched her anxiously. After a moment, Héloïse looked up and held out her hand to Marie-Victoire.

'Of course you must go, if you wish,' she said. 'But you must promise to come back and tell me how you fare. I will see to it that you are rewarded for your service with me.'

Héloïse watched the relief flood into the girl's face and was glad that she had made the effort.

'The extraordinary thing is,' Héloïse confided to Sophie later, 'Marie-Victoire seemed so much older and wiser than either of us.'

Sophie looked up from her writing. She was always writing these days.

'I rather approve of Marie-Victoire,' she said unexpectedly. 'She represents the new France.'

'Well, the new France may be invigorating, but it is decidedly inconvenient,' drawled Héloïse in a passable imitation of de Choissy, trying to make light of the situation.

Sophie looked surprised.

'You are improving,' she said. 'Can it be that Madame le Comtesse de Choissy has a sense of humour, or indeed harbours liberal sentiments? I will have you declaring yourself a republican next.'

'Never,' said Héloïse firmly. 'I will never be that. And nor will you be, Miss Luttrell, for all your fine talk.'

Chapter 7

Marie-Victoire, May 1792

'Allons, enfants de la patrie . . .'

Marie-Victoire was humming a song which had become very popular in Paris. The tune was infectious and she sang it with a good deal of feeling in a true soprano. She was down on her hands and knees scrubbing the rough floor. Her arms plunged in and out of a bucket of suds and swept the ground in front of her in circles. Slowly but surely the grain of the wood unfolded, liberated from its coat of dirt for the first time in many years. It gave Marie-Victoire a ridiculous amount of pleasure to see it.

Eventually she stood up and stretched wearily but contentedly, and lugged the bucket to the door and into the narrow street outside. She walked a little way down the street to the pump and stood pumping hard. A neighbour called out a greeting and Marie-Victoire responded happily, knowing that the suspicions with which a stranger was always regarded when they first arrive in a small, tight-knit community were beginning to disperse. Not that the Cordeliers or the St Germain area was unused to strangers: they arrived in their droves every year in every quarter of the city, searching for work and for lodgings; some in reasonable shape, others so bent and ill-formed with hunger and toil that they could barely walk. But lately the immigrants had changed: men were now coming to Paris because they had heard talk and they were curious, or committed – on the make.

Well, good luck to them, thought Marie-Victoire.

She stepped over the animal skins and offal heaped by the pump, carried the bucket back to her room and set about the task of washing down the walls.

Since the room was small, it did not require too much effort, but the water was soon black with accumulated cobwebs and shavings of candle-grease which she had to scrape off the wall with a knife. Marie-Victoire stood back after a while to admire her handiwork and rubbed her hands dry on her coarse stuff apron. Eventually, when she had an odd sou to spare, she planned to buy some whitewash and paint the walls over. But that would have to wait for the time being. Still, even to her critical eye the improvement was obvious. She went to the door and threw the dirty water into the street, putting out her tongue at a small boy who shouted an obscenity in her direction. She watched him good-humouredly as he ducked out of sight and decided that all small boys were pests.

Marie-Victoire sat down at a small table which stood at one end of the room and began to make some calculations on a piece of old broadsheet that she had found in the street. Fifteen sous for candles. Twenty-five sous for sugar. Twelve sous for bread. Eighteen sous for soap. Her tongue sticking out of her mouth with the effort, she totted the amount up and set it against the sum of money she had made selling two of Héloïse's cast-off gowns and her mother's silver chain, the one piece of jewellery she had ever possessed. After a great deal of addition and subtraction, Marie-Victoire calculated that she possessed twenty sous to last her for the rest of the month. (The money Héloïse had given her was lying wrapped in a stocking at the bottom of her box of clothes, to use only in an emergency.)

She tapped her stick of charcoal on the end of her nose and left a smudge, but the gesture made her feel extremely businesslike, so she scrawled two decisive lines at the bottom of her sums and pushed the paper aside. It seemed a long time since she had left the Hôtel de Choissy, clutching a parcel of clothes and a purse of money, but, in fact, it was only a little over two weeks. Héloïse had been concerned over Marie-Victoire's arrangements and had suggested coming to see where Marie-Victoire was going to live. But Marie-Victoire had felt an instinctive dislike of the idea, so Héloïse had not persisted.

Marie-Victoire felt churlish about her decision, but she had wanted to walk over the threshold for the first time with Pierre, and she also wanted to begin her new life unencumbered by anything from the old. She felt jealous of her new independence and she certainly did not want to be marked out for speculative gossip by the arrival of Héloïse in her carriage.

Lying just to the south of the Pont Neuf, the Cordeliers district was one of the oldest parts of Paris and the Rue des Sts Pères was situated on its western boundary. Proud of its particular flavour and character, men from the Cordeliers were men to be reckoned with and fellow Parisians from other areas such as the St Antoine or Pologne, or even from adjacent St Germain, were careful not to insult a 'Cordeliers' unless they wanted a fight. In the Cordeliers, the streets huddled together, following the pattern laid down when the terrain was mostly fields and the black-and grey-cowled monks from the great religious orders wended their way to and from the heart of the city. The houses were tall and many were built of wood faced with grey and yellow stone. Here and there the thoroughfares opened out into squares dotted with plane trees where people sat and drank and children played.

It was a busy community, and one that now hummed with added excitement, for many of the men who were involved in the latest events lived in it – Danton, Desmoulins and Marat. Since war had been declared the Cordeliers headquarters were thronged from morning to night with officials caught up in the business of recruitment, and everywhere there were soldiers; draped over mounting-blocks and fountains, drinking in the smelly, smoke-filled *cabotines* and generally making life unbearable for the mothers of countless excited small boys.

For Marie-Victoire these two weeks had been a time of enchanted access into a new world. It had not taken her very long to discover what she had always suspected, that the Rue des Sts Pères was a very different place from the cushioned comfort of the Hôtel de Choissy. It took courage to launch yourself into the stream of life that ceaselessly spawned and died down in the streets, where it was everyone for himself. You lived, or you died, and nobody much cared – one stroke of bad luck and that was it. But for the first time in her life the choices were now Marie-Victoire's to make, and it was a heady freedom.

Pierre came each night and left during the day to do his own work. He appeared to have several business arrangements which involved driving the cart around Paris, as well as a string of contacts and friends, from one of whom he leased the cart and horse. He planned to buy his own as soon as finances permitted, he told her, but meanwhile he was managing nicely with his employers' animals. Marie-Victoire was not sure quite what it all involved, and because Pierre was a little reluctant to discuss his activities she did not enquire too closely. She was still finding out about Pierre, and a little unsure of her ground, so she held her peace. It was enough that she had him at night. Nights that she blushed to remember.

At first, Marie-Victoire had been shy and more than a little frightened, but Pierre's honesty, tenderness and open good humour soon dispelled her fears and embarrassment. She had much to learn, but Marie-Victoire (and she blushed again) was proving a willing pupil, and the times they enjoyed together brought her a happiness and contentment that she had never dreamed would be hers.

Marie-Victoire was hungry, so she hacked at a loaf, broke off a hunk of cheese and chewed vigorously on the gritty bread while she decided what to do next. Even these small gestures gave her immense satisfaction. The joy of being her own mistress and of apportioning her time as she wished! To be alone and free and about to make her fortune . . .

Her meal over, she got to her feet and began to unwrap the material that Pierre had procured at a good price from a warehouse which was selling up its goods to the west of the city. She peeled several layers of dirty sacking from the bundles, which made her sneeze, and revealed three rolls of cloth. A white muslin, a pink taffeta and a beige cotton. None of them was of particularly good quality, but they looked well enough if they weren't inspected too closely. Marie-Victoire pondered and then hefted them, one by one, over to the window that fronted the street. Depositing the contents of the table-top on to the floor, she dragged that over to the window as well. Her face wrinkled with the effort as she carefully lifted the rolls on to the table and draped the material over it.

She squinted critically at her handiwork and then went outside to view it from the street and was disappointed. The window display looked meagre and uninviting. Marie-Victoire did not have any experience to draw on in these matters, but she knew enough to know that she would have to do a lot better to tempt in any customers. She returned inside and sat down.

A thought struck her. Jumping up, she went out into the courtyard that lay to the back of the building where she remembered seeing some bales of straw. She dragged two of them into the room, sighing when they littered wisps of straw over her clean floor, and manhandled them over to the window. Then, with the ease of someone country born and bred, she swung them up on to the table and began to drape the lengths of material around them. With the addition of a clever nip and a tuck here and there she was able to fashion them into something that looked deceptively like ready-made gowns. Folding the ends underneath the bales, she went back outside to take a look.

The change was startling. The window looked just right – inviting, professional and hinting at concealed riches inside. Marie-Victoire rubbed her hands together and sent up a silent prayer that the Rue des Sts Pères would attract enough passers-by with some money to spend. Still, she reasoned, with the optimism of youth, brushing off the straw that clung to her gown, very soon the word would spread.

'Allons, enfants . . .,' she sang again and her voice floated into the street, stopping the man outside in his tracks. He listened

159

for a moment with a smile and then stepped over the threshold.

'You sound happy,' he said, depositing a bottle of wine on the table.

'Pierre!' Marie-Victoire rushed over to him and threw her arms about his neck. 'What a surprise. Why are you here?' she asked, her voice muffled by his shoulder.

Pierre dropped a kiss on to the top of her cap and then buried his lips in her neck, savouring her fresh warm smell. He had been collecting saltpetre and was black with grime.

'Missed me?'

'Of course.'

'Well, then, let's see what you have done today.'

Pierre inspected the room. 'Good,' he said after a moment, and proceeded to open the wine. 'We must drink to this *Santé* Marie-Victoire.'

He swigged a mouthful and, leaning forward, applied his lips to hers and trickled some wine into her mouth. Marie-Victoire melted.

'Delicious,' said Pierre, enjoying the little gasp of pleasure that she gave.

'We will be so happy here,' she said, clinging to him. 'Won't we? You and me. Together against the world. Won't we, Pierre?'

'We will,' he replied, and bent to kiss her again. 'How did I have the luck to find you?' he asked.

Marie-Victoire smiled, the warm, happy smile of a woman who knows she is loved, and settled herself more firmly in his embrace.

His arm still around her neck, Pierre drank more of the wine and wiped his mouth with the back of his sleeve.

'I've got you some stuff,' he said.

Marie-Victoire opened her eyes wide. 'How?' she asked innocently, and then giggled.

'Looted,' said Pierre without going into detail and winked at her.

'*Dieu!* What is it?'

'Material, linen, clothes, you know the sort of thing. But first things first, *ma doucette.*'

He drew her to him and pushed her gently towards the closet that led off the room and served as their bedroom. It was tiny and airless and the walls were streaked with damp. The floor was almost entirely taken up by a mattress and by two cardboard boxes that contained Marie-Victoire's scanty possessions. Pierre seemed to fill the space. His hands roved over her kerchief and loosened the laces of her stuff gown which fell obediently down over her legs. Then, when she stood naked, he ran his hands up and down her body, lingering on her small breasts, and laid her on the mattress.

When Marie-Victoire awoke the sun was high in the sky, and she lay for a moment trying to remember where she was. The closet was stuffy and smelt of their love-making. Pierre's arm lay across her body and she removed it gently. He sighed and murmured and she leant over to kiss the side of his head before sliding noiselessly off the mattress. She pulled on her linen chemise and knelt to say a quick prayer to ask forgiveness for the sin she had committed. The prayer was more for form's sake than anything else. Marie-Victoire had no intention of stopping loving Pierre, but she worried about it all the same.

'It won't make it any better.' Pierre sounded lazy and amused.

'It makes *me* feel better,' said Marie-Victoire, half-defiantly. Pierre's previously avowed declaration that there was no God, confided to her one night when he was half-drunk, made her feel uneasy and she fretted for the good of his soul.

'Come back,' he pleaded, his voice heavy with impatience.

She hesitated and then slid towards him, her prayers forgotten.

An hour later they left the shop, which Marie-Victoire locked behind her.

'There is talk of a riot,' Pierre informed her as they made their way towards the building by the crossroads where he stabled the horse. Marie-Victoire said nothing, but she wrapped her kerchief tightly around her waist and tucked the ends into her waistband. The gesture was not lost on Pierre, who reached for her hand.

'Don't worry,' he said reassuringly.

She squeezed his hand, her anxiety allayed. Pierre slipped his arm around her shoulders and looked at her fondly. He had seized his chance with Marie-Victoire and he wasn't regretting it. One look at her pretty and bewildered face in the Hôtel kitchen all those months ago had told him that here was a girl he could trust. Events had proved him right. But even he had been surprised by the degree of happiness that Marie-Victoire had brought him. Once he had succeeded in persuading her to come to the Rue des Sts Pères, she had thrown herself wholeheartedly into her new life. He loved her for that. The fact that she had had a man before him mattered not a whit. Pierre thought briefly of women he had bedded. Most of them had been very enjoyable. Somewhere, there was probably a brat or two, but he had never taken the trouble to enquire where.

Marie-Victoire was special, and he hoped it would stay that way. She was soft and willing and very good company. She was loving. She was clever with her hands. What more could he

161

want? Of course, she was obsessed with this Maillard fellow, but she had promised him that time in the Tuileries Gardens to forget the man. Pierre did not want to run into him again either. If he did, he wouldn't muck about.

Pierre reckoned he knew how the world worked, and he wasn't averse to twisting it to suit his objectives. It had to be so. Either you swam with the tide or you drowned. Pierre had no intention of drowning. He was going to survive and he was glad that it would be with Marie-Victoire.

'*Allez*,' he said, and patted her rump.

Marie-Victoire felt her spirits rise. With Pierre beside her, the world was rosy. Even the thought of Jacques could not dampen her mood, and she still thought of him, despite her best intentions. It was the one thing that marred her happiness, and try as she might she could never rid herself of the habit. Nevertheless Marie-Victoire grinned up at him. These were stupid fears to have and she did not want anything to spoil her time with Pierre. It was too precious and new, and she was enjoying herself too much. She gave him a playful push. He stopped to drop a kiss on to her nose and they reached the stable in perfect accord. Within minutes, Pierre was driving the cart down the street.

In the main boulevard, life was continuing as normal. Laden with bread and vegetables, housewives hurried on their errands. Here and there a group had stopped for a gossip and the on-coming carts and carriages were forced to pause and make a detour. Pedestrians filed past with more or less good humour and shouted out their encouragement to those who had been obliged to back up their vehicles before negotiating the narrowed passage.

Further down the street they came upon the remains of a baker's cart which had been travelling from the mill to the baker. The wrecked front wheel and traces of flour bore mute testimony to its fate.

'Probably stopped and looted,' remarked Pierre. 'The price of bread is high.'

'I know,' said Marie-Victoire. 'You don't have to tell me.'

She thought of the anger and desperation that the women must have felt at the sight of the laden cart, and tried to imagine herself attacking it, but failed.

'Where are we going?' she said at last.

Pierre grinned. 'To a house,' he said enigmatically.

'But whose?'

'Someone who felt it better to leave France and all his possessions behind.'

He stopped in front of an opening that led off the main street and led her down a smaller street lined with houses whose gardens behind were filled with fruit trees. Two magnificent iron gates came into view, through which Marie-Victoire could see a walled courtyard and a house. She gasped: the house was beautiful – or had been.

The sun reflected on the tall windows dazzled her for a moment, but even so she could see the devastation that had taken place. Spilled all over the courtyard and in the hall opening behind the main door were objects lying in crazy abandon: linen, pictures, china, clothes and shoes. As she peered more closely, she could see curtains that had been torn from their rods hanging askew behind the smashed windows.

Something like shame at what she was about to do rose up in Marie-Victoire, a feeling that she and Pierre should not be there. She sat quite still, a small, irresolute figure, clutching her apron between nervous fingers.

Pierre jumped down and hitched the horse to a railing. He lifted her down and, like the intruder she felt herself to be, Marie-Victoire crept silently after him, her eyes wide with amazement. She was no stranger to a house such as this and, despite her new loyalties, something in her heart cried out at the sight. The once-beautiful silk wall-hangings were now torn and ripped by alien hands, the walls had been gouged by God-knew what instruments and the banisters wrenched from their moorings in the curving staircase. It was a scene of utter and death-like desolation. Marie-Victoire could not help thinking that she was witnessing a kind of death, the murder of the spirit of the house, and it made her shudder. For the first time, she really understood what had happened to La Joyeuse, and with it came real regret.

Pierre cast an approving glance around. He had seen it before, and unlike Marie-Victoire he had no pity to waste.

'Come on,' he said. 'We shall have to be quick, there will be others here soon.'

He mounted the stairs, took his bearings and pushed open a pair of double doors that led into the first-floor salon. The same desolation greeted them, and it was obvious from the dirt marks on the wall that many of the paintings and pieces of furniture had been taken already. Still, Pierre noted with an expert eye, the carpet on the floor was intact and the window drapes had plenty of material in them.

'We'll see to those later,' he said briskly, pointing them out to Marie-Victoire who nodded reluctantly.

The main bedroom appeared to be directly above the salon, and Pierre told her to follow him upstairs. On the landing, he stopped and listened.

'Quiet,' he said, bristling. 'I can hear voices.'

He pushed Marie-Victoire behind him and crept softly up to the doors and peered through the crack. Marie-Victoire saw his shoulders relax. Pierre swung the door open.

She gasped at what lay inside. This clearly had been the room of the mistress of the house. It was now a scene of utter chaos, every trace of elegance and luxury obliterated by the hatred and spite that had whirled through it. The walls, which had been hung with pale green silk, were scratched and blotched; what remained of the furniture tipped at crazy angles; and splinters of glass and wood lay scattered on the floor. The brocade bed-hangings were torn from their moorings and the sheets were strewn on the floor in wild abandon. Someone had made free with the bed and stains of red wine pooled on the white linen and ran down to the floor. The drawers of an antique chest had been wrenched open and everywhere the owner's possessions lay in heaps – swathes of satin, brocade, muslin and silk, bundles of gloves and laces, tangled with pictures, china and even a clock whose smashed face turned sightlessly to the ceiling.

'*Salut*,' Pierre greeted a group of men and a woman who were picking over the goods. They acknowledged him briefly, too busy with their task to pay him much attention. Marie-Victoire was uncomfortably reminded of carrion and tried to avoid looking at them.

Pierre indicated the biggest pile with his hand.

'Make your choice,' he said with a satisfied smile.

Marie-Victoire swallowed hard. She raised her eyes slowly to his face.

'I can't,' she said. 'It's wrong.'

Pierre's eyes narrowed. 'What are you talking about?' he said, surprised.

Marie-Victoire's mouth went dry. 'It's not right,' she managed to say.

Pierre raised his eyebrows, and with that gesture his face transformed itself into something quite different from that of her tender lover.

'I didn't think you were faint-hearted,' he said.

Marie-Victoire stood her ground.

'These things don't belong to us,' she whispered back. 'How can we take them?'

'Listen, Marie-Victoire,' said Pierre angrily. 'I paid good money for the privilege of getting first choice. To help you. You are the one who wants to make a go of your business. Remember.' He picked up a shoe from the floor and examined it. 'Perhaps I should not have wasted my time.'

'Pierre,' she said, miserably aware of her cowardice. 'Don't be angry. Can't you understand?'

'No, I can't. You should have thought of this earlier.' He turned away.

Marie-Victoire sank down on to the floor and ran her fingers through a pile of lace-edged chemises. Her fingers encountered something stiff and matted, and she flinched as though she had been burnt when she saw that the material she was handling was disfigured by a fresh bloodstain.

'Ugh!' She leapt to her feet. 'Let's go. This is a horrible place and horrible things have happened here.'

'Now, listen to me.' Pierre cast a quick glance over his shoulder towards the others in the room and again he lowered his voice. He grasped her chin in his hands and forced her to look directly into his face.

'You are ignorant and poor. All you have is your pretty face.' He spoke very fluently. 'You have spent your life, unlike many I know, in some comfort, but you have chosen to leave it to try to make a go of being your own master. . . . For that you must take credit. But it is more than wishing that will make it happen. Do you understand, my girl? You are not in a position to be prissy-minded.' He dropped his hands and looked over her head. 'Count yourself fortunate, Marie-Victoire, that you have chosen to try your luck at a time when not too many people are going to ask questions. Take the chance, Marie-Victoire.'

He pushed her away impatiently and waited for her to reply. When she said nothing he said quietly, but with a good deal of menace, 'I will make you.'

Marie-Victoire bit her tongue hard and winced. This was a side of Pierre she had never seen and she did not like it.

'Don't talk to me like that,' she said stiffly. 'I may be poor and ignorant, but I know what is right. *This* is wrong and. . . . We are acting like beasts.'

Her breasts heaved up and down beneath her kerchief and her face flushed with anger.

Pierre laughed shortly. 'You don't have any rights at all, *ma vie*, when it comes down to it. Only your wits.'

Marie-Victoire was so angry that she couldn't speak.

'Now, do what I tell you. We need to get the cart loaded up,' he said.

She turned, intent on storming out, and then paused. Common sense laid its cool fingers on her brow and prevented her from making that final move. She knew in her heart that Pierre was right. These beautiful things had been abandoned by their owners. She and Pierre had to make a go of the shop.

165

Surely God would forgive her? In the two seconds that it took her to rethink, Marie-Victoire realised that she had been too hasty.

'All right,' she said slowly, her anger draining away, conscious as it did so that she could never go back.

'Good girl,' said Pierre with a sigh. 'Now choose. We haven't got long before there is a free-for-all.'

Slowly and distastefully at first, Marie-Victoire picked her way through the objects and then, despite herself, her excitement mounted. There was more than enough to keep the shop going for the next few months. She worked quickly, shaking out materials and examining furniture and china. Gradually, a pile grew around her feet. She was still hard at work when Pierre signalled that it was time for them to go. While he went to turn the cart round, Marie-Victoire hauled her trophies down the stairs and stacked them neatly in the courtyard. She did not bother to say anything to the others in the bedroom. She was glad to leave them; they reminded her too much of what she herself was doing.

It did not take long for them to load their booty on to the cart. Pierre fastened it securely with a length of rope and leapt up on to the driving board. He gathered the reins.

Marie-Victoire knew that Pierre was still angry with her and it hurt. On the other hand, she was not going to have him ride rough-shod over her wishes without some sort of say, and she wasn't quite sure if she liked the ruthlessness that Pierre had displayed. It did not occur to Marie-Victoire that Pierre was ruthless because he had learnt the hard way not to look a gift-horse in the mouth. The first quarrel, she thought, hating the idea. She touched Pierre's arm briefly.

'Am I forgiven?' he asked, roughly, so as to conceal his feelings.

He was angry with Marie-Victoire for her squeamishness and angry with himself for wounding her.

'Yes.'

'Then, let us forget it?'

She nodded and held on to him tightly in a rush of remorse, and remained holding on to him for a long time.

The streets were much worse on their return and it was growing late by the time they turned into the Rue des Sts Pères. The traffic was now almost at a standstill and Pierre had to coax the sweating horse between narrower and narrower gaps. Marie-Victoire sat beside him checking every now and again to see that their load was still secure. Finally, they ground to a halt. Pierre jumped down to hold the horse's head and Marie-Victoire picked up the reins. There seemed to be some obstruction ahead and a sound of shouting which came closer and closer.

'Riot?' she called over the clamour.

'I can't tell,' Pierre replied. 'Sit tight.'

Marie-Victoire stood up instead and peered through the mêlée. 'It's soldiers,' she shouted through cupped hands. 'They're marching this way.'

Pierre edged the cart closer to the wall. 'We will just have to wait,' he said resignedly.

'I don't like the look of it.' Marie-Victoire sat down again abruptly. 'There seems to be trouble.'

A group of men armed with pikes forced their way through to the area where Pierre and Marie-Victoire waited. They were followed by more men in varying types of dress. Some were in their shirtsleeves and breeches. Others wore ticken trousers and stout boots and were carrying a weapon of sorts, either a pike or a crude wooden stave. Some had knives stuck at angles into their belts. In the main they appeared to be both surprised and dazed, and only a few were stepping out with any semblance of purpose. Several women ran alongside. They were shouting and sobbing.

'Halt.'

A command rang through the hubbub and the untidy group shuffled to a standstill. Dressed in a stained white uniform with blue cuff-flaps and muddy gaiters, a sergeant pushed his way to the front. Pierre, watching with dawning comprehension, shrank back with a quick movement against the wall. The sergeant turned to consult with a figure who had materialised out of the crowd.

'No.' Marie-Victoire felt the word burst from her, and she could have bitten out her tongue for her stupidity. 'Jacques.'

It was indeed Maillard, looking considerably more prosperous and better-fed than the last time she had seen him. He was wearing a short red coat over his striped trousers and a huge tricolour cockade, and he appeared to be acting in some official capacity. Marie-Victoire lowered her head and prayed as she had never prayed before that Jacques had not seen her.

'Ten more,' shouted the sergeant. 'I need ten more for the honour of serving *la patrie*. If I don't get any volunteers, I'll just have to choose.' He leered expectantly at the crowd, which fell back nervously. 'Come, my friends, is no one going to offer to thrash the Austrians?'

A woman burst into frantic sobs. Marie-Victoire peered at her between her interlaced fingers. She looked neat and respectable but her hair was tumbling in disorder from under her cap and

167

she had obviously been running. A second woman threw her arm around her and told her to shut up.

Maillard considered the scene and then he raised his hand. An expectant hush fell. Maillard pointed a finger at some youths who had had the misfortune – or the imprudence – to be standing quite close to him.

'They'll do,' he said in unmistakably authoritative tones. Marie-Victoire's heart gave a warning thump.

Before they had time to protest, the 'volunteers' were pushed forward by their friends. The sergeant gave each of them a piece of paper and they were chivvied into line with the rest.

Again Maillard raised his hand. Then he paused. As if drawn to a magnet, Marie-Victoire unwillingly raised her face and read in Maillard's the flaring triumph and revenge that she knew would be there. Maillard's hand pointed briefly and it was done.

With a curse, Pierre was hustled by the sergeant forward into the line.

'No!' shouted Marie-Victoire. 'Jacques, no! For mercy's sake!'

Maillard did not answer her but signalled to the sergeant to take Pierre's name.

Pierre thought swiftly. Perhaps he could make a run for it? But that would not serve. Maillard knew who he was and it would be difficult to operate in such a small city as Paris if the authorities were looking for him. Better to let the army take him and then to arrange a convenient, but temporarily incapacitating, flesh wound at a later date and get himself invalided out. It was a nuisance this, and put paid to his plans for Marie-Victoire and himself. Pierre made up his mind definitely to get his own back on Maillard, and not to be squeamish about it. The man was a menace.

Marie-Victoire's nails had made white crescents on her palms and she was gazing at him in agony. Pierre shrugged and mouthed a kiss over the crowd, and cast a warning glance towards Maillard who was affecting not to be watching them. The sergeant barked out the order to march and the ill-assorted band of recruits moved up the streets and out of sight. Only then did Maillard make his way over to Marie-Victoire.

'Why?' she sobbed at him. 'Why did you do it? Could you not have left me alone?'

'You know why, Marie-Victoire,' he replied with a shrug. 'I have been waiting for some time now to get rid of him.'

'Where are you taking him?' she asked through stiff lips.

He ignored her question. 'I will come to get you when I am ready,' he said. 'I am about to move into rooms in the Rue St Honoré. You will live there with me.'

'Never,' said Marie-Victoire and spat in his face. Maillard did not even blink.

'I will allow you that,' he said oddly. '*Au revoir*, Marie-Victoire.'

He left her staring dully over the horse's head, and vanished.

Hours later, Marie-Victoire flung herself on to her mattress and lay wide-eyed and motionless, too exhausted to sleep. It had taken all her energies to get home, unload her wares and see to the horse. Not that she cared about them now.

She thought of Pierre, and then for some reason of her mother, and the future stretched out ahead of her, dim and frightening. The tallow taper beside her mattress flickered and spluttered its acrid odour into the small room, and little blobs of yellow grease rolled down on to the floor. Marie-Victoire watched them listlessly.

She rolled over and buried her head in the mattress, willing herself to sleep. But sleep would not come. Instead, the phantoms of fear and hunger raised their gaunt heads, pressing down on her with their awful warnings. A horrible picture of Pierre lying wounded on a battlefield took their place. It was so real Marie-Victoire could smell the gunfire and hear the screams. She could feel his pain and taste his life-blood trickling down through her fingers. She moaned and pressed her hands desperately over her head.

She did not, at first, hear the knocking, until it grew more insistent and demanding. At last, she got slowly to her feet and went to unlock the door.

'Who is it?' she asked without interest.

'Pierre.'

Somehow Marie-Victoire made her trembling hands open the door. Pierre stood on the threshold.

'I have arranged it till morning,' he said with a shrug. 'Then I must go.'

She drew him to her and buried her head in his breast so that he should not see her crippling fear. Nothing, she told herself, must betray her anguish – that much at least she could offer. Her restraint would be her gift to him, and her body and her warmth must be the only memories that he took away. Pierre ran his lips down the small face blotched with tears and tasted their salt. He kissed the tip-tilted nose raised up to his and then her sweetly curving lips.

'If I don't come back,' he said harshly, 'get yourself someone else. But promise me one thing. It won't be that bastard Maillard.'

Marie-Victoire pulled herself away to look at him better.

'Need you ask?' she said softly.

'Promise, then.'

'I promise.'

'With all your heart?'

'With all my heart.'

He seemed then to sink into her, demanding her strength and a part of her soul, and she acquiesced. They did not say much through the night that followed. There was no need. It was enough that, entwined in the threadbare blankets, flesh lay on flesh and endowed their small, shabby room with the memory of their passion.

Towards dawn, Pierre rose, donned his army-issue white coat with its blue and red epaulettes and slung a leather strap over his shoulder. He then left, leaving Marie-Victoire huddled on the mattress.

It seemed to Marie-Victoire, lying aching and hollow-eyed, that part of her had gone with Pierre – a small, thin shade who would follow him down dusty roads into green woods and yellow cornfields, like a ghost from the past.

PARIS, July 1792

By the summer of 1792 most of the aristocrats had disappeared from the Assembly. Their place was taken by the Feuillants, Girondins and Jacobins, among the last a precise little lawyer from Arras called Robespierre. The Feuillants wanted a constitutional monarchy. The Girondins were noted for their love of liberty and their wish to sweep away the old repressive social hierarchies. The Jacobins were more extreme but less influential and, unlike the Girondins, anti-war. 'Peace will set us back . . . ,' said Madame Roland, the wife of the new Girondin minister of the interior. 'We can be regenerated through blood alone.'

But with fewer than 140,000 men France was under threat from allied royalist forces. Despite the frantic efforts of the authorities, equipment was scarce, defection rife and mutiny simmering. There was no ammunition, very few officers and little enthusiasm. The results were disastrous for the French.

In Paris the rumours swelled. The war coincided with a serious economic crisis and the government-issued paper currency, the assignat, declined alarmingly. A demand for prices to be fixed grew. Riots broke out. Accusations of counter-revolutionary activity flew thick and fast, and accusing fingers pointed to the Tuileries. 'They are the ones who have betrayed us,' shouted the orators, and a deluge of obscene pamphlets flooded the city, tearing what remained of the queen's reputation into shreds. The clergy went into hiding, terrified that they would bear the brunt of popular fury. The Girondins tried then to force the king to accept a decree whereby all priests who had not sworn the constitutional oath could be deported. The king used his veto to refuse and dismissed his Girondin ministers.

The Parisians decided on their own way of making their feelings plain. On June 20th, 8,000 shopkeepers, artisans, porters, market-women and itinerants came pouring out of the faubourgs. Armed with muskets, pikes, pitchforks and staves, they swarmed into the Assembly. They shouted abuse and waved their weapons (on to one of which was affixed a calf's heart with a notice reading 'the heart of an aristocrat') for upwards of three hours. Then, bored with this sport, they forced their way through the Porte Royale and made for the Tuileries.

They discovered the king in an anteroom. 'Here I am,' he told the mob, as his sister, Madame Élisabeth, threw her arms round him to protect him. The queen hurried to join them and they stood together while their subjects harangued them. The king accepted a red Phrygian cap of liberty and stuffed it on to his head. He was still wearing it when, weary hours later, the crowd dispersed. He sank exhausted into a chair, snatched off the cap and threw it on to the floor.

This time the royal family had survived, but everyone knew that worse was to come.

By July, France had also declared war on Prussia. The alarm guns sounded daily over the city, booming out from the Pont Neuf and the Arsenal. The recruitment teams swept their nets wider, proclaiming the message, 'La patrie en danger.' The watchers yielded up their sons and brothers with bitter tears.

On July 14th, the city gathered once again to celebrate. On the Champ de Mars, eighty-three tents stood arranged around the royal marquee. Outside Paris, a contingent of fédérés, many of them from Marseilles, waited to parade through the fields. They were rough, determined men who had listened to the provincial agitators spreading their gospel of insurrection. . . . The royalists are working for the counter-revolution. The king is in league with the enemy. The queen has sold France to the Austrians . . .

Chapter 8

Sophie, July 1792

To begin with, I understood very little but after a while I began to see more clearly. Here are a people, face to face with Privilege and Corruption, fighting for Liberty and Justice, and my heart cannot but approve . . .

Sophie wrote quickly, her fair head bent low over the paper. She wanted to finish her work before she left for the celebrations.

The time is coming when there is no longer a Distinction between Classes. The Rich will mingle with the Poor and the King will rule in Perfect Accord with the Will of his People. A King there should be, for without a Head of State the Country will be open to Anarchy and Discord. But He must rule with His People . . .

She paused to repair the ravages wrought on her quill by her forceful stabs at the paper and nibbled at the feather. Had she got her thoughts into the correct order? Would Miss Williams consider Sophie's arguments for a constitutional king in France sufficiently well argued? They sounded well enough when she read them out aloud to herself, but she needed to be quite sure.

Sophie had been gratified by the poetess's encouragement of her efforts. She had never intended to confide her secret to Helen – or to anyone – but Helen had prised it out of her at one of her breathless salon evenings which she and William had attended. Helen had swooped with determination.

'Do, please, Miss Luttrell, let me see anything you write. I have a friend who is very anxious to publish the opinions of sensible people. It is so important that we all have a clear view of what everyone thinks. And you, I am persuaded, my dear Miss Luttrell, being half-French yourself, will have a particularly useful point of view. Do say yes to my notion.'

And Sophie, not proof against this charming flattery, could

not but find it in her heart to oblige. She soon discovered that she had an unsuspected talent for neat phraseology, and she had settled down to produce a stream of documents, each divided into headings: *Les Droits des Peuples*, *Lettres aux Anglais* and *Sur les Droits des Femmes*. She presented these faithfully to Helen.

'*Ciel*,' remarked Helen on receiving the last, 'I had no idea you were a feminist and a liberal.'

'No, nor did I,' replied Sophie. 'It was only when I began writing that I knew what I felt. But, truly, I am increasingly of the opinion that the subject of our sex's position in our society should be addressed.'

Helen gave her a shrewd glance. 'So the little one is growing wings,' she said thoughtfully. 'We must encourage you. I shall try to arrange an invitation to Mademoiselle de Gouges. Olympe would be delighted to discuss such matters with you. Even as we speak she is engaged on writing a pamphlet on very much the same subject. Now, and this is important, you must not tell anyone what you are doing. We don't want any well-meaning interference, do we?'

Sophie had agreed and had thought no more of it, rejoicing in the sense of power that her writing gave her. She concluded with some satisfaction that her mind felt stronger and more supple. Writing brought her a new sense of purpose and an opportunity to grasp affairs that were outside her immediate concern. It gave Sophie much to think about and it also comforted her enormously that in this area of her life, at least, there was no confusion.

She did, however, let Miss Edgeworth into the secret, and her governess approved the scheme.

'I think it will do you a lot of good, my dear,' she said after a moment. 'You need to come down to earth a little after all this gaiety. Some mature reflection and application will make a better woman of you.'

Miss Edgeworth, if the truth was known, was becoming a shade alarmed both by the political situation and by Sophie. She was beginning to think it was time she took charge and conveyed Sophie back to England. Or, indeed, that it was time Ned returned. The last, of course, was a concession made only out of loyalty to her employers, for Miss Edgeworth, herself a touch infatuated with William, considered that here, at last, was a man worthy of Miss Luttrell. But, then, Miss Edgeworth was, despite her black silk and corkscrew curls, something of a free spirit. But after a great deal of anxious thought, Miss Edgeworth decided she had no power to influence events and to hold her peace a little longer.

Neither of the women thought to ask what happened to Sophie's documents once Miss Williams had borne them away. It did not occur to them that she might be careless in whom she entrusted them to, or that the men who sweated over the back-street presses were unscrupulous and possibly loose-tongued. As it happened, they should have done. Sophie's reflections on the king and the constitution caught the eye of one such publisher, who sat up all night to set the text. By the next afternoon, it was being hawked along the river bank together with *La Vie Scandaleuse de Marie-Antoinette* and other such interesting documents, where it was bought and read with attention.

One such passer-by – a tall, blond, foreign-looking gentleman – stopped to buy it and perused it idly. What he read made him stop in his tracks. He muttered an oath and shook his head as if dismissing a fanciful notion. Then he re-read a paragraph. It was. It was the very same phrase, the very same turn of words. His eye fell to the bottom of the page and he saw that the anonymous author was billed as a lady of quality and learning. He turned, retraced his steps and demanded of the seller how many copies had been sold. The vendor shrugged and told him he couldn't keep count but he did know that a gentleman prominent in the increasingly influential anti-monarchist Jacobin club had also bought a copy which he intended to show his colleagues. William had damned Sophie's imprudence and sat down to think.

Sophie wrote on in blissful ignorance with one eye on the clock. She must hurry. At eleven precisely, she sanded the paper and folded it. Then she rose and tugged at the bell to summon her maid, and applied herself to the more frivolous matters of her dress.

It had been decided to take a boat down the river to the July 14th celebrations. The party, consisting of the marquis and marquise, Héloïse, de Choissy, William and Sophie, planned to land near the field of the Champ de Mars and to perambulate gently towards the royal marquee. It had taken a great deal of persuasion to make the de Guinots attend the celebration – such an occasion was deeply repugnant to them and went directly contrary to their deepest beliefs. In the end, it was de Choissy who argued them around, pointing out that the king required their support and it was wise to run with the prevailing tide. Héloïse had agreed with him and, anyway, she was required to attend the queen; and Sophie, for her part, wished to observe the anniversary at close quarters.

Seated opposite her in the boat, William watched Sophie

unobtrusively and wondered what thoughts were going through that golden head. Slipping through the sky, the sun played on the green and brown of the water and changed the bubbles of foam into myriad colours. The air was soft with the siren feel of summer and the birds dipped lazily into the spray sent up from their oars. Dressed in bright green, the fruit trees nodded in the well-stocked gardens that sloped down to the water's edge and, behind them, the buildings softened into the summer haze.

Sophie stared around her. To her right lay the Tuileries and its gardens and round the bend in the river to the left the area known as the Champ de Mars. There were cows in the orchards, and vegetables growing in the market gardens and, over towards the Champs Élysées, a long oblong patch of grass. The weed tangled in the boatmen's oars and the boats glided along with the current. Sophie sighed and closed her eyes.

It was hot, and William was reminded of the heat back in Virginia. He wondered briefly how Elizabeth was faring and resolved once again to write her an honest letter.

How strange love is, he thought. What were the pieces that made up the jigsaw? Was it lust and the feel of a body under yours? Was it the little flickers of perfect understanding that passed between two people? Was it the shape of a breast, or the curve of a neck or the sight of a pulse beating on satiny skin? How did you put the picture together, and was there no choice in the matter? Why was it that, day by day, another little detail of Sophie's face became imprinted on his heart, and the sound of her voice stirred in him a deepening desire to take care of her?

William did not know the answers. He knew only that his emotions were no longer under his control. As if she had been listening in on his private monologue, Sophie stirred in her seat and tilted her head in an attitude of artless repose.

'Are you comfortable?'

William broke into her reverie and watched with enjoyment as her grey eyes opened in surprise.

'Indeed I am, never more so.'

He detected a hint of mockery in her reply. It was time he warned Sophie of her possible danger and asked what her plans were. William was thoroughly alarmed. Paris was dangerous, simmering with discontent and subject to violent fluctuations in mood. As a foreigner, one had to be doubly careful – William fingered his pocket where a sealed packet lay containing his latest report – and if you were a woman as well, then it was folly to invite censure.

These things would have to be explained to her, but so far

he had hesitated. First, because the right opportunity had not presented itself, and secondly because William was loath to trespass on territory that was not strictly his. He knew that the figure of Ned still hung over Sophie, a large, angry memory that was not going to be easily placated, and he knew that his success or not with Sophie depended on the fact that he had not pressed her over his feelings. He sympathised with Sophie's predicament – although he would have been horrified to know that Sophie's nights were often made hideous by her guilt over Ned, with the knowledge of her parents' displeasure and, almost worst of all, by the thought that her behaviour might result in her forfeiting High Mullions.

Sophie stirred and waved a white-gloved hand in the direction of the others.

'We are nearly there,' she informed him.

Over on the left bank, the crowd had thickened and parties of boats were negotiating with each other to reach the landing stages. The boatman piloted his craft through the traffic and nudged the prow towards the landing stage. Safely landed, Sophie was waiting for the rest of the party to disembark when William bent over her and whispered into her ear.

'I must speak with you alone, soon.'

Her face was puzzled but she nodded, before moving forward to greet the de Guinots.

The marquise was in a frosty mood, as she so often was these days. Privately, Sophie considered that her manner concealed fear, and she did not blame her aunt, but she knew that Héloïse found her mother very difficult and she was distressed on that account for her cousin. The marquis was his usual courteous self, although obviously distracted and suffering from over-work. He was no longer a minister, the king having been obliged to dismiss him earlier in the year, but he still collaborated closely with his sovereign and the strain of it was beginning to take its toll.

William scanned the field in front of him and his brow furrowed. He mistrusted the atmosphere.

'I know,' remarked a voice at his elbow. 'The Champ de Mars does appear to have a remarkable resemblance to a military camp.'

De Choissy spoke softly, as was his custom.

'Worried?' asked William in an undertone, not wishing the ladies to hear him.

'No more than usual. But I shall trust you, my friend, to take Miss Luttrell and Madame la Comtesse away if there should be trouble. I shall attend to my dear parents-in-law. *Comprenez?*' De Choissy was commanding, not requesting.

177

'Of course,' replied William, making a mental note of the topography. 'Have you spoken to Monsieur le Marquis?'

'I am about to do so,' replied de Choissy and moved languidly away.

The men handed the ladies through the crush towards the royal marquee, which was enclosed by a ring of smaller tents. Beside each of these fluttered a tricolour flag, its bold red, white and blue echoed in the thousands of cockades sported by the crowd. The servants, bearing food and wine, ducked from one to another, sweating in the sun.

On the surface, Paris was *en fête*, alive with a deceptively innocent and carefree gaiety – a swirling mass of colour, noise and movement. Old men sat gossiping under the trees while younger men gathered to discuss the latest events. Their wives went to and fro, organising the food and scolding children who darted and chattered round their feet like starlings.

William's sharp eye saw at once that there were large numbers of the poorer elements in evidence. For each well-brushed coat and pair of breeches there were the trousers and red *carmagnole* waistcoat of the artisan. For each silk gown worn by the well-to-do housewife, there was the plain stuff frock and shawl of the seamstress or the rags of the street drab. For those that cared to do so, he thought, there was plenty to read in their expressions – a fierceness and determination that had not been there before. . . . William told himself to stop being fanciful. Sophie tugged at his arm.

'Look over there,' she said. William turned obediently in the direction of her pointing finger to where a tree stood bedecked with objects. He squinted at it, temporarily blinded by the light. He could just make out a profusion of paper pictures of armorial bearings, crowns, cardinals' hats and St Peter's keys pinned on to it.

'I see,' he said, light dawning. 'Those pieces of paper represent the king, the pope and the aristocracy. I wonder what the authorities mean to do?'

Sophie shrugged, her attention had been caught by a pair of sweethearts. Scarcely more than children, they were wandering through the crowd with arms around each other, so thin and pale that their entwined limbs seemed almost transparent. As she watched, the girl stopped to speak to her lover and Sophie glimpsed a pale face whose papery-dry, bluish skin seemed not to belong to the living. Sophie shivered and her grey eyes widened in sudden apprehension. She turned to William.

'We must join the others,' she said. 'The marquise will be waiting.'

Inside the royal tent, the courtiers stood stiffly to attention while the royal family moved down the line, trying not to notice that the gaps in their once numerous court were becoming more and more obvious. The royal children were very much in evidence. Madame Royale stuck her chin into the air and the little dauphin hopped from foot to foot, impatient for the ceremony to begin. The king peered out on the world from under his wig, his slow, amiable face as usual expressive of nothing very much. He was dressed in a rich silk coat over a thick padded under-garment which the queen had insisted he wear as a precaution against an assassin's dagger. But his sword sat awkwardly at his hip and his white stockings were wrinkled. Even Héloïse, always quick to defend her sovereign, had to admit that, set against the tailored apparel of more fashionable gallants, he looked hopelessly old-fashioned.

Marie-Antoinette was by his side, stiff and haughty – and desperately anxious. She had lost weight and her sapphire-blue dress hung loosely on the once ample frame. Her magnificent hair was thinning and whitening, and the famous Habsburg underlip was bitten raw. Her eyes were red-rimmed from weeping and from hours of deciphering codes late into the night when she wrote frantic missives asking for help to courts all over Europe and letters to the man she loved, Count Axel Fersen. Unconsciously, Marie-Antoinette twisted the diamond rings on her fingers. Héloïse had reason to know that habit well. Click. Click. Click.

'*La pauvre reine*,' whispered Sophie to Héloïse.

Héloïse sighed. It was true, despite her straight back and proudly held head, the queen presented a sad spectacle. All of the royal family did. There was a beaten look about them; and a sense of doom hung over the proceedings. Privately, Héloïse was beginning to be afraid that the unthinkable could happen and France would put aside its king and queen. Even so, she did not wish to admit as much to Sophie, and certainly not in public. She frowned at her cousin. Sophie raised an eyebrow but said nothing more.

At first the singing was only a faint faraway murmur, percolating with difficulty through the clamour. Then it grew louder and more insistent, picking up volume as the voices swelled until the chorus became strong and vibrant.

'What is it?' asked Sophie, tingling in every nerve.

'A new song, my dear, for new times,' said de Choissy. 'It has been adopted by the *fédérés* who, if I am not mistaken, are about to march on to the field.'

'It has travelled fast,' said William in an aside to de Choissy.

179

'Indeed,' he replied.

'How do you know that?' asked Sophie, considerably mystified. 'From where has it travelled?'

William avoided her look. 'Intuition, Miss Luttrell,' he said lightly, thinking of one report his agents had sent him, informing him that a new revolutionary song had been composed and was sweeping the salons of Brussels.

Sophie gave him one of her straight looks, troubled yet again by a feeling that she could not place. The *Marseillaise* reached a climax, and its final cadences were crashed out to the rhythm of marching feet and screaming cheers.

'It does possess something special,' said Sophie, committing the tune to her memory.

The royal party took their places at the marquee's entrance and stood waiting to review the processions. Crammed to bursting, the fields stretched away into the distance, gaudy with fluttering flags and dotted by chestnut trees. Every spare inch of space was taken, and the outlines of thousands of heads – blond, dark and grey – blurred like colours on an artist's palette. Marching briskly, many arm in arm, the *fédérés* shouted in a hoarse patois and waved at the excited Parisians, who shouted back in excitement. Behind the *fédérés* came untidy groups of men carrying models of the Bastille and sheets of patriotic songs which they distributed among the crowd. Behind them marched the re-formed National Guard and the regiments of the line, and a more sober procession consisting of the National Assembly representatives.

Héloïse strained to see Louis and was rewarded by the sight of his familiar figure, mounted on his chestnut horse, leading the detachment. De Choissy's hand closed none too gently around her own.

'I think you should attend Her Majesty,' he told her.

Héloïse excused herself and took her place behind the queen.

He knows, she thought, and felt the goose-flesh rise on her arms.

The courtiers shifted uneasily and clustered round the figure of the king as if they were offering protection, however inadequate. At the given signal, Louis XVI moved slowly forward to initiate the second half of the proceedings. At the steps of a makeshift altar, erected near to the decorated tree, he stumbled, and Héloïse heard the queen's stifled scream. The king recovered himself, took the Oath of Loyalty, watched by thousands of pairs of eyes. A silence fell as he was led by the mayor of Paris towards the 'Tree of Feudalism' and requested to set fire to it.

At this point, Sophie glanced at the queen and saw that

Marie-Antoinette's humiliation was reflected in every line of her body. The queen was staring defiantly and blindly into nowhere and tears which she made no effort to hide streamed down the royal cheeks.

'Poor lady,' Sophie murmured to herself.

With an unexpected show of spirit, the King declined the mayor's invitation and, after exchanging a few cursory civilities, walked back to his family.

'So it's over,' said Sophie to herself, rather surprised at the brevity of the ceremony.

'*Mais oui*. I rather think you are right.' De Choissy beside her spoke reflectively, and it was obvious from his tone that he meant more than the celebrations. 'It's over for us all.'

His gaze followed the king as he was escorted off the Champ de Mars, accompanied by a sullen silence that was all the more marked by the contrast to the cheers that had greeted the *fédérés*.

'A puppet king?' queried William, who had joined them, holding a glass of wine.

'No, my friend, what you are seeing is something infinitely more disturbing.'

'What do you mean, monsieur?' asked Sophie.

'I mean, dear ones, that our sovereign over there is about to become a martyr.'

Neither William nor Sophie found they could reply to that statement, and their silence was more eloquent than any words.

The queen and her children made their departure, followed by the court officials. It was obvious that, free from the constraints of the royal presence, the crowds were going to remain on the Champ de Mars until well into the night. Already there was a smell of roasting meat, accompanied by the sound of shouts and singing, and the convivial crack of campfires.

The de Guinots indicated their wish to depart. Both of them looked pale and careworn. Nothing in their long years as high-ranking courtiers at Versailles had prepared them for what they had just witnessed. The king, at the beck and call of the mayor of Paris, and virtually forced to burn the symbols of his authority! The spectacle had exhausted them and Héloïse was thankful that she had possessed the forethought to insist that they return home in carriages. They bid perfunctory goodbyes to each other and embarked on their separate journeys considerably more dispirited than they set out.

'Thank God,' said Héloïse, sinking back limply on the coach's upholstery, feeling so drained that she could hardly move. De Choissy sat opposite, a gloved hand resting lightly on his cane.

181

She could read nothing in his face, but she knew him well enough to know that he was thinking. Héloïse's stomach lurched and she tasted bile in her throat. She forced herself to take a deep breath. Did it matter, she thought wearily, what de Choissy thought? and acknowledged reluctantly that it did.

Since that night in the bedchamber, she knew, and he knew, that his power over her had diminished, and this comforted her, but not much. De Choissy had welcomed the news of her pregnancy with studied politeness – and a series of questions as to when she anticipated being confined. Héloïse had lied. De Choissy appeared to accept her explanation that it would be born in the spring, but she knew it was only a matter of time before he pressed her further. It was going to take the most careful deception to pass off this baby as De Choissy's and the thought made her spirit quail.

At the Hôtel de Choissy, Héloïse went upstairs to rest. De Choissy announced that he was paying calls and Miss Edgeworth was nowhere to be found. Sophie and William were left together in the drawing room. Sophie went straight to the point.

'What is it you wish to talk to me about?'

William paused, took out an enamelled snuff box and inhaled a pinch.

'Excellent,' he pronounced.

'You sound exactly like Monsieur le Comte,' remarked Sophie.

William instantly became serious and snapped the box shut. 'Miss Luttrell – Sophie – do you trust me?'

Sophie nodded, but there was a hint of reservation in her manner.

'But of course, Mr Jones.'

'Then, I must ask you a question and you must think before you reply, because it is important,' he said, testing his ground.

She looked at him enquiringly. 'Go on.'

'How do your sympathies lie, politically speaking?'

A shade of alarm passed over her face. 'Why do you ask me? We have discussed our feelings on the subject very often.'

'Because I suspect that you are involving yourself in a manner which may be dangerous.'

She was suddenly very still.

'Sophie, answer me.'

'I wasn't aware you possessed the right to cross-question me,' she said very cool.

William dug into his waistcoat pocket and drew out a piece of paper.

'Do you know wha, this is?' he asked.

Sophie took it and smoothed it out. Her hands trembled slightly. It did not take her many seconds to see what it was. She raised her eyes to his.

'Yes, this is mine. I have been writing a little, a few thoughts, nothing so very momentous. I had no idea it had been printed.'

With a swift movement, he captured her hands.

'Sophie, who do you give them to?'

She hesitated. 'Why, Miss Williams, of course.'

William dropped her hands.

'That's what I was afraid of. Don't you realise, my sweet, impractical fool, that Miss Williams is the most indiscreet of women, with indiscreet friends. You have played into their camp and opened yourself up to comment. God knows what danger this may put you into.'

Caught on the raw by his vehemence, Sophie's composure was shaken.

'How did you find out?' she asked in a low voice.

'Because your work is being hawked from every cheap booth and bookstall all over Paris. I saw it by chance and, unfortunately, I am sure I will not be the only one who will discover who the author is.'

William walked over to the window and looked out. The garden was resplendent with summer flowers. Beyond it the roofs of neighbouring buildings jutted up reassuringly as they had done for decades. The prospect appeared to soothe him, and Sophie saw him relax. But when he spoke again, William was struggling with feelings that threatened to overwhelm his composure. Fear for Sophie. Fear for the future. And, over and above those, his wish to carry her off to safety, far beyond the turbulence of Paris.

'Why did you do it, Sophie?'

'I would have thought, Mr Jones, that you are the one person who would have understood and sympathised,' she replied. 'I wished to make a contribution. Being a woman prevents me from speaking publicly and this way seemed the only avenue open. It was so simple to do.'

'Don't, Sophie. Don't air your political views in public,' he said.

Stung by his words, Sophie avoided his look. 'You don't understand,' she said bitterly. 'I thought that you did. But I was mistaken.' Her disappointment was so great that she could scarcely speak. She had imagined that William would sympathise with her efforts.

'If you say so, Miss Luttrell, then I stand reproved,' he said.

183

'But I beg you for your own sake never to allow your work to leave your hands.'

William went to pick up his hat, more shaken than he could remember by her reproof. 'I shall bid you good-day.'

Sophie tried to pour herself a glass of wine from a tray on the console table, but her hand trembled so much that she could not lift the jug. She stood instead with her hands pressed against the table and waited for the door to close behind him.

At the sight of Sophie in so much distress, William's anger faded. He threw his hat into a chair and strode towards her.

'Sophie, forgive me.'

Before she could prevent herself, Sophie reached up to touch his cheek. She wanted so much to touch him, to reassure herself that he was there and to feel his warm and living contours, even though she knew it to be unwise and wrong. William caught at her hand and pressed it to his chest where it lay imprisoned in the folds of his cravat.

'Will you marry me, Sophie? Now. This day. This month?' he said, forgetting everything but his love for her.

He could have cursed, for at his words the light drained out of her eyes.

'How can I?' she said. 'There is Ned.'

'Surely Sir Brinsley and Lady Luttrell cannot force you?'

'No,' she said slowly. 'But they expect it of me. They have always expected it. How can I abandon my duty to them? And what of Ned? I cannot let him down so wantonly. Besides, I have . . . I have the greatest affection for him.'

William released her hand.

'What of Ned?' he said. 'You, of course, must decide, but I can offer you more than Ned. I can offer you a new life. I have a large house and sufficient means. I will inherit money. I will give you children and a country that is made for someone like you, Sophie, where you can write in peace. Think of it, we can leave this old world with its battles and bring up our family in the new one.' As he spoke he drew her close. 'We think alike, my heart. I know we do.'

Sophie felt his breath on her cheek and smelt the masculine scents of pomade, leather and Cologne, and her senses blurred with longing. She tried to conjure up Ned but failed. William stroked her hair.

'You are so lovely,' he said.

She was tempted beyond endurance, and William pressed his advantage. He bent his head, and at the touch of his lips Sophie gave in.

At last, he released her and they stood gazing at each other until William bent once again, this time to kiss her white throat. His lips travelled downwards towards her breasts, found the swelling and lingered. He stopped.

'I apologise,' he said. 'I did not mean to take advantage.'

Her answer when it came surprised him.

'I am glad you did,' she said simply, her face flushed with emotion.

William smiled at her in relief. 'Ought not a gently brought up English girl such as yourself be angry?'

Sophie laughed. 'Perhaps,' she said. 'But this is Paris, and even virgins . . .' She held up her hand teasingly. 'Don't blush, William, I am not ashamed of my condition. Even virgins aren't entirely ignorant.'

'Then, you will marry me?'

Her laughter died, leaving in its place a stricken look. She turned and her skirts swished in a perfumed cloud. Sophie dropped her face into her hands.

'Forgive me, William, but I cannot,' she said through her interlaced fingers.

From outside came the noise of a coach's arrival. A door banged and there was the sound of impatient feet, but Sophie paid no attention. She was fighting an anguish that threatened to tear her in two. William stood still.

'You cannot mean it,' he said at last.

Sophie raised her head and flinched at his expression.

'My parents and Ned must come first,' she said brokenly. 'Forgive me. I should never have allowed you . . . I should not have permitted.'

In reply, he caught her to him with such force that she cried out.

'I shan't let you, Sophie. You are my life. Do you hear me?'

Through her confusion and misery sounded another voice.

'Sophie,' it said, and the inflection was all too familiar.

Goaded beyond endurance, she raised her lips to William's for one last guilty kiss, and then broke free.

'Sophie,' said the voice again.

With a muttered exclamation, William released her, so abruptly that she staggered.

'Sophie,' said the voice for the third time.

Sophie looked up through eyes now blinded with tears and saw Ned, booted and spurred, standing in the doorway. With a sigh she crumpled into a heap on the floor.

William ripped off his coat and sent it flying as he swooped to pick up Sophie's inert form. He cradled her close to his breast and brushed his lips through her hair.

'My poor Sophie,' he whispered, before laying her on the sofa and ringing the bell.

An interested witness to this little scene, Ned bit back an oath and clenched his fists. He bent to pick up William's coat, which he tossed angrily on to a chair. As he did so, a small sealed packet fell out at Ned's feet and he bent to retrieve it. What he read was sufficient to make him glance up with narrowed eyes. Then, without a second's hesitation, he pocketed his find and went over to help William.

Chapter 9

Pierre, August 1792

Citoyenne Marie-Victoire Bonnard
At the house by the pump
Rue des Sts Pères   August 5th, the year 1792

Ma chère amie,

Are you well? Have you sold the things that
we chose? I think of you every day. I am sitting in a barn
writing this to you and I am told that we are near to the forest
of Mormal. Today our detachment surprised the troops of
Monsieur le Prince de Coburg. He is aiming to take Le Ques-
noy, but we will try to prevent him. If we fail, we shall have
to fall back on Landrecies or even Mauberg. Do you know
where they are? I am not sure, but not too far from here. It is
strange being under fire. I get very hot and my eyes become
bloodshot with the smoke. My pay each day is fifteen francs
and three décimes. The corporal gets twenty-three francs and
eight décimes. I must see to it that I am promoted. I enclose
an *assignat*. Use it well.

Marie-Victoire, I miss you. My teeth ache and I must have
the back one drawn. We live well, for the land is filled with
good wheat and vegetables. We drink beer mostly, for wine is
expensive, and there is plenty of milk and cheese. It is said
that the enemy is trying to cross at the river Sambre, but these
Austrians are cowards really.

I long to hear from you. If I had a letter I would read it again
and again. Do you remember me like I remember you? Are
you faithful? Somehow, I feel that you are. The women in this
area are very plain and do their hair in thick plaits under straw
hats and their heads are as big as three-month-old calves. So,
you see, I have no temptation.

I don't like being a soldier. It is hard and boring and I long
to be back in Paris with my cart. We volunteers ('volunteers'

187

is the wrong word, don't you think?) are known as *culs blancs*, or cornflowers. That is how I think of you, Marie-Victoire, so perhaps it isn't so bad. My friends Lafargue, Devismes and Duquet are with me and we look after each other. The musket they gave me is in bad order and I am searching for a trigger. Let us hope I find one before I need it.

Marie-Victoire, has that man Maillard come to find you again? If he has, you must tell me and I will deal with him when I return. Remember your promise to me, won't you? Hide your money where we agreed. If you want more stuff, go to my friend in the Rue de la Harpe. He knows about you.

I am trying to arrange a wound. But I must be careful as it is not easy. I think I shall have to break a toe, or perhaps I will pretend to have the bloody flux. No matter, I will come home as soon as I can.

I send you my greetings and a great deal of my heart.

Pierre Labourchard

PARIS, August 1792

Day by day the news from the battlefront became worse and French pride took a battering from which it was going to take years to recover. In Paris, the authorities in the commune responded by decreeing that any man who possessed a pike should enlist as a National Guardsman. The result: Paris turned into a city under arms, a seething mass of sansculottes, among them bullies, killers, madmen and fanatics.

First set up in April 1792 in the Place de Grêve, and intended as an instrument that would despatch criminals to a decent, humane death, the guillotine was beginning to assume an importance that its inventor never envisaged. It was now perceived by those quick to take advantage as a convenient method to eradicate enemies of the state. Its huge shining blade began to rise and fall with increasing rapidity.

In Koblenz, Monsieur le Comte de Provence proclaimed himself regent and formed a ministry-in-exile. In addition, the Duke of Brunswick, commander of the royalist army, signed an important document in which he threatened to put Paris to the sword if the royal family were placed under any further threat.

The last proved to be the spark that lit the conflagration. When it heard of the manifesto, Paris erupted to the call of 'Aux armes, citoyens'. The Marseillaise burned a new rhythm into files of marching feet on the cobblestones and injected white-hot fervour into patriots' hearts. It was sung everywhere: in the Palais Royal to the sound of cheers and rattling weapons; in theatres; in the opera house; in wine shops and countless drinking dens. Filled with anxious and frightened men, and riven by deep and bitter political divisions, the National Assembly struggled to keep control over the city. They failed.

On August 8th a huge crowd collected once again on the Champ de Mars to demand the abdication of the king. This was the moment the power-hungry Jacobins had been waiting for.

On the night of August 9th, Jacobin supporters made their way to the Hôtel de Ville and announced that the Paris Commune was now dissolved. In its place, they installed a new Insurrectionary Commune

189

composed mainly of artisans whose revolutionary zeal was unquestioned.

The Jacobins had prepared the ground well. There was no one brave, or rash, enough to contradict them. Spread out through the city, their agents provocateurs worked feverishly to whip up tinder-dry emotions in the quartiers. All through the night of August 9th the people continued to gather until there were 20,000 or more.

As August 10th dawned, a day that promised to be of searing heat, the second march on the Tuileries Palace by the citizens of Paris began.

Chapter 10

Jacques, August 9th, 1792

He got drunk again. It was the one licence that he permitted himself. It did him good to feel the coarse wine surge through his veins and turn his legs into heavy pieces of wood. He liked the sensation of the world distancing itself, and his visions, so often lonely and fear-ridden, growing big with importance. It was when he was drunk that he worked out his next move – and thought about Marie-Victoire.

He often wondered why she was so important to him, why his obsession gripped him and never let him free. He had tried sometimes to rip her from his heart, but it never worked. Marie-Victoire was embedded in him, and his desire for her, if anything, grew greater.

He was an unlovable, and unloving, man – he knew that. And he didn't, so he thought, much care. Perhaps it was because Marie-Victoire *had* once loved him, in her fashion, that he refused to let her go. Or was it because she had thwarted him? It didn't matter. Maillard knew that he held one priceless advantage. He was willing to wait for Marie-Victoire and he wasn't going to give up.

Maillard was doing well. He had taken trouble to cultivate friends in the Jacobin club and frequently attended their meetings, where he shouted louder than anyone else. His Jacobin connections had promised to help him to a position in the new commune. Nothing too important, but enough for him to get a toe in the door. Maillard knew it was because they found him useful. There was nothing he wouldn't do, no area of the city too far-flung for him to traverse, and they came to rely on his willingness. With his extra duties came knowledge. With knowledge came power. It pleased him that people were beginning to grow frightened of him. It made up for many things.

Best of all, he would soon be in a position where he could sort out the de Guinots. Maillard was looking forward to that. Getting

191

rid of them would purge the world of those it no longer needed or wanted. And give him his sweet revenge.

At dawn he planned to join his associates and march on the Tuileries. He had spent all day in the streets, whipping up his listeners into a frenzy with his impassioned exhortations. It had proved thirsty work. It was very late, but no one seemed able to sleep. The streets were as crowded as at midday and the summer night hardly seemed to arrive before it was gone. Maillard drank one last glass, heaved himself to his feet and set off in the direction of the Rue des Sts Pères. He was going to allow himself one last look at Marie-Victoire, just in case he did not come back.

He had discovered where she lived by looking up the recruitment records at the section headquarters. The clerk had obligingly recorded Pierre's place of residence along with the others. After that, Maillard often went to spy on Marie-Victoire. He never revealed his presence, and it proved no trouble to keep out of her sight.

Tonight, the door of her shop was open in an attempt to introduce some air into the stifling room. He could see her outlined by the light of a cheap taper, moving around and arranging her things. She looked very small and her waist had thickened, and once or twice she straightened up to rub her back.

The wine talked to Maillard.

'Go and take her, you fool,' it said.

'Wait,' counselled his more prudent side. 'It is better to wait.'

'Take her. Lift those skirts. You have done it once. It won't matter again.'

Maillard stepped forward and, as he did so, Marie-Victoire looked up and saw who it was. Quick as a thought, she banged the door to and bolted it.

'Let me in,' he pleaded.

'Go away. Get out of my life. Leave me alone.' She sounded close to tears. 'Go and ruin someone else's life. You have done enough. You and I are finished.'

Maillard leant against the door, rested his head against the wood and belched.

'You are wrong, Marie-Victoire,' he announced to her and to anyone who cared to listen. 'We are not finished and I shall carry out my promise. Not now, not tonight, my pretty, because I have other things to do. You won't mind waiting, will you, Marie-Victoire?'

His voice caressed her through the door. Marie-Victoire shrank back against the wall and did not reply. She remained motionless until she heard him heave himself upright and stagger down the road. Only then did she dare move. She sat down on a chair and fumbled for her rosary.

Maillard negotiated the streets with varying success, determined not to yield to his drunkenness. By the time he reached the Pont Royal, his head had cleared sufficiently to allow him to remain upright without swaying.

The crowd was dense and angry, and the heat so thick you could have cut it with a knife. All at once, Maillard felt completely at home. This was what he was born for: to be carried by a tide of unstoppable excitement, to feel the blood quicken in his veins, to fondle the sharp point of the pike that someone had pushed into his hands, to hate, to hate so badly that he was willing to thrust it into the body of anyone who thought differently from him.

It was like this that men such as Jacques Maillard spent that long, hot August night before the dawn tocsin summoned the people of Paris to battle and the sound of running feet filled the streets of the city.

Chapter 11

The Tuileries, August 10th, 1792

All day Louis d'Épinon had worked frantically to brief and position his troops, and by nightfall the reports were coming in thick and fast – the mob was marching, it was armed, the Duc d'Orléans rode at its head – and he needed to check what was false and what was true. The order had gone out to the two thousand known nobles still left in Paris to come and defend their king. So far only one hundred and fifty had chosen to answer the call, many of them elderly and infirm.

Louis cursed at the heat and the stupidity of the situation. Uniforms and weapons were slippery with sweat and the gunpowder was hot to the touch. Concerned as always about the loyalty of his men, he was almost sure that many of them would defect to the revolutionaries, and needed to know, above all, what the king planned to do. Would he stay and face the invaders or would he take a more prudent course and leave Paris?

Louis was doubly worried. Héloïse was in attendance on the queen and she had insisted on remaining on duty, despite the queen's express wish that she should return home to her husband. Louis, snatching a brief moment to talk to her, begged her to go, but Héloïse was firm. Her duty, she told him, lay here. Louis had time only to press a kiss on her wrist before, alarmed for her safety, he had returned to his work, where he tried, unsuccessfully, to banish her from his mind.

Inside the royal apartments in the Tuileries the king conferred repeatedly with his officials and paced up and down. The queen, who had just returned from handing out food and drink to their supporters, stood talking to her friend, the Princesse de Lamballe, whose beautiful, vapid face registered an unusual determination. Madame Élisabeth hovered nervously in between. Héloïse sat in a corner of the room, ready to leap up and pack if the order should come.

At 4 a.m. Louis presented his latest report, conscious of a

growing exasperation. Surely the king must take action? But analysing the weak, rather lazy face while he detailed the numbers of the defenders in clipped tones – nine hundred Swiss Guards, two thousand National Guardsmen and his own regimental detachment – Louis knew in his heart that his king would never fight. Surreptitiously, he searched out Héloïse and was rewarded by a faint but reassuring smile.

Finally, as a result of a last hurried conversation conducted with the advisers, it was decided that the royal family would do nothing until daybreak. Summoning up his powers of persuasion, Louis argued forcefully against this decision.

'You must escape, Sire. We cannot undertake to protect you. We will do what we can, but I must tell you that we will be severely outnumbered.' In desperation, Louis dropped to one knee. 'With all my heart, Sire, I beg you to listen and to ensure the safety of your family.'

Louid XVI blinked down at him.

'You must remember, Monsieur le Capitaine d'Épinon, the last time we endeavoured to escape. If you can forget what happened at Varennes, I cannot. I will not be responsible for a second episode. Besides, I cannot abandon my people.'

Out of the corner of his eye, Louis saw the queen shrug in a hopeless fashion. She had spent most of the afternoon trying to persuade her husband to address his troops and inspire their support. But without much success. He rose to his feet and turned towards her.

'Madame la Reine, you have heard what I have said. I can only repeat, you and His Majesty are under threat. Please take this last chance.'

The haughty blue eyes stared back at him, and Louis was reminded of a time not so long ago in Versailles when he had watched Marie-Antoinette, attired in a white gown sewn with sapphires, open a ball. Then those blue eyes had sparkled and the lips had uttered charming witticisms, and the queen had danced without a seeming care in the world. The contrast between that brilliant vision and this tired, strained woman, endlessly clicking her diamond rings round her fingers, was both shocking and painful.

'Monsieur,' she said, 'this is a conflict of forces. We have come to the point where we will know which is going to prevail – the king, the constitution or the rebels. For myself, I would rather be nailed to the walls of the palace than seek protection from those who have behaved badly towards us, and it would be unthinkable to leave our loyal nobles and our gallant Swiss to die alone.'

Before Louis could answer, Monsieur Roderer, the Attorney-General, interposed himself between Louis and the queen.

'Madame, in my opinion it is necessary for you to place yourself under the protection of the National Assembly. By staying here you are endangering the lives of your husband and your children. I will myself go and inform the members of this move, if you will permit me.'

The queen, no longer able to control her tears, looked at the king, who shrugged in a bewildered way. Louis bowed his head.

'I will consider the matter a little longer,' said Louis XVI.

'Then, Sire, I must accept your wishes,' Louis replied. He paused. 'Sire, perhaps you should show yourself to your troops as a sign of your loyalty.'

To this the king did assent, and a flurry of courtiers and ministers descended into the gardens where the National Guardsmen had assembled.

Keeping a wary eye on the rooftops, and straining for every sound, Louis preceded the king down the staircase. The first fingers of dawn were already whitening the sky. It was, Louis saw, that perfect moment, a moment of breathless hush when the world, poised between the concealing dark and the clamour of daybreak, gathers its forces, and even the birds sit silent at their roosts. Like a thick blanket, the heat wrapped the city in its hot breath. Chased by the sun, a few wisps of mist drifted up from the river and dissolved into nothing. Within seconds the moment passed and the shafts of sunlight darkened into brazen yellow. A city smell rose into the air, a mixture of wood smoke, latrines, decaying vegetables and the dry-dust taste of summer. He breathed deeply, hoping to still the little jumping beats of his heart and master the tension in his stomach. Who knew, this might be his last day on earth.

Louis wanted passionately to live, but he also knew that when the fighting began he would be in the thick of it. There was no question of that. Like Héloïse, he knew where his duty lay. At the thought of her he felt better.

The king emerged slowly from the palace and stood still, seemingly dazzled by the light. Dressed in a purple suit, his wig only half-powdered and flattened on one side, his sword bumping with every step, he walked like a man lost towards the troops on the terraces. But halfway there he appeared to change his mind, hesitated, and made his way back to the palace, to the accompanying jeers and shouts of a watching crowd which had gathered on the Terrasse des Feuillants. The king stopped in his tracks and shook his head from side to side, before disappearing from view.

The situation that Louis d'Épinon dreaded was beginning to happen – and the king was doing nothing to prevent it. In despair, he watched as one National Guardsman after another, infuriated by the king's lacklustre behaviour, broke ranks with the evident intention of joining the mob. Some of the gunners even swivelled their guns so their noses now pointed towards the palace, and not a few shook their fists at the retreating king.

Héloïse, watching from a window of the palace, clasped her pregnant belly with a protective gesture. It was as if the king had no will, no energy, no fight, to turn the tide that now ran against him. In his lethargy, she thought, tasting defeat on her tongue, was written their fate.

She made her way over to the queen and waited for permission to speak. Her Majesty was holding yet another conversation with a minister, but she interrupted it to listen to Héloïse.

'If you please, Madame la Reine, I think it would be wise if I arranged for your trunks to be packed.'

Unusually for her, Marie-Antoinette's blue eyes flashed fear before she veiled them with weary lids.

'As you please, Madame la Comtesse.'

And that was all.

Héloïse was glad of something to do. Inside the queen's bedchamber the maids scurried about dropping things and heaving clothes into one haphazard pile after another. Fear was palpable in the room and their pallid faces told their own story. It required all Héloïse's energy to restore some sort of order and to quieten a girl sobbing loudly in a corner, and then she threw herself into a chair to snatch a few minutes' sleep.

By eight o'clock the shouts hailing from the direction of the Place du Carrousel could be heard quite clearly. Their noise interrupted Héloïse's confused dreams and woke her. She sat for a moment listening to the tocsin tolling with a dull beat, trying to clear her buzzing head. She rose and made her way to an apartment that overlooked the Place du Carrousel.

By now the remaining royalist troops on this side of the Tuileries had been withdrawn into the palace, leaving their cannon glistening in the sun. Héloïse could see them quite clearly unattended in the courtyard. On either side of her, muskets poked out of windows and caches, and the blue and white of the soldiers' uniforms appeared behind the casements. Héloïse clasped her hands tight and sent a prayer into the hot air.

'Keep him, O Mary, Mother of God, keep him safe.'

She was, of course, praying for Louis.

It was time she returned to the queen. She hurried back through rooms filled with courtiers and messengers, and pushed her way through the crowd that had collected outside the king's apartments.

'Gentlemen,' she cried out. 'Let me through. I have orders to attend Her Majesty.'

At her entreaty a passage was cleared for her. Héloïse picked up her skirts and pushed open the door. The king was sitting at a table, his hands resting on his knees. The queen was standing in the middle of the room talking intently to Madame Élisabeth and some ministers. As she entered, the king looked up at his wife.

'Let us go,' he said with a heavy sigh.

In utter despair, Héloïse dropped a curtsy in front of the queen. No one could be unaware of what this departure would mean. It was, she knew, too late for the royal family to escape and too late for the king to take charge. So they had to wait – king, queen and the courtiers and servants who would be left behind in the besieged palace – for the escort that would take the royal family away to an unknown future. Once they threw themselves on the mercy of the National Assembly, the Bourbons' power to order their fates would be lost. Sensing the atmosphere, the little dauphin tugged at his mother's hand in bewilderment while his sister stood pale and stiff beside him, a too-mature expression on her young face.

At last, the escort arrived. The king and queen made their farewells and walked slowly through the apartments towards the stairs. At the door the queen stopped.

'We'll be back soon,' she said defiantly.

Then they were gone, leaving their shocked and frightened supporters to look after their own safety as best they could.

The leaves had fallen early this year in the gardens. Released from the stifling palace rooms, the dauphin sank with a delighted whoop knee-deep into the rustling heaps between the lines of trees and kicked at them with childish abandon. One of the soldiers lifted him up on to his back, whereupon the queen gave a shriek, fearing that he had been kidnapped. Héloïse brought up the rear of the party, and kept her eyes focused on the queen's upright figure. A thousand hostile faces were directed on to them from the Terrasse des Feuillants, and she shivered, despite the sweat that trickled down her back. The air seemed to be filled with the tramp of feet, which matched the insistent thuds of the drums and the snatches of the *Marseillaise*. The heat burned its way down into her lungs.

The king entered the Assembly first and, after some confusion, the queen followed him. Not one of the seated delegates made any move to greet them. The dauphin was placed on the secretary's table and Héloïse hastened to disentangle him from the ink and papers that were strewn all over the green baize. The door of the Assembly closed. The Tuileries was left to face the onslaught.

Now they came: surging down from the Rue St Honoré and the Rue du Carrousel, through the Rue de l'Échelle and the Rue St Nicaise; from the Pont Neuf and Pont Royal – a deadly tide that nothing would stop. Cabinet-makers and goldsmiths, servants, clerks and jewellers, water-carriers, glaziers, gauze-makers, locksmiths and carters, shopkeepers, craftsmen. On they swept, faces locked in hate and exultation; fierce, determined and single-minded.

His men grouped in battle order behind him, Louis stood under the peristyle of the Tuileries and watched while the revolutionaries battered at the gate of the Tuileries courtyard. He knew, with a sickening certainty, that it would not take very long for them to breach it.

As he suspected, within seconds the attackers had demolished the gates and were inside the courtyard. Surprised by their easy passage, those in the forefront paused, uncertain what to do next. One of the leaders, bolder than the rest, came running over to the Tuileries entrance and tried to persuade the grim-faced Swiss Guards – without success – to come over to their side. During the ensuing scuffle a Swiss was cut by a sabre.

Louis clenched his teeth, took a deep breath and sang out the order.

'Fire!'

It had begun. The bullets whistled in a smoke-wreathed swathe.

The front line of the attackers took the brunt of the onslaught. Under the rain of lead, it straggled, swayed and opened to let the bodies of those hit fall to the ground. Then it closed again, this time to surge forward with renewed vigour. As they came closer, the blurred mass of faces became more distinct, and for Louis they became distastefully individual. Here was a young man who surely did not deserve to die, a woman who should be at home, a fanatic with his mouth stretched back over his teeth in a ghastly grin. . . . Their cries of *'Trahison! Trahison! Mort aux traîtres!'* rose hoarse and distinct above the sound of their running feet and the guns.

Blinded and confused by the fire, the invaders hesitated for a vital few seconds and Louis took the opportunity to regroup his men in front of the palace entrance. He drew his sword. Out in front of the crowd a man called Fournier, nicknamed 'the

American', harangued the Parisians and then, with an oath, turned and cut his way through the doors. He yelled for them to come on. The mob poured after him.

Louis withdrew further under the entrance. Fournier ran up to the foot of the great staircase situated under the peristyle, seized the pikes of the two Swiss sentries and began to chase them up the stairs. The Swiss, waiting above, lowered their weapons into a fighting position.

'Fire!' shouted someone from the first storey and let loose another hail of bullets. In return the Parisians replied with a volley of shot from the commandeered cannon and the courtyard was soon littered with dead and wounded who screamed in anguish while their comrades ran to take their place.

The battle raged on, its noise thundering into the streets, unnerving all who heard it. In the National Assembly across the Tuileries Gardens the king was jerked into action. Determined that no one should die in his defence he scrawled hastily on a scrap of paper: 'The king orders the Swiss to lay down their arms at once, and to retire to their barracks.'

His message, brought by a sweating runner, was handed to the Swiss commander just as the first wave of invaders had been, miraculously, ejected from the palace. Immediately, in obedience to their king, the Swiss on the staircase shouldered their arms and began to march off in the direction of the Rue de l'Échelle, where they were leapt upon by the mob and torn to pieces.

Unaware of the king's order, the remainder of the Swiss Guards disposed themselves inside the palace. This time, with a renewed surge of energy, the mob succeeded in storming the palace. Swarming up the staircase, the attackers launched themselves at the guards, many of whom, their ammunition exhausted, grappled hand to hand only to be cut down where they stood.

Louis found himself fighting his way backwards up the grand staircase, shouting commands over his shoulder at his men behind – but retreating, always retreating into the interior. Within minutes the mob had gained the upper hand and roared into the apartments and corridors – wrenching open doors, and streaming into rooms to search out terrified courtiers and servants who huddled, shivering with terror, in their hiding places. Rather than be taken, some of them flung themselves out of the windows, to be smashed on the stones below or, worse, to perish on the pikes massed underneath. The air was thick with screams, and low, monotonous animal shouts of hate, and blood of the dead and injured flowed down the staircase and the corridors.

Outside the palace, the mob set to work despoiling and stripping the bodies which they piled in heaps, impaling the heads on to pikes. Some of the royalist fugitives unwisely tried to make an escape across the gardens, only to be hacked to pieces under the fountains. Others tried to climb up the marble monuments. They were soon prodded down by bayonets and set on by the mob. A few, very few, lucky ones managed to leap out from the queen's room and on to the terrace below, where they made for the dauphin's garden gate and so to safety.

Louis brushed the sweat out of his eyes and tried to stanch the blood from a pike cut on his neck. The last of his men had just fallen with a curdled scream. Below him, the Swiss were either dead or in retreat up the staircase. All around, the bodies of the fallen lay abandoned, and, like broken insects, the wounded were endeavouring to crawl to places of safety. The smoke was choking and lay in a thick cloud over the staircase and corridors – looming out of it, the ghostly figures of both attackers and defenders.

But they weren't ghosts, and this was bitter and terrible battle, and Louis knew that the outnumbered royalists, betrayed by their king at a crucial moment and slaughtered in their hundreds, had lost. It was time to rethink.

Louis decided to make a run for it. There was no point in staying any longer and no dishonour in saving himself. He had discharged his duty and there were no more men left to rally. So thinking, he turned and ran two flights up the stairs into a passage that he knew led to the north of the palace and into a narrow corridor, off which led a series of rooms used for storage. Choosing the smallest, Louis pushed open the door and leant panting against it. He would have to force himself to wait until nightfall, if need be, before trying to leave the Tuileries.

By now the mob had discovered the kitchens in the Pavillon de Flore, where they seized an under-cook and pressed him into one of the cauldrons boiling over the furnace. His screams floated out above the uproar and his murderers gorged themselves on food and watched his torment. In the cellars, the once orderly rows of dusty bottles were now a sea of broken glass. Clutching what they could carry, the looters staggered upstairs and collected in the vestibule under the staircase used by the queen, and proceeded to dance amongst the wine and the gore. From somewhere above a violin sounded out, harsh and discordant, followed by a crash as it was smashed to the ground.

Upstairs, men and women ran up and down the corridors, screaming their defiance. The escritoires in the queen's bedroom had been forced and a stream of money, jewels and trinkets were

201

being fought over by some filthy old women. The bed had been torn apart, the great mirror smashed, and someone had brought a hammer down on the clock that had stood on the console table. Plate, books and even chests were dragged to the windows and the contents tipped out to looters waiting below. In the king's apartments, a chandelier was cut from its moorings and went hurtling down in a million flashing pieces while the royal wardrobes were systematically ripped apart.

In the courtyard, a fire had been built and a collection of hags were engaged in roasting the severed limbs of the Swiss Guards over it. Plumes of foul yellow smoke wreathed the August sky and a white rain of feathers drifted silently down from the bedrooms where the quilts and feather-beds were being destroyed. They fell on to the mutilated bodies of the dead, already putrefying in the sun. Clouds of black flies were gathering, and a sickly-sweet odour of blood and decay mixed with the acrid smoke, making it impossible to breathe.

Louis waited in his hiding place for the sounds of tramping feet that, incredibly, never came. He judged that the Tuileries was so vast and so bewildering in its layout that the odds against his being discovered were shortened – or, at the very least, he had bought himself some time.

Later, and he had no idea how much later, the noise abated. In its place reigned a lull, fractured now and again by the cries of dying men and by raucous laughter. Louis' instincts told him that the worst must be over. He decided it was time to act. Opening the door, he scanned the corridor. It was empty. Holding his sword in one hand, he worked his way along it towards a staircase that he knew led down towards the west side of the palace and gave access into the gardens.

He was slithering, light-footed as a stoat, down the treads when a noise caused him to jump out of his skin. Bellowing from the chapel came the sound of an organ: great, booming chords that rang through the palace. A looter was telling Paris that the Tuileries was taken.

Louis leapt down the last few stairs and out into the sunlight. He ran down the steps of the terrace and dodged into the trees, making a bee-line for the riding school and the National Assembly. On the Terrasse des Feuillants, he paused to regain his breath and cast a quick look over his shoulder. To his horror, he saw that a party of looters had seen him and were beginning to give chase. Cursing because his uniform had given the game away, Louis put on an added spurt and dived down the passage that led to the riding school.

Once there, he beat on the door. There was no answer, only a

202

terrified moan from inside. In desperation, Louis set his shoulder against it, crying out that he was a soldier of the king, and heaved. It yielded, and Louis fell into the building and on to the doorman who huddled behind it.

'Bolt it properly, you fool,' he ordered, and made haste to help the man, whose hands were shaking too much to be of any use. It was woefully inadequate, but it would have to do. The riding school had not been intended as a building for defence.

Louis slumped against the wall and breathed deeply, the sweat running in streams down his back and face. When he felt he could speak, he pulled himself upright and walked into the debating chamber where the delegates sat in a petrified silence.

Covered in bloodstains and grime, his uniform in tatters and his face gaunt with emotion and exhaustion, Louis was not a reassuring sight. A ripple of alarm from the hundred or so deputies greeted his entry. Louis searched for the king to salute him but failed to see him either at the president's table or on the benches. Was it possible, after all, that the king had managed to flee?

A movement caused him to swing round, and only then did he see the royal family. They had been herded at the instigation of the president into the tiny shorthand-writer's box set apart from the main body of the room. Directly in front of the box sat Héloïse.

Louis bowed, and the king lifted a hand in acknowledgement. Louis pushed his way through the deputies' benches and gave a brief report to the king, emphasising the bravery of the Swiss Guards. The king sat inside the bars and said nothing. Louis gave a more detailed briefing to the president.

At last he permitted himself to approach Héloïse. She leapt to her feet and, disregarding the stares of the curious deputies, clasped his hands to her breast.

'Thank God,' was all she could say.

Louis stroked her face with his blackened hands and traced the circles of exhaustion that ringed her eyes.

'Ça va, chérie?'

'Of course. And you?'

Louis grimaced. 'As well as could be expected. What is happening here?'

Héloïse sighed and sat down again.

'You can see. They have been sitting there since nine o'clock this morning. No one has tried to help them or give them anything to eat. I have done the best I could. But they are suffering terribly.'

Since the shorthand-writer's box measured only nine or ten

feet square and into it were crammed the king, the queen, Madame Élisabeth, the two royal children and the governess, the long, hot hours must have been excruciating. Although they all sat quietly and with touching dignity, the strain and misery on the faces of the royal captives was plain for all to see.

Once or twice, a fusillade of bullets rattled outside, and a little later shouts echoed from the direction of the Terrasse des Feuillants. Louis talked quietly to Héloïse, instructing her where to hide if it should be necessary. The deputies moved restlessly on their seats, and the queen did her best to soothe the fractious dauphin whose exhausted sobbing frayed nerves already at snapping point. At last, the worn-out royal children fell asleep. The queen remained motionless, wiping her forehead now and again with her handkerchief. The king began to snore. No one dared to offer the royal family any refreshment, not even so much as a glass of water, until, infuriated by the deputies' cowardice, Héloïse went over to the president and begged that he should permit her to offer the jug of lemonade which stood on his table to Their Majesties. After some hesitation, the president agreed and Héloïse had the satisfaction of seeing the queen's discomfort relieved a little.

Dusk fell, bringing with it a measure of relief, and the evening light began to camouflage nerve-racked countenances and cool the furnace of the air. With the threat of violence receding, the tension lessened. Nevertheless, nobody in the riding school was under any illusion that the king and queen were anything but prisoners of the Assembly. At midnight, Louis decided he must do something. Fighting his battle-stiffness and a raging thirst, he approached the president.

'I think the fighting is over,' he told them. The president was sweating profusely. 'It would be best if we tried to convey Their Majesties somewhere for the night.'

The president hastened to agree with Louis and beckoned to a couple of deputies. They conferred with each other, and it was decided that it would be advisable if the king and queen spent the night in the Feuillants Convent. Louis elected at once to escort the party. Indeed, it was expected of him. He went over to offer his arm to Marie-Antoinette. The queen swayed as she rose and nearly fell but checked herself in time.

The royal party filed wearily out of the box. Sweat stained the once dainty robes of the royal ladies and soaked the king's purple suit, and the dauphin whimpered in distress. But they went quietly enough, only too glad to be released from their confinement.

The convent was only a short walk across a garden and the

night air served as welcome, if all too brief, balm. Louis was to remember that journey as one of the hardest tasks he had ever undertaken. He understood only too well that he was leading his sovereign into captivity. Weak though she was from her long incarceration, the queen walked behind the king but insisted, nevertheless, that she carry her son. For her part, Héloïse took the hand of Madame Royale and was shocked at how pitifully it trembled in hers.

Inside the ancient Feuillants building the gloom was unrelieved. Somehow, and Louis never knew how, someone had already procured some dirty – and probably verminous – mattresses which they had thrown on to the truckle beds which occupied the dismal cells. The British ambassadress had also contrived to send over clothes and linen for the dauphin and a former minister to the king had risked his servant's life to send a fresh suit for the king. Otherwise there was little else. Louis stood guard as Héloïse did the best she could to make the beds comfortable. A flurry of voices notified the arrival of the Duc de Poix and the Duc de Choiseul, who had been summoned by the Assembly. They announced that they would stand watch until the morning, when the royal family would be escorted back to the riding school. There was nothing more Louis could do.

He stood in front of his sovereigns for the last time and bowed to them as they sat, beaten and exhausted, on their uncomfortable mattresses. The king stirred himself to thank Louis for his loyalty and courage and gave him leave to make for the royalist armies assembling on the French borders.

Louis found it difficult to speak. Struggling for control, the queen offered him a hand to kiss and, removing one of her diamond rings from her fingers, she gave it to Héloïse. Héloïse clenched her hand so hard around it that the stones bit into her flesh. She curtsied her thanks with tears running down her face. Héloïse's last memory of Marie-Antoinette was of the queen stretched out on her truckle bed crying bitterly for the misfortunes she had helped to bring about.

Once outside, Héloïse sagged against the wall. She closed her eyes and felt her legs turn to water.

'I can't go any further.'

'Nor can I,' said Louis.

He held her against him for a moment and considered. Then he picked her up and carried her down the corridor and into a cell at the end of the passage. It was pitch dark, and he swore as he tried to find a place to lay her down. Héloïse clung to Louis, and willed herself not to faint. She managed to stay upright while Louis stripped off his coat and shirt and spread them on the floor. Then he unfastened her robe, eased it tenderly from her body and laid it on top of his improvised bed. Remembering another occasion when he had undressed her like this, Héloïse sank to the floor without a sound and allowed him to loosen her stays and strip off her stockings.

Gradually, the buzzing in her head quietened. The air on her naked limbs was like cool water. She sighed and lay still. Louis moved around the cell in stockinged feet and eventually lay down beside her. His sword clanked briefly in the darkness.

He smelt of heat, of sweat and of gunpowder. Héloïse touched his damp flesh. It was firm beneath her hand and her own responded. With an effort, she turned on her side and laid a hand on Louis' chest, feeling the muscle and hair smooth beneath her fingers.

'Thirsty?' he asked.

'Very.'

'There is nothing I can give you.'

'*Tant pis.*'

He smiled at her attempt at lightness.

'When did you last eat?'

'I can't remember.'

'Nor can I.'

'Shall we dine on love?'

'We have no choice, but I am not complaining.'

Louis edged his body closer to hers and kissed her.

'Unfortunately, I am too tired to do more than this.'

He kissed her again and held her tight. She thought of the captives down the corridor.

'What will happen to them?'

'Who knows? They should have gone when I told them to.'

'You did what you could. More.'

'Did I, my heart? I hope so.'

'What will you do?' she asked at last.

He rolled over on to his back.

'I must try for the border and the army,' he said bitterly. 'As a soldier of the king, I don't think Paris is the place for me any longer.'

Héloïse crushed her knuckles against her mouth and willed herself to say nothing. She needed to think.

'It is not safe at the moment, Louis. You'll need money and visas. Otherwise you won't get across France.'

'I shall have to risk it without them,' he said. 'What else can I do?'

With an effort, Héloïse sat up on one elbow and stared into the darkness.

'I have a better idea. My house at Neuilly. I could hide you there until we arrange the papers.'

Louis tried to make his tired brain think sensibly, but his mind felt thick and clogged. He understood enough, however, to know that Héloïse was talking sense. It would be far better to go to Neuilly, rest a little, plan and then leave Paris.

'And you?' he asked. 'What about you? I cannot leave until I know you are safe.'

'I shall come to Neuilly, too. With Sophie. And I shall manage it without de Choissy.'

'*Bien*,' said Louis exhaustedly. '*Bien*.'

He pulled her down towards him and buried his face in her breasts.

'The child?'

'Our child is well for the moment.'

Louis tried to smile, but he heard again in his mind confused echoes made up of shouts and screams, of hate and violence, all mixed into a jangling concert of death. She felt him grow tense and wrapped her arms around his head, willing him to sleep and to forgetfulness.

Louis relaxed, the nightmare slackened its hold and he slept. He left Héloïse to stare over his head and to reflect on the strangeness of fate that had brought her to this place. Her eyes closed, but she continued to cradle her lover with infinite care – until sleep bore her away, too, into merciful oblivion.

AFTERMATH

Throughout the night the looting went on amid scenes of indescribable savagery and drunkenness. Drinking and eating whatever they could lay their hands on, the looters piled up their plunder and counted the heads of their enemies.

Round the fires they danced, singing at the tops of their voices. Voices that were hoarse with exhilaration and battle. Many of the women sprawled drunkenly where they fell, their skirts above their heads, and the flickering shadows merged while the men made free with the wares so liberally offered. Every so often a scuffle would break out as somebody tried to steal someone else's booty. Once the horrible sounds of an unlucky thief precipitately hanged from a convenient tree broke into the revelry.

Towards dawn, the Tuileries lay quiet at last. The bodies of the living and the dead lay jumbled together in the courtyards and gardens. The stench of wine and of death was overpowering. It percolated into the adjoining streets and filtered into the alleys, causing citizens to put up their shutters in spite of the heat.

The sun rose over a city that had witnessed a revolution – a bloodbath that in a single night had washed the country free of a king. It was a city that was soon to be deserted by those who had taken its pleasures so lightly; for at first light everyone who considered it prudent to leave Paris began to pack. And there were many. In the embassies and trading houses, the diplomats and merchants chivvied their frightened families into any conveyance they could lay their hands on. In the noble houses, the aristocrats hid their jewels and paintings and burnt their documents.

From this day on the old Paris would be silent. Even as the sky turned from dawn opal and turquoise into bleached white, the Insurrectionary Commune was planning its arrests, and considering how best to deal with foreigners within the city walls. From this day on, no one who had links with the court or those proscribed by the revolutionaries would feel safe.

It was only after dawn had come and gone that the citizens of Paris,

208

the ones who had sat terrified and mute behind their doors, crept out of their homes to wander the Tuileries and to see for themselves what had been done in the name of freedom.

There they saw the grief of the women who searched through the dead for their menfolk, and heard their sobs. They saw the looters, stripping the corpses, and picked their way through the terraces over the recumbent bodies and aggravated the clouds of flies. They saw that their brothers had given their lives to defend their rights and demolish a tyranny, and they committed it to memory – for vengeance feeds on vengeance.

If any of them had chosen to look up, they could have seen the sky stretching out beyond the grey roofs and the glistening river, and heard the birdsong in the trees, and seen the splashes of late summer flowers; and they would have wondered at the contrast between the beauty of nature and the horror of humanity.

Chapter 12

Sophie, August 10th, 1792

In the Rue de l'Université, Sophie paced up and down like a caged animal and ran to the window every second minute. It was five o'clock in the morning, but she had been awake all night, beside herself with worry for Héloïse.

De Choissy, who had also spent a not inconsiderable part of the evening likewise pacing up and down, had finally dismissed Sophie from the salon at two o'clock and ordered her to get some sleep. She had suggested that he do likewise, but Sophie had a strong suspicion that he had stayed up all the same.

She clasped her *robe de chambre* more firmly around her shoulders and strained out of the window, straining to see across the gardens and the parallel Rue de l'Île towards the river and the Tuileries. But she could see nothing.

Yesterday had been hideous, a day full of unbearable tension made all the worse by not knowing. It had been impossible to obtain any news: the streets were clogged and de Choissy had been turned back twice by the press when he had endeavoured to drive over the bridge. He had returned in the late afternoon after his second attempt, his mouth set in a thin line from which all trace of lightness had fled.

'There is nothing we can do,' he had told Sophie, and when William offered to go instead de Choissy had turned on him with unaccustomed sharpness and told him to desist. Ned had said nothing. He had sat, sprawled in a chair, reading a periodical, and Sophie had wanted to shake him.

She dragged a chair over to the window and knelt on it. Where was Héloïse? Would she have survived the horrors that were being whispered about by the servants? Nobody this side of the river knew what exactly, but it was clear that the palace had been under attack. Perhaps Héloïse had been warned in time and escaped to the Hôtel de Guinot? Or even to the west of the city? Sophie knew she had friends there. But perhaps she had not.

There was enough in the rumours for Sophie to know that, if she hadn't, Héloïse's life would have been in danger.

'Oh, Héloïse, where are you?'

Sophie pressed her fingers into her eyes in an effort to clear her brain, and thought.

After a while, she stood up and went into the tiny powder room that served as her clothes press. She pulled open a chest.

'I think I remember,' she said to herself as she burrowed into carefully folded clothes. 'I think I remember. I had just what I want.'

At last, she found what she was looking for, a plain calico gown with a narrow skirt.

It took her a little while to get dressed without help, but she managed it. Stopping only for a straw hat and a pair of cotton gloves, she let herself out of the bedroom and began to descend the staircase. When she was halfway down, the door of the salon opened.

'Where are you going?' enquired de Choissy.

Sophie jumped. He was dressed in the suit he had worn last night and he was holding a bottle and a glass in his hands. So Monsieur le Comte had not gone to bed! His face was drawn and shadowed with stubble and it was obvious he had been drinking.

'I can't sleep,' said Sophie, continuing on her way.

'That is apparent,' replied de Choissy. 'But where are you going?'

'To see what I can.'

'Foolish girl,' he remarked as he followed her down the staircase. 'Don't you realise it is dangerous out there? I had better come with you.'

Sophie was a little daunted by this vision of the normally soigné count.

'I am sorry to see you so worried,' she said gently.

De Choissy frowned.

'What do you expect?' he asked, his tone icy. 'That I rejoice while my wife is probably massacred by the rabble?'

'That is not worthy of you, Monsieur le Comte,' she said. 'I know that you love Héloïse and love her more than you will admit.'

De Choissy trod down the last few stairs towards her.

'How sweet-natured you are, Miss Luttrell, and so innocent.'

Sophie reached out and took the glass and bottle from him. He relinquished them without comment.

'Indeed,' she said. 'Am I at a disadvantage in being so?'

He laughed.

'If I am truthful, no. But perhaps you are right, Sophie. It is not a fashionable thing to love your wife, you know – and I am not at all sure why I should care for her.'

The last was muttered sotto voce, as if Sophie wasn't meant to hear.

'I know I am right,' she said, a little alarmed at her own daring, but sensing that now was the time to say things if she was going to say them at all.

De Choissy cupped her chin with one white finger.

'Are you?' he said hoarsely. 'Do you understand, my dear and beautiful Miss Luttrell, what it is to love?'

Sophie's mouth contracted and her eyes darkened.

'Don't remind me,' she said painfully.

'The dashing Mr Luttrell has been superseded by my friend the clever Mr Jones, but duty forbids you from doing anything about it. Am I right? Of course I am, Sophie, and I admire your principles, even if I can't exactly share them.'

'Nonsense,' said Sophie, not knowing whether to be provoked or not. 'You understand about duty and obligation as much as anyone, you merely pretend not to.'

'Touché! Sharp, straight and to the point. Well, then, Miss Luttrell, we must help each other, must we not? When this is over, that is.'

He reached out and took the brandy bottle from Sophie, poured himself a glass and drank deeply. The white line around his lips receded a little.

'To our compact, Miss Luttrell.'

He placed the bottle and glass on the hall table. When he turned to hand her out of the door, he was back to his normal, impeccably polite self.

All was peaceful in the Rue de l'Université. The early-morning light made them blink. Sophie stopped to pull on her gloves. A water-carrier passed them and a girl was selling fuel outside a shop. De Choissy's silk coat seemed incongruous in this setting, but he appeared not to be troubled by his appearance. They made their way down the street.

At the junction with the Rue de Bac, they turned left towards the river and the Pont Royal.

'It's strange to be walking in the streets,' commented Sophie, for want of anything better to say.

'I never do,' said de Choissy. 'I don't need to. I have at least three carriages and a stable of horses at my disposal.'

'What do you think can have happened?' said Sophie, suddenly impatient with the inconsequentiality of their conversation when there were so many more important things to think about.

'Who knows? It looks as though the palace was taken by the revolutionaries, but what actually happened inside is difficult to say. My secretary has failed to get back to me yet, so I can't even hazard a guess if Their Majesties have survived.'

'What will you do if they haven't?'

'Then, my dear,' de Choissy said, through clenched teeth, 'it is more than time to leave Paris.'

At the river embankment, they turned right and picked their way through the jumble of makeshift huts and houses that fronted down to the water's edge.

'Oh, no,' muttered Sophie, clasping her hand to her mouth and pointing with a shaking finger.

Lying in the shallows were the corpses of two men. Who or what they were was impossible to say, for their bodies had been stripped of clothes and equipment. Only their bloated faces and gaping wounds were left. De Choissy turned her face gently away with his long fingers.

'Look across the river,' he said.

Her arm tucked into his, they stood and gazed across the multi-coloured water to the Tuileries. The hush was complete. A strange, eerie silence that wrapped the city in a fearful grip, telling of things done and promising of things to come. The smoke from the revolutionaries' camp-fires wreathed the sky, garnishing its blue with white and yellow. It tipped the palace buildings in an acrid haze and rolled in clouds over the gardens.

'What have they done?' said Sophie. 'Dear God, what have they done?'

Chapter 13

On the Run, August 11th, 1792

Héloïse woke first, aroused by her raging thirst. She lay for a moment without moving, pinned by the dead weight of Louis, whose head still lay on her breast. Her tongue felt swollen, and stuck to the roof of her mouth.

She sensed that it was already light, though it was difficult to tell in the cell. She could hear movement inside the building – voices were calling out orders – and outside there was the sound of rapid feet. She knew it was time to move, but she wanted to savour for one last minute the feel of Louis. His heart beat on hers and his breath caressed her skin in a gentle sighing. She felt so close to him, blood of his blood and bone of his bone, and despite the fear and uncertainty she had never felt so alive.

Louis groaned and stirred, pressing his face deeper into her breast, as if willing himself not to wake. She reached out and stroked his hair.

'Are you all right?' she enquired tenderly.

Louis was instantly awake.

'*Dieu*. We must get out of here at once, Héloïse. I must get you to safety.'

Sleep had shorn him of his defences and his customary sophistication, and he looked so young and worried, so unlike she had ever seen him before, that she could not answer for a moment, but touched instead the curve of his jaw where the stubble now showed through.

'And you? You *will* go to Neuilly as we planned?'

'Of course.'

It did not take them long to dress, and before long they were retracing their steps of yesterday evening. The door to the royal sleeping quarters remained closed. They walked past it without a backward glance.

'Curses.' Louis stopped once they were outside the convent. 'I forgot, this uniform will act as a beacon.'

He tugged off his coat and stuffed it hastily under a nearby bush, and with it his sword. He stood for a moment looking down at the latter.

'I was fond of that sword,' he remarked, before turning to help Héloïse, who found herself weaker than she had supposed.

Their progress seemed interminable. Héloïse could only walk slowly. She was dizzy from lack of food and water, and clumsy from the night on a hard floor. With every step the light grew stronger, and Louis grew more anxious.

'We must cross the gardens,' he said. 'I know the gate that opens near to the Pont Royal. From there it is a quite easy walk to the Rue de l'Université and the Hôtel de Choissy. But we must hurry.'

Fortunately, there was no one in the passage that led into the gardens and they were able to pass through the gate and down the steps without hindrance. But instead of turning left and walking up the *allée* – the way Héloïse had come the day before – Louis led her through the trees towards the river wall opposite, stopping frequently to watch for signs of life from the huddles of sleeping revolutionaries under the palace walls. They reached the formal parterres and stopped appalled at the sight of so many bodies littering the ground. Héloïse gagged at the stench.

'Oh God,' she whispered. 'Is it possible?'

The presence of so much death was almost too much to take in. At first it was only its physicality that impressed itself: the smell, the horrible sights and the sound of flies. Only later did the details of faces and limbs come back to worry her, and with them the knowledge that each of these men belonged to someone and would do so no more.

A corpse lay blocking their path. Louis stopped and ordered her to stand behind one of the trees.

'Don't look,' he told her abruptly. 'Turn away.'

Héloïse disobeyed, and watched with horror as Louis crouched down beside the body and rifled through its coat pockets.

'*Bien*,' he said, holding up a packet of papers. 'These will be of use.'

Grimacing with distaste at the task, he proceeded to pull off the dead man's coat and shrugged it on. It was too large and there were bloodstains on the sleeves, but it would have to do. Louis pulled the cuffs over his torn shirt and adjusted the neck.

'Come on,' he said.

No one challenged them as they made their way out through the gate and turned towards the Pont Royal. Louis was just heaving a sigh of relief when he saw a group of National Guardsmen walking north across the bridge in their direction.

'Héloïse,' he whispered urgently. 'Listen to me and do exactly what I say. Cross the road and continue walking. Do not look back. You must find your own way to the Rue de l'Université. Do you understand? I am a danger to you.'

Héloïse nodded.

'Of course,' she said calmly, though her heart contracted with pain at leaving him. 'Remember . . .,' she tried to say, and her voice sounded thin and scared, but there was no time.

'Good,' he said, understanding what she was trying to say. 'And I will. Now go, *chérie*, and God go with you.'

He pushed her hard towards the opposite side of the bridge, and waited until the guardsmen were within three yards or so of him. He began to run. Slowly at first, until he was sure they realised what he was doing, and then with increasing speed. The shouts of the men behind told Louis they had taken the bait. He put on a spurt and headed west along the quay which ran the length of the gardens, praying that his path would be clear. After a while the shouts grew fainter as, one by one, the guardsmen decided to abandon their chase. It was too early and too hot, and many of them were still groggy from the night before.

Louis slowed to a walk. He fought to regain his breath, and tried to work out where next to go. At the end of the gardens by the orangery, the wall curved round and ran north before running into the Place Louis XV. Louis shrank against the brick while he debated the wisdom of crossing by the opening into the square. He edged forward. All appeared quiet. There were a few weary-looking people clustered round the statue in the centre of the square, but none of them seemed to be looking towards the river. Louis decided to risk it. Slowly, agonisingly slowly as it seemed to him, he darted into the open space and headed for the wooded area that skirted the Cours la Reine. Once under the trees he turned north, keeping under cover, crossed the Champs Élysées and slipped into the orchard that ran alongside the Faubourg St Honoré.

Safe, if only for the moment, he stopped running, and his strength seemed drained away, leaving him unable to move. His knees buckled and he fell on to the grass beneath the trees. He tried desperately to fight off the dizziness that swept over him, but failed, and with a little groan he fainted.

Louis lay as if dead for many hours. Above him the sun described its scorching arc, shooting out rays that burnt through the foliage and sent dry leaves whirling down over his body. Louis was fortunate in that he lay under a group of the thickest trees, and their shade protected him from the worst ravages of the heat. Towards late afternoon, the air became even stiller, shimmering in mirages in front of the few who ventured outdoors. The streets lay mostly empty until evening, and thus Louis was granted a few extra hours of safety. When night fell the bats flew out of their hiding-places, weaving on silent wings in and out of the trees where the swallows dived and swooped in search of water.

Conscious at last, Louis watched them until the dark sucked their small forms up into the night and the stars shone hard and brilliant over the city. A strange lethargy stole over him, brought on by hunger, tension and fatigue. Gazing into the sky, Louis imagined that he had known no other existence, that the events of the last few days had never taken place and that he would lie dreaming, like a schoolboy, in the orchard for ever.

At last he roused himself and tried to neaten his appearance. He knew he must look an extraordinary sight – bloodstained, crumpled, unshaven and hollow-eyed. He searched his coat pocket for a handkerchief and encountered the stolen packet of papers. His hands were unsteady as he unfolded them and tried to read, but it was useless. It was too dark and Louis was too tired. He stuffed them back for later consideration.

Bent almost double, he weaved from tree to tree and made for the Rue du Faubourg St Honoré. Before long he could see it, running north-west in a straight line towards its *barrière* gate and south-east towards the junction where it became the Rue St Honoré. As far as he could make out, it was quiet. With a bit of luck he could cross it and take cover in one of the meadows that lay to the north, even perhaps raid one of the market gardens for some vegetables or fruit.

'*Diable.*'

Louis exclaimed under his breath and shrank back under a tree. Coming down the road in the direction of the Place Louis XV was a posse of National Guardsmen, holding their pikes erect in a businesslike manner. They moved slowly and peered suspiciously to the right and the left.

Louis held his breath. What were they doing at this hour? Who were they searching for? Were they searching from house to house? The men talked to each other, but Louis was too far away to make out what they were saying. The posse moved on with a clank of weapons.

Louis began to despair. It was going to be harder than he had thought to reach Neuilly. If he went west or north, sooner or later he would hit the *barrière* and that was sure to be guarded. Anyway, with his bloodied coat he would arouse suspicion. If he went east or south to the river, he would find himself back in the city, and a battle-stained man wandering the streets was an obvious target. Louis had no illusions as to his fate if he should be caught. Perhaps, after all, he should have made for Héloïse and the Hôtel de Choissy?

De Choissy! Louis hit his fist into his hand. Of course! There was one alternative, a risky one, but he could try it. Running almost parallel to the Rue du Faubourg St Honoré was the tree-lined Rue de Chartres. Only two or three hundred yards from that was the house that belonged to Adèle de Fleury. Louis knew it by repute. He had also met Adèle once or twice at Versailles.

It took him a long time, and his progress was erratic. Every so often he was forced to stop, either because his knees threatened to give way, or because he imagined he saw figures. But, at last, the huge wall that enclosed the house came into sight. Keeping well into the shadows, Louis skirted its perimeter and came eventually to the gates, which were locked fast. Somewhere inside, a dog barked. He leapt back out of sight and retraced his path, hoping to find a breach in the wall.

He did not have to walk far: a couple of bricks in the grass directed his gaze to a place where the wall had caved in very slightly. Panting with the effort, he pulled himself up and dropped over the other side. He inched forward, accompanied by the murmur of the leaves and the howls of the unseen dog, steering well clear of the direction from which they came. In a very few moments, he was rewarded by the sight of a light. Gradually the outline of a house took shape against the night sky. It was, he had been told, a beautiful house, built at the turn of the century for a favoured mistress by a royal prince who had decided to colonise this more unfashionable part of Paris. Louis acknowledged its distinctly feminine aspect – the lines and curves which had been charmed into elegance by a skilful architect. He saw also that candles burned in the big window on the first floor.

Almost light-headed with relief, he selected a stone from the gravel path and took aim. Careful, he thought: too hard, and run the risk of a nosy anti-royalist servant discovering him; too soft, and Adèle would not notice.

The stone sprang up towards the window in a graceful arc and hit the glass with a ping. Louis waited and then sent up a second. A shadow appeared at the window and the casement was thrown up with a jerk. Someone clad in white held back the drapes and peered out.

Louis strained to see who it was.

'Madame,' he called softly.

The figure froze, and then moved to obtain a better look below.

'Madame de Fleury,' Louis repeated, his voice etched with tension.

'Who's there?' The voice was low and uncertain.

'Louis d'Épinon.'

'Who?'

Louis repeated his name.

'*Ciel!* What are you doing in my grounds?'

Adèle disappeared and returned holding a lighted candelabrum which she raised up high. Louis' tired, dirty face glimmered up at her.

'What are you doing?'

'I am in need of food, shelter and a bed. Can I come up? It is too dangerous to stay here.'

Adèle hesitated and rapidly reviewed the situation. Her husband was conveniently away, and she had just sent her maid to bed.

'Can you climb up?'

Louis grasped the iron drainpipe and gave it an experimental tug. It seemed firm enough. Then he summoned his last ounce of energy and began to inch his way up. Halfway there, the humour of the situation struck him – he was hardly the gallant and dashing lover – and he laughed.

'Shush.'

Adèle stepped on to the balcony and leant over to help him up the remaining inches. Then he stood in front of her, swaying slightly, and even managed a sketchy bow.

The room behind looked infinitely welcoming and he sighed with relief. Adèle practically pulled him inside, cast a glance down below to check if they had been seen, and shut the window with a decided snap.

'Now, monsieur, just what are you doing?'

Louis told her, and as she listened to his account the colour drained from her cheeks and she exclaimed in horror.

'I suspected something had happened when I returned from Versailles yesterday. I was visiting friends in the town and the road to Paris was strangely quiet.' After a pause, she continued. 'I will of course help you.'

Louis sensed that her offer cost her some effort. Adèle was not, after all, in the habit of giving refuge to men on the run.

'It will be difficult,' she said. Her eyes were beginning to sparkle. 'I am not sure that I can trust my maid, but I suppose I will have to have faith in the stupid wench if I am to hide you here. But I am forgetting,' she said quickly, 'you will be hungry and thirsty.'

She lifted a jug from the table and poured some water into a glass. Louis gulped it down, and Adèle took a second glass from a fine silver-gilt set laid out on a tray and filled it with wine. It burned its way down to Louis' lurching stomach and sent welcome sparks shooting through his veins.

Louis set down the glass and threw back his head to savour the sensation. Adèle was pacing the room, the muslin wrapper that framed her neck and bosom emitting soft swishes. Delicate, feminine, pampered sounds, a world away from the Tuileries and Paris. Outside, an owl hooted and Louis, opening his eyes, saw that Adèle was a dangerously attractive woman. Her loosened hair tumbled down over her shoulders and her lace nightcap offered a perfect frame for her features. In the candlelight, she looked almost a girl. As he watched, Adèle put a finger to her lips and nibbled at it gently, an unselfconsciously sensual gesture that would have alerted many men.

At last she spoke.

'I must trust Lucie,' she said. 'And I will keep you here until I can obtain a passport. Where would it be best for you to go?'

'I shall go to Héloïse's house at Neuilly.'

Adèle looked at him sharply.

'Aha!' she said knowingly. 'So that is the way the wind lies.'

Louis got to his feet and executed another bow.

'So be it,' said Adèle. 'I am not one to enquire into the affairs of others, not even when it concerns my brother. My poor Hervé, he will not like it. He ever despised the cuckold, and he is very taken with Madame la Comtesse.'

Louis frowned. Adèle was renowned for her gossiping, albeit she went about it in a more good-natured way than many of her friends. Even so, he felt he could trust her. He leant forward and took one of her hands and kissed it. Adèle smiled and rang the bell. Presently, a small tangle-haired girl appeared in the doorway, rubbing her eyes. When she saw Louis, she uttered a shriek.

'Quiet,' said Adèle sharply.

Lucie stood twisting her nightdress round and round her fingers as Adèle explained the situation and directed her to go and search for food.

'But, madame,' faltered Lucie, 'I must tell you that Antoine has told me that the authorities are planning to visit you tonight.'

'Why didn't you say, you stupid girl?' Adèle was very curt.

'Antoine . . . Antoine . . .,' Lucie faltered. 'He told me not to tell you, and he said he would beat me if I did.'

'How does Antoine know this?'

'He has friends in the section headquarters,' said Lucie, barely above a whisper. 'They tell him things.'

'I see.' Adèle poured a glass of wine for herself and took a reflective sip. If the truth was known she was beginning to enjoy herself, although she had no illusions as to the danger she was courting.

'But careful,' she said to herself. 'Don't get carried away by the sight of a handsome face.'

She glanced at Louis out of the corner of her eye. He was, despite everything, remarkably attractive, and her flesh stirred in pleasurable anticipation.

Louis ate the cold chicken and cheese that Lucie brought, barely tasting them. Adèle rose and came to kneel beside him, her perfume wafting into the room.

'Poor Monsieur d'Épinon,' she said. 'Poor Louis.'

He managed to smile at her and she touched his knee with a soft caress.

'Now, where shall I hide you?'

Louis let his gaze wander round the elegant room and lingered on the bed that dominated it. It was a huge, old-fashioned bed, draped à la polonaise, and had room for at least four occupants. At least four, he thought wryly, of Adèle's lovers.

'I could hide in your bed,' he said, half-idly.

He heard Lucie gasp and saw Adèle's plucked eyebrows arch.

'But of course,' said Adèle with a trill of laughter. 'Why did I not think of it?'

She walked over to the bed and flung back the quilted coverlet, exposing lace-bordered sheets and large pillows.

'You will have to lie across the bed – so,' she said, 'and I will cover you with the pillows and lie back against you.'

There was another shriek from Lucie.

'I suppose', said Adèle, frowning at the maid, 'I shall be forced to cultivate a fever for the few days until I can obtain the necessary papers.' She sighed with mock ill-humour. 'And I have so much to do.'

Louis intercepted a look so full of sensual promise that he quite forgot his fatigue, and quite forgot Héloïse. He felt nothing but admiration for Adèle. Quite obviously, she was a woman with courage and humour and, for all her diminutive size, no weakling. He saw that she was flirting with him and his eyes lit up in response.

'Well, then, madame, we had better go to bed,' he said. He stretched one grimy hand for her inspection. 'You must permit me to wash, otherwise you might not be so ready with your invitation.'

Adèle signalled to Lucie, who led him into the dressing room off the bedroom. She poured some water into a china bowl and left him to wash. Louis plunged his face into the water gratefully. Ten minutes later, cleaned and glowing, he returned to the bedroom and, without further ado, climbed into the bed. Adèle was snuffing the candles, and she saw how tense he was. With a graceful movement she removed her *robe de chambre*. Underneath it she wore a gauze nightrobe which was almost transparent. Once again her perfume filled his nostrils.

'Sleep now,' she said, propped on one elbow. 'I know that you are tired.'

He sighed in gratitude, the dark pressing down on his eyelids, and obeyed her. Adèle lay for a while longer. She had some thinking to do. Only when she was quite clear in her mind did she turn on to her side, away from Louis. The room was quiet.

He was awakened by an urgent tug at his arm.

'Louis.' Adèle's voice was sharp and businesslike. 'They have come. You must hide.'

Already she was pulling the pillows aside. Stifling a groan, Louis roused himself and crawled into the position she indicated. Adèle settled the pillows against him.

'Can you breathe?' she asked. He pressed the curve of her back to show that he had heard.

'Hush now. Not a word until I tell you,' she reminded him.

The sound of voices on the stairs told her that she had not a minute to spare. Adèle glanced at the window and saw dawn was streaking the sky. She closed her eyes and breathed a prayer, not an activity she often indulged in.

There was a tap on the door. Adèle pretended not to hear. The tap was repeated, loud and peremptory.

'Ah,' she moaned languorously, in an excellent imitation of someone roused from sleep. 'Who is it?'

'Madame,' said Lucie, her voice squeaky with fear, 'there is someone who wishes to speak with you.'

'At this hour,' said Adèle. 'Certainly not.'

'Madame, you must.'

Before Lucie had finished speaking, she was brushed aside. Three men walked into the room, dressed in the now familiar uniform of the National Guardsmen. Adèle braced herself.

'What do you gentlemen mean by this intrusion?' she asked in a nicely judged assumption of anger.

The man in a short jacket and striped pair of trousers stepped forward and Adèle saw that he was very young.

'My name is Gaury, citoyenne. We must apologise for disturbing you at so odd an hour, but we wish to search your house for enemies of France.'

Adèle sat upright and adjusted the pillows a fraction.

'Monsieur Gaury, I am not in the habit of harbouring enemies

222

of France,' she remarked in freezing tones. 'Do you have any special reason for choosing this house?'

'We are searching all the houses in the neighbourhood. There have been reports of unauthorised activities near the *barrière*,' replied Gaury.

'Good heavens!' exclaimed Adèle. 'Then, you must search at once.'

The two guardsmen had the grace to look discomfited, but Gaury's regard remained unflinchingly direct. He snapped out an order to the guardsmen, who began to prod at furniture and look behind chairs. Adèle felt Louis stiffen.

Mother of God, she thought. Keep still.

'Forgive me', she addressed Gaury, 'if I do not rise to assist you. But I hardly feel it would be in order.'

As she spoke she contrived to let one side of her nightgown drop over her bare shoulder, almost to one breast. Gaury did not take his eyes off her, and there was no lightening in his expression.

'Your movements, citoyenne?'

'My movements?' Adèle's voice held a note of incredulity at his impertinence.

'Where have you been these past few days?'

'Why, here, monsieur, and today I have visited friends at Versailles. Is that important? You will understand that I am not accustomed to being questioned in this manner.'

Gaury ignored her.

The search of the bedroom having revealed nothing, the men stood waiting for further orders. Gaury directed them to the rest of the house and Lucie was ordered to show them round. Adèle leant back on the pillows and willed that Louis could breathe.

'Who are you exactly?' she asked, and this time a hint of anger crept into her voice. 'I trust your men will be gentle with my property.'

'They will be as thorough as is necessary. They have their orders. I have been entrusted by the Paris commune under the direction of Citizen Jacques Maillard to bring justice to bear against all those who work against *la patrie* and to ensure the safety of all patriots. Your family is one of many under suspicion.'

'Stuff!' said Adèle, losing patience at this rodomontade. 'You are a bunch of brigands, whoever you are, and you would appear to be the most foolish.'

Gaury said nothing. Adèle was unnervingly reminded of pictures of early martyrs she had seen in books in her distant youth. There was the same dangerous single-mindedness to be read in the face, the same ruthless determination. Are they all like this? she wondered. She dropped her gaze and concentrated on gathering her resources. She could feel Louis' warmth under the pillow and hoped that he could hold out. Trapped in the suffocating darkness, Louis struggled to breathe and remain still. Despite his discomfort, he could feel his anger rising, coupled with a growing impatience at the absurdity of his situation.

Gaury sat down on one of Adèle's slender gilt chairs.

'Who are your friends at Versailles? Where did you obtain your papers?'

Adèle enlightened him.

'Are you planning to remain here for the next few days?'

'Indeed,' replied Adèle. 'I need time to recover from this outrage.'

Gaury cleared his throat. It was not a pleasant sound.

'If you have nothing on your conscience, citoyenne, then your recovery will be swift.'

'You know, I could have you whipped,' remarked Adèle conversationally.

'I doubt it, citoyenne. It would not, in any case, be wise.'

The sergeant returned to report that his men had found nothing. Gaury rose to his feet.

'Citoyen Maillard will be disappointed,' he said, adjusting his leather belt. 'We shall be back.'

Adèle nodded. 'I shall be – how shall I put it? – informing my friends of you. They will be fascinated.'

'Your friends, citoyenne, have no more power, if that is what you mean.'

Gaury turned sharply on his heel and left the room with his men. Their footsteps died away down the stairs and after a minute could be heard crunching down the drive.

Adèle waited until she heard them no longer and with trembling fingers pulled aside the pillows. Louis was lying absolutely still, barely breathing. Adèle shook him, but there was no response. She shook him again, harder this time. There was no response. Adèle bent over swiftly and began to blow air into his mouth.

Louis found himself dragged back from the dark embrace into which he had been sucked by the feel of her full, moist lips on his. Without thinking he stretched up his arms and pulled Adèle down towards him, imagining in his confusion that he was with Héloïse.

Surprised, Adèle at first drew back a little, then relaxed and permitted his hands to do what they wanted. After a while, she helped him by sliding out of her nightgown, revealing the seductively rounded body of a woman who had kept herself well. The light was still kind to her curves and hidden places, and her hands were very knowledgeable as they gently removed Louis' clothes. By then it was too late to stop. Their two bodies closed and Louis gave himself up to the delights of the warm, comforting body that took such easy command of his.

Later, when they lay side by side under the tangled sheets, Adèle began to laugh with relief and amusement. She was still laughing when Lucie entered and stopped in confusion at the sight of them in the bed. Adèle merely covered her bare breasts with a careless flick of the sheet, unembarrassed and unworried. Lucie had seen her like this so many times before. Still, it was not the time to linger.

'Now we must plan,' Adèle said.

The following night, Louis slipped out of the back entrance of the house and Lucie locked and bolted it after him. Clad in a clean shirt and the Duc de Fleury's breeches, his coat now washed and pressed, Louis looked like a respectable gentleman who had seen better days. Inside his pocket were the stolen papers which proclaimed that he was one Citoyen Legrand of Rue St Jacques. Under his arm he carried a small parcel of food and wine.

Louis breathed deeply; it was good to be outside savouring the night air again. Following Adèle's instructions, he made his way through the parkland surrounding the house towards the small artificial lake that lay at its centre. Once there, he skirted its bank until he reached a charming little folly built by Adèle in one of her more extravagant moods. The bolt yielded easily to his touch and he entered a circular room with large windows. Louis could make out tables and chairs and, if his eyes did not deceive him, a luxurious day-bed situated at one side. He laughed. Despite her fragile air, Adèle was very well organised. The room was well aired and well maintained. Louis peered out of the window at the quiet expanse of lake and the shapes of the trees. All was quiet except for the sounds of leaves and animals in the undergrowth. Louis sat back and marvelled at the eternal, unchanging peace, worlds away from the horror that still churned inside him.

He thought of Héloïse. Beautiful, steadfast, loving Héloïse. The Héloïse who had held him through that long night at the Tuileries and who had refused to abandon her post. Héloïse, who almost certainly was bearing his child. In the gloom, Louis gave a little smile, half-tinged with regret, but not entirely so. The memory of Adèle was very recent and he had enjoyed his time in the vast bed with her. It had been a moment of passion and abandon, to be taken, relished and then relinquished with good manners. But it had nothing to do with his feeling for

Héloïse, and now he and Adèle would forget the interlude and continue on their separate ways.

When dawn came, a flock of geese landed on the water with a flurry. Their coming rippled up the shallows and broke the reflections into a thousand eddies and refractions of light. Louis woke from his doze and sat eating bread and fruit while he watched them.

At ten o'clock he packed up the remains of his meal and hid it. He locked the folly behind him and slipped into an adjacent copse of trees, and began to work his way cautiously towards the main gate of the house, using the trees as cover. He made good time. Adèle's carriage swept into view just as he got close to the rendezvous. The carriage stopped and the gate-keeper threw open the gates. Lucie opened the door and scrambled out, carrying a basket. She went over to the keeper and appeared to engage him in lengthy and garrulous conversation. Eventually, she offered him the basket and disappeared inside the lodge, still talking hard.

This was Louis' cue. Adèle beckoned from the carriage door and Louis, sprinting as hard as he could towards it, leapt inside. He lay panting on the floor and Adèle threw a rug on top of him. Lucie climbed in, in her haste stepping heavily on Louis. The door shut and the carriage moved forward.

Once the gate was out of sight, Adèle prodded Louis with her foot and he sat up. She leant forward to adjust his cravat.

'Up, my friend. Remember you are the respectable and slightly pompous Monsieur Legrand, a very – very – distant connection of mine.'

Louis gave a slight moue. 'How badly you treat me,' he said with a smile.

Adèle leant back against the squabs. 'All this is very trying for my nerves,' she remarked lightly. 'I shall be forced to leave Paris to take the waters in Plombières.'

All the same, a shadow passed over her face and neither of them spoke for a moment. Louis leant forward and kissed one of her hands.

'You are a brave woman,' he said, and Lucie, in her corner, blushed for her mistress.

At the *barrière* two bad-tempered soldiers stinking of garlic and cheap wine ordered the carriage to halt. They addressed a few surly remarks towards Adèle and peered inside, but appeared to be more interested in returning to the guard-house than in any passenger she might carry. After some debate, they handed back the papers to Adèle and Louis and the carriage clattered under a grey stone arch into the sunlight.

226

PARIS, August–September 1792

After three sweltering days spent in the shorthand-writer's box, listening to the deputies voting for the suspension of the monarchy, the king and his family were herded into a coach and driven at a deliberately slow speed to the Temple, former headquarters of the Knights Templars. At first they thought they would be housed in the delightful little palace contained within its medieval walls – the scene of glittering social evenings and musical soirées in better days – but they were soon disabused. The royal family were to take up quarters in one of the ancient towers. This was prison! Comfortably, but not luxuriously, housed, they settled down to what remained of their existence together.

The Girondins still dominated the government of the country, but in the Insurrectionary Commune one man was beginning to make his voice heard above everybody else's. A huge, bull-necked, roistering lawyer called Danton. Dubbed the 'Mirabeau of the Mob', he was appointed minister of justice, from which vantage point he also influenced the decisions taken in the Ministry of Foreign Affairs and War. It was Danton who saw to it that it was his friends and supporters who were sent out to the provinces to convey the message of the revolution and to tell of the glorious day the Parisians deposed their king.

A circle of iron began to close around Paris. Vigilance committees were established in the city sections, many internal passports were suspended and hundreds of 'counter-revolutionary' suspects were rounded up and herded into the prisons, including a large number of priests. The word 'aristocrat' became a term of abuse hurled at anyone who did not like the idea of a French republic.

The Parisians mourned their dead, and news of the suspiciously easy surrender of the frontier fortress of Longwy to the Austrians did nothing to soothe the bitterness and hatred. Nor did the intelligence that the Vendée area was rising in support of the royalists. France, it seemed, was on the brink of civil war.

'We must fling ourselves on our enemies,' declared Danton, whose thundering oratory never failed to stir those who heard it – 'L'audace,

et encore l'audace, et toujours l'audace.' And those who still supported the king, or who were suspected of harbouring counter-revolutionary sentiments, took fright as they heard his words. They knew that the people of Paris did not need to be told twice.

They were right to take heed. The Parisian authorities were turning an increasingly deaf ear to the mounting rumours that an attack on the overflowing prisons was being planned . . . . Its object: to rid la patrie of her enemies, once and for all.

Chapter 14

La Force, September 2nd, 1792

Armed with a warrant from the surveillance committee, a detachment of soldiers from the section headquarters came for the Marquis and Marquise de Guinot at ten o'clock in the morning. The marquis had just time enough to scrawl notes to Héloïse and his lawyer before he and his wife were conducted outside and told to wait. Watched by the frightened household, then seals were fixed to the doors of the Hôtel de Guinot, and the house declared the property of the republic.

'Stiff-necked lot, these aristos,' muttered one of the guards to another, surprised at the lack of commotion made by the affair. He spat reflectively on to a marble statue of Aphrodite.

A hired conveyance deposited the prisoners at the end of a small street thirty paces long and ten wide. The marquis descended and helped his wife down on to the cobbles. They were conducted past some ancient houses and into the prison of La Force. Here they passed through a narrow entrance and a lobby and into the prison office.

The concierge in charge of La Force was busy and irritable, but not unkind, and he listened with some sympathy to the marquis' politely worded request that he and his wife should be housed together.

'By rights she should be taken to the Petite Force round the corner,' he muttered, pocketing the louis that the marquis had had the forethought to bring with him. 'The women are lodged there.' He finished the registration and sucked at his thumb thoughtfully. The marquis proffered a second coin. 'Well, just for tonight, then,' he said.

His fellow gaolers were considerably rougher, and their tempers were not improved by over-work.

'Hurry up,' barked the largest and most brutal-looking to the marquis. His big, stupid face glistened with sweat from the heat that penetrated the thick stone walls which oozed great drops of moisture. His dog, a mangy, vicious-looking animal, lurched behind him, baring his fangs at the marquise's skirts. The marquise leant weakly against a stone pillar and the marquis put his arm around her to encourage her onwards.

'*Allez, ma chère,*' he admonished in a cheerful voice. 'It can't be far now.'

The gaoler pushed them through the prisoners milling in the central courtyard. Many of them already had a prison pallor scored into their complexions, and sores from lack of fresh food, but others appeared to be still healthy and were engaged in playing cards and arranging assignations.

The marquise permitted herself one icy glare at the gaoler and stumbled on. Eventually they came to a halt in a corridor studded with doors. The gaoler prodded the de Guinots through the nearest.

'You are lucky,' he commented sourly. 'I have been told to put you in here and leave you together.'

'We thank you,' said the marquis with old-fashioned courtesy, and hastened to sit his wife down on one of the two narrow camp-beds that practically filled the room. The door closed behind the gaoler and the de Guinots were left to contemplate their new abode.

'Not much space,' said the marquis, still a little stupid with shock. A stifled sob answered him as the marquise buried her head in her hands. The marquis let her cry for a while and then prised her hands away.

'I think you should rest, madame,' he suggested, helping her on to one of the beds and clumsily loosening her stays. 'You know, *ma chère,*' he said, 'we do have a position to maintain in this place. Others will expect it of us.'

The marquise shuddered. 'I am aware of it, Charles,' she replied with a trace of her old hauteur. 'I shall endeavour to do my duty.'

'We will talk about it after you have had some sleep,' said the marquis. He folded a threadbare blanket over the marquise and tucked in the ends.

Satisfied that she was as comfortable as possible, the marquis left her to rest. At the end of the corridor the passage widened into a large refectory hall. Seated at a long table, the prisoners were eating their dinner, a tough, unappetising stew, composed mainly of bones and old vegetables. The marquis placed himself at an empty bench and reached for a slice of greyish-looking bread which was piled on the table.

'Eat up,' advised his neighbour, pointing to the stew. 'You won't get anything else until noon tomorrow.' The marquis smiled but declined. He had already made arrangements with the obliging concierge to have his meals brought in and his stomach wasn't ready to tackle anything as robust as the stew.

He was sipping at some water when a gaoler appeared. 'Prisoner de Guinot,' he bawled.

The marquis rose to his feet and wiped his mouth with his handkerchief. He followed the man through the courtyard and into a lobby where a familiar figure stood waiting, pale but composed.

'You have fifteen minutes,' said the gaoler, looking Héloïse up and down with a leer. Héloïse did her best to ignore him and dropped a coin into his palm.

'Daughter,' said the marquis, stretching out both his hands.

'I came as soon as I could,' said Héloïse. 'I have brought you linen and wine.'

'Excellent,' said her father, and took the bulky package from her. 'I hope you included some books.'

'Indeed,' she said, and hesitated. It was so unexpected to see her father in this setting.

'What is the charge?' she asked at last. 'By whose orders are you here?'

'The commune,' the marquis replied with a shrug.

'But why?'

'For conspiring against France and for being in communication with the enemy, for anti-republican opinions.'

'I see,' she said flatly. 'But as a minister you had every reason to correspond abroad.'

'It seems not,' the marquis replied.

'De Choissy will do all he can.'

'Good. Tell him I shall count on him and the others of my friends.' The marquis smiled. 'Take heart, my daughter. All is not lost yet.'

Héloïse swallowed. 'And madame, *ma mère*?'

'She is sleeping, I hope. This has come as a shock.'

He indicated a bench by the wall. 'Let us sit down. There *is* one thing I wish to ask you.'

Héloïse sat down. 'What is it? I am at your disposal.'

The marquis thought hard before he replied. 'Would it be possible – and it might not be possible since they sealed the house – for Monsieur le Comte de Choissy to arrange for some of my more valuable paintings and porcelain to be taken to safety? It would grieve me unutterably to think that they might be in danger from ignorant persons.'

'Paintings and porcelain . . .' Héloïse choked slightly. How very like her father!

'My dear, these are things that make life tolerable. I have spent many happy hours studying them in my time and they have never failed me,' the marquis reproved her.

'I will see what can be arranged,' said Héloïse. 'It will be difficult if the house is under seal, but perhaps de Choissy can bribe a member of the section committee.'

The marquis sighed, the first flickers of real doubt troubling his serenity. He was not, however, going to reveal any of his private fears to his daughter, and he set about convincing her that he felt perfectly tranquil about his sudden change of fortune

'One thing,' he said finally, 'and the most important. I feel that it is time that Miss Luttrell returned to England. Now that we can no longer extend our protection, this is the correct thing to do.'

Héloïse's hand fluttered in an expressive gesture.

'I have been dreading your saying so. Sophie has become more than a friend and I love her dearly. But you are right, sir, she should return.'

'Once that is done I shall rest easy,' continued the marquis. 'As you know, Cécile, your sister, has left France, and I wish you to leave now with your husband. You must take the documents that I have deposited with our lawyer and go to Berne or Koblenz. There you will leave these documents with our banks. They will provide you with funds if you have need of them. You must remain out of France until it is prudent to return. Do not, I beg you, leave it until it is too late.'

Héloïse hesitated. She had no wish to disobey her father, or to lie. The marquis leant forward and captured one of her hands. He spoke urgently.

'You must do as I say.'

'Your time is up.'

The gaoler had returned with his dog. Héloïse leant forward and, for the first time in her life, threw her arms round her father, regretting bitterly that she did not know him better. She clung to him until he gently disengaged her.

'Come when you can,' he admonished over his shoulder, and then he disappeared into the courtyard.

The marquise was awake when the marquis returned. He saw that an attempt had been made to render the cell more comfortable. The marquise had pushed the two beds together to make a bigger space to move about in and had placed a stool directly under the window to catch the light. She was saying a rosary when he entered.

'My dear, I have just seen Héloïse,' he told her.

The marquise's face expressed little more than perfunctory interest. 'Is she well?'

232

'Pale. I think the child bothers her.'

'As mine did me. Do you remember?'

'Of course,' the marquis lied. He began to unpack Héloïse's parcel. 'She has done well, our daughter,' he remarked, holding up food, linen, books and wine. The marquis poured some of the wine into a small leather cup and offered it to his wife.

'*Alors*,' he said, drinking his share, 'the sooner I begin writing letters to the authorities, the sooner we shall be out of this place.'

The evening fell and the inhabitants of La Force prepared themselves for another night of incarceration. The sound of voices died away. Those fortunate enough to occupy cells moved quietly around inside them, tending their clothes, letter-writing or praying. In the corridors the nightly scuffles as to who slept in what space were subsiding and the prisoners laid out on long rows of straw pallets grew quiet, only a moan torn from a dreamer breaking the stillness.

The marquis slept fitfully. At one point he imagined he was back at Versailles, consulting with the king. He could hear a babble of courtiers' voices and his own debating some issue. He jerked in his sleep. Above him the painted ceiling of the king's council chamber melted into harsh grey stone and he turned in surprise – to encounter a hard, unfamiliar mattress. The marquis raised himself on one elbow to reassure himself that the marquise was sleeping. She lay motionless, her hair in neat plaits. The marquis settled himself with his face to the wall and thought of his paintings.

The prisoners in La Force slept on.

Near dawn the marquis was torn from sleep by a cry – an unearthly sound filled with pain and terror that sent him crashing bolt upright. The cry came again, sharp and anguished, ending with a terrified choking, and this time the marquis heard the sounds of laughter and a stream of oaths.

He threw back the blanket and groped his way towards the door to peer through the bars set into the wood at eye level. In the gloom he could just make out the outlines of the sleeping figures in the corridors, some of whom, like himself, had been rudely awakened. Once again a scream tore through the air.

'*Qu'est-ce qui passe?*' hissed a voice.

'I don't know,' whispered the marquis from his vantage point. 'But I think it would be best if you pretend to be asleep.'

The tramp of feet interrupted him, and a group of men swung round the corner. They carried flaring torches which cast uneven patches of light and sent demonic shadows up the wall. They moved purposefully along the row of sleepers. The marquis shrank back. He knew at once that these intruders were murderous and that something foul was afoot. One of the men gestured to his companion and leant over to jerk a sleeping figure upright. The prisoner stumbled blearily to his feet and his captor slapped him round the face in order to wake him. The prisoner gave a cry of protest.

'Shut up,' ordered the man. 'And follow me.'

By now six or seven other prisoners were on their feet. The guards prodded them down the corridor and out of sight. The cries began again.

'What is it?' the marquise was awake, hugging her blanket to her.

'Nothing, my dear,' replied the marquis.

'Charles, something terrible is going on. I know it. Listen to those screams.'

The marquise slumped back on the mattress and pressed her hands to her ears.

'We must pray,' said the marquis quickly, and knelt down by the window.

'Dear God,' he began, and as he did so the door swung open. The marquise screamed and the marquis spread his arms out in an involuntary movement to protect her.

'None of that,' said a voice from the doorway. 'We don't want her. Only you.'

An icy chill settled on the marquis, but with it came a stubborn courage. He drew himself to his full height, every inch the courtier. 'You dogs,' he said slowly and with some relish. 'You filthy murdering dogs.'

The gaoler laughed and gestured over his shoulder.

'Here,' he said, 'we have a joker.'

Two of his companions stood in the doorway with torches, and even in the deceptive light the marquis could see the blood smeared on their arms and clothes.

Behind him the marquise was sobbing, terrified. Then she too chose to pull herself together. She got up from the bed and took her husband's arm.

'Charles,' she murmured, and in her voice were the memories of the life they had shared. 'Charles.'

'Marguerite,' he said, proud that she had chosen to bear this moment in a way that he approved. He bent and kissed her on the forehead. She clung to him.

'The children,' he whispered into her ear. 'You must tell them not to give up hope. Nor must you.'

'Go with God,' she said tenderly and pressed her rosary into his hands. The guard gestured towards the corridor.

'Out,' he ordered roughly.

The noise was now deafening in the prison as the prisoners shouted and struggled to avoid the round-up. In contrast, the marquis went quietly. There was no point in resistance.

He was dragged into the concierge's office where a tall, thin, inquisitor-like figure sat at a rough wooden desk. He was wearing red cap, striped breeches and a tricolour sash. He was writing furiously. Rolls of parchment littered the table and lay on the floor.

'Aha,' he said, without looking up. 'I have been waiting for you.'

The marquis said nothing. The voice was one he had heard before, not familiar but recognisable. He struggled to place it.

'Your name, citoyen?'

'Charles Antoine Louis LuDucq, Marquis de Guinot, Chevalier de Brion . . .'

'No more, citoyen,' the man cut him short. 'All titles are abolished.'

'I know you,' said the marquis suddenly. 'Your family lived on one of my estates.'

'Correct, citoyen, at La Joyeuse.'

'You are . . .?'

'Maillard. Jacques Maillard, and I have been waiting some time to deal with you. In fact, I have been waiting a long time to deal with all your family.'

'But why?' asked the marquis in surprise. 'You were always well treated.'

Jacques rose and walked over to his former master, and thrust his face into his.

'I could bear neither your charity nor your pitiful wages. Each winter my family nearly starved – and we were the lucky ones.'

'That is not true,' said the marquis quietly. 'Nobody in my demesne ever starves.'

'How would you know, citoyen? Did you ever visit us in our hovels? Or did the stench offend you too much?'

He caught at the marquis by his hair and forced his head back. 'I am glad that you are going to die,' he said unemotionally. 'And I will see that your family dies with you. I still have this to account for.'

Maillard pulled up his shirt to reveal his scarred torso, patterned with red welts.

'Your daughter ordered this,' he said, and his voice thickened. 'She will pay for it.'

Maillard released the marquis and returned to his desk.

'But I am almost forgetting the point, citoyen. You are convicted of crimes against France and must take the punishment.'

The marquis drew himself up to his full height. 'By whose authority?'

'The people of France.'

'Are you going to kill me?'

Maillard shrugged and pointed in the direction of the door. 'What do you think?' he asked.

It was all too obvious what was happening. The cries of pain and the sound of bodies thudding to the floor were clearly audible; so too were the grunts of the men butchering them. In response to a signal from Maillard, the guard ripped the marquis' coat from his back and motioned for him to step outside.

'You are judged guilty', said Maillard with a smile, 'by true patriots and you must suffer the penalty.'

In the doorway, the marquis shook off the restraining hands.

'I ask only that you spare my family,' he said desperately.

'*Adieu*,' said Maillard his face expressionless.

'You will roast in hell for this,' shouted the marquis, but when he saw the scene outside his voice faded.

He had been taken into a small interior courtyard of the prison, at one end of which stood some men surrounded by bodies. The nearby wall was covered in blood and the air was thick with its rank smell. One man, a huge giant of a fellow, stood leaning on his axe with the body of a still quivering victim lying beside him. He wiped his forehead with the back of his hand.

'Another, Durand,' shouted the marquis' escort, and pushed him towards the wall.

'God's teeth,' said Durand. 'I need a rest. Get me some wine.'

Someone thrust a skin of wine into his hands with a coarse oath of encouragement. Durand raised it to his lips, flashing a grin at the marquis as he did so.

'You don't mind waiting, do you?' he asked.

The marquis' fingers explored the cold stones of the wall behind him. He willed himself to remain silent and then grasped at the rosary so the beads cut into his flesh.

Moved by some obscure stirring of pity, one of the watching guards leant towards him.

'Don't cover your head with your hands,' he muttered. 'It takes longer that way.'

His pulses pounding, the marquis watched Durand put down the wine and take up the axe. He was still clasping the rosary when the blade sliced deep into the space between his shoulder and his neck. The rosary slipped from his fingers and fell with a hiss to the floor.

'Jesus have pity on me,' murmured the marquis.

The axe rose and fell twice. It was over.

236

PARIS, September 1792

The marquis' death and those of his fellow-prisoners who perished with him at La Force marked the beginning of the massacres that swept the prisons of Paris for five days; to begin with as isolated incidents and then as a swelling tide of blood that broke over the city with the avenging hatred of the Furies.

First one prison then another was invaded by a mob intent on destruction. Dragging their victims from their cells, parading them in a mockery of a trial and then butchering them where they stood, the self-styled avengers of France did their work. La Force, La Salpêtrière, Le Châtelet, the Carmelite Convent and the Abbaye . . . the toll grew longer and the murderers madder with collective blood lust. The screams of the dying had no sooner stilled in one quartier than they were taken up by the unfortunates in another. There was no respite, no mercy, only savagery.

In the streets onlookers watched as cartloads of bodies, many still twitching, were drawn through the streets to the burial grounds. At the Conciergerie the assassins and their companions made a pile of their victims in the Cour du Mai and danced around it, dipping their bread into the gore and eating it. At La Petite Force the Princesse de Lamballe, the queen's dearest friend, was one of the first to be murdered and her mutilated corpse and severed head were waved in front of the royal prisoners' window.

'So dies a whore, an enemy of France,' shouted one old crone at the sight.

'Death will come to all enemies of la patrie,*' echoed a brawny jeweller from the Faubourg St Antoine.*

Gradually the fury abated, leaving the authorities to count the cost. Over 1,200 prisoners lay dead, thirty-seven of them women, and the murderers – the septembriseurs *– slipped back to where they had come from, to boast of their exploits in the wine shops and beer cellars.*

Paris returned to a semblance of normality. For a time many citizens had no idea what had happened, and, if they did, they comforted themselves with the notion that the deaths were a necessary evil to save France from her enemies.

Chapter 15

Sophie, September 4th, 1792

'Héloïse.'

Sophie swept into the sitting room that she and Héloïse shared in the mornings. Héloïse looked up. She was drafting a letter to her father's lawyers. De Choissy had tried to dissuade her from such a task, telling her that she should leave such things to him, but Héloïse had been firm. This was something that she could do and she needed the occupation to divert her mind.

Where was Louis? Was he safe? Had he reached Neuilly? These questions nagged at Héloïse day and night. She had had no real rest since that early morning when she had stumbled unexpectedly over the bridge from the sacked Tuileries Palace and Sophie had caught her in her arms. Both Sophie and William were concerned for her health, but Héloïse assured them that she had taken no lasting injury from her experiences. With that they had to be content. De Choissy had said nothing much, except to warn her that their plans for leaving France must go forward. Héloïse had been too shaken to argue.

'Héloïse. We must go immediately to La Force.'

Héloïse put down her quill and sanded her letter.

'Why?' she asked. 'Is there news of Monsieur le Marquis?'

'There are rumours that something dreadful has happened. Miss Edgeworth has just returned from a visit to Miss Williams's and there is talk in the city of killing in the prisons.'

Héloïse stared vacantly at her letter.

'Well, then, we must go at once,' she said. 'You are sure?'

'I hope I am wrong. It is probably nothing. Where is Monsieur le Comte?'

'At the Louvre, I believe. I don't know.'

'Ned has gone out yet again to try to obtain visas for England, but Mr Jones is here and will accompany us.'

'Good,' said Héloïse, and rang for her maid.

'Héloïse.' Sophie chose her words carefully. 'Héloïse, I think you must prepare yourself. It is possible. . . . Remember,' she said in a rush, 'I am here to help you and I won't ever leave you as long as you need me.'

Héloïse was touched. She went over to kiss Sophie.

'I am glad you said that, Sophie,' she said. 'The truth is, I do need you. Perhaps today even more so. It's selfish, I know, but it's true.'

'Not so,' said Sophie. 'I cannot imagine life without you, *chérie* – and I don't want to go home . . . for all sorts of reasons, and Ned is trying to make me. Anyway, if I go, you can always come with me.'

Héloïse retied Sophie's sash, which had come undone.

'*Nous verrons*,' she said. 'Now we must go.'

The road to the prison was choked. Carts, diligences and coaches, filled with anxious relatives, fought with each other for a passage through the streets. Inside the de Choissy coach, Sophie grew worried. The streets seemed worse than she had imagined.

'Perhaps, after all, we should not have come,' she said.

William reached for her hand and held it reassuringly. Privately, he agreed with Sophie and was angry with himself for being foolish enough to allow them to accompany him. Héloïse regarded them both with a determined expression.

'But we must find out,' she said.

'Good God.'

Sophie, who had been looking out of the window, suddenly jerked back and covered her eyes.

'What is it?' cried Héloïse.

'Bodies. A pile of bodies. They were in a cart.'

'Close your eyes, both of you,' ordered William sharply, and pulled down the leather blind.

Then, it's true, thought Sophie. I must stay calm.

Dear God, thought Héloïse, not again.

The coach drew to a halt by the Rue des Ballets and the prison came into view. The three of them alighted.

'Leave this to me,' said Héloïse, as they picked their way over the cobbles towards the prison entrance. William tensed, ready to spring forward if there was trouble, and watched warily while Héloïse went towards the guards. She proceeded to engage one of them in conversation, and a coin flashed before disappearing into the man's pocket. Héloïse beckoned, and they passed without hindrance through the lobbies and into the courtyard.

A guard showed them through yet another lobby into a second, inner courtyard and, as he did so, something warned Sophie to go no further. She stopped abruptly and placed a restraining hand on Héloïse's.

'Don't,' she begged. 'I think it would be better if we go back and leave Mr Jones to do the rest.'

Héloïse shook her off and walked on regardless. The scene that unfolded before her in the courtyard was to carve itself into her memory for the rest of her life. She staggered, and William ran to support her.

'Get back,' he shouted to Sophie, who was behind them. But it was too late. Sophie, like Héloïse, stood rooted to the spot, immobilised by horror.

Heaped against the stone wall in the courtyard were thirty or more corpses. They had been dead for some hours and rigor mortis had already set in. Their wounds exposed gaping expanses of bone and entrail, and their blood had seeped through the paving stones and congealed in pools on the ground. The only noise was the incessant buzzing of flies.

Near the top of the pile lay the marquis. His face was masked by blood and dirt but Héloïse knew him at once from a scar that snaked up his arm, a legacy from a battle fought in his youth. His head lolled in an unnatural fashion, and a grimace distorted his face which was turning black in the September warmth. Héloïse clutched at her stomach as she fought for her breath.

'Citoyenne de Choissy.'

A voice spoke from behind. A voice that was full of confidence and authority. All three of them looked up. Jacques Maillard stood observing them. He looked exhausted and stooped with fatigue, and his face gleamed with sweat.

'How do you know my name?'

Héloïse searched his countenance. Surely she knew him? The stranger awoke memories of La Joyeuse. Surely it was not . . .?

'Maillard,' replied the stranger. 'Jacques Maillard.'

Maillard was enjoying picturing what was passing through Citoyenne de Choissy's mind. He rubbed at his three-day growth of beard with his fingers.

'Have you come to take your father's body?' he continued. 'I will give you permission to do so.'

Héloïse gasped at his audacity. How dare he? A former servant.

'You don't have any choice,' said Maillard with satisfaction. 'If you don't have my permission, then you can't take him.'

'Mr Jones, I must sit down,' said Héloïse faintly. 'I don't feel very well.'

'Come with me,' Maillard commanded, and they followed him towards the prison office.

Maillard swept a pile of documents off a stool to the floor and indicated that Héloïse could sit down if she wished. He went over to the door and barked out an order. A guard appeared carrying a bottle and glasses. Maillard offered it around. All three of them refused. Maillard shrugged and drank himself.

'We shall remove the body of Monsieur le Marquis and then go,' William curtly informed him. 'If you would be good enough to allow the ladies to remain here, I will see to it.'

Sophie shot him a glance. William's tone was not conciliatory.

'As you wish,' said Maillard. 'You have my permission.'

William left the room. Héloïse raised her head.

'Who did this . . . this evil thing?'

'I was in charge.'

A look of mingled cunning and pride crossed Maillard's face, and his eyes burned with a sudden light.

'I don't believe it,' whispered Héloïse through dry lips.

'They were enemies of France.' Maillard rolled the words out with relish.

'If you believe that, monsieur, then you are a fool . . .' Héloïse was icy, and Maillard stiffened automatically at the contempt in her voice.

'We need to protect France,' he repeated stubbornly.

'Monsieur le Marquis worked all his life for his country,' Héloïse replied.

Maillard leant over the table towards her.

'Your father was a parasite, like the others of your kind.'

Sophie twisted her handkerchief round and round her fingers. She prayed that William would return so that they could leave this dreadful place and prevent Héloïse from saying anything further.

'Where did you learn to think like this?' Héloïse was saying.

'At La Joyeuse, citoyenne,' replied Maillard, and observed her face with satisfaction. 'I watched you, citoyenne. I watched you very carefully. You and your big, greedy, careless family, and I saw the misery you made around you. Did you ever think of us, citoyenne, or were you too busy eating your fine meals?'

'Everyone who worked at La Joyeuse was well cared for.'

'You know nothing, and care less.' Maillard was in full flow and traces of spittle flecked his mouth. 'Did you ever give a thought to the hovels that existed by the side of your big house? Or see the hunger of mothers with their children? Or understand the exhaustion that came with work, work, and yet more work? Do you know what it is like to give up the best of your crops, or shiver in winter because you haven't got a coat? No, of course not.'

Héloïse shook her head in disbelief.

241

'Oh, I watched you, citoyenne,' continued Maillard. 'And I learned. I taught myself a great deal while I watched. Then I came to Paris and found that my friends thought like I did. They believed in me and now I am in a position to call the tune.'

Héloïse got to her feet with difficulty.

'You are nothing but a murderer,' she said. 'A cheap, common murderer.'

Maillard levelled his gaze at her and Sophie was struck again by his burning eyes.

'I would be very careful, citoyenne, if I were you,' he told her. 'You no longer have any authority. And' – he turned on his heel – 'I have two scores to settle.' He sat down at his desk and pulled some papers towards him. 'A beating, and Marie-Victoire.'

There was no mistaking his malice – nor his fanaticism.

Héloïse slumped back down on the stool. She remembered events at La Joyeuse quite clearly now. Sophie was by her side in an instant.

'Enough,' she said to Maillard. 'Leave her in peace.'

Maillard looked her up and down.

'If I were you, Citoyenne Luttrell – yes, I do know your name – I would be very careful,' he said. 'We do not like strangers in our city. We don't trust them.'

Sophie ignored his threat.

'Put your head down as far as you can, *chérie*,' she admonished Héloïse.

Héloïse allowed Sophie to wipe her forehead, then she straightened up.

'I am all right,' she told her.

She put out her hand to William, who reappeared in the doorway, and he helped her upright.

'Monsieur Maillard,' she said contemptuously, looking remarkably like her father, and Sophie knew what the effort must have cost her. 'You are not the only one who can be vengeful. We de Guinots do not forget. We shall not forget you. Do you understand?'

Maillard coloured violently, but he chose to laugh.

'Your time has passed, citoyenne. Nothing you can do can hurt me now. I have it in my power to finish the de Guinots.'

'Come,' said William. 'At once.'

He shepherded Héloïse and Sophie from the room.

'Look straight ahead and hurry,' he said. 'It's dangerous in here, and there are men outside I don't trust the look of. Anything might happen.'

They walked out of La Force and into the street.

'Madame – Héloïse . . .' William put his arm gently around

Héloïse. 'You understand, we are taking the body of Monsieur le Marquis with us. Can you bear it?'

Héloïse's reply registered in her face, in which pride, fury and grief were mingled. William understood, and said no more.

The coachman cracked his whip and the coach began to force its way back through the streets. Héloïse supported the marquis' head between her hands and stroked his bloodied hair back from his face. She held him thus throughout the long journey to the Rue de l'Université.

The look of horror and disbelief on Ned's face back at the Hôtel de Choissy warned Sophie that trouble was brewing again in that quarter. But she pushed the notion to the back of her mind. She would have to deal with Ned later. There were more important things to do first.

Strangely enough, it was de Choissy who assumed charge and who brought order into the confusion that greeted their return. He took one look at Héloïse, whose pallor was alarming, and swept her up into his arms. He carried her up the grand staircase to her bedroom, laid her on the bed and sent the maids scurrying for water and wine.

It was de Choissy who arranged for the marquis' body to be laid out in a manner befitting his rank. It was de Choissy who knelt by the body among the black velvet and candles and prayed for hours, his face set with grief and bitterness. It was de Choissy who sent one of his servants running at top speed through the night to fetch a doctor for Héloïse. It was de Choissy who kept a midnight vigil over the feverish body of his wife and commanded Sophie to get some sleep.

Héloïse lay in bed, alternately soothed by a sensation of quiet nothingness and racked by a pain that sliced into her body. Sometimes she heard herself crying. Sometimes she was aware of voices above her. Once she was sure she heard Sophie calling her name. But it was a long way off and she did not have the energy to answer.

'Héloïse,' pleaded the voice. 'Héloïse, listen to me. You must try.'

Sophie's voice trailed away into a place that she, Héloïse, could not reach. After that came de Choissy, standing straight and insolent, or so it seemed to her in her confusion.

'Madame wife. You must pull yourself together. Try harder.'

The voices swelled and merged, until they formed a monstrous cacophony – begging, cajoling, angry and pleading. Héloïse wished to hear none of them. She was too tired and weak. From somewhere else, the marquis added his urging.

'Héloïse. You must listen to them. Go back.'

She felt the marquis push her away. Standing beside him was Maillard, his brown eyes oddly gentle.

'I will be even with you,' Héloïse promised him, and buried her head in the pillow at the sound of his laughter.

Someone was missing. Héloïse tried to search for him, running down long grey-stone passages and through the Parisian streets. Where was he?

'Louis,' she moaned.

'She's delirious,' said de Choissy to Sophie. He bent over his wife.

'Héloïse,' he said.

Her hot, flushed faced stared up at him.

'Oh, it's you,' she whispered desolately.

'Yes,' said the count grimly. 'It is. Do you feel any better?'

But Héloïse was too far away to answer.

When she was better Sophie sat with her for much of the time and Héloïse spent hours staring at the carved bedposts and tracing the line of panelling in the room. She would gaze at Sophie's golden head bent over her writing and study the dreaming look that often replaced a tense little frown. Héloïse knew what put that frown on Sophie's face and resolved to try to help her when she felt better. Though what she would say, she wasn't quite sure.

Once, her hand wandered down to her belly and discovered a bandage swaddling it flat. She let it rest there until she understood that she had miscarried, and then she cried. Sophie comforted her.

'There will be others,' she said.

Héloïse remembered something.

'Madame la Marquise. Is she alive?'

'Monsieur le Comte has managed to see her,' replied Sophie carefully. 'She is as well as can be expected. The situation is still too dangerous for him to arrange matters for the time being.'

'And . . .' Héloïse found it difficult to frame the question.

'And Louis?' Sophie finished for her, stroking Héloïse's hair lovingly back from her face. Héloïse nodded, relieved and glad that the pretence between them was over.

'I have sent word as discreetly as I could, after I received this.'

Sophie drew a folded piece of paper from the bosom of her dress. Héloïse reached out her hand and noted with interest how transparent it was.

'*Mignonne*,' she read. 'I am safe. Come when you can. L.D'E.'

Héloïse felt tears trickle down her cheeks, tears of thankfulness and relief. Sophie wiped them away.

'It was his child, you know.'

'I guessed as much,' replied Sophie quietly.

'Did I give anything away?'

Sophie hesitated. 'Not as far as I can tell. But, Héloïse, I must tell you, Monsieur le Comte nursed you so tenderly that I could not help thinking . . .'

Héloïse turned her face away. 'Don't,' she said.

Sophie desisted, not wishing to distress Héloïse and bring back her fever.

'Don't worry,' she said soothingly. 'I will not discuss it further.'

Héloïse considered.

'Sophie. I told you that my father wished you to return to England – for your own safety. I also told you that I wanted to keep you here and you said you would. I don't hold you to that promise. I want you to think very carefully about leaving.'

Sophie knelt by the bed and took Héloïse's hand.

'Now, more than ever, I will not consider abandoning you,' she said, the thought of it gripping her heart.

'But you heard what that monster said. He would get rid of all the de Guinots. We are a danger to you.'

'I did. It does not make me change my mind. Listen, Héloïse, I am too much part of it here. I cannot go back to what I was. Ned will argue otherwise, but I don't want to listen to him. I hate myself in many ways for the pain I am causing others, but I cannot leave you – or Paris.'

'Or Mr Jones?' said Héloïse. 'Will you marry him instead?' she persisted when Sophie did not answer. Sophie tried to find the right words.

'I don't know, Héloïse. I am confused about my feelings for Mr Jones and concerned about Ned who won't be put off for much longer. I need more time.' She paused. 'Sometimes', she said awkwardly, 'I feel . . . I feel that I am incapable of love, otherwise all these questions would be easy to resolve. You see, I thought I loved Ned.'

Sophie rose and went to pour out the cordial specified by the doctor into a pretty fluted glass. She slipped her hand behind Héloïse's head and helped her to drink it. Héloïse reached up and touched Sophie's cheek, deeply concerned by her cousin's confession. She longed to help. She also knew that Sophie was wrong: her beautiful cousin was made for love.

Héloïse settled back on to the pillows, holding Louis' letter tightly against her breast.

'Neuilly, then,' she said, and her lips curved into a happy smile. 'But first I must rid myself of de Choissy.'

*

De Choissy was uncharacteristically curt over Héloïse's plans when she tried to discuss them. How strange, she thought, with a new intuition born out of her happiness, I think he is disappointed. He is so difficult to fathom, but, yet, I believe I am beginning to understand him a little.

The count regarded his wife with his inscrutable eyes. Héloïse was lying on the day-bed in her bedroom, looking much better. She had made her toilette for the first time in days and Sophie had threaded a blue riband through her hair. Pearl earrings hung in her ears, and her thin fingers were clasped round a porcelain tea-bowl.

'I suppose I must acquiesce,' he said. 'I can't stomach ailing females for too long and you are too weak to travel far. You have, if you will forgive me for pointing it out, my dear, quite lost your bloom. I suppose the house is yours to visit how you wish. I shall come when I can,' he added drily.

'Can you organise the papers?' asked Héloïse. 'I would like to go as soon as I can. The doctor says I may travel in three weeks' time.'

'I shall get the papers for you on one condition.' De Choissy made a calculated pause. Héloïse waited. 'That you agree to leave France with me as soon as you are fit to travel. And, if I were you, madame, I would see to it that it is soon. I can't answer for what will happen otherwise.'

Héloïse traced a pattern in the embroidered cushion by her side.

'I never thought you would take the émigré road,' she remarked. 'But I was wrong.'

'Don't be flippant.' De Choissy was annoyed.

Héloïse took a sip of tea.

'I was merely remarking that I considered you to be the last person to abandon your king, despite the fact you would like to pretend otherwise,' she said.

De Choissy got up from his chair.

'The king will die.'

'Are you sure of that?'

'Don't be a fool, Héloïse. You know what is happening. You have experienced the mob. I could accuse you of several things, but never of stupidity.'

Héloïse changed her tack.

'Where does your loyalty lie?' she asked, curious to know.

'Primarily to myself. And to you,' he added disconcertingly.

Héloïse raised her eyebrows.

'But, of course, Héloïse, my concerns lie with you.' De Choissy was impatient with her unspoken implication.

'Do you not consider it your duty to remain here as long as His Majesty is alive?' she asked.

De Choissy moved to the window.

'The king, my dear,' he said from over his shoulder, 'is a fool. And so is his very dear consort.'

'Perhaps,' Héloïse countered. 'But they are still entitled to your loyalty.'

De Choissy turned round to face her and leant back against the window-sill. His fingers played with the tassels that trimmed the drapes.

'Does it not occur to you', he said, 'that I can serve him just as well outside France?'

'Or yourself.'

Héloïse set down the tea-bowl on a black japanned tray on the table by the bed.

'And myself,' he acknowledged.

'Let me understand this correctly,' said Héloïse. 'Are you leaving France to serve the king better there, or to ensure your neck is saved?'

'Are you being deliberately obtuse, Héloïse?'

De Choissy moved over towards her. He bent over and grasped her face none too gently, forcing her to look up at him. Héloïse met his gaze, taking in his elegant suit and his handsome, dissipated countenance.

'Listen to me,' he said. 'The situation is worse, much worse. You know that. You have seen it and suffered. The old order is doomed. It vanished when the king left Versailles. The harpies of the new so-called republic can't wait to get their hands on people like you and me, and, let it be said, my dear, on our possessions. Strange things are happening to France. And we should take note of when the odds are stacked against us.'

'Spoken like a gambling man,' said Héloïse, removing herself from his grasp. 'Nevertheless, I shall not come with you.'

De Choissy sat down on a chair facing her.

'Now why?' he reflected, deceptively placid. 'What can possibly keep you when your duty lies with me?'

Héloïse lifted a blank face towards him.

'How can you understand?' she said.

His eyes narrowed and she wondered if she had gone too far. He was unpredictable and she was fighting on territory that was new to her. She wondered if he was enjoying this encounter. Whether it aroused the primitive streak of cruelty in him that she so often had cause to know. Was it unwise to provoke him into direct confrontation? After all, he was her husband and she knew he wouldn't hesitate to assert his rights over her.

'You may be right, Hervé,' she said smoothly, a little surprised at her own duplicity. 'But I do need time to rest. I shall go to Neuilly and, of course, you are welcome there. But the doctor did say . . .' She paused delicately. 'I would hate to think your journeys were in vain,' she finished.

De Choissy rose to his feet and smoothed down his tail-coat. He was not pleased.

'You have no need to worry, Héloïse. I have plenty of business to occupy me in Paris.'

He looked down at her, an odd little smile stretching his thin lips.

'Go to Neuilly to, er . . . rest. I shall allow you that. But not for long. The situation changes daily. As soon as you return, we shall go.'

While Héloïse was talking to de Choissy, Sophie was out riding with Ned for the first time since his sudden arrival back in Paris. She had avoided being alone with him purposely but, to do her justice, it had not been entirely her fault. There had been several visits from friends in Versailles, the marquis' funeral, condolence correspondence to answer on behalf of Héloïse, and Héloïse's illness had also occupied much of her time. Ned himself had ridden to Neuilly on an errand for Héloïse, and while there he had been taken ill. When he returned he had spent day after day trying to obtain visas to return to England. But now she could no longer avoid him. Nor should she.

The situation she now found herself in was so convoluted, and Sophie was so weary. Compared with their recent experiences, she knew her fears, and her subterfuges, to be shallow and unworthy and she understood it was time to abandon the luxuries of indecision. But the choices were difficult. Ned or William? England and all that she loved, or America and a country she did not know? It would have helped if she had been clearer as to her feelings for Mr Jones. Her heart told her she loved him – her unruly heart that leapt in anticipation of his visits and cherished the things that he said. But Sophie wasn't entirely convinced that her heart should be trusted. William came from a different country, and in order to marry him she would have to cut the ties that bound her to those whom she cared for most.

She lay racked with anxiety at nights, and rose the next morning fully determined to refuse William and to marry Ned, only to find as the day progressed that she couldn't actually bring herself to say the words. Ned had brought her messages from High Mullions. A blistering missive from Sir Brinsley which ordered her to return at once, and a tear-streaked document from her mother which gave her the greatest anguish of all.

'*Ma fille*,' it read. 'Come home. We can resolve things better when we see you. We cannot force you into a marriage that you do not want. Nor will we. But to marry without us approving the gentleman is neither wise nor right. You must come.'

On reading this, Sophie felt her cup was full. To humiliate Ned was a sour entry on her slate. To leave Héloïse at this point unthinkable. To say goodbye to William worse – but to ignore her duty at the express pain and disappointment of others was a burden that almost strangled her.

She found she could not even talk to William. Angry, but not surprised, by Ned's return, William had tried to understand, but he was preoccupied with his own work. Jacobin spies were everywhere, and counter-revolutionaries were forcing up the price of information by scattering money all over the city and thus undermining his own network. He had also received an overdue message from General Washington, ordering him to return to America as soon as he could put his affairs in order. The directive plunged him into anxiety. Leaving France was no easy matter and he was dubious as to how Sophie would react. The situation was certainly not helped by the presence of Ned. So he remained deliberately in the background while he considered his options, which upset Sophie even more.

How calm life at High Mullions now seemed compared to the treacherous quicksands that lay ahead. Sophie often reflected on just how far she had travelled. From an innocent girl to the woman she now considered herself to be, a woman, moreover, who had seen sights to depress the most optimistic. She had witnessed violence and death. She was no longer ignorant of complicated feelings. No longer so impetuous. She had been tried severely by what she saw as her own inconstancy and unable to resolve a situation that should have been simple to deal with. How was she to make sense of it all?

Thus it was with a heavy heart that she had consented to go riding with Ned after he had cornered her in the salon that morning and suggested a picnic outside the city walls. Sophie had agreed because she knew she must.

De Choissy had lent them his horses and his groom. The day was fair and, despite herself, Sophie felt her spirits rise as she swung up into the saddle. It had been a long time since she had been on such an expedition. She knew she was looking her best in one of Mlle Bertin's exquisitely cut riding habits which was trimmed with steel buttons. Perched on her head was a black high-crowned hat with a curving plume. Her gloves were made of the finest leather and her boots shone. Ned leaned over in his saddle and caught at her reins.

'Quite like old times, Sophie,' he remarked.

She removed the reins from his grasp.

'Thank you, Ned, but I can manage. Yes, it is, isn't it?'

They swung down the Rue de l'Université and the Rue Dominique, picked their way over the Champ de Mars and made for the *barrière* gate and the road which led south-west out of the city. The burning heat of summer had softened and there was a hint of autumn in the air. The leaves crunched underfoot and once outside the gate (a protracted negotiation which had taken all of Sophie's skill to conclude) there was an intoxicating feeling of freedom. The air was fresh and sweet and they urged their horses onward, galloping between farmhouses and vine fields and finally into a long, open meadow.

Shouting and laughing, their differences momentarily forgotten, they trotted over to a clump of trees and dismounted. Ned handed Sophie to the ground. She sat down on the rug that the groom had spread out and waited for Ned to open the hamper.

'Hurry up,' she said. 'I'm hungry.'

It was true, she felt hungrier than she had done for months. Ned watched her cut herself a piece of chicken and he drained a glass of wine. Paris lay before them and Sophie paused between mouthfuls, pulled back into the present, and wondered how anything so beautiful could house so much horror and sadness.

When she had finished, he spoke.

'Sophie, I want no more of this nonsense.'

Sophie set down her glass of wine. She did not have to ask what he meant.

'I have waited long enough,' he continued. 'And I now have the correct papers. Miss Edgeworth and I are in agreement. It is time to leave.'

Sophie raised an eyebrow.

'Miss Edgeworth? I wasn't aware she had discussed her views on the matter with you.'

'Of course she has.' Ned spoke impatiently. 'And don't get high and mighty with me. She is a sensible woman and she agrees that your adventure in France is over.'

'Leave Miss Edgeworth out of this, if you please.' Sophie was angry. 'I shall speak to her when we get back. Much as I admire and rely on her, this is not a matter for her.'

'You forget,' said Ned, leaning back on the rug. 'She is in Sir Brinsley's employ and must carry out his wishes.'

'*Ciel!*' said Sophie. 'So it is Miss Edgeworth who decides my affairs.'

Ned sat up. 'You are in danger of becoming impossible,' he said. 'It is not worthy of you.'

Sophie subsided, a little ashamed of her outburst.

'Now, listen, Sophie. You shall be made to see sense, if I have to beat it into you.'

Sophie shrugged, disliking his tone.

'Spare me your bullying, Ned. It does not become *you*.'

'Sophie. Do I have to spell it out to you? You are an unmarried woman. You don't have the right to set yourself up against your father's wishes. Nor, for that matter, mine. You must obey us.'

Sophie looked up at him and there was a great deal of pity in her eyes. Ned had spoken to her from another world, a world she believed she had left behind. She picked a daisy out of the grass and rolled it between her fingers. Suddenly she understood: it was no longer enough to be a dutiful daughter and wife. There had to be something more in her life. Sophie wanted the liberty to choose her own destiny. A key had turned in a door and she had arrived at a truth.

It would not be easy, and Sophie was aghast at her own daring, and not a little afraid. But it was quite clear to her that she could never surrender herself to a man such as Ned. The pieces of the jigsaw that had eluded her during the past few months now fell into place and she saw, at last, where all her worry and confusion had been leading.

'I shall not marry you, Ned,' she said quietly.

Ned put down his chicken leg.

'It's that man, isn't it?' He was furious and acid. 'He's seduced you. I should never have allowed you to remain in Paris. I thought perhaps if I left you alone you would come to your right mind, but I should have taken you away the minute I suspected . . .'

Sophie raised her hand to stem his tirade.

'Stop,' she said. 'It does you no good. I have not yet decided whether I will marry Mr Jones or not, but I have decided that I cannot marry you. I am deeply sorry.'

Ned got to his feet.

'If you marry him, Sophie, you will never see High Mullions again. I shall forbid you the place.'

Sophie leapt to her feet and seized Ned by the arm. He had touched on the spot where he knew it would hurt.

'You forget, sir, that you are not master of High Mullions until my father dies.' Her anger spurted up. I will go back if I wish. I will be returning in the spring. My father will receive me, I know. If I am still there when he dies, then well and good. But until that day you have no power to say such things.'

Ned had put on a little weight over the past year and he looked older and more careworn. He was frowning with the effort to control himself. Her anger faded and she hated herself for the hurt she knew she was causing him. Ned grasped her by the shoulders. Sophie recoiled, but forced herself to look into his eyes.

'I think you're lying to me about Mr Jones,' he said, 'and I'm astounded by your treachery.'

Sophie flinched.

'Harsh words will not make me change my mind,' she replied. 'But I own you have a perfect right to be angry.'

Ned wanted to shake her.

'I am trying to make you understand what you are doing,' he said, modifying his tone. 'You are throwing away your future and your reputation for a whim – a stupid notion that has fixed itself in your head.'

'Ned, I am quite able to make my own decisions.'

'You don't have the right, Sophie,' he flung back at her. He paused. 'Do you know what this Mr Jones does?'

'Of course I do.'

'Well, you don't,' Ned said, taking his time.

Sophie's heart contracted. Ned obviously knew something she didn't. He searched in his pocket and produced a packet.

'This, my dear girl, is what your Mr Jones really does. He is nothing more or less than a common spy,' he said, holding the packet in front of her. A magpie flew out of the trees directly in front of her. Sophie observed it while the ground appeared to shift under her feet. She took the packet from him.

'I don't believe you.'

'Read it,' said Ned. 'On second thoughts, you won't be able to, the papers are written in some kind of code. But I have. From what I can make out they are written to his government and appear to give details of naval fortifications and financial transactions in the Ministry of Foreign Affairs. Now, what have those to do with a land agent? Mr Jones, it would seem, has a secret life.'

'How did you get hold of them?'

Sophie held the documents by her fingertips.

'It doesn't matter,' said Ned impatiently.

Sophie threw them back at Ned.

'Take them,' she said. But a pit had opened up in her heart. William a spy. A man with a double life. The thought was unbearable. A spy was someone who lied and pretended. A spy was also not to be trusted. And she valued trust and honesty.

But even as the thoughts raced through her mind the doubts

252

began to make themselves heard. William was always so well informed. Who was that odd man at White's Hotel? How had he known about the *Marseillaise* being sung in Brussels?

'It *isn't* true,' she whispered, willing herself not to believe it.

'But it is,' said Ned, stooping to pick up the packet. 'The proof is here.'

Sickened by his expression, Sophie turned away.

'How dare you come to me with this?' she said scornfully. 'I thought better of you.'

In contrast to the shadows that lay between them, the sun continued to shine down into the meadow.

'Sophie. I have not . . .' Ned had the grace to look at his feet. 'I have not always treated you well. I know that. But that is in the past. I feel differently now. I cannot permit you to make this mistake. Come home with me and we can forget all this.'

She looked at the man who had so often occupied her thoughts, at the strong body which was already coarsening, brown hair and wide mouth that was smiling defensively – and realised that they no longer possessed any power to move her.

'I can't pretend what you have told me is no longer welcome,' she said. 'But it does not in any way alter my decision not to marry you.'

Goaded beyond reason, Ned pulled her to him.

'Indeed?' he said, and began to kiss her. His tongue filled her mouth and his body pressed hard against hers. Sophie drew back, gasping at the intimacy.

'You are making a mistake,' he said. 'Remember that I was willing to marry you, despite your flirtation.'

Sophie shook herself free and bent to pick up her crop.

'That is almost the stupidest thing you have said, Ned,' she said, in a shaking voice. 'Though I thank you for the sentiment. When I am a careworn old maid – if I am – then I shall remind myself of it.'

'Sophie.' Ned realised that his anger had allowed him to go too far. 'Please think again.'

To her horror, she saw that there were tears in his eyes.

'Please don't speak to me again,' she said, wanting only to have done with this encounter.

Ned was silent.

'Then, don't ever come back begging for forgiveness,' he said finally. 'Because you won't get it, and I meant what I said about High Mullions.'

'So be it,' replied Sophie. 'I think you will find I am as resolute as you.'

She led the way across the meadow and to the waiting groom.

Without addressing a word further to each other, they rode back into the city.

Two days later, Ned left Paris for the last time and took a protesting Miss Edgeworth with him. Sophie felt she had no choice but to let her governess go, and she bade her farewell with more than a few tears. To Ned she said nothing, fearful that her guilt and her confusion would betray her. Nevertheless it was with a heavy heart that she watched the equipage draw out from the courtyard from behind a window, and raised her hand to them in silent farewell.

Chapter 16

Pierre, September 20th, 1792

Pierre lay looking up at the darkening sky, which was strange because it was not long after one o'clock. Around him the noise of battle went on and on – the thunder and whistle of bullets, the sudden silences and the sound of cannon hitting soft ground. And the screams that always came afterwards.

It was hot and dry. Above him the forms of his fellow soldiers wavered at him through a shimmering mist and the grass was stained red and black. Pierre tried to move and failed. This was the second time he had tried. The first time he had put it down to the shock of being thrown to the earth after a cannon ball had scythed its way through the French ranks quite close to where he stood. This time he understood what was wrong, and he bit his lip in anger and despair.

But it was no use wasting these minutes in useless emotion. He had to think. What was happening to the battle? He remembered a force of 82,000 Frenchmen facing 131,000 men of the royalist and imperial armies under the command of the Duke of Brunswick. He remembered how someone had called out 'Long live the nation' and how the French had sung *Ça ira*. He remembered the French centre of operations had formed the apex of a right angle, just by the village of Valmy's windmill. It was there that Pierre had felt a strange displacement of air and a hot, rushing wind before the earth had swung up to meet him.

One of his mates bent over him.

'Keep going, *mon vieux*, we're chasing the buggers off the field.'

Pierre's fingers scrabbled at the front of his tunic.

'Can you do something for me?'

His friend understood and reached inside Pierre's shirt and pulled out a folded piece of paper.

'Send it,' Pierre whispered, his breath labouring. 'My dying wish.'

The face above him nodded.

'Of course. I must go. Good luck.'

Pierre was left with the sensation of wool binding his limbs and cloaking his brain. He wanted Marie-Victoire, so he tried to summon her picture up in his mind – a pair of gold-flecked eyes, a rounded shoulder, long brown hair streaming down a white back – but it was no good. She was sinking further and further away, and he couldn't chase her.

A sob rose to his lips. He could feel his blood seeping out of the huge wound in his back and out of the jagged gash in his leg. Was it so very wonderful, he reflected, as it trickled down his leg, to die for an ideal? Slowly the haze in front of his eyes grew darker. The heat sucked at him, and his legs stiffened.

At last the sky grew black. Pierre sighed once and lay still.

PART THREE

The Terror
January–September 1793

PARIS, January 1793

On January 21st, the king was woken at five o'clock. Already the drums were sounding in the cold dawn. He dressed, heard Mass and walked out to his carriage.

It was a long journey to the guillotine and it was not until half-past nine that the procession inched its way into the Place Louis XV, now renamed the Place de la Révolution.

The king got out of his carriage, allowed his captors to cut his hair and removed his brown greatcoat. Guards tied his hands behind his back, and Louis mounted the scaffold. He tried to address his people, but the drummers prevented his words from being heard. All too quickly, he was hustled to the plank of the guillotine and the great blade came down.

A hush seemed to grip the city, impressing those waiting to enter outside the closed **barrière** gates. It seemed that, for a moment, Paris stood still. Then in the Place de la Révolution the crowd rushed forward. They threw their hats into the air, screamed their joy and fought to dip their handkerchiefs into the blood.

France was without a king.

Chapter 1

Marie-Victoire, January 1793

Marie-Victoire shifted from one foot to the other. The wind was bitterly cold and whipped among her skirts and through the folds of her shawl. She was tired too, and her legs ached, and there was a pain in her belly just where the child sat heaviest. She could feel it kicking inside her with the abandon of someone who is warm and fed. 'Trust it to wake up now,' she muttered, for she had hours of waiting still to endure. The queue outside the baker's snaked down the street, and the women who waited in it were sullen. Each one had staked out their place and anyone who tried to jump the queue was harangued by wives and mothers driven to despair by the prospect of hungry faces at home. The bread queues were a daily sight and Marie-Victoire was finding that she needed to leave her shop for longer and longer periods each day in order to obtain her ration. Not that it mattered, she thought miserably, the shop was not prospering and, after Pierre had left, her interest in it had dwindled.

For the thousandth time that week Marie-Victoire wondered where Pierre was. If he were alive, and if he would come back. She had received only one letter from him, which she kept under her pillow and read every day. She had heard nothing else except for gossip on the streets – the French armies were on the run, they had won a great victory, the troops were deserting. The rumours varied and she had found them confusing, bringing her hope one minute, despair the next.

Marie-Victoire fingered her dog-eared ration card proclaiming her entitlement to just two pounds of bread, and then pocketed it when she saw a tough-looking young woman next to her eyeing it. She cupped her hands round her belly in the familiar gesture of pregnant women and rubbed where it ached. The bread queue was a long way from the time when she had walked so blithely from the Hôtel de Choissy, determined to make her way with Pierre. A long, long way. And for what? It had all been so much harder than even her worst fears. Nobody had any money, certainly not in the Cordeliers. People wanted to sell their possessions in order to buy firewood, flour and sugar, and if they came into the shop it was to persuade her to buy yet another pair of stockings, or a chemise, or an apron. Without Pierre's careful counselling, Marie-Victoire had used up her money, including her emergency hoard from Héloïse, and her pride wouldn't let her apply to Héloïse for more. She had begun to understand a certain look on some women's faces. A look that spoke of vanishing hope and bodily exhaustion. Marie-Victoire had never imagined that she would be the same. But now she was.

'When will it be born?'

The young woman who had eyed her earlier spoke with genuine interest.

'In the spring, I think,' replied Marie-Victoire, grateful for the chance to talk.

'One more mouth to feed, is it?'

'No, this is the first.' And the last, she added to herself.

'I have four. Borne seven, though,' said the woman.

Marie-Victoire looked at her curiously.

'So many,' she said. 'Does your husband have work?'

'Him!' The woman snorted. 'He's gone. Didn't fancy having so many children to feed. Fucked himself silly and didn't like what came of it. I should have known.'

'How do you manage?' asked Marie-Victoire, a chill running through her.

'The usual way, *ma fillette*. Two sous against the wall, five lying down. Anywhere and everywhere, Jeanne will give you good value.'

She made a coarse gesture and hitched up her skirts to display a pair of surprisingly good legs. At that point, the queue moved forward and Marie-Victoire found herself clinging to Jeanne for support.

'Here, lean on me,' said Jeanne, 'I'll look after you.'

By the time they had obtained their loaves of coarse, lumpy bread and accused the baker of hoarding the best, a friendship had developed. Clutching their precious ration, they left the shop together, talking hard. Marie-Victoire found herself thawing. It had been such a long time since she had engaged in anything so simple and satisfying as a gossip. Jeanne was happy to impart her knowledge of the area, and was prodigal with bits of information that Marie-Victoire stored up for future use. At the junction of the Rue St Benoît and the Rue des Sts Pères, they stopped.

'Can I come and visit you sometimes?' Marie-Victoire asked diffidently. 'I would like to see your children.'

'If you like,' said Jeanne carelessly, but she looked as though the idea pleased her.

Considerably cheered, Marie-Victoire returned home. But soon the silence and loneliness claimed her again and she found herself slipping back into a semi-comatose state from which it was impossible to rouse herself. At nights, though, she would lie sleepless, trying to forget the feel of Pierre's warm back and the sound of his breathing, only to rise wearily in the morning to fetch wood and water. These were things that she had to do, but as her body grew heavier and her mind duller, Marie-Victoire found them harder and harder. There were days when she did not bother to open the shop, but lay on her mattress, fingering her rosary and gazing at the ceiling. From time to time she heard the tocsin pealing and her curiosity flickered briefly.

The price of food rose and then, as a cold spell gripped the country, spiralled. Violence in the streets became commonplace and Marie-Victoire never went out after dark – not that she wanted to. She took less and less interest in what she ate or wore and had to force herself to queue for bread. Sometimes her state of mind worried her, but not even the thought of Pierre's disapproval was sufficient to jolt her back into activity. She was cold, always cold, and the baby bothered her.

'After it is born,' she promised herself, 'it will be better.'

One day in late January she was lying as usual on her mattress, wondering if, after all, she should return to the Hôtel de Choissy and throw herself on Héloïse's mercy. Darkness was already setting in. It was freezing and the footsteps outside in the street rang on the cobbles. She had no more rushlights or wood for the fire. She contemplated going out to beg for food since she had not eaten all day, or the day before, but she felt sick at the thought. Her back was aching and her feet were like blocks of ice. She eased herself on to her side and wished that she was dead.

There was a knock on the door. Marie-Victoire sat up. The knock was repeated. She dragged herself upright, flung her shawl round her shoulders and went over to the door.

'Who's there?'

'Jeanne.'

Marie-Victoire opened the door. Puffs of dust rose in the draught. Hugging her shawl tightly around her, Jeanne walked in.

'I thought I would see how you were doing. I haven't seen you around.'

Marie-Victoire shrugged and, to her shame, tears began to trickle down her cheeks.

'Here, let's look at you.'

Jeanne swung her round to the light and stared at her.

'You seem poorly.'

'I feel it,' Marie-Victoire admitted.

'You're not starting?'

'I don't know. My back is hurting and I'm losing.'

'Ah, well,' said Jeanne knowledgeably. 'I should think you are.'

Marie-Victoire wiped her tears with a grubby hand. The arrival of Jeanne had made her feel better.

'I think there is half a bottle of beer somewhere,' she said.

'Let's drink it,' said Jeanne, hunting on the shelf. 'It's a good thing I decided to look you up. Is there any news of your man?'

'None.'

Marie-Victoire's desolate voice made Jeanne pause in her search. She could remember, just, what it was like to feel like that. Pity made her brisk.

'Come on, then, down with it.'

She poured the beer into a cup and gave it to Marie-Victoire.

'Looks flat to me, but it will do.'

After her first swallow, Marie-Victoire knew that she was going to be sick. She set down the cup and stumbled to the door and retched. Suddenly, she felt moisture gush down her legs. She clung to the doorpost and clutched at her belly.

'*Dieu*,' she gasped as a pain cramped her muscles.

She allowed Jeanne to guide her over to her mattress and to lie her down. Jeanne flipped back Marie-Victoire's skirts and ran her hands over the swollen body. Marie-Victoire moaned. The pain came down again, enfolding her into a private world, and Jeanne was blotted out.

Some time later Marie-Victoire raised herself on to her elbow. Jeanne was sitting at the end of the mattress watching her. To her surprise, the room was growing light.

'How long?' she managed to whisper.

'You've been at it some time,' replied Jeanne. 'But you've got a little way to go yet.'

Marie-Victoire slumped back and closed her eyes.

'It was good of you to stay,' she muttered through her raw lips. 'What about your children?'

Jeanne laughed. 'They are used to looking after themselves.'

The agony began again as Marie-Victoire's body laboured to relieve itself of its burden. At the moments when she felt she could take no more, her body relaxed, and her mind wandered through the woods and fields that Pierre had told her about in his letter, trying to find him. But before she could do so an iron band tightened once more round her stomach and Pierre would disappear.

'Pierre,' she pleaded. 'Come back.'

A little later she screamed. Jeanne busied herself between Marie-Victoire's legs and, to the sound of her mother's distress, Marie-Victoire's daughter fought her way into the world on to a crumpled heap of sheets. She lay there with her tiny mouth open, as if registering surprise at her arrival, while Jeanne cut the cord and wrapped the baby in a torn-up shift. Then she placed the baby in her mother's arms.

Marie-Victoire peered down uncertainly, and quite suddenly the pain was only a memory. Peace stole through her battered body – a calm so perfect, so profound and so joyous that she never forgot it. The baby mewed, flicked her big, blue eyes open for a moment and settled back into her mother's arms. Her tiny, still bloody crown peeped out of the wrappings and Marie-Victoire lifted her free hand and stroked it gently.

Jeanne scooped up the afterbirth, wrapped it in a piece of sacking and took it away. Next she attempted to straighten the sheets and rub away the stains. She went out into the street and returned with a fresh pitcher of water, and proceeded to bathe Marie-Victoire's face and thighs with a rag.

'I ought to bind your stomach,' she remarked as she worked, 'but I am too tired.'

Marie-Victoire looked up and saw how weary her friend looked. Jeanne's hair had tumbled out from under her dirty cap and her skirts were stained.

'You have done enough,' she said gratefully. 'How can I ever thank you?'

'Don't,' said Jeanne. 'I'll call on you one day.'

She dipped a crust of bread which she had found in her pocket into the water and held it to Marie-Victoire's lips.

'Eat,' she commanded. 'Then feed the baby.'

Marie-Victoire obeyed. She placed the baby to her breast and, after a moment, felt the first tug at her nipple. The baby sucked sleepily at first and then with increasing urgency, and Marie-Victoire gave herself up to these new sensations with a dawning wonder and delight.

'What will you call her?' asked Jeanne, bending over to look more closely.

'Marie, after my mother,' replied Marie-Victoire, tracing the curve of the baby's chin with her finger.

'Marie it is, then,' said Jeanne. 'Now I must go. Will you be all right?'

Marie-Victoire watched Jeanne let herself out and resumed contemplating her daughter. She remained like that for some time, before falling into a deep sleep, still clasping Marie.

Marie-Victoire was never again to feel the rapture of that moment when she fell in love with her baby. Lack of food and warmth drained her already depleted body, her nipples were sucked raw, and she worked herself up into a pitch of anxiety over Marie who was always hungry and restless. Tired as she had been before the birth, she was doubly so afterwards. And never had she been so alone as on those endless freezing nights, when she dragged herself upright to nurse a hungry Marie.

By the time Marie was a month old, Marie-Victoire had plunged, once again, into a deep depression. It was only by the greatest effort of will that she forced herself to take care of the baby. That much did register in her mind, but all other considerations disappeared. Once again, Jeanne came to the rescue and whisked Marie away to her minute room on the Rue St Benoît, where she was welcomed by Jeanne's children and began to thrive. When Marie-Victoire felt better, thanks largely to Jeanne's good-natured bullying and practical help, she often wondered why she had chosen to befriend her so thoroughly.

But she was too grateful to protest. Instead she took a coin she had discovered knotted into her skirt hem, slipped into the nearest church and lit a candle in front of the Virgin. She felt guilty about it, knowing she needed the money and that Pierre would have disapproved, but she wanted to make this gesture in recognition of her safe delivery. Besides, she felt different. Becoming a mother had changed her. She could not explain how exactly. Perhaps it was something to do with understanding a different kind of love. Perhaps it was a greater reverence for life. Perhaps, now that her health was restored, it was a renewed desire to cling on to it. But she wanted to tell the Virgin that she understood the blessedness of giving birth, and was grateful. Reassuring and serene, the Virgin's painted face shone into the incense-laden gloom of the church and Marie-Victoire knelt at her feet for a long time and felt at peace.

She thought of Pierre less each day. He belonged to another part of her life that was over now, rather like La Joyeuse and, as she hoped, Jacques Maillard. It did not mean that she had forgotten Pierre, or that she did not long for him to return, only that the first tearing sense of loss had faded into a dull ache. Marie-Victoire told herself it was for the best: she could no longer afford to suffer so intensely for someone who wasn't there. Life was too hard, and she must concentrate on finding food and work.

In desperation, Marie-Victoire packed up the remaining stock in the shop – a roll of material (slightly waterstained), a pair of brass candlesticks, gloves, a shawl, a pair of torn stockings embroidered with clocks, two chemises and a serviceable leather travelling case with most of its contents intact – and on Jeanne's instructions carried them down the street to a certain Monsieur Quivebeck. There she stammered out her request.

Monsieur Quivebeck was not overly anxious to help her. He had other, more lucrative business to attend to. In the end, however, he could not resist the appeal of her worn but still pretty face. Sighing deeply, he took the things and told her that she was never to mention anything of what passed between them. He told her to sit on a bench. Marie-Victoire did as he asked and listened to Monsieur Quivebeck issue a stream of orders through a leather curtain. Shortly afterwards, he dived through the curtain and disappeared.

After an hour, he reappeared. He thrust a ration card and some coins into Marie-Victoire's hands.

'Here, it isn't much, but you didn't have much. I have taken most of it in payment for the card.'

Marie-Victoire clutched at them and tried to thank him, but he made haste to show her out as quickly as possible. She examined the card outside, hardly daring to believe her luck. The forgery was excellent. Made out in the name of Citoyenne Bonnard, the card entitled her to an additional ration of bread, a whole two-pound loaf extra. Trembling with excitement, she tucked it into her pocket and went into the street, almost bumping into a tall, heavily veiled woman who was hurrying into Monsieur Quivebeck's house. Marie-Victoire heard the discreet clink of money and saw the flash of a diamond ring before she carried on, her eyes averted.

It was Jeanne who solved the problem of work. She arrived at the shop one day in March. The place was in a mess. Marie-Victoire's once clean floor and windows were filthy and her belongings scattered everywhere, but she never seemed to have time to put them right. She indicated a stool by the wall and told Jeanne to push the clothes on to the floor. Jeanne's eyes sparkled.

'I've found you a situation,' she announced.

Marie-Victoire looked up from her suckling and lifted a sleepy Marie on to her shoulder to wind her.

'Shush,' she said, 'I think she might be going to sleep.'

'Listen, you wooden head. I have found work for you.'

Marie-Victoire tucked a shawl round the baby and settled her in the cardboard box that did as a cradle.

'Where?' she asked.

'At Monsieur Danton's.'

Marie-Victoire whirled round, and her jaw dropped open. Everyone had heard of Monsieur Danton, and indeed few who lived in the close-knit community could have failed to have seen him or to have heard his booming voice in the Cour de Commerce.

'You will give up this place,' said Jeanne with decision, 'and live with me. I'll mind the baby in the day and you can look after my children at night when I go out.'

She chuckled coarsely and winked. Marie-Victoire regarded her friend for a moment and then went over to the stool and kissed her on the forehead.

'Thank you,' she said simply.

Jeanne said nothing, but she blushed and looked distinctly gratified.

So Marie-Victoire packed up her few possessions, including the pamphlets that Pierre had given her so long ago, and locked the room for the last time in the Rue des Sts Pères. Holding Marie tight to her bosom, she deposited the key with the old lady who lived opposite, with strict instructions for her to pass on her new address in the Rue St Benoît should a soldier ask for her. Then she walked down the streets towards the peeling stone house that was to be her new home. She had not, deliberately, allowed herself time to consider that she was taking a step backwards. That her dream of independence was as far away as ever. Somehow, it did not matter so much any more. What mattered was Marie and keeping alive.

The Dantons lived in a house situated in the heart of the Cordeliers in the Cour de Commerce. Marie-Victoire passed through an entresol, up a stone staircase and found herself outside a pair of doors. She had no idea what lay ahead of her.

A diminutive maid answered her knock and ushered her into a good-sized anteroom which was furnished with two walnut cupboards, a table desk and a mahogany chiffonier. Beyond that was the salon where the windows, draped in cotton, overlooked the street. Marie-Victoire could see an elegant arabesque wallpaper pasted on to canvas, two fine mirrors and a console-table. At the far end of the room was a sofa upholstered in straw silk, six armchairs covered in green satin and a number of lyre-back chairs with straw seats. Later, she was to get to know the bedroom containing two low beds, hidden by yellow curtains, and Danton's study containing a large polished desk with copper fittings and an enormous number of books which overflowed the shelves.

Madame Danton received Marie-Victoire in the main salon. She was heavily pregnant and obviously ill and distraught. Monsieur Danton, she informed Marie-Victoire, was away in Belgium on government business. She herself, she said, twisting her chatelaine round her large, square hands, she was waiting to be confined and required someone to take on some of her household duties while she was incapacitated. Marie-Victoire nodded, her compassion stirred by the sight of this sad and nervous lady, and she agreed to help out as a personal maid for as long as madame wished. Gabrielle Danton's mouth twitched into a smile and Marie-Victoire fancied that she relaxed a little. She followed her new employer down to the kitchen.

The kitchen was ruled over by Marie and Katherine, two friendly-looking young women. It was admirably stocked and maintained, and a delicious smell of beef stew wafted out from a pot suspended over the fire. If nothing else, Madame Danton appeared to be an excellent housekeeper. The girls welcomed Marie-Victoire and proceeded to regale her with titbits from what promised to be a fund of gossip.

Through them, Marie-Victoire learned that Monsieur Danton was a devil (but an exciting one), that he liked his home comforts, that he neglected his wife (indeed, the rumours of his womanising were all over Paris), that madame was pining and feared this coming child would kill her and that she often spent the night sobbing alone in her bedroom. Marie-Victoire listened and exclaimed at appropriate intervals, secretly relieved that Danton was away from home.

'Do they have many visitors?' she asked at last, for want of something to say. Katherine sharpened her knife on a whetstone.

'Endless,' she confirmed. 'Madame has to give dinner at least once a week and the talk goes on and on.' She lowered her voice. 'Politics, you know. It bores me and I don't understand it. Still, we have the work and madame is a good mistress – poor thing.'

She wiped her hand over her forehead and her peasant face shone with good humour. She slapped a chicken down on a board and gutted it with enthusiasm.

'You'll like it here,' she told Marie-Victoire. 'They treat you well.' She went over to the pot on the stove and lifted the lid. Marie-Victoire's stomach rumbled. 'Here,' said Katherine kindly. 'Have some of this,' and she shoved a plateful of beef stew towards Marie-Victoire, who did not have to be asked twice.

At first, she was unhappy. She missed the baby more than

he had imagined. Marie-Victoire had grown used to being with her and to attending to her every whimper. She worried, too, that Marie missed her. Mutinous at the change in routine, her breasts ached and a tell-tale stain spurted on to the front of her own whenever she thought too hard about her. At the end of each day, when she got back to the Rue St Benoît, Marie-Victoire would snatch up her daughter, rip open her bodice, and then both of them would settle back with a contented sigh.

Jeanne offered no comment, except to remark that Marie was fine and did not appear to miss her mother at all. Half of Marie-Victoire did not want to believe Jeanne, and she had to stifle an occasional pang of jealousy. It was for the best, she told herself firmly, and, gradually, she came to believe it.

If Marie-Victoire was truthful, she enjoyed being back in a well-run household among nice furniture and pretty objects. Her work was not onerous and Madame Danton was a gentle and undemanding mistress. Much of Marie-Victoire's day was taken up by ministering to her ills and helping her through the last stages of a difficult pregnancy. Once that was done, she was free to arrange her time as she pleased. There was plenty to do and she began, once more, to take pride in her work.

'Eh bien,' she said, as she dusted the china that was arranged on the table in the salon. 'It could be worse.'

She gazed thoughtfully at her reflection in one of the mirrors. Except for her full and milky breasts, she was slimmer than she used to be, but not unpleasingly so. The haunted look on her face had disappeared, and, thanks to helpings of Katherine's stews, she looked clear skinned and well fed. True, her face was thinner, but it suited her. The girl from La Joyeuse had gone. In her place stood a woman.

Marie-Victoire tucked a stray strand of hair under her cap, then decided it looked too severe and pulled it back again. That was better. She twirled and peered over her shoulder at her back view. The effect was not so pleasing. Her skirts were rumpled and there was a large black stain by the hem. She was so busy trying to remove it that she did not hear the front door slam or the salon door open. When she did look up, her hand was arrested in mid-air.

He was lounging against the door frame, smiling the smile she knew so well and had hoped never to see again. His face was almost skeletal and the brown eyes shone with a mad light. He looked like a man eaten up by hatred and by obsession. All trace of humour and compassion had gone and in their place burned the determination and single-mindness of a zealot. Here was someone who had tasted blood and would not be satisfied until

he had tasted more. Marie-Victoire crossed herself and began
back away, her hand over her mouth.

'No,' she said disbelieving. 'No.'

Maillard pushed himself upright. As surprised as she was
the encounter, he was in no hurry. This was the moment he ha
waited for, and he had every intention of savouring it to the fu
Besides, he enjoyed seeing the fear on her face, it gave hi
confidence and the feeling that he was in control. He had grow
accustomed to fear in his presence. In fact, he relied on it;
offered him as much nourishment as his daily meals. More. Th
time, Marie-Victoire would not escape.

'What are you doing here?' she faltered.

'I came with a message for Citoyenne Danton from Citoye
Robespierre,' he replied. 'Little did I think I would kill two bir
with one stone.' He held out a hand which she ignored. 'Come
he said, 'I have been thinking about you a lot. I have been bus
lately, but a friend of mine told me where you're living and
knew you were working in the area, so it was only a matter
time. Did you really think you had given me the slip?'

Marie-Victoire's mouth was dry. 'You devil,' she said.

'Perhaps,' he said, 'but a faithful one. You are mine, Mari
Victoire. I had you first, remember?'

'How could I not?'

'I have been very patient, Marie-Victoire, and now that I ha
found you, I think the time has come for action.'

'You have no power over me,' she cried.

'But I have. I have a great deal of power. I am not the Jacqu
you flung aside any longer. I have friends in high places and
reputation for getting my way.'

He indicated the tricolour sash that was slung across his she
coat and tapped a finger against his lips in a gesture that w
almost obscene.

'I have an apartment on the Rue St Honoré quite close to whe
Citoyen Robespierre lives. It is waiting for a mistress. I did t
you that I wanted you to come.'

Marie-Victoire shook her head violently. 'Never'.

Maillard took a step towards her and she shrank back agair
the console-table.

'Go away,' she panted. 'A *foutre* on you.'

He continued to move towards her until his body pressed u
against hers. She could feel his warmth and smell the garlic ar
tobacco on his breath.

'You will never say that to me again,' he warned.

'A *foutre*,' she spat at him.

His face tightened and Marie-Victoire tensed, waiting for tl blow to fall. It never came. Instead he released her and flung himself down in one of the chairs.

'I don't think you understand.' Jacques was quite calm now. 'You will be coming with me because, if you don't, you will be putting others at risk.'

She looked bewildered and Maillard laughed.

'Where have you been all this time, Marie-Victoire? Have you not seen what is happening? Think, my pretty. You are living with Jeanne *la putain* are you not? An immoral woman. You used to be in the employ of one Citoyenne de Choissy, known to me as Héloïse de Guinot. Citoyen de Choissy, her husband, is not known for his republican views.'

He laughed again, and Marie-Victoire found herself clutching the table with enough force to mark it.

'Citoyen de Choissy has been greedy, like all of his kind. He has tried to transfer his money out of the country. A mistake. Luckily, the matter has not been investigated by the authorities – yet. But it is only a matter of time . . . unless . . . unless I forget to put the case in front of them. Equally, your friend Jeanne could find that the authorities take exception to her activities and decide that prison is the place for someone like her. Do you understand what I am saying?'

Marie-Victoire pressed her hands to her ears.

'What has happened to you, Jacques?' she asked. 'How can you say such things?'

Maillard rose to his feet and seized her by the waist.

'You did,' he said hoarsely. 'You did when you left me like a dog in a ditch. I knew then that the world had no mercy unless you were bigger and stronger than everybody else. I learned that if you don't take where you can, then you have nothing. I want to take as much as I can from *canaille* like the de Guinots and I want to make you suffer for leaving me.'

'And if I don't come?'

'Do I have to spell it out?'

Marie-Victoire wrested herself from his grasp. She thought of Héloïse and Jeanne. Surely she did not owe them this sacrifice? Marie-Victoire looked down at her hands, then up at Maillard, remembering Héloïse's concern for her welfare and Jeanne's tired, kind face, and she knew she could never repay them in this manner. She could never be responsible for another's danger. It was no use finding her own way, if it was at a price that would haunt her for the rest of her life.

Before she could say anything, a bell jangled in Madame Danton's room. There was a sound of running feet and a scream rang through the apartment.

Marie-Victoire started.

'It's madame,' she said. 'I must go. The baby.'

Maillard caught at her sleeve and held it tight.

'No, you don't,' he said. 'I want an answer.'

She tried to pull herself free.

'Yes or no, Marie-Victoire?'

'Do I have any choice?' she asked desperately.

'None.'

'God in heaven,' she whispered.

Maillard tightened his grip until her body was jammed against his. His fingers bore into her flesh and she felt the bruises sprout under his touch. With a cry, she ceased struggling and allowed him to place a hand under her elbow. To the sound of Madame Danton's moans, Maillard hustled her through the door and out of the house.

Chapter 2

Neuilly, January 1793

'My dear boy, it is not that much to ask,' remarked the Comte de Choissy as he descended the curving staircase at the Hôtel de Choissy. 'After all, you have been my guest and will continue to be so when you accompany madame my wife and Miss Luttrell to Neuilly . . .'

'Of course,' said William, 'what you say is true, and in normal circumstances I would be the first to offer. But I cannot afford to risk anything just at the moment.'

De Choissy sighed.

'And I had grown to count on you,' he said, with more than a hint of sharpness. 'As a friend and as a businessman.'

His words stung William, and it pricked his pride to consider that he was allowing himself to fall beneath his standards of honour and friendship. But it had to be. De Choissy was dangerous, both for what he was and for the clever business speculations that William suspected that the count and his friends were engaged in. It would be an act of foolhardiness to consent to de Choissy's request to smuggle money and bonds to London en route for America – even if William could arrange it. It was not that William disapproved of de Choissy's complicated financial transactions, or his desire to safeguard his wealth. If he had been rich, he would have done exactly the same. The count was not alone. Most of the rich were either speculating or secretly transferring what they could salvage of their fortunes into sympathetic banks in Germany and Switzerland. William suspected, in fact he knew, that de Choissy was using his money to fund counter-revolutionary activities in ways that the American government would be fascinated to read about when they received his report. Not that William actually named the count – that would be taking his duties too far.

Transmitting information across the Atlantic had become more and more dangerous. William's carefully planned postal drops

were vulnerable, and his spy network liable to penetration b
informers and revolutionaries, and he dared not put too muc
detail into his reports in case they fell into the wrong hands. Th
situation was delicate and it was volatile, and required the utmos
discretion. William was determined not to stack the odds again
Sophie's safety. Or his own.

It worried him that he had never found the packet he had lo
on the day Sophie fainted. The packet had contained a great de.
of information and a list of names, including that of the Chevalie
Floyd. William had not seen the chevalier since their encounte
at White's Hotel, but he had heard a snippet of gossip from a
agent operating in the Ministry for War which indicated that th
chevalier had not forgotten the incident. The authorities in th
commune would be delighted to obtain such a prize documen
as William's report, if indeed it had fallen into their hands, an
if the chevalier had also carried out his threat and bandied hi
name about in the Hôtel de Ville, then William was doubly a
risk. He went over and over how he could have been so inep
as to have lost it, and prayed that it had fallen into the Rive
Seine.

De Choissy showed him out of the door into the courtyard.

'Monsieur le Comte,' he began, and then stopped, appalle
by the coldness in de Choissy's eyes. 'Monsieur le Comte, if th
price of your hospitality is this, then I fear I must decline makin
further use of you . . .'

He never finished his sentence, for de Choissy took hi
arm and hustled him to one side, out of earshot of the waitin
coach.

'Listen to me, *mon cher*. You will be so good as to do what
ask. Others are depending on you, and I need hardly say wh
they are.'

William stared at him, suddenly suspicious of how much th
count knew.

'If it is money that you want' – de Choissy spoke with all th
arrogance of his class, and William flushed – 'there is plenty. Bu
I urge you to think clearly about the political situation and to as
yourself, American though you are, if France is on the right road
and to consider in the light of that whether your skin is s
precious. There are reasons why I wish to do this, and I will no
bore you with the details, but they are good ones, my friend
Once you have accomplished your task you need never think (
it again.'

William pulled on his gloves. The count was very insisten
and he did, in truth, owe him much. But he owed Sophie more

'William, I beg you to do this for me.'

William glanced up. All trace of de Choissy's sarcasm had deserted him and he was in deadly earnest. William hesitated, torn between prudence, professional considerations and his better nature. De Choissy sensed his advantage.

'You will do it?'

William bowed.

'Let us say, Hervé, that I will return to Paris as soon as I need to make arrangements. We will then discuss the matter further,' he replied, hoping that it would never come to that point.

'*Bien*.' There was no mistaking the relief in the count's voice. 'I would as lief use you as anybody.'

He took a pinch of snuff and inhaled it. The two men stared at each other.

'Now for the ladies,' the count said at last, as if nothing had passed between them. He peered in through the coach door. 'I trust you have everything, my dears,' he said.

Wrapped in a sable rug, Sophie and Héloïse nodded simultaneously. Sophie held out her hand.

'Goodbye, Monsieur le Comte,' she said, and gave him her hand to kiss. De Choissy patted it. Sophie had been very quiet since the recent departure of Ned, and her high spirits had quite gone.

'You must rest at Neuilly,' he said with his smooth good manners, but his eyes veered past her to his wife. 'Goodbye, madame,' he said. 'We will meet again soon.'

Héloïse gave him her hand and he kissed it. It trembled a little in his grasp, but she permitted him to hold it for a little while longer.

'Goodbye, monsieur,' she said lightly. 'I trust that you will take care.'

'But of course,' he said, and stood back.

The coach door banged shut and the coachman sprang into his seat. The horses' breath steamed into the chill air and they pawed at the stones, restless to be off. A sharp command, and the coach began to move forward, the horses slipping on the cold flags. De Choissy raised a hand in farewell, and then disappeared.

After an anxious journey, which had involved a long wait at the *barrière* gate, the coach crossed the bridge at Neuilly and turned west towards St Germain-en-Laye. Three miles later, after negotiating some ill-made roads, it drew up outside an elegant-looking house built twenty-five years or so ago which was perched on an incline. The drive skirted a well-tended garden and curved around to the front of the building through a carved stone arch. The house blazed with light and a figure stood in the entrance.

With an impatient little sound, Héloïse threw back the fur rug and strained forward to see who it was. The coach halted, the door flung open and Louis reached over. He lifted Héloïse out, and with a joyous cry she flung her arms around his neck. Louis carried her into the house and placed her gently in a chair in front of the fire in the salon. He knelt to peel off her gloves and remove her cloak, and chafed the thin fingers that stretched out to the warmth.

'You have come, *mignonne*,' he said.

'But of course,' replied Héloïse. 'Did I not say I would?'

'We will enjoy these weeks, I promise,' said Louis softly. 'No regrets. No fears. No tomorrow.'

'No tomorrow,' she agreed, and pressed his head to her slight breasts.

Left outside, William and Sophie drank in the quiet with a profound sense of relief. With each yard, the oppression of Paris had lifted and the nightmare receded. A profound feeling of peace stole over them both.

'How wonderful,' said Sophie, relaxing for the first time in a long while. 'How remote it feels here and untouched.'

The sounds of the coach clattering into the stable yard drowned William's reply. On an impulse, Sophie lifted her skirts above her ankles and ran towards the garden. Her feet crunched over frost-sharpened pebbles in the path and left black imprints on the frozen lawn. William went after her and they arrived panting at an old sundial that stood on a square of grey stone. She stopped to regain her breath. William slid his arms around her waist with a hungry gesture. Sophie tensed.

'Please don't,' she said, terrified that she would lose control.

William released her immediately.

'What is wrong, Sophie?'

Sophie did not reply.

'There is something. I can tell.'

Still Sophie said nothing. She willed herself to push her deepening doubts about William to the back of her mind. She wanted above everything else to keep this stolen time free from recriminations and, in her heart, she admitted to not wanting to face the truth. But, however hard she tried, the secret that Ned had told her preyed on her mind. How can I be such a coward? she questioned herself. Have I no principles at all?

'It's nothing,' she said quickly. 'An angel has passed over my grave.'

William shivered. He bent over to kiss the junction of her chin and neck, and buried his face in the ruffles of her high-necked travelling costume.

'Don't talk of death,' he said.

Sophie allowed herself to be turned so that he could kiss her properly. If I knew the truth I could not allow him to do this, said a little voice in her head. I cannot bear the thought of losing him but I cannot accept . . . what he might be.

'I should not be taking advantage of you,' said William, his voice muffled, 'but, then, I am always saying that.'

Sophie remained silent, but her hands crept up his body to hold him tighter and tighter as if to banish the demons of distrust. The rising moon shone on her hair and turned it silver.

'We must go in,' she said, muzzy from his kisses. 'They will be expecting us.'

'Wait,' said William. 'I want to give this to you.'

He searched in the pocket of his tail-coat and produced a signet ring.

'It belongs to my family,' he told her. 'I wish you to have it.'

The gold gleamed yellow and heavy on his outstretched hand. Sophie picked it up and examined it. It was of a curious design and very ornate.

'How beautiful, and how unusual,' she said, genuinely intrigued. 'It must be very old.'

'It is.'

She dropped it back into his palm and pressed his fingers over it.

'No,' she said. 'I cannot accept it.'

'When will you?' William sounded very distant.

'Please,' said Sophie, 'give me a little more time. I need to think and I need some peace. I shall have both here. I can't make my mind up about something so important unless I have time to think.'

'Remember we may not have much time.' William spoke soberly and his face was grim.

He replaced the ring in his pocket. 'Very well, Sophie, I shall do as you ask and not press the matter. I had thought since you had sent Ned away that I could hope . . .'

William didn't finish his sentence. She felt his anger like a heavy hand laid on her heart. Her own answering spurt of irritation was directed more at herself and her lack of honesty. She had failed to question him when she knew she should have done before the atmosphere grew poisoned and she must expect the consequences.

William succeeded in swallowing his disappointment.

'Have you done what I requested,' he said, changing the

subject with an effort, 'and destroyed all your political writings?'

'Yes, I have,' she replied, retracing her steps to the house, 'and I have desisted from writing any more since you last talked to me.' She hesitated before going on. 'I feel a little ashamed. I was dabbling in things that I knew nothing about.'

William took comfort from the fact that she trusted him enough to make such an admission.

'I admire that in you,' he said, to her surprise. 'I think we should hold views and we should express them. Only now, and in this country, it is unwise and dangerous. When you come to America I predict you will start a new tradition of lady writers.'

Sophie saw that he was not entirely joking.

'Oh!' she said wrathfully. 'You are *quite* impossible. When I reach America indeed.'

She swept off towards the house.

The supper the four of them enjoyed before the fire in the tiny salon that evening was the first of many such gay and intimate occasions. Both ladies had agreed on the principle that no one was to dress formally, to which Louis and William acceded, and they lingered until late over cards and wine, often helpless with laughter. It proved to be a golden time, a time for friendship and levity, and for pushing away dark thoughts and darker fears. During the day they would ride, turning always from Paris towards the forest to the west, and they raced each other over the hard ground. Héloïse very often won, her light hands and excellent horse allowing her to outpace even Louis. Sometimes, but not often, they made an expedition to some site. Once they ventured as far as Versailles, but drew back from entering the grounds. They preferred to leave the palace, slumbering in its silence, to others. Chilled by the icy weather, they would return for dinner and read and write until supper was served. After supper they played expensive games of piquet or loo, until, sleepy from the fresh air, they made their way to bed and to the luxury of uninterrupted sleep.

Héloïse loved that moment at the end of the day best. She would lie in bed and watch the door. Louis would enter, holding his candle. Then he would be beside her, and they would have the long night to themselves. They would awaken in the late-winter morning, entangled in each other's arms.

'You are sure the servants are to be trusted?' he said sleepily one night.

'As far as they can be,' replied Héloïse. 'I picked them myself.'

'And Monsieur le Comte?'

'He will never know.' Héloïse was not a good liar.

'He knows,' said Louis, kissing a strand of hair. 'If I understand Monsieur le Comte correctly, he is playing a game. Your idyll in return for leaving France.'

'Perhaps,' said Héloïse, as his hands slid down her body, 'but I will have had my idyll.'

On another occasion Louis asked Héloïse to tell him about de Choissy.

Héloïse told him a little. Louis tightened his grip round her shoulder.

'*Ma pauvre,*' he said, shocked at her recital. 'What a strange man. He hates women, and yet he needs them. He hates you, yet he loves you. Do you understand?'

'No,' replied Héloïse, and pressed her cheek into his chest. 'I don't want to understand. I tried to begin with, but he sickens me too much.'

'He is beneath contempt,' said Louis after a moment.

Tantalisingly brief, the weeks slid into spring. The days grew longer, and snowdrops and anemones began to appear under the trees. Still Sophie said nothing to William, and hated herself for it. 'It might be the only time we ever have,' she wrote in her journal. 'A spy is always an object of hate and suspicion, and I am not immune from that feeling.' And added: 'I think I read somewhere that revolutions have a habit of devouring even their own children. So perhaps we are doomed anyway.' She allowed yet another day to pass.

William had an inkling of the truth after Sophie asked him if there had been spies in the Roman empire. Then he dismissed it. Sophie could not possibly know, there was nothing that could have given his game away. Still, he was puzzled and hurt by her attitude, knowing that while they appeared on the surface to be in perfect accord a barrier lay between them. A frown line began to etch itself over his eyes.

De Choissy sent regular missives from Paris with the latest news, and Héloïse always replied that she wasn't as yet fit to travel.

'I have received news that Général Dumouriez has won a battle at Jemappes, and it is said that the republic will go on to annex Savoy, Nice and Belgium. This will incite England to declare war, if I am not mistaken,' he wrote in January.

'As I predicted, France has declared war on Britain,' he wrote on February 3rd. 'This is good news, for perhaps the republic will take a beating.'

Towards the end of February, his letters took on a more urgent tone. 'You must be very careful,' he warned. 'There are informers everywhere. Even when you think you are safe.'

On March 11th, he wrote again. 'I have been summoned to the Hôtel de Ville for questioning. Do not worry.'

'I am sure Monsieur le Comte will be safe,' said William as Héloïse read out his letter. 'But he is right,' he continued, glancing down at the broadsheet he was reading. 'We have been foolish in permitting Monsieur d'Épinon to ride with us.'

Louis looked grave.

'I will remain inside from now on,' he agreed. 'It's too dangerous. And the time has come to make some plans.' He stretched his hand across to Héloïse. '*Ma mie*, we must face facts.'

Héloïse replaced the cup of chocolate she was drinking on the table and looked steadily at Louis.

'But of course,' was all she said. 'I will help you.'

Louis' fingers tightened on hers.

It was a considerably more sober party who adjourned to the green salon for the morning. The men went out to inspect the horses and Sophie picked up a piece of embroidery.

'Ugh, how I hate it,' she murmured.

'Then, why do it?' asked Héloïse, pacing up and down the room.

'Habit,' said her cousin with a long-suffering sigh, 'and the memory of Miss Edgeworth.'

The peaceful scene outside seemed to mock Héloïse, and she flung herself down in one of the chairs arranged at the side of the room, only to spring back to her feet to continue her peregrinations. Sophie sewed on, lovely and seemingly tranquil, but wrestling again with what she should say to William.

'Don't move,' she said at last, biting a thread off.

Héloïse, surprised, did as she was bid.

'Exactly the same,' said Sophie.

'What do you mean?' Héloïse's eyebrows flew up.

'The portrait.'

Héloïse looked up at the wall. Above her, in a massive gilt frame, hung the portrait of her great-grandmother.

'You are so alike.'

It was true. The same shaped bones and dark eyes shone out of a rather wilful countenance, and except that her great-grandmother appeared to be enjoying her life at the moment of painting, surrounded as she was by her children and dogs, the two women were the same.

'She was very wicked,' commented Héloïse. 'And had many lovers.'

'Like great-grandmother, like great-granddaughter,' said Sophie, and laughed at the outrage on her cousin's face.

'I'm teasing you,' she pointed out. Héloïse sat down and forced herself to smile.

'You know,' remarked Sophie, 'you're behaving like a caged animal.'

Héloïse was gathering her wits for a suitable reply when a scratching at the door interrupted them. One of the servants proffered a letter on a salver. Sophie took it, and saw with surprise that it was addressed to her. She broke the seal and a second, smaller, packet fell into her lap. She picked it up. It was from Ned, and the covering note, dated the afternoon of March 11th, was from de Choissy.

'My very dear Miss Luttrell,' she read out, 'I hasten to enclose this letter which has arrived for you. I trust everything is in order. I remain, of course, your very obedient . . .'

Sophie laughed. 'How very like Monsieur le Comte,' she commented, and took up Ned's letter. It was dog-eared and stained and she had an odd presentiment that it had passed through many hands.

'Sophie, I write in haste,' Ned had scrawled in his large hand. 'I am about to embark for England, but I must warn you that I have been searched and some documents were taken from me. The same documents that I once showed you. You know what I mean. Tell Mr Jones that I sincerely did not mean this to happen.'

It was dated October 20th, 1792.

'Over four months ago,' said Héloïse, reading it. 'How curious. What could Ned have that belonged to Mr Jones?'

'I don't know,' lied Sophie, and Héloïse watched in surprise as she almost ran out of the room.

Sophie found William in the stables, discussing the finer points of one of the horses with the groom. When he saw her he came forward to greet her

'Superb, isn't he?' he said, indicating the glossy black back of the horse with satisfaction. 'I wish I could take him with me.'

Sophie indicated that she wished to speak to him alone. The moment she had dreaded had now come. She had to talk plainly.

In English, she said, 'This letter has arrived from Ned.'

William frowned and drew her towards the door. 'What can Ned want?' he said, his pleasant mood shattered.

'Read it,' said Sophie briefly.

She observed his face carefully as he did so and saw for the first time the side that he normally kept hidden from her.

'Aha,' said William under his breath. 'I should have known.'

'William. It is time for the truth. Ned showed me those documents before he left.'

William bent to pick up a curry comb from the floor. This, then, was the key to Sophie's behaviour.

'So that's it. Now I understand your manner towards me,' he said with regret.

'You should have told me, William.'

'Sophie,' he said, 'this is not for you. Truly.'

She faced him. 'There you are wrong. If I am to marry you, it does concern me.'

William looked away. He ran his hand thoughtfully over the horse's back. 'Easy, boy,' he said, avoiding Sophie's eyes.

Sensing the tension, the horse whinnied and stamped. The warm smell of the stable battled with the sharp air from outside. In the adjoining stall, a groom moved about his business and then departed, casting a curious glance over his shoulder at the English mademoiselle and the American monsieur. At last, William spoke.

'Please don't say anything more,' he asked. 'It is better if we don't discuss it.' He tried to take Sophie in his arms.

She shook herself free.

'I have to know,' she said. 'Don't you see this secret of yours is as much about us as anything? These are difficult things to say, and I have waited too long to say them, but there must be trust, and truth, between us if we are to understand one another. And I want to understand, William, by all that I believe in, I do. But I cannot if you are not honest with me. I think you owe me an explanation. I have done my part in sending Ned away. Not without cost to my reputation, and to my self-esteem, and not without misgivings. Now you must trust me.'

William kicked at a heap of straw. Sophie's appeal had stirred up uncomfortable feelings, and they threatened to fracture his calm. He knew she was right and he wanted to tell her his secret, but he couldn't. Discretion was the first rule, a rule that applied never more so than now. It was a price he always knew he would have to pay, but until now he had not understood just how high that price would be.

'Come here,' he pleaded. Sophie swallowed but stood her ground.

'Are you a spy, William?'

William dug his hands into his pockets. 'I cannot make you, of course,' he said, ignoring her question.

'No,' said Sophie.

She sat down on a bale of straw and began picking out the wisps.

'You have disappointed me,' she said. 'How can I love a man who cannot confide in me?'

William sat down beside her.

'Don't, Sophie,' he said. 'I don't think I can bear it.'

He laid a hand on her knee. For a moment Sophie's hovered above his, wanting to reassure him that everything was all right, but her pride intervened. After searching her face, William got to his feet. He dusted down his breeches.

'Not a very elegant sight,' he observed.

Sophie could not even raise a smile. William had chosen to ignore her plea and it left her sick at heart. It also made her feel cheated. Quite obviously, he did not consider her worthy of his trust – and yet he was willing to marry her. It was not the first time a woman had been put in her place, and it would not be the last. It was an unpalatable fact, Sophie decided, and one, in this case, she did not have to accept.

William cleared his mind with an effort. There were things he must do at once. Chief among them was to obtain passports and travelling visas and to get Sophie and himself out of France. Once that tell-tale document was deciphered by the authorities – and it only needed someone like that Maillard to be snooping round – then they were in the greatest danger. William cursed Ned under his breath for the stupid idiot he was. He bent to lift Sophie to her feet and began to remove the straw from her fashionable china-blue lutestring gown. She allowed him to do so in silence. He felt her hostility and, in a last effort to make her understand, he took Sophie's chin in his hand and raised it so that she was forced to look into his face.

'Listen to me and listen well.' He spoke rapidly. 'We no longer have much time. Yes, I do work for my government in a secret capacity. I cannot tell you what exactly, not because I don't trust you but because if I told you I would be both betraying a promise and putting you in danger.'

'I see,' said Sophie slowly. 'The American government requires first-hand information about France.'

'No different and no less than any other government, Sophie. We cannot afford to be naïve.'

'Very well,' Sophie spoke more coldly than she felt, but she did not care for the tone he had adopted. It reminded her of Ned.

William dropped his hand.

'I will not wilfully put you into danger, Sophie, nor is it proper that I should tell you details that are nothing to do with you. If you cannot accept that, then I am sorry. I am going to Paris now, and if I am successful I promise you that I will tell you something of the matter. If I do not return . . .,' he went on, and saw the colour drain from her face. 'If I do not return, you must promise me one thing.'

He waited for her assent before continuing.

'It is becoming imperative that you leave France with or without Monsieur and Madame le Comte and Comtesse. When they leave is, of course, something for them to decide – although it may not be much longer that they have that option. But you, Sophie, must leave. If I am not with you, you are to go to Sir Robert Brandon in the Rue de Richelieu. He knows all about you and has his instructions from me. He has become', William's face softened, 'a very good friend of mine, and is a noble-hearted gentleman. He has lived for many years in Paris and built up a successful wine business. Trust him, he will do all he can to help you.'

Sophie stood back.

'I see,' she said. 'I thank you for your concern.'

She was battling with both anger and disappointment, neither of which made her feel like extending an olive branch. 'But please don't return on my account. I shall be travelling to England as soon as I can. Alone. I am sorry, but our association is at an end. Goodbye, Mr Jones.'

'Sophie!'

She quitted the stables without a backward glance, leaving William frowning after her retreating figure. He pulled himself together. Later, when this was all over, he would have time to think about it, but not now. Turning sharply on his heel, he shouted for the groom to saddle up.

Within the hour he had gone, and was galloping up the main road towards the city wall.

Left behind to wait, Héloïse, Sophie and Louis discussed the position in the rose-garden: it seemed safer to be out of doors and away from interested ears. Louis outlined his tentative plans to leave Neuilly and skirt south round Paris where he would strike out for Châlons-sur-Marne, Verdun and the border. Knowing that she could no longer refuse de Choissy's request to leave, Héloïse made Louis promise that he would try to reach Koblenz. For her part, she would make every effort to persuade de Choissy to aim for there too.

'But I shall not do anything until I know that Sophie is taken care of,' she added.

'If necessary, I will escort Sophie to a port,' said Louis, considering his strategy. 'We cannot leave you to travel on your own if Mr Jones is not here and it would be foolishness to travel with Héloïse. You and I could perhaps try to make for La Rochelle instead of the north, but if the English are still blockading the coast we will make for Bordeaux.'

'I had better travel light,' said Sophie, in a vain attempt at a joke.

'It is a strange ending to your French visit,' said Louis, staring over the fields that lay beyond the house. 'You came when France had a king and occupied the highest position in Europe. Now France has committed an act of madness which has made her the object of loathing in Europe. I ask myself how this can be. But I cannot find the right answers.'

'There are many answers,' said Héloïse, and took his hand. 'But only one path for us. We must keep faith and we must survive. But, if necessary, we must also die.'

Louis kissed her fingers one by one.

'A stoic philosophy, Héloïse. D'accord. But we will add something to it. We must endure and, if called, we must die – but not without a fight – to restore the king.'

Héloïse cradled his hand to her cheek. They were in perfect accord. Sophie, forcing back her tears, wondered why she felt so out of patience with their sentiments. Of course, she condemned the execution of the king and abhorred the bloodshed. Her memories of the latter would never leave her and she was bitterly disillusioned that change was bought at such a high price. But could they not see that France needed to shake out the cobwebs of ancient malpractice and begin afresh? Sophie found herself thinking that William would have agreed.

She left them together and went to inspect the newly dug vegetable beds. The damp earth had a sharp tang and the rows awaiting their onions and potatoes looked reassuringly ordinary. Sophie stood for a long time staring down. Her adventure, begun so gaily at Héloïse's betrothal, had turned into a painful disaster which would result in her returning to High Mullions in disgrace. Now she must forget William, leave France and go home. Alone and unhappy. She wondered how she would ever resume the life she used to think was all she ever wanted: the prospect of her parents' disappointment, Ned's angry proximity and the enjoyment her imminent spinsterhood would give the gossips filled her with the blackest depression.

William was not expected back until the next day, and Sophie got up in the morning prepared to ignore him. But as the hours went by and no William returned she began to feel anxious. Héloïse did her best to comfort her.

'These matters take time, chérie. When one negotiates, it is necessary to talk, to reflect and to be patient. One cannot be in too much of a hurry and William certainly must not look as though he is.'

Louis bent to put another log on to the fire. It was after dinner and the afternoon, although lighter than a few weeks previously, was beginning to get cold.

'*Reste tranquille, mademoiselle,*' he said affectionately, for he had grown to love Sophie. 'If I know anything of Mr Jones, he will be back. He is a slippery eel that one, and he has many resources.'

Despite their reassurances, Sophie slept very little that night. If William was a spy and he was discovered, then his life was in danger. If, on the other hand, she had been revealed as the author of that stupid pamphlet and William was known to associate with her, then he was again at risk. So was she. An awful picture of William being herded into prison, of William pleading for his life in front of a judge, of William being led towards the bloodstained guillotine filled her mind. She sat bolt upright and attempted to light a candle. It took her some time but in the end the light flared up and she was comforted. Ashamed of herself, she picked up a book and tried to concentrate, but it dropped on to the sheets unread. Why had she let William go without a word of support? Why had she not told him that she understood? That she didn't mind about his work, whatever it was? That what mattered was William? Why, oh, why had she not told him that she loved him? In the quiet, mysterious night silence, Sophie acknowledged the truth.

She slipped out of bed, threw a wrapper round her shoulders and pulled back the shutters from the window. If she hoped to see a figure moving through the garden, she was disappointed. All was still, and only an eerie light played on the landscape below. Sophie replaced the shutter and threw herself into a chair, shivering with cold. She stared into the gloom and watched the candle with eyes that were beginning to burn with exhaustion and worry.

Of course she loved William enough to forgive him. How could she have been so blind and so stupid not to have seen it? What a fool she had been. How could she live with the knowledge that her stiff-necked pride had got in the way if he failed to return? By now, Sophie was shuddering in earnest and she clutched her wrapper tighter and tighter across her breast in an agony of remorse. Questioning and cross-questioning, alternating between hope and fear, she remained sitting where she was until daybreak when, at last, she fell asleep.

She awoke, stiff and numb, to find Héloïse rubbing her hands.

'*Sophie*, what have you been doing? You are freezing.'

Sophie tried to get up, but her legs were so cramped that she fell back. Héloïse began to rub her feet.

'You should have woken me,' she said tenderly. 'I would have come. You must not upset yourself like this. Think of William.'

'I *am* thinking of William,' said Sophie, and burst into tears.

Héloïse drew her cousin's tousled golden head on to her shoulder and cradled it.

'I have been such a fool, an overbearing fool,' wept Sophie into its comforting warmth. 'I let William go without . . .'

'I have been meaning to tell you, *mignonne*, that this is no time for playing games,' said Héloïse carefully. She had been intending to talk to Sophie about William, for she had sensed that her cousin was not happy.

'You are right,' said Sophie, raising a strained and tear-streaked face. 'This is no time to dice with things that matter – with things that might mean life or death.'

'Shush,' said Héloïse, stooping to kiss her cheek and holding her close. 'It is not too late.'

'Pray God it is not,' said Sophie, her tears falling faster. 'For I owe it to William.'

'Does this mean you will marry Monsieur Jones?'

'If he will have me.' Sophie choked on the words.

Over her cousin's head, Héloïse smiled.

'Well, then, you must be patient.'

She stood up. 'I am going to send for some breakfast and I will sit with you while you eat it.'

While Sophie tried to force down her roll and drink her chocolate Héloïse wrote a letter to de Choissy.

'I shall instruct the cook to make a bouillon for your dinner, *chérie*. I think you are in need of something nourishing,' said Héloïse at last, when she had finished.

'Thank you,' said Sophie mechanically, 'but I am not hungry.'

'You will do as I say,' replied Héloïse firmly.

Sophie thought it wiser to say nothing. She sat thinking hard. Then she threw back the bedcovers and stood up.

'I am getting dressed,' she announced.

Héloïse glanced up.

'I trust you are not planning anything unwise,' she remarked, folding her letter. 'I don't trust that look on your face.'

Sophie fixed an earring into her ear.

'Would you always use the same gate going from Paris to Neuilly?' she asked.

'Probably,' said Héloïse, mystified. 'It is the most direct route.'

Sophie adjusted a second earring.

'You love Louis? Yes?' she asked a now wary Héloïse.

'Of course.'

'More than life?'

'More than life.' The last was said with a great deal of feeling.

'Then, you will understand,' said Sophie, disappearing into the dressing room that led off her bedroom in search of a pair of stockings. 'Are you prepared to fight for him?' she called through the door.

'In my way, yes,' replied Héloïse, thoroughly alarmed.

'Then, we are agreed.' Sophie's head peered briefly round the door. 'And I am going to fight for Mr Jones.'

Sophie was very silent during an early dinner. Héloïse and Louis talked quietly and afterwards they retired to the salon, where Louis began to plot a possible route on a map which he had found in the library. At three o'clock Sophie got to her feet and announced she was going riding.

'I am coming with you,' announced Héloïse. 'Wait for me.'

Sophie followed her into the hall.

'Héloïse,' she said, and hesitated. 'Héloïse, this is no ordinary ride.'

Héloïse stood with one hand on the banisters, a foot poised to ascend.

'I am not stupid,' she said unhooking the first of her buttons on her sleeve. 'I know that. That is why I am coming with you.'

'I am going to the *barrière* to watch for William. If he is in trouble, he will probably wait until the last minute before the curfew when it is getting dark. If he doesn't come today, I shall go tomorrow. And the day after that, if need be.'

'Of course,' said Héloïse. She leant towards her cousin. 'On one condition. Louis is not to suspect. It will be dangerous and he is likely to insist on coming too, and I cannot allow that.'

Sophie agreed at once.

'Hurry, then,' she said.

Twenty minutes later, the cousins, having denied the services of a groom, rode out of the stables and pointed their horses towards Versailles. The road took them down a gentle incline but once the house was out of sight Sophie reined in her mount. Clad in a grey riding habit, cut in the most severe and flattering lines, Héloïse trotted up behind her.

'Where do we go from here?' asked Sophie.

Héloïse pointed her whip to the east. 'Follow me. I know the paths quite well from when I rode here as a child.'

'You do understand, don't you?' said Sophie. 'If William has to run for it, we can provide a diversion, or if he is on foot, we help him get away.'

'Yes,' said Héloïse.

She swung her mount round and led the way down the road until she found an opening. She raised her arm and beckoned to Sophie before plunging down a narrow track bordered by a high, scrubby hedge. Sophie followed her.

Despite their circuitous route, the *barrière* was in sight within three-quarters of an hour. They picked their way cautiously along the side of a field and Héloïse indicated with her crop that they should make for a clump of trees about two hundred yards from the city walls. They urged their horses forward.

'We will wait here,' Héloïse announced when they were under the cover of the trees. 'I think we are out of sight. But, Sophie, I warn you, as soon as the gates are closed we will return.'

Sophie nodded and strained to see through the darkening afternoon, every nerve-end primed with tension.

'Stay here with the horses,' she whispered. 'I am going to take a look.'

She slid down off her mount, tethered it to a branch and groped her way towards the edge of the trees. As far as she could see, everything appeared normal. A few carts were making their way home after selling their wares in the market and she could hear their drivers cracking jokes with the guards who stood at their posts by the gates. A coach clattered down the road towards the city and stopped. Sophie saw a hand holding a sheaf of documents stretch out of the window, and within minutes the coach lumbered through the gateway and out of sight.

Then nothing. Only the outline of the city, guarded by its grey stone walls, and the muffled conversations of the bored guards.

Sophie was cold. A frost was chilling the air and night was falling.

'You must come,' she prayed. 'William, you must come.'

She glanced back over her shoulder and saw that Héloïse had dismounted and was rubbing down the horses with a handful of grass.

A shout from the *barrière* made her turn around. Something was happening. One of the guards was endeavouring to drag shut the heavy gates and was shouting furiously to his companion who had wandered out of sight. There was a scuffle, a stream of curses, and a horse broke away from the gate and galloped towards the watching girls. Two figures clung to its back. Sophie recognised de Choissy and, perched precariously behind him, William.

Regardless of the danger, she picked up her skirts and ran towards the road, waving her plumed hat. The rider reined in his horse and swerved.

'It's Sophie,' yelled William. 'Stop!'

De Choissy brought his sweating, terrified beast to a halt and William jumped down and ran towards Sophie. Careless of anything else, they met and clung together.

'You came for me,' he panted.

'Yes,' she said brokenly.

'No time,' shouted de Choissy. 'Get going. Tell my wife I had to go. I will make for the border.'

He jerked savagely at the bridle and, turning, drove his spurs into his horse's flanks and disappeared across the fields.

Sophie caught at William's hand and pulled him towards Héloïse. Bent almost double, they sprinted towards the trees, Sophie's skirt making her stumble and nearly to fall. Héloïse stood waiting there, the horses ready. She swung up on to her horse and William swept Sophie up on to hers and then scrambled up behind her.

'Follow me,' said Héloïse, and urged her horse into a furious canter back the way they had come. The whole incident had taken only a few minutes.

William clung on to Sophie's waist and ducked to avoid the trailing branches. Sophie stooped over her horse, concentrating on keeping her seat, and kicked her overburdened mount to greater and greater speeds. It took all of her skill to stay on and more than once William's hand saved her from falling. Choosing the quickest routes across the fields and through the woods, Héloïse led them on without faltering. At last, she turned west and began the descent to the house. Their speed slackened. Close to the gates, Héloïse stopped.

'Get down,' she whispered to William. 'Follow the wall round to the left and go through the kitchen garden. No one will see you. I will let you in through the door into the library. It is better so. Just in case one of the servants is not as reliable as we supposed.'

William vanished into the falling dusk.

Back in the stables once more, Sophie and Héloïse slid off their horses and handed them over to the surprised groom.

'I am afraid we over-exercised them,' remarked Héloïse lightly to Sophie, loud enough for the groom to overhear. 'We must take more care in future.'

Sophie forced a laugh like a tinkling bell. 'Quite so, cousin. How careless we are.'

William was waiting outside the library. He slipped inside like a ghost.

'Upstairs,' said Sophie. 'We'll talk upstairs.'

Louis met them at the door of the salon.

'What the devil . . .?' he demanded, and stopped in his tracks when he saw William. He seized Héloïse by the arm.

'Where have you been?' he asked tight lipped. 'I've been worried.'

'Later,' said Héloïse. 'I will explain everything. Let William talk.'

Paris was in turmoil, William informed them. A revolutionary tribunal had just been set up to try all the so-called enemies of the state and they included foreigners suspected of working for enemy governments, émigrés and those who had tried to smuggle their capital out of the city.

'The category includes Monsieur le Comte,' said William quietly. 'When he presented himself at the Hôtel de Ville, he discovered that he had been denounced. By a former servant of your father's. I believe, Madame Héloïse.'

Héloïse gave a start.

'I am sorry, madame,' continued William. 'I am truly sorry because this puts you in danger also. Monsieur le Comte managed to arrange to return to the Hôtel de Choissy. I met him here, and I managed to hide him for a day up in the Place Royale. Then we stole a horse and made for the gates. We were lucky to break through the guards. He will make for La Tesse, and he told me to tell you he had plenty of friends who will help him.'

'So,' said Héloïse, 'Monsieur le Comte and I are enemies of France.'

'I am afraid so, madame. If it comforts you at all, you are in good company.'

Héloïse shrugged. 'This is a cross I must bear,' she said, determined to keep her sense of humour at least.

'As for me – for us,' William corrected himself and glanced at Sophie, 'I have had no luck in obtaining visas. I shall have to return and try again.'

Sophie shuddered.

'Not yet,' she said. 'We must think and plan before you go back.'

Her relief was so overwhelming that she could think of little else. Even the knowledge that her happiness was gained at the expense of Héloïse's did little to dim it. Joy flooded her, and a lightheaded excitement that flushed her cheeks and lit up her grey eyes.

Later that night, she bathed in front of the fire and asked that her hair be brushed until it shone. She left it flowing in a cascade down her back and dabbed perfume on to her wrists and neck. She dismissed the maid and scrutinised herself in the mirror. She wanted to remember this moment. Then, holding candle in her hand, she crossed the corridor and knocked at the room opposite.

William was sitting by the fire in his shirt sleeves. His hair was still tied back but his shirt hung open at the neck, revealing smooth, unblemished skin. When he saw who it was, he drew in his breath and got to his feet.

'I have been hoping,' he said, and drew her close. Sophie laid her cheek on his shoulder.

'Am I forgiven?'

'There is nothing to forgive.'

His lips were travelling down her neck.

'Sophie. If you knew how much I have longed for this.'

She smiled and raised her arms. Her nightdress fell open her breast. William tightened his grip.

'Are you sure? Are you absolutely sure?' he asked her.

She was trembling as she pressed closer to him: with desire and with her own daring.

'I am sure,' she said. 'But you will have to help me.'

She did not have to worry. William was tender, passionate and careful. Careful to allow her to find her own way toward knowledge, he led her towards an oblivion that left her shaken with passion and gratitude. And Sophie, tasting the limits of the flesh for the first time, found that there were no limits, only endless love and delight, and that what had seemed to her narrow pathway was, in fact, an enchanted land.

There were her tears and William's words of love sounding gently in her ear; there was the feel of his strong shoulders and narrow thighs, the bruising on hers, the touch of his fingers and surrender of her body beneath his – these were impressions that added up to something greater.

Gazing down at her tangled hair and graceful limbs, running his hands down over her breasts and curving waist to the golden down below, knowing that intelligence and courage lay behind the closed eyelids, William knew he had been right. Sophie was his, and his for life.

'You know what this means?' he said many hours later when at last, she lay quiet in his arms.

Sophie sighed and stretched a hand up towards the ceiling. 'Tell me.'

He reached across her to the table beside the bed and opened the drawer. Taking her hand, he pressed the signet ring on to her finger. It hung loosely, so she was forced to clench her fist.

'It's yours.'

She kissed his mouth.

'If you are asking me to marry you, I will,' she said.

'Soon?' he asked.

'Soon,' she said drowsily.

They were asleep when the knocking began at the door.

'Get up,' called Louis from outside. 'Someone has betrayed us. They have sent from Paris. I must go. Goodbye.'

Héloïse appeared, her face drained of colour.

'They have come to arrest us. All of us.'

PARIS, Spring 1793

Europe united against the regicidal French republic, and soon France was at war with England, Holland and Spain. This coalition was also joined by German and Italian princes. Under the Prince of Coburg's banner, a new spring offensive was launched against the 'murdering' French. Pressed on all sides, the French armies, who had made considerable inroads into Germany and Belgium after their victory at Valmy, now found that their progress was considerably harder.

At home the cost of living rose sharply, the assignat fell in value and food was short. The call for a conscription of 300,000 men caused widespread discontent. In the Convention, formerly the National Assembly, extremists, or enragés, struggled to gain the upper hand over Girondins and Jacobins. In the Vendée, thousands of peasants took up arms against the Revolution and declared their intention of opening the port of Rochefort to the British fleet. Elsewhere, in the cities of Lyons, Nantes and Marseilles, violence simmered and tensions reached breaking point.

Desperate to maintain authority, the Convention decided to act. In doing so, it laid the seeds of the Terror. Captured rebels bearing arms were to die. Émigrés returning to France were to meet the same fate – and there were many slipping back into France in order to beat the sequestration orders on their property. Foreigners were to be closely watched. Priests were to be deported.

Most sinister of all was the creation in March 1793 of the Revolutionary Tribunal – 'to judge without appeal the disturbers of the public peace'. 'Let us be terrible,' thundered Danton, remembering the September massacres, 'to spare the people being so . . .' Under the auspices of Fouquier-Tinville, the new public prosecutor, the tribunal went to work in the Grande Chambre of the Palais de Justice. Fouquier-Tinville was permitted to prosecute either by virtue of his office, or on the accusation of the authorities, or simply on the denunciations of ordinary citizens. Letters addressed to him were posted free of charge, thus ensuring that all citizens could reach him. The first sitting of the tribunal began on

April 6th, 1793. It ushered in one of the most bloodstained periods in French history.

The extremist element in the Convention was slowly gaining an upper hand. In April the Committee of Public Safety was set up, with Danton as one of its nine members. In time, it was to exercise a terrifying power. By now, the influence of the Girondins was on the wane. They were further discredited when Général Dumouriez, with whom they were closely associated, defected to the royalists. The Girondins had also tried too obviously to whip up support for themselves in the provinces. The Girondins, however, made their biggest mistake when they denounced Marat, an extremist and a popular figure with the sansculottes. Marat undertook his own defence in front of the tribunal and the jury acquitted him. Borne shoulder-high through the streets, amid cheering crowds, Marat and his cohorts won the day.

From then on, it was a spectacle of dog eat dog in the Convention. The Girondins steadily lost ground and credibility. The enragés whipped up support among the sansculottes and demanded Girondin blood. Playing one faction off against another, the Jacobins, with Robespierre as their leader, sat waiting in the wings. In June the Girondins went on the run, pursued by warrants for their arrest.

Chapter 3

Jacques, May 1793

Without saying goodbye to Marie-Victoire, Jacques banged the door shut behind him and turned left into the Rue St Honoré. At the Rue St Denis he turned right and walked towards the bridge and on to the Île de la Cité. His stomach tightened in anticipation of the day ahead. Since it had been set up in April of that year under the direction of the prosecutor-general, the tribunal had grown in power, and its very name struck fear into the hearts of all those who passed under the portals of the Palais de Justice.

Being a judge on the tribunal suited Maillard admirably, a crowning touch to his ambitions. It took courage to stand up and be counted, and Maillard was not short of that commodity, unlike many of his confrères who preferred not to accept such a dangerous honour. But when he had been called from his position on the commune, he had not hesitated. Maillard straightened his sash and quickened his pace. This was his finest moment. It mattered nothing that Maillard and his fellow judges were ignorant of law – one of them was an agriculturalist, the other had been, successively, a naturalist, a surgeon and a gunner in his time. Maillard knew, as those who toiled to process the increasing number of suspects knew, that justice in the real sense had very little to do with the proceedings. What, after all, were the refinements of a properly conducted trial when the future of France was at stake? In his eyes, nothing. His part called for him to eliminate traitors as fast as the law allowed, and now the law had been made conveniently flexible. So be it. Maillard did not care. It seemed to him supremely right that he could sit and pass judgement of death. Particularly when it came to scum like the de Guinots. He was a long way from the boy who had risen, bloody and ashen, from the whipping ordered by Héloïse, to vow vengeance.

Truly, it had worked out better than he had ever dreamed. He had finished off the marquis and his wife would rot away in prison. Now all he had to do was to continue his investigations into the ci-devant Comte de Choissy – investigations that would, of course, include his wife. Citoyen de Choissy had disappeared. With a bit of luck, he was still in France. Meanwhile he had the wife confined to house arrest, and the English woman too. The Committee of Public Safety would be interested in her. Maillard's appetite for power had grown with his influence, and he was quick to appreciate how his political ambition had so neatly dovetailed with his private vendetta. He took enormous pleasure in explaining the ironies of it all to Marie-Victoire.

Poor Marie-Victoire. She had not stood a chance. Not with him to contend with, and she was foolish to have thought otherwise. She was also very naïve to have imagined that he would give up the idea of persecuting the de Guinots.

In the courtyard of the Palais de Justice, known as the Cour de Mai, he stopped to talk to one of the women who sold cheap souvenirs from her booth. He then entered the building, and the guardsman on duty in the *greffe* greeted him with an oath. Maillard replied in kind. It was as well to keep these people in good humour. He made his way up the stairs.

The tribunal sat in the Grande Chambre, which overlooked a dark courtyard, and even in summer its tall windows permitted only a little light. The floor was paved in black and white marble and the room still bore traces of its recent despoiling by the authorities. The beautiful velvet draperies had been ripped down, the oak ceiling roughly plastered over and the carved wainscotting destroyed. At the north end were arranged the judges' table and chairs. To one side of those were four wooden benches for the accused and on the other sat the clerks and the stocky, pock-marked figure of the prosecutor-general.

The clerks had been up since dawn transcribing names and filling in indictments. There was an air of barely suppressed excitement in the room, and already the spectators were jostling for space in the public gallery, anxious not to miss one minute of the spectacle. Maillard went over to confer with Fabricus, the chief clerk, and then sat down in his seat. He was soon absorbed in the task of reading the pile of documents requiring his attention. He read slowly and hesitantly, forced more often than not to skim over the legal terms. He was thus absorbed when the first prisoners were ushered to the benches.

'*Prisonnier de Clinchamp,*' announced the clerk, and a ripple of expectation broke out in the public gallery.

'*Prisonniers Luttier et Gaveaux . . .*' The roll-call of names mounted. There was plenty to do today. Maillard settled his legs into a more comfortable position under the table and motioned to a clerk to fetch a glass of wine. The president got to his feet and read out the indictments. A woman sobbed on the prisoners' benches.

It did take long to sentence the ex-prior, Jean de Clinchamp.

'*Ah, mon Dieu!* I shall at last see your face,' the condemned man repeated again and again.

Luttier, a soldier, lost his temper when he heard his fate and cursed his executioners. Gaveaux begged to be allowed to spend a few moments with the woman he loved. Maillard reflected, thought the better of it, and indicated a curt negative. Accompanied by some sympathetic cries from the gallery, the prisoners were ushered out to take their last walk through the Conciergerie where they would wait for the tumbrils to arrive at the end of the session.

Yes, this will be a good day, thought Maillard as he drank his wine, a very good day.

Chapter 4

Hôtel de Choissy, June 1793

The waiting room in the Hôtel de Ville was unbearably hot and crowded and William had been sitting for a long time. He glanced at his watch. Only two hours left.

The section authorities had given him permission to leave the Hôtel de Choissy in order to obtain his travelling papers, but he had been sworn to return by four o'clock. As he, Sophie and Héloïse were under house arrest, and had been since their enforced return from Neuilly, William felt he had no option but to comply. He did not wish to jeopardise Héloïse's position, which grew daily more precarious. A frown was etched into his forehead and he puzzled for the thousandth time how to resolve the impasse. Their movements were limited, a guard was posted permanently at the gate of the Hôtel and Héloïse was forbidden to leave the house under any circumstances. By order, they had been told of the special surveillance committee.

Naturally William did not seriously consider abandoning Héloïse and, anyway, Sophie would not hear of it. His frown deepened. Sophie was now pregnant and the baby was due to be born in December. William was determined to get her out of France somehow before it became too difficult for her to travel. Héloïse, too, if he could arrange it. Where Louis was, no one knew. As far as they could tell, he had avoided arrest at Neuilly by hiding in one of the outbuildings and they prayed he had made it to the border. Privately, William felt rather doubtful. Louis had had neither money nor papers on him when he left them, nor was he properly dressed, and it was unlikely he had managed to return to the house without incurring serious risk. Héloïse, however, surprised both of them with her optimism

'He will manage,' she said. 'We hid some papers and clothes in the woods at the back of the stables for just this possibility.'

But her face grew more drawn and, at night, Sophie could hear her pacing her room into the small hours.

William shifted on the uncomfortable bench and watched while a young woman tried, unsuccessfully, to reason with a clerk who was smoking a villainous-smelling pipe. After a while, the woman gave in, gathered her children and departed. William was struck by the look of desperation she cast at him. He looked round the room at the selection of anxious and exhausted men and women. He supposed that some of them might be queuing for their own life, others for someone they loved, and the toll on their emotions was obvious from the profusion of nervous coughs, snapped comments and whispered conversations. He passed his tongue over his lips. Would they get out of Paris alive?

The clerk sat at one end of the room at a desk under a window from where he would issue summons from time to time. William stretched out his long, breeched legs and leant on his cane. His nonchalant attitude appeared to attract the attention of the clerk, who sent over his aide. William rose, adjusted his hat and sat down in front of the clerk.

Obviously, the passion for dirt affected by revolutionary extremists reigned supreme at the Hôtel de Ville. The man had not been near water for months. Layers of grime rimmed his fingernails and he sported a tidal mark where his collar met his neck. His hair hung in greasy locks down to his shoulder and his equally dirty Phrygian cap was jammed unceremoniously on to the top of his head.

'Yes,' he barked, in a voice hoarse from cheap wine and tobacco. William explained that he wanted a passport in the name of Mr and Mrs William Jones, for America, via passage to England. They would be accompanied by his bride's governess, a Miss Edgeworth, and he wished to obtain papers for her too. William hoped that Héloïse's English would be up to the deception. The clerk's hostile eyes flicked at him, noting the quiet elegance of William's dress and his composed bearing.

'Your reasons?'

'I wish to return home with my bride.'

'A French citoyenne?'

'No, English.'

'Name of?'

William supplied further details and watched the clerk scrawl them on to a long roll of parchment. He disliked giving out so much information but there was no help for it.

'When do you wish to depart?'

'As soon as possible.'

The clerk scraped back his chair and went into another room

where William could hear him conferring with a colleague. The clerk reappeared.

A second and, apparently, more senior clerk emerged from the back room, holding a bundle of documents. On top of them protruded a familiar-looking packet with its seals undone. William recognised it at once. He leant over and pretended to wipe at some dust on his boot while he thought. When he straightened up, ready to bluff his way through any questions, his face was as bland as he could make it.

The senior clerk stank as badly as the first and was even less accommodating.

'Your request is refused, pending some investigations,' he informed William. 'You and the English woman are not to leave Paris until your purity as a friend of *la patrie* is proved. We wish to consult a citizen patriot on some details of your case. Meanwhile, you will remain where you are until further notice.'

William inclined his head. His relief was so overwhelming that he was sure it must register in his face. He had a little more time.

'As you wish,' he replied politely. 'But I am sure it will not be long before the citizen clerk will be making out our passports.'

The clerk spat a stream of yellow tobacco juice into the straw on the floor.

'Perhaps,' he offered. 'Perhaps not.'

Back in the Rue de l'Université, William hustled Sophie into the bedroom they now shared. Most of the house had been sealed up by the officials – de Choissy property now being declared a possession of the state on account of his suspected émigré status. The only rooms available to live in were the smaller salon and three bedrooms overlooking the back of the house. The servants had fled, all of them, even the ones that Héloïse had trusted and counted on, and it was proving impossible to employ a girl from the neighbouring streets. As a result, Sophie and Héloïse were contriving to live as best they could, sending out for meals, fetching water and struggling to heat it.

'Miss Edgeworth would approve. She always maintained I needed to work harder,' Sophie had said when it became obvious they would have to look after themselves, tackling the unfamiliar tasks with more energy than skill. She had evoked a rare laugh from William.

He was not laughing now, as he explained to Sophie the latest position.

'There is nothing else for it,' he told her. 'We must leave. I will make use of Sir Robert. I only wanted to as the very last resort, and the time has come. I managed to arrange a pass to the Rue de Richelieu.'

Sophie held up a pair of red and blistered hands.

'You had better make out that we are humble farmers,' she said. 'I am the part to the life.'

'So is your swelling belly,' said William, running an ardent hand over her stomach. He grew serious.

'I must take care of you, my Sophie, and I must find a priest who is willing to marry us.'

'I wish this had not happened quite so soon,' said Sophie, looking down at her waist. 'I'm worried that this makes me an extra burden.'

'A scandal, you mean,' said William, smiling, and tilted her chin up towards him. He smoothed down an odd strand of her golden hair with careful, tender fingers. 'When she hears of it Miss Edgeworth will shudder in her bombasine.'

'Miss Edgeworth might surprise you,' countered Sophie.

Neither of them mentioned the painful subject of her parents.

Sir Robert Brandon was reached on the Rue de Richelieu. An Englishman who had chosen to reside permanently in France, he had lived in the same house for the past twenty years, from which he ran a successful wine-exporting business. Tall and inclined to embonpoint, he was a shrewd businessman and a generous host whose sleepy air hid a mind of exceptional sharpness. William knew him to be successful, prudent and adept at survival. Sir Robert counted both revolutionaries and royalists among his friends, even though William suspected that he was involved in secret political intrigue of a very dangerous nature. But Sir Robert was a kind and honourable man who kept his promises and had never been heard to utter an opinion that was remotely political. So convincing was his persona that the authorities left him alone; indeed, some of them came to his house to mix with bankers and financiers of all persuasions. Thus it was that Sir Robert's drawing room was the centre of many gatherings where financial matters were discussed and acted on and – if William was correct – royalist fugitives secretly gained help.

No, thought William, there was not much that escaped Sir Robert's benevolent eye; details that would be welcome in émigré circles. William had never dared tax him on the subject, nor would he do so. But, after all, it was in the interests of counter-revolutionaries to make the republicans appear as corrupt and greedy as possible. However they orchestrated it, he reasoned, and the ways were many and devious, counter-revolutionaries would be united in their efforts to undermine the republic's

302

social and political programmes by hastening a financial crisis. Sir Robert's house was a perfect forum into which they could feed rumour and speculation – and obtain an excellent meal to boot.

Sir Robert was only too glad to receive him. He liked the tall, serious young American and, being childless himself, had rather taken to fancying William as the son he might have had. Over a glass of excellent port, he agreed to obtain the documents for the three of them.

'Is it necessary for you all to leave?' was all he asked. 'It is difficult contriving for so many.'

William nodded. 'I could not leave Madame la Comtesse alone,' he said. 'But your price, if you please, for this favour?'

Sir Robert smiled at William's directness, and refilled the glasses.

'An excellent vintage,' he remarked, holding it up to the light. 'Are you of the opinion that your fellow countrymen would enjoy such a wine?'

'Indeed, sir,' replied William, savouring the bouquet.

'Well, then, my boy, that is my price. I shall look to you when you are back in America to further my interests. Is that fair?'

'Perfectly,' said William.

'Now,' said Sir Robert, suddenly very serious as he opened a concealed drawer in his bureau. 'This is what you must do.'

Two hours later, William slipped into the courtyard at the Hôtel de Choissy and made his way to the stables, a little surprised that the guard had left his post at the gate. The stables now lay empty, their horses dispersed by the local section, and most of the equipment had been stolen or removed. But some sacks of bran and oats still remained, partly hidden at the back of the building. William went over to them and, plunging his hand deep into the feed, deposited some documents inside the sack. Then he dragged the sack against the wall so that it was concealed by the others. He dusted his hands and checked to see if the guard had returned. He was preparing to slide noiselessly back into the house when he stopped in his tracks. A party of National Guardsmen were descending the steps of the hôtel, holding Héloïse by her arms. Behind her followed Sophie.

Héloïse said something to the sergeant, who gave the command to his men to release her. Héloïse ran over to Sophie and the two of them clung together until the guards dragged them apart. William could restrain himself no longer. He strode out of the stables and confronted the sergeant.

'What are you doing?'

Sophie cried out in English. 'They are arresting Héloïse.'

William understood her warning and immediately modified his tone.

'By whose authority do you do this? May I see the documents?' he asked.

'My orders, citoyen, come from the Committee of Public Safety. The citoyenne has been denounced as an enemy of the republic.' He waved a paper bearing an official seal in front of William.

'Can she not remain under house arrest?'

'The committee has decided not. They wish to make a thorough investigation, and they are pursuing their enquiries with regard to the citoyenne's husband.'

'Can you tell me where you are taking her?'

The sergeant, who seemed a reasonable man, looked William up and down.

'I am not permitted to give out such information,' he said finally.

At that moment the clouds parted and the sun came out. For a moment, the scene taking place in the quiet courtyard belonged to another world. William pulled himself together.

'It would be a kindness to tell me, and I am sure the lady concerned will remember with gratitude.'

The sergeant hesitated. '*D'accord*,' he said. 'The citoyenne will be taken to the Abbaye prison on the Rue St Marguerite.'

Sophie gave a gasp. Héloïse said nothing. She was relieved that she wasn't being taken to the Conciergerie, from which few emerged alive.

'Thank you,' said William to the sergeant. 'May I have a few words with the prisoner?'

Obligingly, the sergeant stood aside and William bent to embrace Héloïse.

'Do not despair,' he said *sotto voce* in English. 'We will work for your release.'

Héloïse indicated that she had heard.

'Have you packed anything?' continued William, switching into French.

'Enough,' replied Héloïse. 'I will send word when I need more.'

William kissed her on the cheek.

'Goodbye for now, dear friend,' he said, and stepped back.

Héloïse twisted her head round.

'Sophie,' she called. 'I love you. If you see him, tell the other I love that I am thinking of him. Always.'

Sophie lifted her hand in a despairing gesture.

'Au revoir,' she said, choking back tears. 'Au revoir.'

The party filed out of the courtyard, Héloïse's slight figure dwarfed by the men beside her. At the gate, she paused and sent them a smile that was full of courage. Then she disappeared from view.

William supported Sophie back into the house.

'So stupid,' she murmured, 'but my legs won't seem to hold me.'

In the salon, William chafed her limbs. Despite the warmth of the day, they were cold to his touch and he made her drink a glass of brandy. Sophie obeyed. Presently her hands and feet stopped feeling like blocks of ice and she felt better. Neither of them said much. The big house was empty and silent, harbouring as it did the memories of its past life and of the people who had now gone. Huddled among its wreckage and its sealed rooms, they felt like intruders.

'We must leave,' said William at last, and held up his hand to ward off Sophie's protests. She struggled to stand but he held her down. 'I know what you are going to say and, in part, I agree. We will do what we can to get Héloïse released, but after that we will go.'

That night Sophie could not sleep. She lay tossing and turning, aware of the growing discomfort of her belly. William was beside her, breathing very lightly. She knew he had stayed awake for a long time planning the next move. Sophie raised herself on to her elbow to look at him. With his hair spread out over the pillow, William looked different. Less complicated and more peaceful. Almost boyish.

'Sleep on, my love,' she whispered, and brushed his shoulder with her lips. He moved, muttered something and flung out a hand. Gently, so as not to disturb him, she slid out of bed and went down the stairs to the salon.

It was a bright early-summer night. The light streamed in at the window and pooled in silver patches on the floor. At the big window, Sophie stood and watched the stars wink and shimmer over the city and wondered if Héloïse was awake too. A melody from a song swam into her head, and she hummed a bar from it before a noise in the courtyard below made her pause in mid-phrase. Someone was out there, moving towards the house. A shadowy outline inched its way past the sleeping guard and moved on panther-soft feet towards the steps. Sophie dodged behind the drapes. The figure remained quite still for three minutes or so, then ran up the steps and disappeared. Sophie heard the sound of something being scraped along the window ledge and a muffled sound of broken glass. Her stomach tightened in apprehension, but she thought it best to remain hidden. She listened to the slow, cautious sounds of someone mounting the staircase. A thief, she thought, her mind slow with fright, or perhaps it is one of the old servants returning to take refuge? Someone has been talking about the hôtel and a sansculotte has come to plunder it. With each new footstep her courage ebbed. Why, oh, why hadn't she gone to fetch William?

The moon disappeared behind a cloud and the room was plunged into darkness. The walls loomed black and suddenly threatening and she felt suffocated. She shrank further behind the curtain. A slight rasp from a hinge on one of the folding doors told her it was opening. The noise broke into the silence. The intruder slipped like a shadow into the room. Sophie inched her body back against the wall. The man was moving from object to object as if searching for something. He picked up some papers and tried to read them. Then he swooped down and held up William's swordstick to the light and examined it minutely. What he saw seemed to satisfy him. As he bent to replace it, the moon reappeared and shone on to his face.

With a sigh, Sophie fell limply against the wall. Then she held out her hands.

'Louis,' she called.

The figure stopped in its tracks and whirled around.

'*Dieu!* So you are here. I was almost giving up hope.'

Sophie ran towards him and caught him in a long embrace.

'But how did you . . .? Where? And for how long?'

'Take a look at me,' Louis invited. '*Regardez!* The new Louis d'Épinon. On second thoughts, just Louis Épinon.'

Sophie looked at him hard. A sansculotte stood before her. More gaunt than she remembered, he was dressed in a short coat, ragged trousers and even the obligatory cap.

'My disguise. In the Rue St Antoine, my dear, I am regarded as something of a patriot. No questions asked: provided I shout louder and speak faster than the rest.'

'Did you reach the border?' asked Sophie, fascinated by this apparition.

'I did, and then I volunteered to work in Paris organising resistance. I had to come back for Héloïse.' Louis grasped Sophie's hands in a hard grip. 'Is she here?' he asked, his longing sounding quite plain in his voice.

Sophie was silent.

'I see,' said Louis after a moment.

'Louis, you must be brave. They took her today to the Abbaye,' said Sophie, and turned away.

He sank into a chair and buried his face in his hands. Sophie knelt down beside him and touched his shoulder.

'Courage, Louis. It is not the end yet.' But her words sounded false even in her own ears.

He stirred.

'It's what I feared,' he said. 'But I had hoped and prayed . . .'

'I know,' said Sophie.

She went to wake William. The two men hugged and began to exchange news. By the time Sophie had found some bread and wine, they were deep in conversation, and she was glad to see that Louis was relaxing. She went over to pull the window drapes closer together, worried that the candles might alert the guard, and sat down on the sofa. Before she could prevent herself, she fell asleep.

As she awoke, the candle guttered and went out. Louis was still talking to William, who was occasionally interjecting. They were planning Héloïse's escape.

'I can bribe one of the women who send in the meals to the prisoners to take in some clothes and a letter to Héloïse,' said Louis. 'Then I can bribe a second woman to exchange places with her. The two women won't know each other so they won't make the connection and the second woman can stay in the prison overnight.'

'It's dangerous,' said William. 'Can you find the right woman?'

'Money helps,' said Louis acidly. 'I have a roll of double louis d'or round my waist.'

'I'll take in the clothes,' interrupted Sophie.

William came over to her. 'So you are awake. How long have you been listening?'

'Long enough,' she replied. 'If I visit Héloïse, I can smuggle in a package. My name will be on the list at the section headquarters and I am known to be confined here. It would be obvious that I would apply to visit Héloïse.'

'No,' said William. 'I forbid it.'

Sophie twisted a strand of her hair through her fingers. 'You can't,' she said mildly. 'I am not married to you yet.'

'As good as.' William was sharp. 'And, it seems to me, the sooner the better. Louis, if I am to help you with your plan, it is on condition that Sophie plays no part in it.'

'Of course,' said Louis. 'I would not have it any other way.'

Sophie glared at them.

'You will have the goodness not to decide matters for me,' she said.

William kissed her hand. 'Please, *chérie*, think of the baby, if not of me.'

'At least, let me find the woman and talk to her.' Sophie could see the sense in William's argument. 'I will be able to do better than either of you.'

'Agreed,' said Louis.

After a moment William nodded. 'I don't like it,' he said, 'but perhaps it is better so.'

'Héloïse's life is in danger,' she reminded him.

'Yes, I know,' he replied. 'But so might be yours.'

Shortly after nine o'clock the next morning, Louis and Sophie let themselves out of a little-used entrance to the hôtel, made their way through the garden and out through a gate in the wall that led into a side alley off the Rue de l'Université. Then they headed in the direction of the Rue St Marguerite and the Abbaye prison. Neither of them excited any interest, nor were they supposed to. Unshaven and dishevelled, Louis had a pipe hanging from his mouth and a knife tucked into his leather belt and, after a thorough search through some chests in an attic into which they had managed to force an entry, Sophie had unearthed a grey stuff gown large enough to accommodate her stomach. She had pushed back her hair under a large cap that had seen better days and golden tendrils hung untidily to her neck. She carried a small bundle of clothes which, if their plan went correctly, Héloïse would wear to make her escape.

It was warm, and Sophie found that she had to stop every now and then to regain her breath. The baby seemed very heavy all of a sudden and she was reminded with every step of her lack of sleep.

'It's not far,' said Louis solicitously, offering her his arm. She took it gratefully.

The square in front of the prison was very busy by the time they arrived. Every inch was occupied by stalls and booths which sold everything from the latest political tract to umbrellas. At the prison gate a harassed soldier was failing to stem the tide of lawyers, relatives and officials clamouring to gain entry.

'Wait here,' said Louis, settling Sophie on to a bench near the stall selling refreshments. He ordered a flagon of beer. Sophie toyed with a wooden cup and watched Louis push his way towards a group of women who stood chattering by the gates, many of them holding heavy baskets containing meals ordered by the better-off prisoners.

Louis examined their faces as carefully as he dared and then edged his way as best he could towards an older woman who stood a little apart from the others with her basket at her feet. Choosing his moment, Louis let his pipe drop to the ground and, bending to retrieve it, knocked the basket over. The content spilled out – a bottle of soup, some ham and bread wrapped in a napkin and two peaches.

'*Pardon*,' said Louis as the woman bent to retrieve her wares with a cry. 'I am sorry.'

The woman snatched up the soup and held it fiercely to her chest.

'*Vaurien*,' she snarled. 'Can't you see what you're doing? I'll lose my money if I don't deliver this.'

'Here, let me,' offered Louis and, clumsily repacking her basket, returned it to her. 'Which prisoner is the lucky man?'

The woman looked at him. 'None of your business,' she snapped.

Louis' smile was ingratiating. 'Then, at least let me buy you some beer for your pains,' he said. The woman paused, torn between hostility and the temptation of a free drink.

'All right,' she said reluctantly.

'Over here,' said Louis, shepherding her through the crowd towards Sophie.

Sophie leant forward.

'Your old clumsy self, I see, Carpeaux,' she snapped at Louis. 'My apologies, citoyenne, my husband is not to be trusted outside the house.'

She shrugged, and pushed the beer towards the woman.

'Drink,' she offered. 'You must need it.'

The face opposite her sagged with fatigue.

'I have been up since dawn preparing the food, and I am not about to lose my commission because of your fool of a husband,' said the woman.

Sophie nodded, all eager sympathy. 'Have you many to feed?' she asked.

'Five.' The woman drank the beer and wiped her mouth with the hem of her skirt.

'I expect money is short,' continued Sophie.

'We all need more.'

Sophie sighed in agreement. 'Do you come here every day?'

'Since summer last year. It is as good a way to make money as any. And if I lose a prisoner to *la mère guillotine*, there is always another one.'

The woman drew her hand across her throat with an ugly gesture.

'The guards must know you well, then, and trust you?'

'I should say.'

Sophie pushed the beer across the table and watched the second cup go the way of the first.

'The odd thing is,' said Sophie carefully, 'I have a commission

309

that needs doing, and I am looking for someone to do it for me
– for payment, of course.'

The woman put down her cup.

'Now you're talking,' she said, darting a glance over her
shoulder.

Sophie swallowed.

'I don't want to tell my husband,' she whispered, and
motioned for the woman to lean over the table. 'I want to send
some clothes in to my niece, who's in there' – she jerked her
shoulder in the direction of the Abbaye – 'but he, the true patriot
he is, doesn't like the idea. But I can't bear to think of her without
any clean clothes.'

Sophie's hand opened on the table to reveal a pile of coins,
then she shut it again. The woman licked her lips.

'You must be fond of her to pay that,' she said.

'I am.' Sophie wiped a convincing tear from the corner of her
eye. 'Will you do it?'

'Who shall I ask for?'

'Prisonnier de Choissy.' Sophie pushed the bundle of clothes
she was holding over the table towards the woman.

'Who?'

'De Choissy.'

In an instant the woman was on her feet. Her beer spilled on
to the ground.

'That don't sound a name for the likes of you or me,' she said
slowly, and the suspicion rose into her face. 'Who are you? I
don't like it. Here, take your things back, I am going to . . .'

She backed into the crowd and shouted at one of her friends
to summon the guard. In a second Louis was at Sophie's
side.

'Run,' he hissed. 'Down the street.'

Sophie did not wait to be told again. She was on her feet and
pushing her way as hard as she could through the throng. The
shouts redoubled behind her.

'À moi,' she screamed, as the pressure of bodies threatened to
crush her.

Louis stretched out a hand and Sophie clung to it.

'I can't move,' she managed to say.

Louis was mouthing something to her over the noise. 'The
prison carts – transferring prisoners,' he said. 'They are coming
through the gates. Get ready to run.'

It gave them their chance, while the attention of the crowd
was focused on the faces in the carts.

'Stop them!' came the cry from the woman. With a quick
movement, Louis hoisted Sophie over his shoulder.

'*Ma femme*,' he shouted, as loud as he could. '*Enceinte*. The baby is coming.'

'Stop them!' came the cry again, but the confusion was so great that no one knew any longer who was being chased.

'Let me through,' bellowed Louis. 'Another patriot is on the way.'

Sophie hung lifelessly over his shoulder. The crowd fell back and Louis was able to push his way up the street.

By now, the first batch had driven out of the Abbaye. Sophie, raising her head, had an indelible glimpse of the wooden cart, rumbling on hard, uneven wheels. The noise was deafening. She fell back against Louis. He shouldered her up the street as far as he could manage. Then he put her down.

'Sophie,' he said into her ear. 'You must walk as fast as you can. You must not think. Just do it. Hold on to me.'

Sophie did as she was told. But with every step, a pain pulled at her belly.

'The baby,' she gasped. Louis put his arm round her and frogmarched her onward.

'Keep going.'

After a minute or two they ducked behind a lime tree. To their right lay a side street. Louis hustled Sophie down it until they reached a crossroads where she leant against a doorway and tried to regain her breath. Louis stood fretting, beating his fist into his hand.

'*Nom de Dieu*, it should have worked.'

Sophie, fighting to control her panic and discomfort, felt the uselessness of his words. Louis would not give up hope. That she knew and understood. She also knew that the odds were stacked against him, but she bound herself to silence.

She squared her shoulders and lifted her chin. William would be waiting and she did not want to give him one second's more anxiety than she could help.

'Don't,' she said to Louis. 'Don't think about anything until we are back in the hôtel. We have yet to get past the guard.'

311

Chapter 5

A Letter, June 1793

To Citizen Rochefort
The Committee of Public Safety
Paris   June 30th, 1793

Dear Citizen,
        I have received your directive to investigate the
château of La Tesse and I have hastened to carry out your
orders.
    On arriving there, we found the château almost deserted
and in a state of considerable neglect. As far as we could tell,
only the concierge still remained with his son. On questioning,
they appeared to be admirable patriots and worthy of our great
republic.
    They say they have not seen the former Comte de Choissy
for many months, nor have they been in communication. I
arranged for the rooms to be searched, but we found nothing.
However, there are reports from the neighbouring village of
lights in the windows of the château at night. I will, therefore,
continue the investigations and inform you immediately of
any developments.
    If we do find the *ci-devant* count, I will arrange for him to be
conveyed to Paris immediately.

                            I remain your obedient servant,
                                    Joseph Lescot

Chapter 6

Marie-Victoire, July 1793

That night she dreamed of Pierre, a loving, happy dream. They
had gone to dine in one of the inns in the suburbs and eaten
heartily of a stew, fragrant with goose fat and plumped out with
white beans. They had drunk deep of the rough red wine and it
coursed through her body, giving her life and warmth. Pierre
had leant over the table and whispered words of love and she
listened with a tender smile and returned them with a lightly
blown kiss.

'Marie,' he had said. 'You must teach her good republican
virtues and bring her up to live in the new world. I rely on you,
Marie-Victoire, to do this for me.'

And Marie-Victoire had nodded, unwilling to let anything
spoil the moment.

She had woken sobbing and crying out his name. A baby was
wailing, and she realised it was Marie wanting her food. She
shifted in the bed, still half-dreaming, and felt the outline of a
back. For a second she thought she was with Pierre. Then she
remembered and recoiled. Beside her, Jacques Maillard slept on,
tired out from his previous day's work at the tribunal.

Marie-Victoire lay still; Marie was quiet now. Katrine would
have seen to her. One of the many things Marie-Victoire hated,
and there were many, about her new life was Maillard's insistence that they hire a girl to look after the child. Marie-Victoire
had protested, but in the end, weary of his obstinacy, she had
given in. She had been too despairing to fight, but deep inside
her burned one more bitter, festering resentment at Maillard.
One day she would rid herself of him once and for all, she
promised herself. But not yet: she had neither strength nor
energy enough. The grey fog that had dogged her after the birth
of Marie had returned and wrapped her in misery, and it took
all her resolution to keep going through the long days.

She got cautiously out of bed, reached for her shawl and let herself out of the bedroom. Her feet tensing on the floor, she flitted down the passage and into the salon. The sight that greeted her was as she expected. Maillard had given one of his suppers which had gone on late into the night and a stale smell of drink and tobacco hung over the room. She picked her way through the bottles and glasses which littered the floor to the window and flung it open. The morning air filtered in and she sniffed it tentatively. How she longed for the fresh, sweet smells of the country. How she longed for the peace of the fields and the sound of the wind in the trees. Paris seemed to stifle her now, it was full of noise and the hot, muddled clamour of greed and political ferment. It was a city in which there was no peace, only terror and sadness. Marie-Victoire wanted above all to escape from it and take her baby back to the simpler traditions of living close to the land: the ways she at last understood were the ones that were right for her.

She sank to her knees and rested her head against the wall of the room. She wanted her mother. Marie would have helped her, but there was no Marie and no way out of the hell her life had become. Somewhere, somehow, she had lost her way and her hopes had vanished, along with Pierre. What remained was the effort of getting through the day, and then the next, and the next. To live with Maillard was purgatory, but a purgatory that Marie-Victoire seemed to have no will to resist. It was not easy to cast aside food and shelter, and she had now tasted of hunger and felt the hand of want. Besides, if she had refused him, he would have taken Jeanne and Héloïse. In the face of such a threat, she felt powerless indeed.

She clasped her hands together.

'O Mary, Our Lady of Mercy,' she prayed, 'I know I am a sinner. Have mercy on me.'

She shut her eyes and bowed her head, willing the images of divine forgiveness to soothe and comfort her as they had done so many times before. When, at last, she opened her eyes, Maillard was looking down at her. He was already dressed in his judge's costume of unrelieved black from head to foot. A tricolour sash streaked diagonally from his shoulder to his waist and he wore a short cloak. He held his hat in one hand. With the other he leant forward to jerk her to her feet.

'What are you doing?' he asked coldly.

Marie-Victoire got to her feet.

'Nothing that need concern you, Jacques,' she replied.

'If I catch you praying again, I'll take steps to stop you.'

'Perhaps,' said Marie-Victoire, an odd little smile playing about her mouth, 'but you cannot order my thoughts.'

Remembering her state of undress, she pulled her shawl tighter around her body, having no wish to incite his lust at this hour. Maillard ran his eyes over her, noting for the hundredth time the exciting swell of her bosom, and swallowed. Marie-Victoire was unwilling, but the challenge stimulated him, and he piqued himself on the notion that, despite everything, she did not remain entirely cold in his embraces. He knew that she thought of someone else as he roamed unrestrainedly over her body, and the little moans that sometimes escaped her were not for him. But that, he considered, did not matter. The truth was that she was now lying with him and would be as long as he had the power to arrange matters.

Nevertheless, she had to obey him in some things, and for a woman of one of the judges from the revolutionary tribunal to be seen praying was dangerous.

'You have work to do, Marie-Victoire,' he said. His gaze swept over the litter of the room. 'I shall require supper for a few of my friends again tonight. See that it is done.'

Her golden-lashed eyes stared at him indifferently and he mastered an impulse to crush and hurt her. Anything to make her acknowledge his presence in a way that mattered. Then he relaxed. Marie-Victoire's capitulation would come later, he was sure of that. It was just a matter of time.

'I must go to Marie,' she said, turning her back.

'*Bien*,' said Maillard, buckling his belt and donning his hat. He stood tall and cadaverous, the black plumes nodding over his face. Already, his mind was on his work.

He left as Marie-Victoire was dressing and her heart lightened at the sound of the closing door. She got dressed in a blue gown of good cotton and brushed her brown hair and pushed it under her cap. For the moment, she did not much care how she looked. Although it was nice to have new clothes again, they did not delight her as once they would have done.

She was preoccupied with the tasks of the coming day, and worried by the baby who seemed flushed and restless. Katrine merely shrugged when Marie-Victoire tackled her and suggested that Marie was teething. But Marie-Victoire was sure that something wasn't quite right and she wanted to get through her tasks as quickly as possible so that she could spend more time with the baby.

The house on the Rue St Honoré had been built by the convent of Les Dames de la Conception in earlier years, and leased out when it was no longer used for its original storage purposes. It was a modest two-storey building with an entrance on to the street and a shop on the ground floor. At the back, it had four

315

windows in all which faced down into a narrow inner courtyard flanked on the opposite side by the convent itself. Maillard had rented the whole of the first floor, which consisted of two bedrooms, a salon, a kitchen and a small closet. The apartment was cramped, noisy and dark, assaulted, on one side, by the noise of the traffic in the Rue St Honoré and, on the other, by the carpenters who worked in the courtyard. Marie-Victoire hated it; the rooms oppressed her and she was sure the area was bad for Marie, who had failed to thrive since she had been wrested from Jeanne's rough and ready care.

Apart from that, she was beginning to dread the increasingly frequent processions of carts that made their way down the Rue St Honoré on the way to the Place de la Révolution and the guillotine. She expressly forbade herself from questioning Maillard on the subject, but the fact that he was helping to send these people to their death did nothing to help her peace of mind. Nor did the cries of the crowd, who seemed to enjoy the sight of the swaying prisoners enduring the torture of that last ride.

Only yesterday, one of them had glanced up from the tumbril to the window where Marie-Victoire, drawn by an awful fascination, was watching: a young girl barely into womanhood, dressed in a costume from the south. She was declaiming a prayer in a patois that Marie-Victoire did not recognise. In the few seconds permitted by the slowing down of the cart, the two women exchanged glances, the pity and horror registered in Marie-Victoire's being returned with a kind of simple acceptance by the other.

No, thought Marie-Victoire, this cannot be right, to send such a one to her death. And before she could stop herself she raised a wooden crucifix that she kept in her pocket so that the girl could see, and then as quickly hid it. The condemned girl turned a face glowing with thankfulness up to her benefactor. The cart rumbled on.

Marie-Victoire smoothed the sheets on the bed and pulled a woollen blanket over them. She went over to the window, poured the dirty water from the pitcher into the street and shut the wooden chest which contained her clothes. An odour of lavender and rosemary filled the room and she stooped to crumble a leaf between her fingers.

The kitchen was in as much disorder as the salon. Two cooking pots hung at angles over the stove and dirty dishes were piled high on the table. Marie-Victoire issued a sharp order to Louisette, a slatternly girl from the neighbourhood who came in to prepare their meals. Louisette was more of a hindrance than a help, but Marie-Victoire had found no one else to take her place, nor was she likely to. She knew the mixture of fear and dislike with which Maillard was regarded, and actually Marie-Victoire did not much care. As long as Marie was safe, she could put up with anything. Louisette brushed a filthy hand across her apron and picked up the water bucket.

'*La petite* has been crying again.'

'Where's Katrine?' asked Marie-Victoire.

'Out.' Louisette jerked her head in the direction of the street.

Marie-Victoire put down her shopping basket and hurried down the corridor to the second bedroom, where she bent over the wooden cradle. Marie had cried herself to sleep and lay flushed and sweating on the mattress. As Marie-Victoire watched, the little body tossed and turned as if searching for a cool place to settle. A tremor shook Marie-Victoire and her throat constricted. She reached out to caress Marie's cheek and exclaimed at its heat. On each of the baby's cheeks burned a bright red spot. Where the lashes fanned out in a semi-circle on Marie's alabaster skin was white. She touched them with her fingertip: Beneath them she knew, with the passionate possessiveness of a mother, lay little blue veins as delicate as a spider's web and the sparrow-like bones that formed the perfect oval of Marie's face.

Marie-Victoire picked up her skirts and ran to the kitchen.

'Heat me some water,' she ordered Louisette, 'and then go and buy meat and vegetables for the bouillon and a chicken for tonight. Hurry.'

She pushed the unwilling girl towards the stove, opened the cupboard where she kept her linen and pulled out an old shift. Using a kitchen knife she tore it into strips. Pocketing the knife, she then searched in the cupboard for a shawl.

She poured the warmed water into a bowl and carried it into the bedroom. With infinite care, she began to bathe Marie's face and hands. Halfway through, the baby woke with a wail and began to cry in earnest. Marie-Victoire crooned to her in an effort to keep her quiet, and continued in her task. When she was finished, she was relieved to see that the baby seemed easier. Marie-Victoire wrapped her in the shawl and, cradling her head on her shoulder, walked her up and down the room. She talked to Marie, telling her of her grandmother and of La Joyeuse, and described the woods and fields of her childhood and the animals that lived in them.

Marie's body burned in her grasp, but the sound of her mother's voice seemed to soothe her. The baby slipped into a fitful doze, but her breath sounded alarmingly hoarse in Marie-Victoire's ear. At last, Marie-Victoire settled her back into her

317

cradle and stood watching her anxiously. Marie lay still. Marie-Victoire returned to the kitchen to supervise the making of the bouillon.

She was dicing carrots when Marie wailed, a piercing, terrified sound. Marie-Victoire dropped what she was doing and ran to scoop her up in her arms, but the baby's body was so convulsed that Marie-Victoire had difficulty in holding her.

'Louisette,' she shouted. 'Go at once to the doctor and tell him to come immediately.'

Louisette's head appeared around the door.

'Go!' screamed Marie-Victoire and Louisette disappeared.

'Marie,' she begged her. 'Please get better. You are all I have. Without you there is nothing. Please, please, listen to me.' Tears began to spill down her cheeks. 'Listen to me, Marie. I love you. You must try. You must get better. Please get better.'

Her voice trailed uselessly into the room while the baby tossed in her arms. Fear slashed at her heart.

'I must do something,' she cried desperately, and cast a wild glance around the room. Seizing the cloth, she bathed Marie again and swept back the downy baby hair from her forehead. Marie sighed and turned her head from side to side. Marie-Victoire went over to the window and flung back the casement. No sign of Louisette or the doctor. She bit her lip and went to sit beside the cradle.

An hour went by, the longest hour of Marie-Victoire's life, and it seemed to Marie-Victoire that the angel of death settled over the room, his wings outspread. Once Marie flung out her hand and Marie-Victoire clasped it in her own, willing life and strength back into the small fingers. Then the baby lay quiet again.

The doctor arrived. Brisk and self-satisfied, he offered no comfort.

'Keep her cool,' he ordered. 'Guard her against the night air, and if she gets worse I will bleed her. There is nothing else I can do.'

Marie-Victoire stared at him, hating his well-fed outline and bland face, and directed Louisette to give him a coin from the chest in the salon, hardly caring that Louisette would more likely than not take one for herself while she was doing so.

Towards noon, Katrine staggered back into the apartment. It was obvious she had been drinking, and Marie-Victoire let her have the full force of her anger. Under the whiplash of Marie-Victoire's tongue, Katrine turned mutinous and gave as good as she got. She then ran into the courtyard where she was sick. A few minutes later, she reappeared and made her shamefaced

ologies, offering to keep watch while Marie-Victoire worked
the kitchen.

Marie-Victoire forgave her and gave up her place. Somehow
e chicken became a stew and the bouillon was made. Marie-
ctoire managed to get some down Marie, who sucked it thirst-
. Then, feeling utterly exhausted, she threw herself down on
r bed.

When she awoke it was dark and the apartment was quiet.
e sat up and pressed her hands to her aching head. Her mouth
s dry and her eyes burned. She swung her feet to the
or.

Katrine was watching over Marie. Marie-Victoire saw how
ncerned the maid looked.

'I bathed her again because she was sick and she has slept a
le,' she informed Marie-Victoire.

Marie-Victoire knelt down by the cradle. Even in the short
ace she had been sleeping, Marie seemed to have wasted.
ite obviously, she was no better.

'Will you help Louisette prepare the supper for Monsieur
aillard and his friends?' she said dully. 'I must stay with Marie.'

She sat staring at Marie, dwelling on every curve and shadow
her baby's face, until she heard the door bang and the sound
feet on the stairs. Then she went out to meet Maillard.

Maillard was in a good humour, and he smelt of wine.

'Marie-Victoire,' he said, giving her his hat. 'Citoyens
ntane, Théry, Souberbielle and Naury have come to supper
I promised.'

Marie-Victoire indicated the salon with a nod.

'*Entrez*, citoyens,' she said. Then she turned to Maillard.

'You must tell them to go,' she said. 'Marie is ill. I think she
ay be dying. Tell them to go.'

Her voice rose and tears choked the rest of her sentence.

'*Merde*,' said Maillard. He hustled Marie-Victoire into the
by's room and glanced down at Marie.

'She looks all right,' he said indifferently. 'You're hysterical.'

Marie-Victoire grabbed at his arm. 'I tell you she's very ill,' she
ed. 'Get rid of them. Do something.'

Maillard shrugged. 'I don't think a sickly baby is a good enough
ason for me to offend my friends, do you?' he told her.

Marie-Victoire picked up Marie and backed away from him.

'You are a devil,' she hissed, dropping kisses on the baby's
otesting head. 'There is nothing human in you any more. I
ought perhaps there might be something, but I was wrong.
u belong to the devil.'

Maillard advanced on her.

319

'Put the child down,' he commanded. 'Put her down and p
yourself together. I wish supper to be served. Now. If the ch
is still ill tomorrow, I shall call the doctor. You will leave her h
and attend to me.'

His eyes bore into hers, willing her to obey. Reluctant
Marie-Victoire did as she was told and stooped to kiss Mar
'*Reste tranquille, ma fleur,*' she told her as she tucked the sha
round her and caressed her tiny head. '*Reste tranquille.*'

Forcing herself to be calm, she followed Maillard out of t
room and went in to the kitchen. She worked automatical
Every so often, she would drop everything and hurry in to che
on Marie. The baby lay quiet. By ten o'clock the men were
drunk that they were flinging glasses into the fireplace. All
them had dined hugely and they sprawled, replete and win
flown, across the chairs and on the floor. One of them w
singing a popular obscene song and Maillard was expoundi
on a highly satisfactory day's proceedings. None of them ga
Marie-Victoire a second glance. Fed up with her frequent disa
pearances, Maillard had forbidden her to watch by the baby.
had need of her services, he said drunkenly, and she sat, froz
with hatred, in the corner. Maillard caught her eye and beckon
her over.

'More wine,' he demanded, and forced his hand into
bosom of her gown.

'Don't touch me,' she said, loud enough for his friends to he
and pushed him away. He tightened his lips and gave he
warning glance.

'Mind your tongue.'

On her way back from the kitchen, she defied Maillard a
looked in again on Marie. The room was curiously hushed a
very still. Marie-Victoire's heart missed a beat and she dropp
the flagon. The wine spread over the floor in a red pool. S
approached the cradle. Marie was rigid and she had lost all
colour. Marie-Victoire felt for signs of life and found none.

'No,' she said. 'No.'

In an instant, she was through the front door and runni
into the street, heedless of the curfew and of the danger, runni
as she had never run before.

'Please, please,' she sobbed as she banged on the docto
thick wooden door until her knuckles were raw. 'Please h
me.'

A surly, sleepy maid opened it a crack.

'The doctor,' Marie-Victoire begged. 'My baby.'

The doctor finally appeared. His plump, irritated face
nothing to reassure Marie-Victoire.

'Go away,' he said, shielding his taper. 'Come back in the morning.'

Marie-Victoire summoned her remaining strength.

'If you don't come, I will denounce you as refusing to attend to a citizen judge,' she spat.

Even in the murky light she could see the doctor's face turn a pale shade of green.

'All right,' he gave in angrily. 'Wait here.'

He banged the door in her face and Marie-Victoire sagged back against the wall.

'If she dies, Lady of Mercy,' she prayed, 'then I shall know that you have no mercy. If she dies, I will never forgive you and will curse you from the depths of my soul. Do you hear me, Lady? I shall not forgive.'

There was no answer from the black night above, not even a glimmer of the moon, only the silence of the street.

Muffled in a long cloak, his bag bumping at his side, and glancing frequently over his shoulder, the doctor cursed as Marie-Victoire urged him on.

'Hurry,' she cried. 'Hurry.'

The house was silent when they made their way up the stairs and through the door. Marie-Victoire snatched a candle from the table in the hall and tried to light it.

'I'll do it,' said the doctor, and then waited for her to lead him into Marie. Once there, he made Marie-Victoire shine the light full into the baby's face.

Marie was exactly as Marie-Victoire had left her, a small waxen statue from whom life had apparently fled.

'This child is dead,' the doctor said, straightening up. 'You have called me for nothing. A malign fever, there was nothing I could do.'

He caught at the candle as Marie-Victoire slid to her knees and into the abyss that awaited her.

When she came to, Maillard was supporting her head and the doctor was forcing some brandy down her throat.

'There, citoyen,' he said. 'She is conscious now. It was a passing seizure. I will take my fee and go back to my bed, if you please.'

Maillard fumbled in his coat pocket and threw a coin at the man.

'Go,' he said.

The doctor did not need telling twice. He picked up his bag and left the room, anxious to leave such misery behind him. Not, he reflected sourly as he picked his way over the cobbles, that it was the first time, nor undoubtedly the last, that he would encounter such.

'You fool,' said Maillard to Marie-Victoire. 'Did you have to go waking the neighbourhood and disturb the guests? I am sorry about the child, truly, but you will have others. Don't waste your feelings. There are plenty more where she came from.'

Marie-Victoire raised her hand to blot him out of her sight.

'You murderer,' she said blankly. 'You filthy murderer. I can' believe what you are saying. The life of my child meant nothing to you, nothing, and yet you pretend to love me. You are a liar to the depths of your black soul. You love nothing and no one. May you rot in hell.'

She got to her feet.

'I never really found out what happened to you, Jacques. Oh I know you got a beating and I left you, but that wasn't enough was it? One woman's body and your stupid lust and it ends in this. Where did you lose your soul, Jacques? And was your revenge on me worth it?'

Her voice cracked and despite himself Maillard was forced to look away from her misery.

'I tell you,' she continued in the same strange tone, 'I shall have mine, for now I have nothing to lose. You took my innocence, then you took Pierre and now my child.'

Maillard leant forward to flick the shawl over Marie's dead face but quick as an arrow Marie-Victoire forestalled him.

'Don't you touch her,' she said. 'Don't you dare.'

'I didn't kill her,' he said defensively.

'As good as.'

Maillard shrugged. 'As you like.' He made to leave the room

'As to my soul,' he threw back over his shoulder, 'I lost it the day you left me in the orchard. If anyone is to blame, it is you Marie-Victoire. Think on that. The child is dead because you abandoned me and I took another path, an infinitely more rewarding one. Death is of very little importance.' He stopped at the door. 'I pursued you because it suited me, and because I needed you to remind me of my past and because I wanted your body. Because', he added softly to himself, 'I could not let you go.'

'You lie, Jacques.' Marie-Victoire spoke in a tone he had never heard before.

He turned once more to face her.

'You lie. You loved me and still do.'

Her eyes glittering and with one hand buried in her skirts, she moved towards him as sinuously as water over stones. 'Take me in your arms, and tell me it isn't true, and then I will believe you.'

Her body swayed towards him in the half-light, mysterious

and sweetly curving. Her hair streamed down her back and her gold-tipped lashes veiled eyes that had gone misty with anguish and desire. He took a step forward, drawn like a moth to a candle, and pulled her body into his, closer and closer – until he felt the knife she produced from her pocket sink deep into his neck.

'For Pierre,' she said, as he staggered and flung up a hand to ward off the next blow that sliced up into his breast.

'For Marie,' she said, and struck him again.

'And for me,' she intoned as the last thrust struck deep into his heart.

He sank without a sound to his knees, blood filming his vision and streaming down his shirt. She stood above him, her knife dangling from nerveless hands, and let it drop to the floor.

'Now we are both damned,' she said, and watched Maillard's blood mingle with the spilt wine on the floor. He sighed once, raised his head and tried to speak. Deliberately, she turned her back and waited until the bubbling breaths died away into nothing. Then she stopped to close the staring eyes and mop the blood with a strip of linen. Wiping her hand on her dress, she went to kneel beside Marie.

'It is over, little one,' she whispered. 'All the pain and the worry, and soon it will be for me, too. I shall not be with you because I have sinned, but I will think of you where I am going and know that you will be safe. If God is merciful, Pierre will be with you too.'

She drew nearer till her lips rested on the transparent cheeks.

'Perhaps it is better so. Perhaps I could not have managed to look after you, however hard I tried.'

She kissed the now icy forehead, traced the lines of Marie's feathery eyelashes and attempted to straighten her fever-twisted limbs. Then, carefully lifting the body into her arms, she stepped over Maillard, sat down in the chair by the corner and cradled it to her.

'I have until morning to say goodbye to you, Marie,' she told her.

Settling back in the chair, she whispered to her dead baby until the dawn streaked the sky and a rumpled Monsieur Théry appeared at the door to bid his farewells and awoke the household.

PARIS, Summer 1793

Slowly but surely, the Jacobins seized the advantages of their opponents
disarray, took control, and ruled the country through the increasingl
sinister Committee of Public Safety.

Not unnaturally, the provinces came to resent the Parisian dominanc
of the revolution and demanded that the National Convention exercis
its full weight in deciding social and political policy. In Paris itsel
egged on by Marat and others, the volatile sansculottes demanded wag
rises, price controls and punishment for hoarders. Always there was th
ever present threat of foreign invasion. The Prussians were advancing
the Spanish were threatening to cross the Pyrenees and the British ha
besieged Dunkirk. The situation degenerated when royalists in Lyon
assumed control, and in Toulon counter-revolutionaries handed over th
French fleet, the arsenal and the town to Lord Hood, the British admiral
As a result, Danton, who had tried by diplomatic means to defuse th
crisis, was thrown off the Committee of Public Safety. He was replace
by Maximilien Robespierre.

The Jacobins had to work hard. Popular unrest increased after th
murder of Marat by Charlotte Corday, a young woman of Girondis
sympathies, which gave the people a potent martyr. Danton and hi
supporters were still men to be reckoned with, and so were the follower
of Hébert, who had set himself up as a radical figure with the sansculottes

The committee responded with decisive measures. The army wa
purged of undesirable generals and the devastation of the Vendée wa
ordered. Revolutionary authority was imposed by force in the provinces
the trial of the queen was ordered and the call went out for the entir
country to take up arms.

On September 5th, Paris echoed once more to marching feet a
Parisians made their way to the National Convention to demand brea
and higher wages. In the confusion, a cry went up from the Jacobin sid
– 'Let terror be the order of the day.'

On September 17th, the convention passed the Law of Suspects. Al
those who showed themselves by thought, word or deed to be 'advocate

324

of tyranny' or 'enemies of liberty' were suspects. The categories included those whose 'civism' was unproved and whose loyalty to the revolution was questionable, those who did not have a legal means of support, those with relations abroad, and those who had emigrated without being acquitted before the law.

The reign of terror had begun.

Chapter 7

Marie-Victoire, September 1793

What made me do it? I don't know. I can no longer think or feel. I can only remember that a madness came over me and I wanted to drive the knife in as deeply as I was able. How strange he should die like that! Jacques always cherished his knife back at La Joyeuse so long ago.

They've taken me to this place and told me that it wouldn't be long, but I think they've forgotten. To kill a patriot is parricide, they said, and they predicted I would wear the red shirt.

It's dark in here and there is no peace. It smells. They smell. So do I. I can never be alone. Except in my mind. I know there will be no mercy for me, especially not from God. I have sinned so terribly. I have killed, I have lain with a man when my heart belonged to another. And today, for the first time, I stole some bread. It was easy. I was surprised how easy.

Blessed Virgin, you deserted me. I wasn't the most obedient of your children but I did love you, but when it came to it I loved Marie more and you took her from me. Why did you do it? How could one small, very small, baby have made any difference to you? I don't understand, and now I never will.

I hope they come for me soon . . . I hate the dark . . . and my head hurts. Lady, look down from your throne and pity me. I am without anyone. If there is any room for forgiveness, think of me. You were a mother once.

My feet are dirty, my hands are dirty and my hair is stiff with grime. I cannot keep off the lice any longer. Every night the rats come and I wake when they run over me. When I remember all the lotions I used when I was with Madame Héloïse and the perfume I dabbed on my wrists, then I laugh. I have Pierre's letter and I read it every day. Was he true to me when he described the girls with their plaits? I think so. In his way. I am sure he is dead. Where does he lie? I wonder. I hope it is in a cornfield sprinkled with bright red poppies where the birds swoop after the sun has gone down in the evening. His eyes will have faded now and there will be earth in his black hair. At least he is in the fields. I shall be confined between grey-stone walls, and the sky that will look down on me will be hazy with city smoke. And there will be no poppies or cornflowers over my body.

Pierre said I was like a cornflower. He never knew he had a daughter. I had a daughter. Her name was Marie and she was so beautiful.

Will the dark ever go? Blessed Virgin, forgive me.

Chapter 8

The Conciergerie, September 19th, 1793

The gates of the Abbaye prison opened to let the cart through. Outside, the driver began to negotiate his way through a jumbled assortment of stalls and shops.

It took time. Most of the figures in the cart sat quietly and raised their heads to the sun. Nobody talked much, they were too preoccupied with their thoughts. One of the prisoners, her dark hair coiled in a mass on top of her head, took a quick look round and then fell back into her reverie. Her fingers fiddled with her white dress, and she coughed once or twice, but she seemed calm enough. She did not even look up as the cart began to rumble down the streets towards the river, and through the places she knew.

The driver flicked his whip, pleased with his progress. Today the transfer of prisoners from the Abbaye to the Conciergerie was going very well. If he was quick, he might even have time to visit the wench who lived over the wine shop on the Île St Louis.

The sansculotte who stood watching the cart, half-hidden behind a group of women, remained where he was until the cart was out of sight. Then he turned on his heel and began to walk in the direction of the Rue de l'Université.

In the Cour de Mai, Héloïse got down from the cart, clutching her bundle of possessions. She walked through the grille, down a flight of steps, across a small courtyard and into the Conciergerie prison. As the door banged behind her, it closed out the sun and severed all contact with the world outside. She closed her eyes for a moment. It was impossible not to know what entering the prison meant. The sudden drop in temperature made her shiver and the cold inside extended its fingers down the opening of her dress.

The prison registry was divided in half by a wooden grille.

Héloïse and her companions were ordered into the part where a clerk sat at a desk strewn with papers. The clerk looked up and mouthed something under his breath at this latest batch. Did they think he was a machine? These days there was no time for anything. The prisoners kept on coming and he, Jean-Baptiste, was supposed to make out the correct documents and compile the lists for the prosecutor-general. It was too much.

They were all the same. A selection of frightened people who tried to disguise it. Sometimes with anger; sometimes with bluster; sometimes with rudeness. He began to write their names in the book and glanced up at Héloïse. This one seemed as if she had herself well in control. She was trembling, though, and that made him regard her a little more kindly. He could sympathise with that much better than anything else.

She answered his questions quietly and efficiently, only once casting a look through the grille where two prisoners, who had been condemned too late the evening before, were waiting to be conducted to the tumbrils. They had been stripped of their coats and their hair was shorn. One of them was drunk and called out for more brandy. He lay sprawled on the floor where he had spent his last night. The floor was littered with his clothes and the remains of a meal. His companion endeavoured to comfort him, but his efforts were greeted by drunken abuse. Héloïse looked away and prayed that she would have strength, if the time came, to approach her end in a more dignified fashion. The door reopened and four more prisoners entered the registry. Before she had a chance to see if she recognised any of them, Jean-Baptiste threw down his pen and shouted to a companion to take her away.

The stench in the corridor into which the turnkey led her was horrible – a combination of decay and badly attended latrines, of illness, misery and the close, sickening miasma of too many bodies crowded together. The corridor was packed with prisoners who milled up and down, exchanging gossip, cultivating friendships and striking bargains. Some were in rags, but many, those with funds, were dressed with the careful refinement of people who had nothing else to occupy their time. Well-bred voices mixed with the harshest of patois, and the noise was intense. The turnkey's dog snapped at anyone who was unwise enough to brush against him and he tore a ruffle of Héloïse's dress. She protested.

'Quiet, Ravage, or I'll throttle you. *Pailleux* or *Pistole*?' enquired the turnkey, driving his truncheon savagely into the dog's side.

'*Pistole*,' replied Héloïse quickly. At all costs she must have a cell to herself. 'With a window.'

'Ten livres.'

'Five.'

Héloïse knew better than to use up her stock of money all at once.

'Ten or nothing.'

'I have it in coin – that will interest you.' She allowed him to see a gold coin.

The turnkey snapped his fingers to bring his dog to heel. 'Why didn't you say before? You pay each week. I want two weeks' worth now.'

Héloïse smiled a wan smile. Her incarceration in the Abbaye had taught her a few valuable lessons.

'Come back in a week, if I am still here,' she said. 'The money will be ready.'

'You are fortunate,' said the turnkey. 'I have a vacancy next door to the Citoyenne Capet. The very best of accommodation.'

He laughed mirthlessly. Héloïse followed him down the passage and left into a corridor that ran the length of one side of the women's courtyard. He stopped, jangled his keys and indicated with a nod that she was to enter the cell. Héloïse held her bundle tighter and went inside. The turnkey held out his hand.

'Prisoners' cells are unlocked at six in the morning and locked at eight in the evening. Make sure you are in the right place. If you need anything, I am sure I can arrange things for a suitable fee.'

'A woman,' Héloïse hesitated. 'I would like someone to attend me.'

'If you ask in the corridor, there will be someone willing to work.'

She placed a coin in his outstretched hand. With that he departed, leaving Héloïse to survey her new abode. The cell was a narrow rectangle and from its dark stone walls rose a chill that would be unbearable in winter. The window opening on to the women's courtyard was barred and open to the air, and the meanest of beds stood ranged against one wall on which was folded a verminous-looking blanket.

Héloïse sat on the bed and placed her bundle beside her and stared into space. A sob rose to her lips. She bit it back, angry at her weakness. It would do no good to weep, but her desolation and her longing for Louis threatened to swamp her good intentions.

Unbidden, a memory stole into her mind, the memory of the garden at La Joyeuse. There, lulled by warmth and the drowsy sound of bees, the roses lay turning their blooms to the sky. Behind them massed the startling blue of the lavender beds and the green of the close-clipped hedges which blended with the grey of the statues and seats. The peace was infinite, and Héloïse, clad in her muslin gown, wandered light as a feather through the garden to pick the roses. She could smell their perfume and feel the glossy roughness of their leaves on her fingers. She caressed them, rejoicing in their firmness and cleanness. . . . It was all so real that she almost cried out. She buried her head in her hands.

'Louis,' she whispered. 'Where are you?'

Later, she lay on the bed tracing the scrawls on the stone walls left by the women who had occupied the cell before her.

'*Je suis innocente*,' wrote one in a hand that wavered and trailed into nothing.

'*Vive le roi*,' wrote another. 'The scum can have me.'

'To lose your head does not mean you will lose your soul,' wrote a third, in a bold and dashing manner.

'I am Madame de Lavergne,' said the fourth, 'and I no longer wish to live.'

She had dated it August 15th, 1793.

Héloïse stared at them for a long time, comforted by the shades of these women who refused to go silently into eternity.

'Your courage shall be mine,' she said aloud into the emptiness of her cell.

By the time she had roused herself to arrange her things, the cell door had banged shut for the night and it was too late to venture out for food. Her stomach, which had tasted nothing since early morning, growled with hunger. She did not even have a candle to read the book she had brought with her.

On impulse, she dragged the bed to the wall under the window and peered through the bars into the courtyard. The sounds of captivity floated out from the huge building: cries and whispers, a muttered prayer and the sound of desperate sobbing. Here and there in the deepening shadows a shape loomed – someone, having outwitted or bribed the gaolers, was visiting someone else, and in the recess opposite to her cell she was sure she could hear a muttered conversation. A dog barked once or twice. The light faded slowly, deepening into shades of opal and aquamarine and then into the violet of the September night. Its colours mocked the misery of the prison below. It seemed to Héloïse, kneeling on her narrow bed, that a million hopes and fears rose up into its velvet blackness and then vanished for ever. She thought of the queen, incarcerated beside her, and of how that royal lady must look, now a bewildered widow, grieving for her children and perhaps glad at the prospect of death.

Would Louis mourn her own death for long? Héloïse felt that

331

it could not be far away. Perhaps de Choissy would spare her a Mass – her strange, unfathomable husband whom she had hated. Where was he? Had he made it to the border? She pressed her face against the bars. There was no time left to hate, nor was there cause any longer. Many things had become clear to Héloïse during the past weeks. Her love for Louis had softened and chastened her pride, and she realised now that, as much as de Choissy had taken her peace and caused her to suffer, she had failed to try to give him either her trust or her liking. If she had, it might have been different.

Huddled in her blanket, she slept at last and did not stir until the door was flung back with a jangle of keys. Héloïse rose, struggled out of her dress and removed her chemise. Her body gleamed as white and fragile as it had ever been. She was thinner perhaps, and her skin was a little more transparent, but she had been lucky in remaining so healthy up to now. She picked up her spare chemise, glad of its cleanness, and wondered if she could pay someone to wash her clothes. Over the chemise she laced a petticoat of Indian *bazin* decorated with little stripes and over that she threw a dishabille which she fastened with a green sash. This, and the dress that she had worn the day before, and a cotton gown *à collet*, was the total sum of her wardrobe, but they would have to do. Luckily it was so warm at the moment that her two pairs of stockings could be worn in the evenings only and she had a good supply of cambric handkerchiefs. To finish her toilette she wound a muslin kerchief round her shoulders and tucked the ends into her sash. Her hair presented more of a problem, for she had no cap. She solved it by combing it out down her back and then twisting it up as high as she could with a couple of combs. She smiled as she did so. Perhaps she would begin a fashion for the ladies.

With her money tucked into her bosom, she made her way with her laundry to the corridor that ran between the men's and women's areas of the prison. It was already filled with prisoners, notaries and officials and money was changing hands on all sides as clients briefed their lawyers. She stopped to ask one of the turnkeys the whereabouts of the larger cells and was rewarded with a jerk of his head in the direction of the women's courtyard.

Héloïse found it difficult to get her bearings and almost impossible to move. The Conciergerie had been designed to house less than a third of the detainees who spread into every nook and cranny of its odoriferous cells and passages, and it was rabbit-warrened with corridors and cabins into which no light ever penetrated. To the right lay the notorious 'Rue de Paris' where the poorest slept and fought off the rats that crept up at night through the sewage tunnels. Off that lay the 'mouse-trap', a labyrinth of dungeons and cells that even the gaolers were afraid to penetrate. The women's area lay to the left, surrounding the women's courtyard. Prisoners who wished to speak to the women in the courtyard could do so at this point through a wide iron grille which was set into the wall at a junction of two vaulted arches. Truly, she thought, it was a place of no privacy and no mercy for the ill or unwary, only of misery, disease and despair.

Héloïse retraced her steps back into the women's courtyard and made her way to a door under an arch. She stepped inside. Almost immediately, she retched. The smell was worse here: a foul contagion of vomit, excrement, rotting food and moisture-sodden straw. Inside, what light there was filtered through an inadequate window and bathed the inmates in a green light.

Every square inch of the cell was occupied. The lucky ones had wrested a few extra inches from their neighbours and sat propped up against the wall or huddled in the corner. The rest were jammed together in a parody of patriotic equality. Some of the women were screaming, and at the furthest end two of them were fighting like wild animals. Others were too weak and numb to do other than gaze about them with expressions of despair. They were all ghostly pale and many of their faces were covered in sores, and vermin crawled through their hair. A few mothers were suckling babies whose limbs were more often than not twisted by disease. It was like a charnel house out of hell.

Héloïse fought to control her stomach, feeling it was beyond her powers to go on. But her pride made her, a pride that told her she must face the worst and survive it. She pushed her way onwards. A howl from a hag near the door greeted her passage.

'A visitor, my friends. A fine lady, if my eyes don't deceive me.'

Héloïse ignored her taunts. She paused while her eyes adjusted to the gloom and made for a corner where a group of women sat trying to darn their clothes. There was something familiar about one of them. She bent over and tapped the girl on her shoulder.

The face that raised itself to hers was pale and thin and streaked with grime. Huge, purple-rimmed eyes peered up at her, and beneath them lay a mouth that betrayed suffering and knowledge beyond her years. There was a world of feeling written into those well-known features – grief, spent passion and a blankness that said their owner had finished with life.

Puzzled by the interruption, Marie-Victoire dropped the rags that she was trying to cobble together with the help of a nail. The woman who hovered in front of her straining vision swam up out of the past, stirring bitter, longing memories.

'Madame,' she said with disbelief. 'Is it you?'

Heedless of the filth, Héloïse dropped on to the straw beside her.

'Marie-Victoire,' she breathed. 'It cannot be you, can it?'

She reached out to touch her in order to tell herself that she was no phantom. 'What have you done to be in this dreadful place?'

'Murder,' said Marie-Victoire blankly. 'I murdered a patriot. I should have been dead a long while ago, but they said I had to wait for a trial.'

'Murder?' said Héloïse, truly surprised, and swept by pity. 'Oh, Marie-Victoire, what has happened to us all?'

Marie-Victoire fumbled with the rags. There were no answers, certainly none that she could give, nor did she have the spirit to find any.

Héloïse got to her feet.

'You are to come with me,' she said. 'You will share my cell. Come.'

She put out a hand to help Marie-Victoire upright. Marie-Victoire stumbled as she rose. She was wraithlike and covered in sores. Using as much force as she dared, Héloïse ushered her to the door and out into the courtyard. Marie-Victoire gasped in the light and covered her eyes with her arm, but managed to walk steadily enough back to Héloïse's cell. Once there, she dropped on to the bed and burst into tears. Héloïse comforted her, and told her that she was safe for the moment. Then she covered Marie-Victoire with the blanket and departed to arrange things with the turnkey.

After a sleep, the first real one she had enjoyed for months, Marie-Victoire seemed better and more disposed to talk. It did not take long to relate her story and she told it simply and unemotionally, only breaking down at the part where Marie died. Héloïse listened without saying anything, holding one paper-dry hand in hers, until the finish, and she thought her heart would break for Marie-Victoire.

'So, you see,' said Marie-Victoire, 'there is nothing left, madame. It has all gone, everything that I ever had, and once Marie went, then I wanted to go, to die too.'

'But if you get out of here, you could make a new life for yourself,' suggested Héloïse gently.

The look that met hers was in its turn filled with infinite pity for Héloïse's naïvety.

334

'You have heard what they say about the Conciergerie?' asked Marie-Victoire. 'The hell from which there is no route save by the little window of the guillotine. I am a murderess and there will be no mercy for me. It is no matter.'

Marie-Victoire circled her neck with her fingers. 'It is quick, and I can't feel more pain than I have already done.'

'Eh bien. Then, perhaps we will go together. There is comfort in that thought, is there not, Marie-Victoire? We must practise courage together.' Héloïse spoke more cheerfully than she felt and went to kneel at the window. 'We must first of all arrange to eat. I have money that will suffice for both of us.'

She was looking into the yard as she spoke.

On either side of the grille that divided the women from the men, benches were being arranged to form a dining table, the centrepiece being the iron bars. On each side of the grille, baskets of food brought in by the women who ran commissions for the prisoners were being unpacked by the recipients. The benches filled up, and the sound of laughter and banter filled the court.

'I think I'll go and see what is happening,' she told Marie-Victoire.

Down in the courtyard, Héloïse discovered there was a spare seat at the impromptu table and she sat down. She ventured to ask her neighbour, a good-looking woman dressed in the height of fashion whom she recognised as a distant acquaintance of de Choissy's, if she could buy some of her food. The woman agreed at once and told her to make free with what she had. Héloïse thanked her, cut a piece of cheese for herself, bit hungrily into it and listened while she ate to the flow of repartee that passed from one side of the grille to the other. The men on their side vied with each other to pay compliments; the women returned them with wit. From time to time, a particular delicacy – a ripe peach, or a glass of wine – was handed through the bars and the accompanying sallies had most of the diners shaking with laughter. Héloïse replied to her benefactress's enquiries, promised to rendezvous with her another time and bundled up some food for Marie-Victoire in her handkerchief. The meal had done much to lighten her mood and she felt she was among kindred spirits. She almost forgot the overflowing cells that lay out of sight around her.

That evening, when the cell door had clanged shut, she and Marie-Victoire sat propped on the bed until late. The darkness loosened their tongues and its blanketing anonymity permitted the luxury of confidences, and they talked as they had once done long ago. Héloïse spoke of Louis and poured out her love

for him. Marie-Victoire listened and was reminded, with a pain
twist of her heart, of how she had felt for Pierre.

'I don't know where he is, and the worst part is that he do
not know where I am. If I had one wish, it is to see him again
Héloïse finished.

Marie-Victoire was curious.

'Where is Monsieur le Comte?'

'He had to leave in a hurry. He had planned to go to Germany

'And he sent no word?'

'It was not possible.'

'Do you not wish to know where he is?'

Héloïse reflected.

'Yes, I would like to know if he is safe. I owe him that. Bu
am glad that I am facing this alone.'

She indicated the cell.

'I would like to know if my mother is still alive, and I a
anxious about mademoiselle, *ma cousine*. She should have l
Paris by now, but I am worried that she will try to persua
Monsieur Jones to do something rash.'

Héloïse wrapped the blanket more firmly round Mari
Victoire's shoulders, for the chill was deepening.

'And you? What do you wish, Marie-Victoire?' she asked.

'I wish to know where Pierre lies buried,' she replied, 'fo
am sure he is dead, and to say a Mass over the grave. I wish
see La Joyeuse again and to see the fields and lie in the lo
grass down by the orchard. I wish to hold Marie once more, b
that I shall never do because I am damned.' Marie-Victoire
voice cracked.

Without thinking, Héloïse gathered her into her arms.

'Hush. Our God is merciful, is He not?' she told her. 'If
pray, He will hear us, I know He will, Marie-Victoire. We m
trust in Him to preserve our souls.'

The girl's sobs quietened. She clung to Héloïse and felt h
warmth seep into her. Gradually, she relaxed, and her he
grew heavier and heavier until she slept, leaving Héloïse
watch over her.

The two of them quickly established a routine. In the mornin
Marie-Victoire washed their clothes at the fountain in the cou
yard and Héloïse would dress in her dishabille and arrange
a woman to bring in their meals. At noon, those women wl
could retired to dress in their cells, to assume a more form
attire. Marie-Victoire would help Héloïse into her cotton gov
and sweep her mistress's still shining hair up on to the top
her head. The afternoon was spent promenading around t

336

courtyard and in conversation with other prisoners. Héloïse knew some of them already, and with each day that passed more and more recognisable faces appeared. Towards evening, Héloïse would once again retire to her cell where Marie-Victoire waited to lace her into her white dress. Then they would eat, sometimes alone, sometimes in the company of others. Occasionally, Héloïse joined in a game of cards – and often won – or in the popular charade, 'Mock Tribunal', which ended with a prisoner being bound to a plank and 'executed'. At first, Héloïse had wanted nothing to do with something so macabre, but then the fascination of it drew her into its grip.

'It is as well to rehearse,' she informed Marie-Victoire who, aghast at the joke, had protested. 'I am learning fast.'

Marie-Victoire shrugged, and her gesture told Héloïse that she thought she was mad. And so I am, thought Héloïse; mad with the horror and the fear of this place.

In this way, five days passed. The weather held fine, and sent down seductive rays of sun into the women's courtyard and painted the sky with a bright cerulean blue.

'If you look up,' remarked Héloïse on the fifth day, 'you can almost believe you're somewhere else.'

Marie-Victoire followed her gaze and Héloïse was thankful to see that a tinge of colour had crept into her cheeks and that her bruises had faded a little.

'Where would you like to be, madame?'

'At Neuilly,' replied Héloïse, 'riding through the forest.'

'And I with Pierre in the country somewhere,' said Marie-Victoire.

The sound of the Conciergerie gate swinging shut for the hundredth time that day sounded into the afternoon.

'I wonder who will be next?' said Héloïse. They were waiting for the daily roll-call of names to be summoned to face the tribunal. She squeezed Marie-Victoire's hand. 'Will it be today?'

'Prisonnière de Choissy, you are wanted.'

The turnkey came up and spoke to Héloïse. He jerked his head in the direction of the men's area. Surprised, Héloïse got to her feet and threaded her way over to the grille.

'Héloïse,' said a voice, and a hand on which reposed a well-known gold ring beckoned through the bars. 'Over here, where there is room.'

Héloïse slipped through the bodies and peered through the grille. Her knuckles whitened.

'You are here, too,' was all she could say.

Pressed up against the grille, de Choissy extended his hand and bent to kiss her lips through the bars.

337

'Indeed, madame my wife. It seems that we are not to b[e] parted in life, nor perhaps in death.'

Bereft of speech, Héloïse stared at him, so bitter was h[er] disappointment that her summons had not been a message fro[m] Louis.

'I thought you were safe,' she said eventually, realising s[he] must say something.

'And so I was, *ma belle*, for a time. Safe – in a manner [of] speaking – at La Tesse. Unfortunately, they came looking f[or] me, so I had to make for the border where I was taken.'

'What is the charge?'

'Counter-revolutionary activity. Émigré status. Taking mone[y] out of France. You can see they enjoyed themselves with me.'

'Is it true? The first part, I mean?'

His smile faded. 'Are you interested? Why, then, yes, m[y] dear. It is. While I was hiding in La Tesse, I managed to shelt[er] a few fugitives.'

'I see,' said Héloïse, impressed by his courage despite hersel[f]. 'What happened then?'

'La Tesse became too dangerous. Someone in Paris ke[pt] badgering the authorities in the town to keep searching th[e] house. In the end, I felt I could not expose Cabouchon an[y] longer. He had risked enough. So I decided to make for Koblen[z]. However, my disguise was not good enough. Nor were m[y] papers. The obliging clerk told me you were here when I arrive[d]. He remembered your name.'

He took her hand and pressed it to his cheek.

'Are you well, Héloïse?'

She grimaced as her neighbour fell against her and trapp[ed] her arm in the grille. It was difficult to talk.

'I will arrange to come and see you,' he said. 'Have you money[?] They did not take all of mine.'

'Enough.'

Then he was gone, caught up in the press behind him.

'Tonight,' she heard over the hubbub.

Héloïse rejoined Marie-Victoire, and now it was the turn [of] Marie-Victoire to comfort Héloïse and to hold her.

'I don't want him,' Héloïse cried with despair. 'I wa[nt] Monsieur d'Épinon and I want him so badly that I think I w[ill] die before they kill me.'

At last the shadows lengthened and the prisoners began [to] prepare for the evening. A card game was in play in one of th[e] cells. In another the mock tribunal was yet again being r[e-] enacted. Héloïse sat by the fountain and reached over to dribb[le] the water through her hands, her white dress showing pale i[n] he dusk. The gate rattled, a dog snapped and then he was beside her.

'I've only got half an hour,' he told her, and drew her into one of the shadowy corners of the courtyard. 'Now, listen,' he said. You know nothing about any of my movements and I will tell you nothing more, so it will be the truth. You are to say we are virtually estranged – not so uncommon, my dear – and you have no control or knowledge of my financial affairs whatsoever.'

Héloïse nodded. 'If you consider that will help, I will do as you say.'

De Choissy hesitated. There was a day's stubble on his chin and his hair had shaken loose from its ribbon. He was dressed neatly, but lacked his former magnificence, and sported buffskin breeches, leather top-boots and a coat with a turned-back collar.

'Voilà my disguise as a stoutly patriotic merchant,' he said, interpreting her gaze correctly. 'You had no idea I could play the trader.'

Héloïse managed a smile.

'I had no idea about many things about you,' she remarked. 'Not, if I am honest, that I wished to.'

He leaned forward and took her by the shoulders.

'Try to understand,' he said, in a tone she had rarely heard. Try before it is too late.'

'Why?' she asked. 'What does it matter to you? When have I ever mattered?'

'I have had time to reflect. We are facing death.'

'How selfish you are, Hervé. You wish to square your conscience, that is all. But, if it makes it better, I no longer hate you as I did. I, too, have learnt some things.'

De Choissy shrugged. 'Can't you accept that I grew to love you – in my fashion?'

She moved out of his grasp.

'You surprise me, monsieur,' she said thoughtfully. 'We did not have much to bind us together. We married out of duty, as is the custom, and I gave you what was required.'

'Not a son,' he said, before he could prevent himself.

Héloïse flinched. 'It was as God willed,' she said.

De Choissy drew her towards him, more gentle than she ever remembered.

'Don't think I don't know about Monsieur d'Épinon,' he murmured into her hair. 'I know all about it. But Monsieur le Capitaine is not here. I am. Let us try to make something of it.'

'That is true,' replied Héloïse with an effort. 'He is not here. But', she added, 'I have no wish for him to be so. Surely you cannot imagine that I want him in this place.'

339

He released her and she moved away so her face was in the shadow.

'Forget him, Héloïse.'

'Never! That is asking too much.'

'Then, promise me that you will think over what I have said'

The gate into the courtyard opened and a figure with a do moved towards them. De Choissy rose to his feet.

'I must go.' His expression was difficult to read. 'But you wi not escape me, Héloïse. I promise you that.'

Héloïse allowed him to kiss her hand, more affected than sh would admit.

'As you say, Hervé, I will not escape you.'

That night, the moon rose over the prison and its radianc seemed to jeer at the buildings. It was worlds away from th suffering that was confined within the walls below.

Chapter 9

Louis, September 19th, 1793

'Of course you must go.' Louis spoke with decision. 'Now Héloïse has been transferred it is even more important that you leave Paris.'

The three of them sat talking in the salon of the Hôtel de Choissy. The clock had already struck ten and the remains of their meal – bread, olives and cheese – lay on the table, and the two men were making inroads into a bottle of wine.

'Sophie,' William questioned her. 'Do you agree?'

She stirred and felt a sudden movement of the baby. She knew the answer to his question. She longed to be free: to leave the fear and terror and to escape to wild, cool spaces where she could breathe again and give birth in peace; to start a new life with William and forget the nightmare. But she was torn in two at the thought of abandoning Héloïse. That would be a bitter betrayal of her cousin, and Sophie could not actually bring herself to give her assent.

Louis read her thoughts.

'Héloïse would want you safe,' he said. 'Consider how she would feel if you put yourself or the child in danger. She often spoke of it.'

'I understand,' replied Sophie. 'But to leave her alone . . . in that place . . . it does not bear thinking of.'

'She won't be alone,' Louis announced. 'I'll be there.'

Both William and Sophie stared at him.

'You are not planning anything unwise?' faltered Sophie, her suspicions growing. 'That would kill her as surely as the guillotine.'

Louis smiled reflectively.

'I shall look to my skin, if that is what you mean,' he said. 'But if you are asking me to abandon her while there is still hope, then you are asking too much.'

He set down his glass on the table.

341

'Now, listen,' he said. 'I have a plan. I will leave almost immediately and I will use the door we used before – it's lucky the guard hasn't noticed it so far, but I think it is only a matter of time. I will return à la sansculotte and begin drinking with the guard. When I have got him drunk, I will signal to you and you must go at once. I will keep him talking as long as I can in order to give you as much headway as possible. Once out of here you will be on your own and you must make your way to Sir Robert's as best you can. I cannot help you. I will give you a few days before I do anything, just in case. William, you know the rest.'

'Agreed,' said William. He picked up his tail-coat and searched in the pocket.

'I think you should have these,' he said, holding out two keys. 'This one is the key to number 7 in the Place Royale and this one opens a safe which is concealed in a cupboard. You will find clothes, money and papers, and you have my permission to use anything you wish. All I ask in return is that you destroy anything you don't use and you never speak of it to anyone.'

Louis raised his eyebrows. He was a little surprised but he was not going to question William further. 'Thank you, William,' he said. 'I am grateful. This will buy me time.'

'So it is goodbye,' said Sophie. 'It is true. We must go. Paris is finished for us. I know that.' She held out her hand to William who took it in his own. 'It is as well, my heart,' she said, to reassure him. 'I will do as you ask because I know Louis will do his best for Héloïse. Only if she dies, it will lie on my conscience for ever that it was . . . that it was alone.'

William bent and kissed her.

'I understand, Sophie,' he said, 'but it is a risk that I must ask you to take. I regret that my own position puts you in more danger, more than you realise, but as an English national you are a target.'

William had already explained to them both in a very sketchy way the situation regarding the Hôtel de Ville and his confiscated documents. He was surprised that he had got away for so long. He turned to Louis.

'I gather from the news-sheet that the British fleet is mounting offensive operations in the Mediterranean. Paris will like its British visitors even less. Who knows, the authorities might even begin to arrest the British? I think it is possible.'

Louis shrugged.

'You are right, my friend. Paris is no place for either of you.' His expression softened at the sight of Sophie's unhappy face. 'Don't despair, Sophie. I promise you I will do my best for Héloïse.'

342

William refilled their glasses.

'You are a brave man,' he said with feeling. 'And I salute you.'

Louis raised his own glass in response.

'It has been my honour to count you as my friends.' And it was the courtier and army officer who spoke to them. 'There are many things that divide us. Our nationality, our politics – and our future – but we have shared much and I shall never forget you.'

He raised his glass to his lips. Sophie grasped hers.

'Until we meet again,' she said.

'D'accord,' Louis agreed.

William drank in silence. He had few illusions as to just how probable it was that they would meet again, and it saddened him. But already his mind was busy with his own plans and he sent up a silent prayer that he would be equal to the task. The three of them made their farewells without lingering. Then Louis slipped out of the Hôtel de Choissy and disappeared.

Within half an hour, he was back as he had promised, carrying two bottles of wine. It did not take much to distract the bored and sleepy guardsman, who was only too glad to pass the time of day in a friendly drink with a well-disposed patriot. Before long, the two of them were roaring out songs into the street and howling with laughter. Out of the corner of his eye, Louis saw the drapes at the salon window twitch. He clutched his red Phrygian cap in his hand and waved it nonchalantly in the air. It was the signal.

The wine had given him a sore head, and his footsteps were not altogether steady as he bade the guard farewell and weaved his way along the river embankment towards the Île de St Louis. Louis stopped once at a street pump and plunged his face into the water, willing its coldness to restore his wits. He walked through alleys and over mud flats, crossed waste spaces and threaded between rows of derelict houses and decaying huts, until he reached the Rue St Antoine. The Place Royale was only a minute or so away.

William had thought of everything. There was fuel by the fireplace. Wine and candles on the shelf and hard-tack biscuits in the cupboard. Louis dared not pull back the shutters and only lit the candles for minutes at a time. He opened the safe, and it was then he understood about William. The light was bad but he managed by working methodically to read the papers contained in it. Then he selected a couple of forged identity cards and a certificate of residence from the pile. The rest he removed from the safe.

Kneeling down by the fire, he began to tear the documents, one by one, into shreds and fed them into the flames.

343

Chapter 10

Sophie, September 19th, 1973

The fiacre deposited Sophie and William at Sir Robert's door. William ran up the steps of the house and sounded the knocker. The door opened at once to reveal a servant who showed no surprise at the visitors. He led them through the hall, obviously the floor given over to offices, and indicated they were to wait in the back study. Sir Robert arrived within minutes, his good-natured face more than usually anxious. He went over to Sophie and bade her welcome with such unaffected good manners that Sophie began to relax.

Over a glass of wine, the three of them discussed the next move. Sir Robert was adamant that they should leave that very afternoon, and assured them it was perfectly possible.

'I fear your writing activities may have been exposed,' he said gently to Sophie, 'and I think your name is on the section lists sent into the committee which deals with public safety. So . . .' He left her to digest the implication. 'I am sorry that this has taken so long to arrange,' he continued. 'I warned you that it might. It takes time and money to get up a chain of contacts and to brief them. However, all should now be well. Do you have your documents?' he asked William.

William patted his coat-tails.

'I hid them in the stables, but luckily I retrieved them two days ago,' he replied. 'Miss Luttrell and I are now word-perfect in our new identities.'

Sir Robert turned his attention to Sophie.

'And you, my dear Miss Luttrell, are you strong enough for the journey?'

Sophie, acutely aware of how irregular her situation must appear, blushed. Nevertheless, she was not ashamed of her condition. She shrugged.

'I had better be,' she said, in an attempt at gaiety. 'Or, rather, the two of us had better be.'

Sir Robert laughed, and his face told her that he approved her spirit.

'That reminds me, my friend,' he said, looking at William. 'I have arranged what you requested and the person concerned can be here within the hour. You are fortunate. I am the one person in Paris who can oblige you in the matter!'

'Good,' said William, smiling at Sophie's puzzled expression. 'I have not as yet informed the lady in question, but I will now hasten to do so.'

Sir Robert tactfully withdrew at this point, in order, he claimed, to put the final touches to the preparations. William waited until he had left the room and then surprised Sophie by dropping to one knee.

'Miss Luttrell,' he said, his eyes dancing. 'Behold me! I am here to do the honourable thing by you and ask you to marry me. And all things considered' – he looked pointedly at her stomach – 'it is about time.'

'Marry me!' exclaimed Sophie. 'Now?'

He nodded.

'I have arranged it with Sir Robert. A Protestant priest is on his way over here.'

Sophie stared at him, the unexpectedness of William's plan leaving her breathless. Through her mind swept a jumble of images – among them, her parents and the hotly protesting shade of Ned. She felt once again the tang of English rain on her face and the sun in the brick-walled garden, and smelt the wet, leaf-strewn earth of the woods around High Mullions. She saw her room, a white sunny place for a virgin girl, and heard Miss Edgeworth's voice drone through the long afternoons when she longed to be outside. These things she was giving up, to live far away.

'Sophie, please.'

William swam before her vision, jealous of the look on her face. She looked down seeing the frown that ruffled his forehead and the anxious curve of his mouth. For a moment, his expression of bewilderment and baffled tenderness resembled Ned's. Then his face snapped back into focus and she knew for certain that William was nothing like Ned. The baby stirred inside her.

'Sophie, answer me.'

Her face cleared. 'Of course,' she said. 'Of course I will marry you. Today.'

And so it was that Sophie Luttrell married William Jones in a grey stuff gown that strained at the waist in a dusty, paper-strewn room that did duty as Sir Robert's library. There had been no time to do anything except brush her hair into its golden waves and find a clean fichu from her bundle of luggage, and if she regretted her abandoned piles of exquisite dresses and lace chemises, or that she had no loving embraces of friends and parents to cheer her on her way, she showed no sign of it.

The disapproving voice of the pastor rose above the hurly burly of the street. How lucky I am this is not England, though, Sophie; he would have run me out of the parish by now. The baby kicked forcefully and Sophie wondered at the strangeness of life that turned out so very different from what she had been led to expect. Who would have foretold that she would have stood, pregnant and shabby, on the run from the Parisian authorities, marrying a man who would take her over the sea and far away?

Not I, thought Sophie, and turned with a radiantly happy smile to kiss her groom.

Chapter 11

Louis, September 26th, 1793

Louis hitched his belt higher, patted his waist where the roll of double louis d'or lay concealed under his shirt, slicked back his cropped hair and pulled down his coat. His well-made figure attracted some admiring glances, and one woman went out of her way to bump into such a handsome-looking patriot. Louis quickened his pace.

The Cour de Mai was crammed with men, women and children, and the refreshment booths were doing a brisk trade. The tricoteuses were already in place on the stone steps of the Palais, where they waited to pour down insults on prisoners being herded into the Conciergerie and to scoff at the condemned who, later in the day, would emerge from the prison to take their place in the carts. Louis looked at them with loathing. They were a hellish breed, and the thought that any one of them had shouted at Héloïse was more than he could stomach. He gave the steps as wide a berth as he could and made for the prison entrance in the north-west corner. The turnkey was in a surly mood and Louis decided to wait until another took his place. He flung himself down against one of the pillars, pulled out a hunk of bread that he had thoughtfully provided himself with and began to eat.

The talk flowed around him. Closeted in one corner, a party of lawyers were busy disputing the merits of a case. To his right, the anxious relatives of a prisoner were debating whom to approach first, and in front of him lounged a detachment of National Guardsmen, very much at their ease. As he ate, Louis took note of the prison buildings, although from where he sat it was difficult to ascertain much. Somewhere inside them was Héloïse, and the very fact that she was there, unseen and unknowing, stirred up a mad desire to storm the gate and carry her way to safety. Louis bent his head, in case his face betrayed too much, and concentrated, instead, on what was being said around him.

Much of the gossip concerned the queen. When she would face trial and when she would die. That she would, was taken for granted.

'Oh, yes,' claimed one savant, 'the widow Capet will feel the blade of *la mère guillotine*. And I shall be there to watch it bite into her neck . . .'

Louis' gorge rose. The prospect of these bloodsuckers gathering to watch the death of the queen he had had the honour to serve was so distasteful that he could listen no longer. He got to his feet and made his way for the second time to the prison gate. As he had suspected, the turnkey had been changed. He waited until a fresh group of prisoners had been ushered through the door and began his negotiations. It was as difficult and tedious as he had imagined. The man was suspicious of Louis' money and worried that someone dressed like him should have so much. But in the end the gold coins did their work and Louis was permitted to enter. He stepped through the *guichet*, which shut behind him.

'*Allumez le miston*. Take note of this one,' the turnkey sang out.

The clerk in the registry looked up from his work and flicked a questioning glance at his colleague. The turnkey gave a thumb up and nodded. The clerk subjected Louis to a hard, searching stare and then held out his hand.

Louis placed two coins in it and said, in a low, deliberately hoarse, voice, 'Until tomorrow. I will give you two more when I leave.'

The clerk jerked his head towards the prison interior and spat in Louis' direction.

'If you last that long,' he remarked sourly, and returned to his papers.

Delighted that he had got so far, Louis kept his face blank as he followed the turnkey through two more doors. Once inside the turnkey turned to him.

'You are on your own now,' he said. 'Mind that you make no disturbance. If you do, I will denounce you and it's my word against yours.'

Louis nodded. 'We understand each other,' he said ingratiatingly. 'You'll have your money, I'll have the woman. No questions on either side.'

The turnkey gave a short, barking laugh.

'A fuck before facing *la mère guillotine* is as good a way to go as any.'

Louis laughed with him, but his soldier's eye was already scanning the corridor, trying to assess the geography of the prison.

The turnkey moved off with a shrug of his shoulders, muttering under his breath. Louis blew a sigh of relief and leant against the wall while he planned his next move. The sight of so many people did nothing to reassure him, and the unsavoury closeness of his surroundings gave him an unpleasant feeling and warned him to be careful, very careful. He took off his red cap and stuffed it into his pocket. Then he pulled at his shirt and wound a modest cravat around the neck. These simple ministrations, as he knew from practice, had the effect of turning him from a villainous sansculotte into something more respectable and therefore less noticeable.

Where was she? From now on, every second mattered. Louis forced himself to remain motionless. His observations soon told him that the men's part of the prison lay to his right and the women's to his left. Through a couple of iron grilles at the end of the corridor there appeared to be a staircase that led up into the Palais interior, and the endless procession of clerks up and down it suggested to him that these were the steps to which the prisoners were led when the time came for their trial . . .

It was difficult for Louis to tell who were prisoners and who were not. The air was thick with different accents. Merchants and bankers paraded up and down with as much grave concentration as if they were at their places of business. Priests moved through the press, spreading their words of comfort, and flushed red complexions betrayed the rural origins of many. The dandies were in evidence, singing their modish songs and mincing foppishly from side to side to avoid the prostitutes who accosted them with their challenging glances and reddened lips. There was a feverish air to all this activity and noise, a frenzy of hope and despair, anguish and anger. He could smell it – a smell of humanity at bay, mingled with an odour of decay and illness which permeated even the stones.

His stomach growled with nerves, and, notching his belt even tighter, he moved as best he could down the passage towards the grille that separated the men from the women. The crowd was thickest at this point and the daily interchange between friends and lovers was in full swing. Louis elbowed his way through. The women's courtyard was packed. Louis peered through the bars and searched the sea of faces that swirled round the confines of the small square, swearing with admirable fluency at anybody who tried to take his place.

He was prepared to be patient, convinced if he stood there long enough he would be rewarded by the sight of Héloïse. As he waited, the iron gate into the yard opened and three of the prison turnkeys strode out into a small enclosed area near to the grille. One of them pulled in his dog, the other two consulted their lists. It was obvious they had been drinking and they were having trouble focusing on their papers. Louis glanced at his watch. This must be the roll-call of women prisoners selected to stand trial the next day.

'Quiet, you scum.'

The grating voice of the turnkey managed to penetrate the hubbub and a hush fell, a few apprehensive gasps cutting into the silence. The dog barked, and one of the turnkeys aimed a kick at its face. It subsided, whimpering.

'Ravage is not so well today,' called out one bold spirit from Louis' side of the grille. 'He doesn't like the accommodation.'

The jeers and sallies that greeting this witticism caused Ravage's owner to frown.

'Get on with it,' he shouted to his companion.

'Jeanne-Marie Clain, Juliette Cailleau, Thérèse Olivier . . .'

A shudder went through the waiting company, and a neatly dressed woman fell to her knees. Her companions hastened to help her to her feet. The turnkey hesitated, peered at his paper and swore.

'I can't read this,' he announced to the other two.

'Claire de Herry,' he hazarded at last.

There was no response. No one stepped forward to claim the name.

'Claire de Herry.' The turnkey was livid. 'Which one of you is it?' he shouted, the spittle flying in a stream on to the stones.

'If you don't own up, I'll take one of you anyway.'

'I am Athenée de Thierry.' A voice spoke from the crowd. Louis drew in his breath as a young woman pushed her way to the railing that separated the guards from the women.

'Perhaps, it is me that you want,' she suggested.

'You'll do,' said the turnkey. 'I need ten.'

Athenée de Thierry reached out to take the indictment from him and placed it in her pocket.

'Le voilà,' she said, patting it with a smile. 'No need for alarm, mes amis.'

'Teynière, Aimée; Marie-Jeanne de Lescalet; Bonnard, Marie-Victoire; de Choissy, Héloïse; Laville, Violette . . .'

It was over for the day.

'Oh God.'

Louis heard Marie-Victoire's involuntary cry, and felt the relief of the waiting women who had escaped – this time. The lucky ones moved off to reassume their places round the fountain or to retire to their cells if they had them, some of them supporting their stricken friends.

Louis could see both of them now. Marie-Victoire was calm after her outburst, but as white as a sheet, and he saw with a painful tightening of his throat how Héloïse's hand tugged nervously at her dress. She was dressed in a simple cotton robe, and her hair, swept up by her combs, revealed the mysterious planes and shadows of her neck and face. She was even more lovely than he remembered her. The two women embraced. Then Héloïse disengaged herself and disappeared. Louis was only prevented from shouting out her name by a supreme effort of will. Behind him the babble was even louder as the men discussed the roll-call and fought to gain a space at the grille. Louis shrugged off the most importunate and grasped the bars harder, willing Marie-Victoire to come closer.

Obedient to his silent entreaty, she looked towards the railings and walked towards them.

'Marie-Victoire!' Louis hissed her name.

Marie-Victoire started in surprise and came closer.

'Monsieur,' she breathed.

'Quiet,' he said sharply. 'I am Louis to you.'

She nodded, understanding at once what he meant, and an unselfish joy spread over her features.

'I will fetch her,' she said simply. 'I am so glad.'

'Marie-Victoire,' he said, 'tell her I am not a prisoner and I've only got a little time.'

Without saying anything further, Marie-Victoire sped out of sight.

And there she was, a whirl of skirts, a rapturous face and huge dark eyes masked with tears of joy. She sobbed and murmured his name again and again while she clung to the grille.

'You have come. You have come to see me.'

'Did you not think I would?' and, ignoring the bars, Louis bent to kiss her mouth, tasting the salt of her tears, and the softness. For a minute there were no words, only an exchange of hands and a tracing of beloved features with their fingers. They pressed closer and closer together, heedless of the cold iron – until it seemed as nothing.

Louis wiped the tears that streamed down her face.

'You look hungry,' she said as he did so, and pressed his hand to her cheek.

'You too, Héloïse,' he said, his eyes dwelling on the sharp curve of her shoulder under her bodice. 'Is it so bad?'

'Not now,' she replied. 'Nothing matters now. I can face anything. It is enough that I have seen you and know that you are well.' She cast a quick look round. 'You must go at once. If

351

you are found out. . . . It is the end for me, I know it, but not for you.' She kissed his hand again and again.

'Not yet, Héloïse.'

'Only one more minute, then. Are you safe?'

'Thanks to William, I have protection.'

'Sophie?'

'They are on their way.'

'Thank God. Louis, no more. There are spies.'

He kissed again. 'It's been so long, Héloïse.'

'Louis, I order you to go.'

'I am not leaving you. Not if it is the last thing I do.'

'But it may be.' In her desire to make him understand, Héloïse raised her voice and was subjected to curious stares.

'Shush, *ma mie*. There is no argument,' Louis told her.

'De Choissy is here. If I have been called, it is likely that he has been too. He was arrested on the border. If he sees you . . . Louis, I don't trust him.'

Louis frowned. He had not counted on the presence of de Choissy.

'Curse him,' he said savagely, and then thought better of it. After all, he could not deny that Héloïse was de Choissy's wife.

'Where is he?' he asked.

Héloïse indicated the men's part of the prison.

'Who knows? He is trying to obtain a cell for his accommodation.'

Louis tried to picture the fastidious de Choissy among the alleys and foul cabins, and failed.

'You must wait for tonight,' he told her. 'I have bribed the turnkey to let me into your part of the prison. Tell me where you are and he will leave your cell unlocked. You must place a handkerchief on the handle.'

Pressed up against her side of the bars, Héloïse considered: the men and women were locked into their separate areas at night, but it was not unknown for a lady's *cher ami* to bribe his way through the women's gate. Illicit meetings were dangerous, but not impossible as long as they were conducted discreetly, and several had slipped the net to snatch comfort in the concealing darkness. Accept, urged her inner voice. The worst might happen tomorrow and you must take what little time there is. Louis has risked so much for you that you cannot deny him now. Nor did Héloïse wish to. She wanted him so urgently, so selfishly, that tomorrow did not seem to matter any more. Only today had any meaning, and the rest was lost.

Louis was waiting for her answer. When at last Héloïse said yes, she was rewarded by his expression.

'I would have come, even if you said "No",' he told her. 'I made a promise to Sophie, and to myself, that I would not leave you.'

'Enough, madame,' a voice spoke beside Héloïse. 'If you will be so kind as to let me into your place, I must speak with the gentleman through here.'

A polite, but firm, prison inmate indicated with a wave of her hand that Héloïse must relinquish her turn. With a little sigh, Héloïse released her hold on the bars and stood back. Louis sent her a private smile and mouthed a kiss. He waited until she had crossed the yard before giving up his place and melting back into the corridor.

When Héloïse informed Marie-Victoire of Louis' plan, Marie-Victoire sprang into life.

'Madame will remain here,' she announced. 'I will fetch water and we will wash your hair and then I will make you a very special toilette.'

She was as good as her word. From somewhere (God alone knew what it cost her, thought Héloïse), Marie-Victoire procured a piece of scented soap. Héloïse seized it and sniffed at it with the hunger of someone who had almost forgotten that such things existed. Marie-Victoire lugged a bucket of water up from the yard and insisted that Héloïse strip down to her bare skin. She proceeded to scrub Héloïse from top to toe, until Héloïse stood breathless and pink from her treatment.

'Luckily, I have a clean chemise ready,' said Marie-Victoire as, finally, she began to comb out the mass of Héloïse's wet hair. For a moment, Héloïse quite forgot where she was and imagined that she was back in her bedroom at the hôtel. Then she laughed at her fancy. All that luxury had vanished with the wind, never to return. But it was good to feel so clean again. She turned to Marie-Victoire, who was laying out her robe.

'This is almost like old times, Marie-Victoire.'

The girl said nothing, her face serious and preoccupied.

'How strange that we two should begin together and end up together,' Héloïse reflected. 'There is a divine pattern that has woven us into the same cloth and seen to it that you and I shall not be parted.'

'I am glad it is so,' said Marie-Victoire. 'It is the only thing left to me.'

The sadness in her voice caused Héloïse to swallow, suddenly ashamed of her joy.

'Without you, Marie-Victoire,' she said and paused, 'I could not have been so strong. I want you to know that.'

She smiled up at the pale face and, on an impulse, touched her

353

cheek to one of Marie-Victoire's rough little hands. Marie-Victoire flushed and bit her lip. But she returned the smile and there was a fleeting glimpse of the old Marie-Victoire in her look: the younger Marie-Victoire who had once stood, flushed and dreaming, in the gardens of La Joyeuse.

In the passage outside there was a sudden clamour and a shouting of orders. Marie-Victoire disengaged her hand and went to look out of the door.

'I think it is something to do with Madame la Reine,' she reported over her shoulder.

'Poor lady,' replied Héloïse, who had often thought of her royal mistress in the next-door cell. 'Madame de Lamotte told me only today that they are preparing her trial. She heard it from her brother.'

'They seem to be moving her,' Marie-Victoire reported. 'I did hear they wanted to keep her under closer watch.'

Regardless of her damp hair, Héloïse leapt up to see. Thin and exhausted, but still elegantly dressed, the queen walked slowly out of her cell, down the corridor and out into the main body of the prison. A hundred eyes watched with Héloïse's, many praying, some plotting the impossible dream of rescuing her, others indifferent and contemptuous. Marie-Antoinette appeared neither to see nor to heed them, but kept her eyes fixed ahead, lifting her dress over the refuse to reveal red prunella shoes of excellent quality.

'God go with you,' Héloïse breathed after the departing form, and wished that somehow she could have comforted her sovereign and former mistress.

Marie-Victoire resumed her ministrations.

'What else are they saying in the prison?' asked Héloïse, knowing that the prison network was by far the most efficient method of gaining information.

'They are having trouble finding a defence lawyer for Madame la Reine and many of the documents have gone missing.'

'Perhaps, then, it will not be possible to try her,' replied Héloïse. 'Unlike us,' she finished, as the thought of the morrow struck both of them.

'Madame.' Marie-Victoire sank to her knees. She spoke hesitantly and with obvious emotion. 'Will you help me? I am not afraid to die. At least, I think I am not. There is nothing left for me to live for, but I fear them. Those men . . . and the carts . . .'

'How can I help?' Héloïse leant forward, touched by Marie-Victoire's appeal.

'Will you help me not to appear weak?'

Héloïse thought carefully before she replied, because she

354

wanted to choose the right words. In the short space during which they had been reunited, Marie-Victoire had come to mean much to her, not just as a face from the past but as a friend. Six months ago, Héloïse would not have considered Marie-Victoire in that light, but now she did. It was a friendship that was born out of their mutual need, but it was also much more; it was the meeting of two women, changed and moulded by experience, each recognising in the other a similar spirit.

'I will help you, if you are prepared to help me.'

Marie-Victoire was surprised.

'I help you, madame?'

'I, too, am afraid, *chère amie*. I need you to support me, and we should support each other as long as we are able.'

Marie-Victoire blinked at the unaccustomed endearment, which sounded sweetly in her ears. Her haunted look faded, and in its place dawned a peaceful expression. Marie-Victoire got to her feet, dusted down her ragged grey cotton skirt and resumed her combing of Héloïse's hair.

'If you need me, madame, then all is well. I am content to die.'

She picked up a lock and smoothed it softly and expertly.

'Madame will look *ravissante* for monsieur by the time I have finished with her,' and a smile curved at her lips that had no envy or bitterness in it.

Marie-Victoire was as good as her word. By the time dusk sent its first probing fingers over the yard, Héloïse stood gowned in her white robe, her hair piled high over her head and falling softly to her shoulders. Marie-Victoire tied a velvet ribbon round her neck.

'Madame should be wearing her diamond necklace,' she remarked as she did so, but Héloïse only smiled and passed her hand over her neck as if brushing away the memory of something so trifling. Marie-Victoire stepped back.

'Monsieur will be pleased.'

Héloïse stood up and stretched out her arms as if to embrace the very walls, and in truth nothing before had ever made her feel so beautiful or so exquisite as her prison toilette. From her fragile fingertips to her feet shod in a pair of shabby, black high-heeled shoes, she was alight with throbbing, insistent life – a figure that flung defiance at the spectre of death.

Already the gates were closing, each one sending an echoing note into the evening air. Crash, crash; followed by the thud of many keys and the isolated oaths of turnkeys in haste to finish their job. The two women listened to the footsteps crunching in

355

the passage outside and the clanging of cell doors, each one nearer than the last. The footsteps stopped at their door and they heard the pant of the turnkey's dog, but after long seconds the feet moved on up the passage. Héloïse gave a sigh and went to stand by the window.

An hour passed. The Conciergerie lay quiet. Two shadows loomed briefly in the light of the torches burning high up in the embrasures, and melted back into the dark. Each of them was making their way towards Héloïse's cell. The taller reached the entrance to the passage first and with a glance over his shoulder disappeared. The second followed a little later.

One torch only hissed and spat in the passageway, sending sparks on to the stone walls. Louis moved slowly along the corridor, holding his clogs in his hands. His eyes searched for Héloïse's signal. The handkerchief gleamed back at him. Noiselessly, he pushed open the thick wooden door and stepped inside the cell. Marie-Victoire flattened herself against the wall. She saw Héloïse raise her face to Louis' and then she slipped quietly away. But once outside she gasped and her hand flew to her mouth.

'Monsieur,' she faltered. 'You're here.'

'That's right, Marie-Victoire,' replied de Choissy, bearing down at her out of the dark. 'Now let me pass.'

She flung her body against the door.

'No, monsieur,' she said. 'It is not for you in there.'

'You are mistaken, Marie-Victoire,' said de Choissy. 'Madame la Comtesse is my wife.'

'No, I will not let you,' cried Marie-Victoire in a determined whisper.

'Don't try me, my dear, this is neither the time nor the place.' He pressed his face up against hers and his eyes were dangerous. 'Get out of the way.'

He pushed her roughly to one side and she raised her arm in self-defence. As she did so, the cell door fell open to reveal Héloïse and Louis.

De Choissy brushed past Marie-Victoire, knocking her against the wall. He addressed Louis and his voice shook.

'Get out,' he ordered.

The two faced each other. De Choissy quickly recovered his poise and waited for Louis' response.

'I should have known,' said Louis in an undertone. 'I should have known that you would trouble Héloïse as long as there was breath in your body.'

'Louis, no.' Héloïse interposed herself between the two men, her hand held up in warning. 'Remember, no noise.'

'He was too strong for me, madame,' said Marie-Victoire. 'I'm sorry.'

'It does not matter,' replied Héloïse, and turned to her husband. 'What do you want?'

The rage died out of de Choissy's face. He adjusted the cuffs of his shirt and straightened his coat.

'Why, you, Héloïse. Who else? Is that not obvious? I had planned on spending a little time on what might be my last night on earth with my wife.'

Héloïse stiffened. 'You have been called, then? The same as I?'

'Of course. Is it not natural we would go together?' He took a step closer to her. 'Did you not think, Héloïse, that I might wish to see you? That, indeed, I mattered?'

She regarded him steadily.

'No, Hervé, I did not consider that. Despite what you told me yesterday, what reason do I have to imagine that your presence here is anything more than an impulsive gesture?'

'Close the door, Marie-Victoire,' Louis took charge.

He turned to de Choissy.

'Monsieur le Comte. You do, of course, have the right to see your wife, that I must concede and I must give you time with her. But I ask you, as an honourable man, then to leave us.'

De Choissy narrowed his eyes.

'Monsieur le Capitaine is in error,' he said. 'It is not for him to decide the rules of this matter.'

Héloïse suppressed a hysterical laugh. The scene was absurd. Did neither of them remember that they were no longer in Versailles but in a prison, and that time was running out?

'Enough,' she said. 'You must go, Hervé.'

De Choissy stood quite still.

'Héloïse,' he said. 'It is not too much to ask?'

Héloïse swallowed, angry that her precious minutes with Louis were vanishing, and at de Choissy for invading them. She had not wanted to think about her husband, or to be reminded of him. But things had happened differently and she knew it was up to her to salvage some dignity out of this strange and embarrassing encounter.

'I cannot pretend that you haven't surprised me, Hervé,' she said. 'And I think I must believe you. If you had told me something of your feelings earlier, our lives might have been different. But you did not. Instead, you did your best to hurt and humiliate me.'

'My dear, it is so unfashionable to love one's wife,' said

357

de Choissy mockingly, and Marie-Victoire was shocked by the bitterness in his eyes.

Héloïse held out her hand.

'Can you take this in friendship?' she asked. 'That is all I can offer. I bear you no grudge – what would be the point? But that is all.'

De Choissy took her proffered hand and held it in his.

'*Touché*,' he said wryly. 'You have developed a fine line in put-downs, my dear. However, I am accounted something of a fighter by those who know me best, strange though this may seem to you, and I won't give up. Nor, though you would not admit it, do you wish me to.'

He caressed her fingers, and Héloïse felt the skin on the back of her neck prickle.

'Go back, Monsieur le Comte,' she said. 'We will meet soon enough tomorrow.'

She felt for Louis' hand and slipped her hand into his.

'I am yours in name only, you must understand that.'

Marie-Victoire opened the door cautiously and waited for de Choissy to leave. Ignoring her, de Choissy pulled Héloïse to him.

'You belong to me,' he said, lacing his fingers hard around her wrists. 'Whatever you think, and whatever monsieur here tells you. Both in law and by affection. As you know very well, I do not permit my heart to be worn on my sleeve and I fully appreciate it is as difficult for you to believe as it is hard for me to tell you, but it is the truth.'

'You bastard,' Louis cursed under his breath.

De Choissy released his wife.

'Spare me your invective, Monsieur le Capitaine,' he said, with more than a hint of menace.

Héloïse shook her head wearily.

'You never loved me, Hervé. Perhaps it wasn't your fault, but I was only a vehicle for your strange desires. That is all.'

His eyes searched her face for any sign of yielding, but none came to his gaze.

'Not entirely true, my dear, and I think you know it.'

Héloïse leant against the wall and closed her eyes.

'If you love me, you will go,' she said, desperate that he should do so.

De Choissy flicked his finger over the sash of her dress.

'I once put a rose in there, did I not, my dear? I am afraid there are no roses here to give you.'

'Hervé, please.'

He straightened up with the expression that she knew so well and bowed to Louis.

'It seems, monsieur, that you win – for the time being. But consider, my dear Capitaine, tomorrow you will be gone – unless you wish to play the martyr as well as the lover, which I assume you do not – and I shall have her. You see, your triumph will be short-lived. It is I that will stand with Héloïse in front of the tribunal, not you. It is I that will ride with her to the guillotine, if we must. Not you.' He moved slowly to the door. 'Remember that, my brave Capitaine.'

With that, he was gone. Marie-Victoire closed the door on Héloïse and Louis and resumed her self-appointed place outside the door. She began to say her Ave Marias.

PARIS, Autumn 1793

The prisons filled up. L'Abbaye, Madelonettes, Porte-Libre, La Force, Sainte-Pelagie, Les Anglaises, Bicêtre, the Luxembourg, the Plessis, St. Lazare, Les Carmes. . . . Having being moved to and from various sites the guillotine now took up permanent residence in the Place de la Révolution, and each day the tribunal sent it more victims.

This was the era of the forger. Wishing to save their money and property, many of the richer émigrés had returned to France. Others needed certificates, issued by the commune, attesting to their 'civism'. White ones for Parisians. Red ones for strangers. Or they might require the cards to nail on their doors stating the name, age and vocation of every inmate. The forgers were not choosy and Paris housed many. Forged residence certificates, false passports, forged assignats – an industry sprang up overnight. Speculation was rife: from the bargains struck on street corners to transactions involving staggering sums. The passeurs, men who purported to be merchants or traders and who ferried money and jewels across the border, became legends, and the sympathetic notary was someone to be cultivated.

As the Jacobin republic strengthened its grip, the tribunal speeded up its work. At first, Fouquier-Tinville concentrated on the émigré, but as the Law of Suspects began to bite, his dragnet threw up a motley of men and women. Young, old, rich, poor, royalist, anti-Jacobin. Guilty and innocent. Fear began to roam the streets, suspicion was the order of the day and there were many old scores that were settled by the simple act of denunciation.

Some went to their deaths in bewilderment, others tossed defiance into the teeth of their enemies. Others impressed Sanson, the chief executioner, with their courage. But all of them faced the ride in a tumbril through crowds not yet sated by blood. If any escaped their fate there are no records to show it.

Chapter 12

Escape, September 19th–21st, 1793

In the Rue de Richelieu, Sir Robert was anxious for them to go.
'You must forgive this haste,' he said, 'but it is in your best
interests.' He indicated the serviceable wooden cart on which
were stacked several wooden wine barrels in the yard. 'Behold
our going-away carriage,' he said, as he helped Sophie up into
the seat in front and settled her. '*Voilà*, Madame Lacroix, you
are the picture of a wine-trader's wife.'

Sophie leant forward and held out her hands, very conscious
of William's ring that now reposed on her left hand.

'You have been so kind,' she said. 'We can never properly
thank you.'

Sir Robert nodded. 'I will receive my thanks in due course, I
have no fear of that,' he said, adding: 'You had best remove that
ring, madame, it does not fit the part.'

Sophie exclaimed, removed the tell-tale ring and tucked it into
her bosom. Sir Robert gave a few last-minute instructions to
William and held out a roll of coins. 'You must take this,' he
said, 'it is all in small coinage.'

William grasped his hand warmly. 'My wife has expressed my
thoughts. I cannot thank you enough.'

He swung up into the driver's seat and took the reins. Sir
Robert stepped back and the cart swung out of the yard and into
the road. Sophie looked back over her shoulder at Sir Robert. He
lifted his hand in farewell.

Sophie suppressed a giggle.

'You look so strange,' she told her husband. 'I am not used to
seeing you dressed like that.'

It was true. After the wedding, William had changed into the
disguise provided by the thoughtful Sir Robert, and instead of
his neat breeches and tight-fitting tail-coat, he now sported a
pair of velveteen breeches, rough white stockings and a short
corduroy coat. Round his neck he had wound a scarf of a

particularly virulent hue, and on his head was a hat that ha
seen better days. William grinned, flashing his white teeth, an
wagged his finger at Sophie.

'Not as odd as you, madame wife. I can highly recommen
that gown; you resemble nothing so much as a fishwife.'

Sophie gasped.

'How dare you, sir?' she expostulated. 'The impoliteness.'

William leant across to give her a kiss.

'Madame wife, you have never seemed so beautiful.'

It was true. In his eyes, at any rate, nothing could take awa
from Sophie's beauty, not even a badly cut gown and a fraye
cap. She grinned back at him, allowing herself to enjoy the
adventure while it still remained in the realm of a game.

Their mood quietened as they approached the *barrière*.

'Remember,' warned Sophie. 'I shall do the talking.'

They had decided that, even though William's French wa
now excellent, it would be better if he remained silent, just i
case a trace of his American accent betrayed him.

More by luck than by skill, William negotiated his way up
the gates and reined in the horse. It clattered to a halt. He jumpe
down and went to its head and busied himself with the harnes:
Sophie waited until one of the guards approached her, and the
proffered her documents, her heart beating hard. The guard too
them and began to read. After a while, he scratched his hea
and called out to his colleague.

'Where to?' he addressed Sophie.

Sophie named a town to the north of the city.

'Why?'

'To deliver the wine. The citizens have need.' She shrugge
her shoulders. 'The republic makes for good business; we ar
constantly being asked for more.'

Too late, she realised her mistake.

'Then, why have I not seen you before?'

The guard spat out a stream of yellow tobacco on to the road
narrowly avoiding the cart.

'I can't say I know your face,' the guard said suspiciously
thrusting his into Sophie's. The blast of his breath hit her an
she willed herself not to recoil in disgust.

'We use the other gate, more often than not; we have frienc
that way.'

'So.' The guard was not convinced. 'Get down.'

Sophie obeyed and stood waiting while the second guar
proceeded to search the load on the cart. He was rough an
uncaring and thrust his pike deep into the spaces between th
barrels. The force of his blows almost splintered the wood.

'Tell him to take care,' Sophie pleaded with the first guard. 'He will cost us money.'

The guard appreciated this argument and issued a command to his companion, who desisted. William went to inspect the damage. The guard gestured towards him.

'Talkative, ain't he?' he remarked.

'He leaves the talking to me,' said Sophie, fluttering her eye-ashes at him. 'Can we go now? I think our papers are in order.'

But the guard kept them a while longer. There was something about this pair that did not smell quite right, and he couldn't put his finger on it. Perhaps it was the woman, apparently in charge of her silent companion, that stirred his suspicions. Whatever it was, he wasn't going to let them go yet.

'I need to examine your papers further,' he announced, and withdrew into the cabin that lay abutting the wall.

All traces of her light-hearted mood quite vanished, Sophie stared after him. The normal traffic went to and fro around her, and comments were being exchanged by the pedestrians crowded into the sides of the road. She felt very vulnerable and was glad when William finished checking the ropes and rejoined her. They said nothing, only exchanging a glance to reassure each other.

William pulled at his neckerchief. The two guards were obvi-ously examining their papers minutely, and they could hear their rapid discussion inside the cabin. William indicated a side-street with a jerk of his head and Sophie understood him to be saying that that was the route they must take if they had to run for it. She nodded.

She was checking the provisions provided by Sir Robert in a basket when the guard returned. He held out their papers and with relief Sophie heard him say that they could go, providing they returned within twenty-four hours. Sophie agreed at once, even going so far as to tell the guard that she was looking forward to renewing their acquaintance. The guard leered and, when William wasn't looking, made an obscene gesture in Sophie's direction. Sophie blushed, giggled convincingly and nudged William to whip up the horses.

The cart rolled forward. Sophie clung to the side as William negotiated the narrow gateway and out into the road beyond. There was only just enough time for her to mutter a brief farewell under her breath to the city in which she had seen so much, and to say a prayer for Héloïse. Then they were away, plodding northwards.

Sophie looked back only once. The guard had followed through the gate and was staring after them. Behind him, girdled by its walls, the city faded, remote and beautiful – a place of the past. A memory of gilded rooms and gay, extravagant people. They had all gone, she thought. Fled abroad or in hiding, or crowded into prison. The shutters had closed in the grand houses and sabots no longer clattered in their attic rooms.

William whipped up the horse. He was anxious, more anxious than he had allowed Sophie to suspect. The way ahead was not easy, and he was concerned for Sophie's health. Jogging about in a wooden cart was not the best mode of travel for a pregnant woman. She already looked tired.

He concentrated for the next few hours on finding his way. Once or twice he stopped to consult a rough map that Sir Robert had provided, and then urged the cart onward. Late in the afternoon, they stopped to eat and fell upon their provisions. Towards nightfall they drove into a small village. William helped a stiff and battered Sophie to alight and went to enquire at an inn for a bed. He re-emerged five minutes later looking worried.

'They are very suspicious,' he said in a low voice. 'Something to do with the papers.'

'I can't go any further,' said Sophie, rubbing her stomach. 'We will have to stay here.'

Luckily, the innkeeper's wife took pity on Sophie and bore her off to the bedroom with a scolding directed at her surly husband for being so uncharitable. Soon Sophie was settled on the bed among woollen blankets and being fed a cup of soup. She sipped at it gratefully, feeling its warmth chasing some of the tiredness from her bones, and permitted her dress to be loosened. She sank back on to the hard bolster as if it were the softest of pillows. She was dozing when William came back. He stood smiling down at her.

'So far, so good,' he said, and sat down to remove his shoes.

'This is a strange wedding night,' remarked Sophie, running her hand over his shabby coat.

William sat up.

'When we reach America, I shall give you a proper wedding night,' he promised.

'If we do,' said Sophie, shaken by a sudden doubt.

'Listen to me, Sophie,' he said. 'When you reach America there is a house waiting for you. It lies at the end of an avenue of trees, and beyond it stretches the forest, as far as the eye can see. Inside, there are rooms – beautiful rooms – and they are waiting for you to take possession of them. There is peace, there is quiet, there is plenty. That is where I will take you for our proper wedding night. I want you to think of that, to think hard and remember in the days to come.'

Touched by his fervour, she smiled and tried to comfort his disquiet.

'It is only my condition that is making me like this,' she said. 'It is nothing.'

He began to kiss her. After a moment he stopped.

'Do you want this?' he asked. 'You are very tired.'

Sophie understood.

'Yes,' she replied. 'Yes, I do, William, very much, more than I can tell you . . . we must take this moment – just in case.'

He was very gentle with her, turning her on her side to avoid the baby, and husbanding his passion until hers had time to grow and match his. Then he shuddered and was still. Damp and entwined, they lay, cradled in tenderness and wrapped in a web of spent desire that succeeded in shutting out the world. Before she drifted into sleep, Sophie reflected that, strange as it might seem, she wanted no other kind of wedding night. What she had shared and enjoyed with William in the small dim room of a countryside inn was more than enough.

After that, their luck was sporadic and the hard realities of moving through a country where the people were nervous and restless became increasingly apparent. They abandoned the cart and its exhausted horse, in the town that Sir Robert used as one of his many depots, and gratefully accepted the meal provided by one of his efficient contacts. They changed into a second set of clothes and hid their first set of papers in William's shoes. No questions were asked, and they spoke very little. It was safer that way.

At noon of the same day, they wended their way to the centre of the town, and waited for the diligence to Calais. Their papers now proclaimed that they were a certain Monsieur and Madame Rutant travelling to Calais on legal business. William was dressed in the sober clothes of a typical notary, and Sophie, ostensibly accompanying him to visit relations, wore a serviceable blue dress suitable for her station.

They boarded without any incident, and sat uncomfortably cheek by jowl with farmers and housewives returning from market. Sophie was fortunate enough to obtain a place by the window, and she occupied the time by staring out of the window. Nothing had changed, it seemed. Bordered by their untidy hedgerows and winding lanes, the fields rolled out and merged into clumps of woodland and forest. Groups of men and women worked at the crops or sat talking to each other under the shade of a tree. The flowers were everywhere, in splashes of red, blue and palest yellow, clumped under hedges or sprinkled in dots amongst the grasses and trees. It was a serene and lovely landscape, untouched by the passion that raged through the land; a reminder, Sophie reflected, of the timeless verity of such things.

At Amiens the diligence clattered to a halt. A uniformed National Guardsman poked his head through the door and ordered them to descend. Sophie alighted first and waited for William, and they were told to present their papers at the guardhouse in the adjacent Mairie. In the Mairie, a small, irritable clerk sat at a desk strewn with papers. He motioned to William to add his documents to the pile and pointed to the wooden bench where the passengers were to sit. William and Sophie did as they were bid. Presently, a more senior official entered the room. He wore the obligatory trousers and short coat and sported a tricolour sash across his chest. Sophie sighed. She was beginning to be very familiar with petty officials such as this. Her apprehensions were justified. The official was not going to let them go quickly. He took his time to work through the list. At last it was their turn.

'Name?'

William obliged.

'Where are you going, and why?'

William gave as brief an explanation as he dared.

Their interrogator cleared his throat.

'Your relations in Calais?'

'My wife's aunt.'

'Where do they live?'

'In the Rue Jacob,' supplied Sophie, thankful yet again for Sir Robert's prescience.

'I know Calais well,' the official said thoughtfully, 'and I don't remember anyone living in the Rue Jacob of that name.'

Sophie shrugged with a charming little gesture.

'Perhaps monsieur forgets,' she murmured.

The official frowned. 'It is not in my nature to forget,' he remarked sharply. 'I would like to question you further. You will wait.'

Sophie sat back uneasily, and watched while the remainder of the passengers departed, one by one, to rejoin the diligence. Under the pretext of searching in the basket that Sophie held on her knee, William managed to whisper.

'We shall have to run for it.'

Sophie nodded.

'Just follow me.'

An hour ticked by, then another. Sophie thought of Héloïse, and then of the baby. At last the official returned, accompanied by two guardsmen.

366

'I don't like the look of this pair,' he said to the soldiers. 'Take them, if you please, to the house of the citizen deputy.'

William gave Sophie a meaningful look and squeezed her hand.

'You will walk between us,' ordered an official, indicating the open door.

The town square had filled up since their arrival and the afternoon traffic was heavy. Their captors cleared a path and escorted the two of them towards a building situated on the north side of the square. In order to reach it, the party had to pass by a narrow alley which opened into a small street. Just as they drew level with the row of houses that flanked it a shriek went up from the middle of the square. Sophie's head jerked round towards the sound. A carriage had lost control and had careered into a fruit vendor's stall. The air rang with screams and the horses were threatening to bolt. William wasted no time. The guards had been diverted by the accident and William, taking advantage of the situation, pulled Sophie into the alley. He told her to run. With fear lending her wings, Sophie obeyed, praying that the baby would take no harm. They pounded down the alley and darted out of sight down yet another side-street.

It took the guardsmen a second or two to realise what had happened – precious, vital seconds that gave them a lead. But not for long. Behind them the shouts increased and the sound of running feet told them that the guardsmen were gaining. At its furthest end, the street widened and William, who was faster, saw that a river ran at right angles to it. He waited for Sophie to catch up, and then propelled her down to the water's edge and along the towpath that snaked beside it. It was a dank and muddy place and the houses, which huddled almost to the water, hampered their progress. Sophie was panting hard and her breast heaved painfully. She stumbled over a log that lay on the path and, with a moan, sank to her knees. William jerked her upright and searched for somewhere to hide. His eyes lit on a small boat moored to a wooden post by one of the houses. He dragged Sophie down the bank and pulled on the rope. The boat came swinging in towards them, sticking a little in the black mud. William pulled harder. He splashed into the water, pulling Sophie with him, and thrust her towards the boat.

'Get in.'

Sophie climbed in with difficulty and dropped on to the narrow plank that served as a seat.

'Hurry,' she called.

William let go of the rope, jumped aboard, seized the oars and began to row down the river. Luckily the current was strong and the river fairly wide at this point. They were just in time, for he saw the guardsmen emerging from the street and pulled even harder. Mercifully, the bend in the river hid them from sight.

He rowed steadily onwards, guiding the boat under a bridge and around a second bend. Suddenly the town dropped away and they were gliding between empty water meadows. Sophie was shuddering with exhaustion and fright. William rowed on, not daring to stop and comfort her, determined to put as many miles as possible between them and the town.

It was dusk when he pulled in his oars and slumped panting over them, too tired to speak. The boat drifted towards a bank and bumped gently into the shallows. After a moment, William got out and tethered it to a convenient tree. Then, a little unsteady on his legs, he shepherded Sophie over the side and up into a field.

Chilled by a cold white mist that rose off the water, they lay close together under a tree, without speaking. Sophie chafed William's hands and they endeavoured to get their bearings. To their right lay a large wooded area and a little further to the right of that she could make out a church spire and the outline of a village.

'Have we any papers at all?' she asked.

William pointed at his wet shoes. 'The Lacroix papers,' he replied.

'Good,' said Sophie, 'we can at least use those.'

William began to count his money.

'We have enough for food, but none extra for travelling,' he announced. 'I shall have to sell my watch.'

Sophie got shakily to her feet.

'You will have to help me,' she said, and stretched out her hand. He took it in silence.

Their progress was very slow because Sophie held them back. The baby pulled at her muscles. Her breasts ached and her nose ran and she was tired. So tired.

'Are you sure you are all right?' asked William for the tenth time. He was supporting as much of her weight as he could. Sophie had no energy left to reply. They skirted the wood, and made for the houses. The village lay in a flat plain encircled by fields. A broad, well-made road ran towards it.

'We'll make for it,' said William, not at all sure what they would do after that. They crossed a final field that lapped the first buildings of the village and turned left on to the road, relieved to be no longer hampered by earth and grass. Sophie's dress was streaked with mud and heavily water-stained. She stopped to repair the ravages as best she could, but felt too weak to do more than dab perfunctorily at the material.

William brushed down his own coat and tried to pull his hair into its usual neat order. He glanced south down the road as he did so, and straightened up, his eyes narrowed.

'God in Heaven!' he exclaimed. 'There are soldiers. We must get off the road.'

Sophie felt tears of fatigue prick at her eyelids and her knees began to buckle.

'Where?' she asked hopelessly.

'Sophie,' said William urgently, grasping her hand. 'Don't give up. I beg you. Look, over there! There's a barn.'

Can I? thought Sophie. Can I do it? I think I have come to the end. She tasted the bitterness of defeat on her tongue and the impotence of weakness.

'Come on,' said William. 'One.'

Her limbs responded, each step taking an age to perform.

'Two.'

Her arms jerked and her legs moved.

'Three. *Come on*, Sophie.'

She plodded on, head bent, half-fainting, cursing the treacherous body that threatened to betray her.

They reached the barn and William set his shoulder to the door. It yielded with a groan of rusty hinges to reveal an interior heaped with hay. He pushed Sophie inside and eased the door shut behind him. The peace poured over her like a balm as Sophie collapsed on to the hay, smelt its sweet, musty smell and felt the scratchy edges bite into her skin. She closed her eyes and drifted into a blankness just as the detachment of soldiers clattered by on the road outside.

When Sophie next opened her eyes, dawn was sending its first rose-coloured streaks through the small window high above the door. She stirred, puzzled by her unfamiliar surroundings. Then she remembered. Her clothes were damp and she felt heavy, useless and frightened. She turned her head to discover that William was watching her.

'You are very beautiful when you sleep,' he remarked, leaning over to kiss her, and grimaced with pain.

'It's all right,' he said at her alarm. 'I'm only stiff. The real problem is these.' He held up his blistered hands for her inspection.

She exclaimed in horror and, with tears running down her cheeks, cradled his poor raw hands in her own. What could they do? Here they were, trapped in a barn, without food, with little money and forged papers. It would take such an effort of will to get out of this impasse, such courage and luck; and, although

369

she knew William would act for both of them if need be, her spirit almost gave up. If it all went wrong, what then? The indifferent stares of some petty Jacobin bureaucrat, the officious bundling into a conveyance to Paris, the dank enclosing walls of a prison, and a slow stifling of hope? She shuddered and buried her face in her hands.

'Listen to me.' William spoke with an angry determination she had never heard before. 'You are not to give in now. I have known you many things, weak, foolish, unfair even, but never a coward. Sophie Luttrell a coward. Never! In all things that we have shared you have never been that, and I am surprised at you now. Remember Héloïse and how she smiled at us as she was taken. Think of Louis doing God knows what. Even de Choissy – wherever he may be. They did not fail us, or themselves, so why are you weakening on me now? As Sophie Luttrell, it surprises me. As Sophie Jones, it angers me.'

His voice threaded through to her with the force of a slap.

'Angers you?' she flared up at him. 'Have I ever let you down? Is it so very surprising that I feel as I do?'

'That's better,' he said unexpectedly. 'I wanted to make you angry.'

Sophie glared at him. Then her rage subsided. William began to brush down his coat, a smile hovering at the corner of his mouth. All at once, Sophie was repentant. She saw the truth in what he said.

'I'm sorry,' she explained. 'It's just that . . .'

He came to sit beside her and slipped his arm around her waist.

'*Courage*, my lady wife. All is not over yet. I'll find someone in the village to help us.'

Sophie begged his pardon again for her behaviour. William settled himself beside her and said, 'Rest a little more and then we will go.'

Chapter 13

Héloïse, September 26th–27th, 1793

Héloïse laid her finger on Louis' lips.

'No,' she told him. 'We have no time. Forget he was here.'

With a sigh he drew her towards him.

Her dress lay crushed on the floor. So did her chemise and Louis' clothes. Louis raised himself above her on the bed and bent to kiss her breasts. Delicate white limbs waiting in delicious abandon. Hair like a raven's wing, spread over coarse ticking that should have been silk. A narrow waist, bones that were too sharp, ankles so small he could circle them with a hand, and pale, pale skin which should have been flushed by the sun. . . . Louis tried to hold all of the things that were Héloïse and capture her for ever.

Almost crushed by his weight, Héloïse waited for his arms to slide round her back. It didn't matter where they were, and there was so much to remember.

'I love you,' he said over and over again, and Héloïse's replies echoed in counterpoint.

'I love you more than life.'

When it was over, she lay quite still.

'How can I fear death when I have had this?' she asked him.

Her lips brushed as light as thistledown over his mouth, and he caught at her wrist.

They did not sleep. There was too much to say. Time was feverishly sweet and cruelly indifferent. The hours were to be tasted with thankfulness, and the imprint of body on body. And never to be forgotten.

At last, Héloïse stirred.

'Louis, I have one request to make of you,' she said.

He raised himself on his elbow.

'Ask it, Héloïse.'

'If tomorrow brings the worst, will you be with me? Will you stay until the end?' She faltered, and then continued. 'You need not worry that I shall be frightened. I will be . . . a little, but if you are out there somewhere, I can bear it.'

He did not reply at once. Wild schemes chased through his mind: of rescuing her. Somehow. Anyhow. Of dying with her. Of taking her away if the tribunal acquitted her. None of them, he knew, made much sense. What Héloïse asked of him was no light thing. It would mean watching as she was driven through jeering crowds . . . watching her mount the platform steps. . . . Héloïse tugged at his shoulder.

'You must not pretend,' she said, reading his thoughts. 'There is no use. Will you do this for me?'

Louis lay down. 'As I told you, I promised Sophie I would not abandon you. Nor would I.'

Héloïse was content. She could ask no more of the strange adventure that had been her life.

'One more thing,' she said. 'A priest. If you can find a priest to bless Marie-Victoire and me as we go, then we can die with clean hearts.'

Louis ran his finger down her neck.

'If you *are* to die, then I will do as you ask,' he said. 'But I haven't given up hope yet. Nor must you.'

Their voices filtered through to Marie-Victoire outside. Her head fell forward on to her breast and she dreamt her old dreams of Pierre and Marie. She awoke with a start and her dreams dissolved. It was time that Louis went back to the men's quarters, and she wondered where Monsieur le Comte had, in the end, spent the night. She got to her feet, listened at the door and went inside.

They were already dressed and they turned at her entry. Marie-Victoire blinked. She did not think she had ever seen such happiness before. Louis picked up his belt and buckled it on. Héloïse reached up to arrange his hair.

'Au revoir, Héloïse.'

'Au revoir, Louis.'

He took her hand and kissed it in the old manner. Then he nodded to Marie-Victoire, thanked her and was gone.

PARIS, September 27th, 1793

In a simple room in the Rue St Honoré furnished only by a table, a chair and some deal bookshelves, a man in an apple-green coat bent low over a notebook. His hair, swept neatly into an old-fashioned style, was white with powder, and small flakes of it dropped on to the table in front of him. His thin lips were set and his eyes were sharp.

'What is our aim?' he wrote, and gave the answer.

'It is the use of the constitution for the benefit of the people.'

'Who are likely to oppose us?'

'The rich and the corrupt.'

'What other obstacles are there to the achievement of freedom?'

'The war at home and abroad.'

'How can we end the civil war!'

'By punishing traitors and conspirators, especially those deputies and administrators who are to blame; by sending patriot troops under patriot leaders to reduce the aristocrats of Lyons, Marseilles, Toulon, the Vendée, the Jura and all other districts where the banner of royalism and rebellion has been raised; and by making a terrible example of all the criminals who have outraged liberty, and spilt the blood of patriots.'

Robespierre smiled to himself and continued writing well into the night.

Chapter 14

The Tribunal, September 27th, 1793

'I love you till death and beyond,' Héloïse had told Louis.

'I love you as no other,' he had replied, trying to make her understand how much she meant to him. 'There will never be anyone else but you.'

She had taken his hand. 'It is enough that I have known you,' she said again. 'All else matters so little.'

Héloïse was reliving each word, each gesture and murmur of the night, when at nine o'clock precisely she was led with the other prisoners up the stone stairs and into the Grande Chambre. So vivid were her thoughts that she did not notice the crowd that swarmed into every corner or the shops spread down the corridor. Nor did she register the cat-calls that greeted the prisoners' appearance. Beside her was Marie-Victoire, who felt tired and ill, and ached for Marie. But Marie eluded her, drawing further away with each step, until her tiny ghost vanished into the noise and confusion.

The crowd was excitable today. They pushed and shoved to obtain the best seats in the spectators' gallery inside the Grande Chambre, and called out noisy abuse. The clerks were frantically ferrying papers to the judges. This was the largest batch so far to be tried in one sitting and they did not possess the resources to cope with it. The prosecutor-general was already at his chair, hunched over his cartons of documents, his large pock-marked face impassive. He looked up as the women were escorted to the banked *gradines* that he had ordered to be built, and which lay to one side of the room, and Héloïse saw the satisfaction in his face. All was as he had arranged. For the first time, Héloïse experienced a feeling of hatred towards those who were responsible for bringing her here, and she determined not to show the slightest indication of fear. Two rows behind her, Marie-Victoire prayed that it would soon be over.

Five minutes later, the male prisoners arrived, among them

de Choissy. He waited until the other prisoners had settled and then indicated that he wished to be placed by his wife. His request was received with scant attention, but de Choissy persisted until one of the guardsmen shoved roughly at Héloïse's neighbour and ordered her to make room. De Choissy sat down and inclined his head in a parody of thanks. He was pale and composed, but his eyes were bloodshot from fatigue. Héloïse noticed that he held several papers in his hand. He turned to speak to her.

'I have arranged for Monsieur Vilain de Lainville to defend us,' he told her.

There was no reference in his steady gaze to the night before, and his tone was non-committal.

'How?' Héloïse was surprised that de Choissy had worked so fast.

'I have my contacts, my dear, and this is the time to use them.' He shifted slightly to get a better view of her face. 'Are you well?'

Before she could reply, the chief clerk got to his feet and began to call out the names of the accused. Héloïse answered to her name mechanically and heard Marie-Victoire breathe out her answer.

The five defence lawyers sat in front of the prisoners. Opposite, and sitting behind the clerks, was the jury. To the left sat the president of the court and the three judges. The public prosecutor had taken up a position at the foot of the judges' bench. Detached and impersonal, their faces hovered in front of Héloïse, safe in the knowledge that it was not they that faced this court. The jurymen took their oath, accompanied by encouraging shouts from the public gallery. The president raised his hand for silence. The hecklers subsided and settled back to enjoy the spectacle.

Athenée de Thierry was the first to give her name, occupation and address. She was cool and composed. The witnesses called to testify against her were led in, one by one. Since the court had had less than twelve hours to assemble them, they were mainly composed of paid volunteers from the street. Documents relating to her case were read out, her lawyer gave a peroration – and all the while a contemptuous little smile played around Athenée's features.

When she sat down, the second woman prisoner was called and the procedure was repeated. Then the third, and the fourth. Roped in behind the partition, the crowd was in high spirits and called out frequently to the vendors for more drink. The better-dressed bought oranges from the orange-girls and sipped at liqueurs while they chatted to each other behind their gloved hands. Héloïse searched for Louis among them, and when she saw that he wasn't present she did not look at the spectators again. They reminded her of animals at the kill. She turned once to smile at Marie-Victoire. Marie-Victoire sent her an answering smile and Héloïse was reassured.

De Choissy spoke into her ear from time to time on legal points that he felt needed clarifying. He swore a couple of times under his breath when some particularly obvious travesty was allowed to go unchecked. Héloïse made no comment and concentrated on the jury who, she concluded, were neither bad nor malicious, merely ordinary men caught up by events they perhaps did not fully understand. As such, she sensed, they were doubly dangerous.

'Marie-Victoire Bonnard.'

Marie-Victoire felt quite calm as she got to her feet and gazed across the sombre room to the black-robed judges. The shaking that had afflicted her knees earlier had stopped and her heart beat in a regular pattern instead of in thumps. She stood quietly and waited.

The president listened to the indictment and a shudder ran through the waiting crowd. A murderess.

'This is what you are accused of,' he pronounced. 'You will now hear the evidence which is to be produced against you. Usher, call the witnesses.'

Marie-Victoire did not even move as Messieurs Montane, Théry, Souberbielle and Naury walked confidently into the court, followed by the plump, unmistakable figure of the doctor.

Under the questioning of the prosecutors, Marie-Victoire's story unfolded, the story of a mother driven to the brink of madness. The audience shuddered pleasurably, although one or two women wiped away tears and shouted out their encouragement to a sister in distress. Monsieur Théry's testimony was vivid, and gave in voluptuous detail the scene he had discovered that early morning. Listening to it, Marie-Victoire felt a veil interpose between her and the world. It seemed so far away now, the passion and grief so old and distant, and she wanted no part of it any more.

The doctor stumbled over his words in his haste to condemn the prisoner.

'She was mad,' he declared. 'Battering on my door in the middle of the night and crying out dreadful things. She even threatened me – me, a respectable patriot – with denunciation. I knew no good would come of it. And all for a child who was already dead.'

Marie-Victoire's lawyer wasted no time on unnecessary words. He could see that the case was hopeless. He spoke briefly on the

376

necessity for clemency and of the quality of mercy for a deranged girl and begged the jury to put themselves in her place. But that was all. He sat down and buried his head in his papers. The prosecutor addressed Marie-Victoire.

'Do you deny this charge of murder?'

Marie-Victoire stirred and ran her fingers over her threadbare gown. Then she lifted her head and replied quietly.

'No.'

'Then, you agree you are guilty of murder. Worse, of the murder of a true patriot. Of parricide, in fact?'

What can I do, thought Marie-Victoire, to end this? To stop the torment. I am so tired and I long for peace and no more suffering.

'I am guilty,' she said, and there was unmistakable pride in her voice. 'I killed Jacques Maillard. He deserved to die.' She raised a hand in a gesture of defiance. 'He deserved to die, messieurs. No one is worth the life of a child. No one is worth the life of my child.'

Her soft country-accented voice sounded thin but clear. Amid the gasps of astonishment that greeted her declaration, she sat down again, and the hall erupted. The president fought to regain control. One of the prosecutors shot to his feet and shouted to the judges.

'You have heard the woman, messieurs. She is condemned out of her own mouth. I demand death.'

With a supreme effort, Marie-Victoire climbed up on to the bench.

'*Vive le roi*,' she shouted above the tumult, her figure dominating the room.

Héloïse leaned frantically across the benches and pulled her down.

'Don't, Marie-Victoire,' she begged. 'Don't be so stupid.'

But it was too late. Marie-Victoire had created a sensation, and spoken words that could not be unsaid. Marie-Victoire tapped her finger to her mouth.

'You do now know me,' she whispered urgently. 'Turn round.'

Héloïse sank back and order was restored in the court. She understood the impulse that caused Marie-Victoire to cry out, but it was mad and foolish. The passions simmering below the surface were sparked, the crowd was growing ugly, and the jury could not fail to be influenced by their mood. De Choissy dropped his head into his hands, and when he looked up it was with a look of despair.

'How ill-considered,' he said under his breath. 'The prosecutors have the case on a plate.'

Nothing so sensational greeted the examination of the remaining women, which was conducted at indecent speed. The jury coughed and scratched. Héloïse waited for her case to be called. Then she realised, with a shock, that she was to be tried with de Choissy.

The first of the male prisoners was dealt with summarily, then the second, third, fourth and fifth. Two were ordinary journeymen, another a jeweller, yet another an engraver indicted for forgery. The last was a merchant, accused of trafficking in money and working for the counter-revolution. The witnesses came and went, each intoning their litany of damning facts. The judges' black plumes nodded and swayed. Of a surety, though, Héloïse wearily, there is no justice here, and because there was no point in listening, she let her mind drift to thoughts of Louis.

'De Choissy, Hervé Christian Louis and Héloïse Violette.'

Jerked back into the present, Héloïse rose to her feet, de Choissy beside her. He reached briefly for her hand and then released it to attend to his papers.

'You stand accused of émigré status, of removing money from the republic and counter-revolutionary activities. Your wife stands accused as party to these crimes. Guilty or not guilty?'

'Not guilty.'

De Choissy spoke clearly, his voice carrying easily over to the spectators' gallery, now electric with tension and excitement.

'Not guilty.' Héloïse said her words without stumbling.

A feeble light struggled to penetrate the windows opposite. The judges' line of black, unrelieved except for their tricolour sashes, was bathed in shadow. Héloïse looked so young, so beautiful, and so remote in contrast, that even the most hardened of the onlookers shifted uneasily in their places. Beside her de Choissy's finely modelled figure exuded an ease that betokened his birth and breeding, the faint hauteur of his thin nostrils and sculptured eyebrows marking him as a figure from another age. There was no fear in his eyes, and no compromise either. De Choissy, it seemed, was ready to fight.

The first witness was a clerk from the bank which the de Choissy family had patronised for years. In a halting voice, he gave chapter and verse of the sums the defendant had drawn out over the past two years. Amounts that made the spectators gasp. When asked what he was doing with such large amounts of money, de Choissy merely shrugged and said that his estates were in need of repair and his marriage had necessitated some expenditure. When asked to prove it, his eyes narrowed to slits.

'Surely, messieurs,' he said, 'the onus is on you to prove that it was not so.'

378

'Citizens,' shouted the prosecutor. 'Do you believe this man?' An animal-like roar greeted his questions. The prosecutor turned back to de Choissy.

'You lie,' he said. 'But we will leave it for the present. Do you deny that you have tried to leave the republic during the last nine months?'

'I do indeed,' replied de Choissy. 'I have documents to prove it.'

He held up a well-thumbed certificate of residence and passed it over to the prosecutor, who passed it to the jury.

'I submit', said the prosecutor, 'that this document is forged.'

He raised his voice so it carried to the end of the hall. 'Citoyens, this document is forged. You know as well as I that there are certain persons who will stop at nothing to deny our republic its life's blood, and here is one of them. I can prove it.'

De Choissy grimaced. 'I trust they have not taken the forger. It says I have been living in Nice since March. Don't mention La Tesse.'

'Bring on *mère* Bonnet.'

A large, untidy woman was led into the court. She was joking with the ushers and the grin on her over-red face indicated that she was enjoying herself. She waved to the public gallery and flapped her apron in mock outrage at a particularly ribald sally.

'*Mère* Bonnet, tell us what you know,' asked the prosecutor triumphantly.

The woman leaned confidingly over the witness bar. 'I keep the beer shop near the Palais Royal,' she stated, 'and one evening in March when I had finished eating, this man walked in. He was already drunk, but he wanted more, so I gave to him. He was waving a fistful of louis d'or in his hand so I asked him where he had got so much money. He replied that he had just done a good turn for an aristo' and forged a paper to say that he had been in France when in fact he was planning to leave. I didn't pay much attention. I get all sorts, saying different things, but this one was so drunk that his tongue rattled in his mouth. I heard the name "de Choissy", which doesn't mean anything to me. Why should it? Then I thought about it, and I grew angry at this terrible thing that had been done to our glorious country, so at the first opportunity I went to tell the authorities.'

The prosecutor executed a bow in her direction.

'Thank you, citoyenne.'

Mère Bonnet acknowledged his thanks with a broad grin. The prosecutor turned to the jury.

'Citoyens,' he said. 'You have heard this good woman and

379

what she has had to say. Now let us address the citoyenne de Choissy.'

Mère Bonnet was led cackling to the spectators' gallery, where space was made for her ample form. Héloïse waited quietly.

'Citoyenne de Choissy, can you swear that you knew nothing of your husband's financial affairs?'

Héloïse gave an affirmative.

'Citoyenne, can you swear that your husband has been resident in France since August 1792 until now?'

'As far as I know. My husband and I have not always lived together.'

'Was he with you for any, or part, of that period?'

'Yes, he was.'

'When exactly?'

'Until December 1792, when I retired to the country in order to convalesce after a serious illness.'

'So you did not have exact knowledge of your husband's movements?'

'I received regular letters from Paris . . . and from Nice.'

'You think they were from Nice? Not from his château of La Tesse?'

'Monsieur, I know so.'

The prosecutor tried again.

'Where was the prisoner from March of this year?'

'He was in Nice. At an estate he has there. He quite often goes to oversee his lands.'

'If that was so, why was he arrested on the German border?'

Héloïse said nothing.

'You cannot answer that, citoyenne?'

The prosecutor was like a cat ready to pounce. Héloïse waited for the noise to subside.

'Surely, monsieur,' she questioned, 'it is not a crime to travel the country?'

'It is, citoyenne, it is – if you are a counter-revolutionary,' said the prosecutor with relish. 'Consider, citoyens, what we have here. A former comte and his wife, whose father was a minister to the deceased Capet. A wife who cannot answer fully regarding the whereabouts of her husband. We have forged papers, and large sums of money which have disappeared. Consider well, are there not here two prime examples of the people we should fear, aristocrats who are determined to keep their wealth at the expense of the people, royalists who scheme to return a king . . .'

His skilfully chosen words worked as he wished. The gallery erupted into jeers and shouts of rage, drowning de Choissy as he tried to speak.

'To the guillotine.'

'Let them look through the little window.'

'Try on *père* Sanson's necktie.'

The prosecutor-general rose and went over to the president. The two men conferred and the president signalled for the jury to depart. They filed out obediently and disappeared from view. De Choissy turned to Héloïse and shrugged his shoulders.

'All is up,' he tried to say, but she could not hear him for the noise. Marie-Victoire tugged at her arm.

'Madame, what is happening?'

'The jury have gone to decide their verdicts.' Héloïse reached for Marie-Victoire's hand across the benches. 'We must wait, but let us not hope.'

'I cannot hope,' replied Marie-Victoire returning the clasp, 'but perhaps you can, madame.'

The roar of the crowd rose in deafening beats to the white-washed ceiling. Down below, the prisoners huddled together on the *gradines*, and counted the seconds. It is such a short time, to seem so long, thought Héloïse, realising with surprise that it was still only early afternoon. The ushers strove to keep the spectators behind their partition, ducking to avoid the missiles thrown by more adventurous spirits that rained down over the court. I am glad, Héloïse's internal monologue went on, that you are not here, Louis. It is the one thing that has kept me strong, the knowledge that you are out there in those anonymous streets – still free.

The sound of the president's bell peeled through the air, cutting through the clamour with the sharpness of a knife. The jury returned and stood behind their benches, facing the president. One by one the names of the prisoners were called out, and one by one the jury returned their verdicts.

'Guilty.'

'Guilty.'

'Not guilty.'

'Guilty.'

'Not guilty.'

'Is Marie-Victoire Bonnard guilty?'

'She is guilty.'

Marie-Victoire's pale face went even paler.

'De Choissy, Hervé?'

There was a pause. 'Guilty on all counts.'

'De Choissy, Héloïse?'

'Guilty on all counts.'

As at Versailles, de Choissy's arm stole round Héloïse's waist. She felt it circle her body in a dream.

381

The judges rose and settled their black-plumed hats more firmly on to their heads. The president asked for their judgements, and on hearing them also donned his hat. Two prisoners were condemned to transportation. Five were acquitted. The rest – and that means Marie-Victoire, Hervé and me, thought Héloïse – were for death.

'Death by guillotine. The parricide among you will wear the red shirt,' intoned the president, and, as if in response, a cloud passed over the square of sky revealed by the window.

De Choissy's arm tightened and he drew Héloïse closer to his side.

'You are mine now,' he said. 'I have you.' And he laughed at the horror and incomprehension on her face. 'Did I not promise your lover that I would win you in the end?'

Héloïse had no reply.

'Prisoners first.'

The guards were shouting for the public to remain where they were, for the fight to quit the chamber and to gain the best vantage points in the Cour de Mai had begun. The clerks were once again rushing all over the room with lists of the condemned which were destined for the executioner and waiting journalists.

'Quick. On your feet.'

The sergeant in charge was jumpy and nervous. He did not trust the public and he was in no mood to pander to anyone he considered already dead. He ordered his men to chivvy the prisoners into a file. De Choissy ignored him.

'Justice,' he said bitterly, 'you are not known in this place.' He raised his voice. 'Your turn will come,' he called out in the direction of the judges, 'and the deaths of your victims will haunt you.'

He had the satisfaction of watching two of the judges go quite pale. A soldier shouted at de Choissy to get into line, and this time he obeyed. The procession moved towards the door. After his outburst, de Choissy was silent and looked neither to the right nor to the left. Marie-Victoire glided in front of Héloïse, her hands twisted together, but otherwise composed. Héloïse thought of all that she was to leave.

'No,' one of the women suddenly cried out. 'No. I can't.'

Her shriek died into sobs. One of the soldiers prodded her with his foot.

'Get up,' he said, and began to drag her across the floor. The woman's screams intensified, agonising and almost unearthly. Marie-Victoire paused and tapped the soldier on the arm.

'Let me,' she asked him, and bent over. 'You must have

ourage, madame,' she told the woman. 'I will support you.'
he laid her hand on the woman's head. 'Listen to me.'

The woman raised her tormented face to gaze at Marie-Victoire.

'How can you?' she asked in a choked voice.

'Like this,' said Marie-Victoire, and held out her hand. 'It's
asy.'

The woman took her hand and got slowly to her feet. Marie-
ictoire helped to support her.

'Come, madame,' she said, 'we will walk together.'

'Marie-Victoire sets us an example,' said Héloïse to de Choissy.

'I believe she does, my dear,' he replied.

He drew himself up to his full height and offered his arm to
éloïse.

'Please,' he said.

After a hesitation, she reached out and placed her hand on his
leeve.

The prisoners filed out silently, past the spectators, into the
alle des pas perdus, through the door that led into the *galerie des
risonniers*, down a narrow staircase and into the prison that
aited below.

Chapter 15

The Road to Calais, September 21st–27th, 1793

William's watch said it was nine o'clock when they let themselves out of the barn and made for the road. Sophie had made an effort with her dress and, although it was creased and stained, it sat neatly enough on her rounded form. She had scraped back her tangled hair and bundled it under her cap. William had been less successful with his clothes and he would present an odd appearance to a curious onlooker. But there was nothing much they could do about it, except to brazen out any questions.

Sophie walked slowly, leaning heavily on William's arm. Her head ached and she was surprised to discover that she had developed a tendency to jump at unexpected noises. The baby did not make her feel any better either. It sat stone-like inside her and a pain had settled into the small of her back. My baby she thought with a sudden, fierce and protective emotion.

It was market day in the village, which turned out to be larger than they had expected. Its main street was busy with people making their way between the loaded booths and trestle tables and crowded with marketeers selling their wares. Sophie's stomach rumbled at the sight of fresh bread, yellow and white cheeses and the mounds of fruit laid out for inspection in a riot of red, green, orange and purple, often with the bloom still clouding their glossy surfaces. Paris had had nothing so plentiful to offer for a long time, and her eyes feasted greedily.

She sat on the edge of the stone ledge surrounding a pump and savoured the luscious taste of the grapes that William had bought with some of their remaining money. William material ised out of the crowd and indicated with a jerk of his head that she was to follow him.

'I've made contact with someone,' he whispered. 'He's willing to help us. He has offered us a hiding-place until he can arrange transport.'

William jerked his head in the direction of a villainous-looking

384

ansculotte whom Sophie had previously noticed observing her. Ie was lounging against a wall, chewing a wisp of hay. Sophie hrank back and laid a restraining arm on William.

'Can you trust him?' she whispered back.

William tapped his finger to his nose.

'There are ways,' he said. 'Look at his coat.'

Sophie was puzzled. There was nothing extraordinary to ob-erve in the man, except that he was more than usually dirty nd greasy and sported a large and very stained cockade.

'Look at the lapels on his coat, Sophie,' William said into her ar. 'You will see a small V cut into the material. For those who now about these things, it is a signal.'

'A counter-revolutionary?' she asked.

'Shush, not here. We will discuss it later.'

Sophie had no choice but to follow. William began to walk up he street. As soon as he saw which way they were going, the ansculotte straightened up and began to walk in the same lirection. At the first crossroad, William stopped and pretended o engage Sophie in conversation, and watched out of the corner of his eye as the stranger sauntered past.

'Are we mad?' whispered Sophie.

'There is little else we can do,' said William grimly.

The sansculotte took a turning to the left and plunged down network of alleyways. Sophie gasped for breath at the pace he et, and was profoundly relieved when the sansculotte halted in ront of a small courtyard, at the back of which was a tumbledown uilding.

'Ask for Angèle,' he said and pointed at a door. 'Say I sent ou.'

And with that he disappeared back up the street from where hey had come.

'I still say we are mad,' said Sophie. 'What if this is a trap?'

'There is honour among spies and counter-revolutionaries,' eplied William. Or you must pray there is?

He took Sophie by the arm, led her through a yard littered vith bales of straw and old agricultural machinery and pushed pen a green-painted door.

'If there is trouble, make your way back to the square,' he rdered her before they went inside.

They found themselves in a long, rectangular room at one end f which stood a printing press. Paper lay everywhere: on the loor, on the benches and stacked in heaps on the trestle table y a high window. Pegs secured bundles of it to the wall and he black ink, smeared and blotched across roughly printed ages, jumped out at him and made him blink. A youth in a

leather apron sat by the window talking to a plump, middle-aged
woman. A bottle and several glasses joined the confusion on the
trestle table and the youth was explaining some point with
extreme vehemence, raising his glass repeatedly to his lips.

'Are you Angèle?' William asked cautiously.

The woman glanced up and smoothed her apron over her
round stomach.

'Your friend has sent us,' said William, approaching her. 'He
said you would help.'

Angèle licked her lips and William noticed a flicker of hostility
(or was it fear?) run over her face.

'Yes,' she admitted reluctantly. 'What do you want?'

William decided that he had to bluff through with this encounter, although on the face of it it did not seem hopeful.

'Can you shelter us?'

He indicated Sophie behind him. Her face was pale and stained
with sweat.

'We need to rest.'

As he spoke, Sophie staggered slightly and William just caught
her as her knees gave way. She sagged against him, with the
effort of keeping upright. Angèle shrugged her shoulders and
opened her mouth to reveal a row of blackened teeth.

'If *he* said so. But I don't like it. We'll all end up on the
guillotine.'

She inflected the 'he' with a good deal of contempt and dislike.
William held out his watch. Angèle took it, bit it and tossed it to
the youth. She went over to a door in the wall and indicated that
they were to ascend the staircase behind it. Sophie tried to walk
but failed, and William was forced to drag her upstairs on to a
landing above. Angèle fumbled at the latch of a small wooden
door, so small that it looked more like a cupboard. She pushed
it back to reveal an airless closet with a mattress and a bucket
stacked against one wall.

'In you go,' said Angèle. 'I'll come back later,' and with that
she locked the door and left.

Sophie shivered uncontrollably at the sound of the key turning
in the lock, and waves of ice ran through her veins. Her head
hurt, and stabbing pains went shooting at intervals through her
abdomen. William ripped off his coat and tried to cover her, but
she wouldn't let him. Now she was burning hot, her numbed
limbs turning suddenly into furnaces, and she wanted above all
to search for a cool space on the mattress.

'I must have caught cold in the boat,' she said incoherently
before the whirling shapes and familiar ghosts enfolded her in
their embrace.

386

They lured Sophie away into another time and another place. A region where the scent of apple blossom wafted tantalisingly in her nostrils, and the pink-white petals drifted down. Only to change, as she reached to grasp them, into drops of blood. Somewhere, far off, there was a roar of a crowd and the crash of a huge knife down on to a wooden plank, and Héloïse's face, dancing white and transparent, smiling her farewell smile. She moaned.

William could do nothing except watch helplessly as Sophie gasped and twitched and cried out from time to time in a fever-racked voice. He loosened her laces and smoothed back the tangled hair, and prayed as he had never prayed before that help would come soon.

The night came and went. William managed to doze from time to time, jerking awake when Sophie's cries became too loud, when he tried, without success, to soothe her. By morning she was no better and William was desperately anxious by the time he heard footsteps on the stairs.

The door opened and their saviour of yesterday stood blinking into the gloom. He held out a basket to William.

'A doctor,' said William, taking it. 'Can you get me a doctor?'

'My name is Maurice,' said the man. 'I will help you all I can but the town is full of republicans, that is why I have chosen to hide you. You must stay here for a couple of days until I can arrange transport. It is not easy. I can't bring the doctor because I can't trust him. You will have to fend for yourselves.' He turned to go. 'Goodbye, my friend. Don't panic,' he said, and added, 'Tell Angèle nothing if she comes, she is not entirely trustworthy. I will deal with her.'

The door closed for a second time on them both.

'By the way,' said Maurice through the keyhole, 'there is plenty of water in the basket for the woman.'

That, at least, was something, William reflected as he hastened to dip his cravat into it and bathe Sophie's face and wrists. Its coolness appeared to bring her some relief. She grew quieter and eventually slipped into a doze. William listened to her breath labouring through her cracked and bleeding lips. He made some calculations. As far as they knew the baby would be born in December. It was now September. Assuming they made it to Calais, would Sophie be fit enough to embark on the Channel crossing before it was born? He rather thought not. On the other hand, how would they find a roof to hide under?

Throughout the day William analysed the options, turning over one plan in his mind then discarding it for another. He even considered returning to Paris to elicit Sir Robert's help yet again.

Every so often, he sipped at the beer provided by Maurice and tended to Sophie. His own hands were troubling him and he found it painful to touch her. Once when he bathed her head she cried out and gazed up at him with unseeing eyes. He paused and his anxiety deepened into a fear that the long, torture-filled hours did nothing to help.

Towards nightfall, Sophie's cries became weaker and her racing pulse dropped, and he thought he saw death in her face. She opened her eyes and murmured 'No more,' in a voice that wrung his heart, so full was it of anguish. Then she sank into an unconsciousness from which William could not rouse her.

In that hot little room, stuffy with fever, slops and the smell of their unwashed bodies, William learnt the meaning of despair. In his desperation, he knelt by Sophie's inert form and gathered her up, cradling her hot head with a gentleness he never knew he possessed. If Sophie was going to die, at least he would ensure that it was in his arms.

When he awoke from an uneasy sleep, it was nightfall again. Sophie lay motionless, her body heavy against his numb shoulder, and he could not even hear the rasp of her breath. He squinted down at the face on his breast and saw that a look of infinite peace had stolen across her features, washing them clean of suffering. It was, he knew, the peace of death. William closed his eyes to blot out that hateful room and cursed out aloud at the waste of his life. Tears pricked behind his eyelids. He had come to the end.

It was only after Sophie moved for the second time that his brain registered the fact. A tiny, fluttering movement of her hand and an imperceptible jerk of her head. He sat stupidly for a moment, hardly daring to hope until he gave a definite sigh and murmured something so low he could not hear it.

'Sophie,' he said wonderingly, and eased her down on to the mattress so that he could look down at her face. 'Sophie?'

She opened her eyes, the effort appearing to exhaust her, and looked up. This time she recognised him. Sweat beaded her forehead, but she managed a travesty of a smile.

'Water,' she croaked. William hastened to lift a mug to her lips. She took a sip, and another, and then lay back, closed her eyes and slipped into a healing sleep.

By the time Maurice returned for a second time with food and water, Sophie had endeavoured, with William's help, to sit propped up against the wall for a few minutes. Maurice stayed only to tell them that his arrangements were still being made, and that they must be patient. William felt in Sophie's dress for his ring and gave it to Maurice, and asked him to sell it if possible.

They would need money to pay for the crossing. Maurice took it without a word. Left alone once again, William began to pace up and down. Two paces up, turn, two paces down, his impatience and anxiety thickening the atmosphere. Once or twice he beat his hands against the wall and stood with his head bowed over his painful fists. Sophie watched him without comment and willed herself to stay awake.

'William,' she whispered at last through the fuzziness that seemed to cloud her brain. He stopped in his tracks and saw how the baby jutted out from her body in an obscene contrast to its thinness.

'Come here,' she said.

He dropped on to the mattress beside her and took one hand in his.

'*Courage*,' she said haltingly, every word requiring enormous thought. 'You remember how you told me that. Now it is my turn. Do not give up. We will make it to Calais.'

The effort drained her feeble strength and she could say no more, but her words appeared to have some effect on William, for he quietened and eventually smiled at her.

'You're right,' he said at last. 'Oh, Sophie,' he went on, and his voice shook, 'to think I might have lost you. I don't think I could have gone on.'

'Kiss me,' she said, and he bent to do as she asked. Her breath was foul with fever, and her body was so wasted that he feared it would break at his touch.

'If I loved you before,' he said, drinking in every line of her gaunt features. 'I love you so much more now.' He sat up. 'Now I must concentrate on making you well.' He settled her more comfortably on the mattress. Sophie sighed and fell asleep.

They remained in the closet for nearly a week. Every so often the noise of the printing press would start up below them and the yard would be filled with the sound of vehicles. They kept very quiet at these times, afraid that the least noise would give them away, and spoke very little. By the end of the week, both of them knew every crack and cobweb in the room and every line of the rough wooden floor. Sophie vowed to herself that she would never voluntarily enter such a place again.

Maurice came for them at dawn on the seventh day.

'Get up,' he ordered them, 'and follow me.'

William had just enough time to snatch up Sophie's cap and a few articles of his own clothing.

'Take these,' he told her, swept her up into his arms and carried her down the stairs to the cart waiting in the yard.

'Put her in the back,' said Maurice.

William deposited Sophie carefully on to some thick sacks and the two men arranged bundles of vegetables around her so that she was partially hidden from view. Sophie lay, on her side, without comment, letting the blessed cool of the outside fan her cheeks and breathing in great draughts of fresh air. William got up beside Maurice, who flicked his whip at the horse, and the cart made its way out into the street.

Long afterwards, Sophie thought of that journey as one of the most important events of her life. Perhaps it was the knowledge that she had been so close to death, perhaps it was the calm and silence of the autumnal countryside, bathed in life-giving sun and awash with colour and the scent of ripeness, but every slow, jogging step brought relief and peace, mingled with deep thankfulness.

Sometimes William got out to walk beside her. Once Maurice swung off the road to avoid some soldiers, and another time they were forced to take refuge in a field for a whole afternoon. It was then that Maurice told them a little about his work, but refused to divulge where he got his funds to carry it out. Neither William nor Sophie pressed him on the subject.

At night they slept in the cart, huddled together, and awoke under dew-damp sacks. Each day brought Sophie new strength, and new colour back into her wan cheeks, and each day took them further and further away from the nightmare. They would make it to safety, she was sure. It would not be easy, because danger still lurked on the roads and in the streets, and would do so until they boarded the ship for England, but she knew in her heart that she and William were survivors. Sophie was content, for she had been lucky and, in the end, far more richly rewarded than she suspected she had a right to be. She could ask no more.

When at last Maurice stopped to point out the first rooftops of Calais, Sophie was able to sit up and gaze her fill.

Chapter 16

The Last Ride, September 27th, 1793

The figure of Sanson, attired in his customary tightly buttoned riding-coat and English-style hat, strode through the Cour de Mai. He had finished his preparations in the Place de la Révolution and the guillotine stood ready and waiting. He consulted his lists and gave the order for two extra carts. At his word, his assistants went running in all directions.

It was half-past three and word had been passed that the carts would leave within the hour. Already the crowd was massing outside the big wrought-iron gates and overflowing on to the quays. The mood was excited and volatile. Paris had still not become inured to the carts rolling through her streets, and the spectacle was still enough of an event to tempt whole families to come and watch. Once it was known that the tribunal had given its verdicts and the executions would take place that day, the Parisians took to the streets and fought for the vantage points on the Place de la Révolution (the best seats were going for five sous). The better-off took their opera glasses and made sure they ordered a meal at the restaurant sited opposite the guillotine where, it was said, the names of the condemned for the day were printed on the back of the menu.

Louis had been busy. His mission had not been easy and he had set about it with a bitter heart. Even while he hoped, he knew he must resolve to prepare for the worst. It had necessitated him activating a contact about whom he was none too sure, but he had to take the risk. The contact had proved helpful and, after money had changed hands, directed him to the home of a woman located in a small street beside the Palais Royal. The woman was young and frightened but courageous enough, and when Louis gave her the password she led him up to a small attic located under the eaves. Louis' knock was answered by a middle-aged man dressed in ordinary clothes but whose close-cropped head bore the traces of a tonsure. He listened, blinking short-sightedly, to Louis' request, and then sighed.

391

'Assuredly, my son, I cannot refuse you. I shall be on the corner of the Rue de la Monnaie and the Rue St Honoré at four o'clock. As soon as the carts have passed on their way, I shall go, without saying anything further.'

When Louis tried to press some money into the man's hand, he refused.

'My work is for God,' he remarked mildly. 'But if I ever have need, I shall call upon you.'

With that Louis left him and returned as fast as he could to the Cour de Mai. When he reached the Pont Neuf the towers of the Conciergerie swung into view, soaring above the haphazard jumble of buildings that abutted its walls, and Louis' heart tightened as he thought of what lay inside. The crowd was thicker and his progress slower. But he persisted, determined to be there when the gate of the Conciergerie swung open. It was a small gesture, but it was all he could do. It was impossible to reach a position close to the prison door, and so he contented himself with waiting by the wooden tumbrils lined up in the Cour de Mai. The *tricoteuses* had already rolled up their knitting, packed up their baskets and sat waiting. At the foot of the steps swirled a medley of officials, lawyers, sightseers, children and guards in Phrygian caps. Louis bowed his head and, for the first time in a long while, sent up a short prayer to a God who appeared to have deserted the land.

Inside the Conciergerie, Sanson's assistants were at work. The male prisoners were being made ready. Two of them sat on stools while the assistant, Desmorets, hacked at their hair with a pair of scissors. As soon as he had finished he handed them over to his colleagues, who bound their hands behind their backs. De Choissy watched impassively, only calling out for a glass of brandy which he downed at a gulp. Desmorets turned to him.

'*Alors*, citoyen,' he said, and gestured to the stool.

De Choissy sat down and permitted his cravat to be wrenched from his throat. The scissors felt cold and hard against the nape of his neck and for a single instant the fear rose, almost choking him. As he strove to master it, his hair fell with a soft thud to the ground, leaving him curiously light-headed and free. With every further snap of the scissors another layer seemed to peel away from the wrapping that enclosed his wayward and complicated heart and, for the first time in his indulged life, de Choissy felt liberated. It pleased him that he had won his last battle over his flesh – something he had never managed in his life. De Choissy smiled to himself, a smile so quixotic that a fellow prisoner checked the words of encouragement that hovered on his lips and turned away.

The two priests sanctioned by the authorities waited by the prisoners to offer their services. De Choissy ignored them. They were priests who had taken the constitutional oath and he wished to have none of them, but some of the men, needing words of comfort, knelt for their blessing. De Choissy allowed his hands to be tied behind his back and joined the group which stood waiting to file outside.

It was very dark in the room set aside for the women, and the smell of excrement that emanated from the *griaches* in the corner almost overwhelming. The pale faces of the women swam up at each other in the gloom, each one expressing a different nuance of emotion – from fear that stifled all else, to bitter sorrow, regret, and a desperate clinging to every second that remained.

'My children,' wept one. 'They are so young.'

'I must pay my debts,' Athenée de Thierry told the gaoler. 'Can I ask you to accept responsibility?'

'May I have paper?' asked Héloïse. 'I must write a letter.'

Fortunately the gaolers were not entirely without pity and they granted Héloïse's request. And as Marie-Victoire sat on the stool and submitted herself to the rough ministrations of the executioner's assistant, Héloïse balanced a piece of paper on her knees and wrote.

My Sophie,

Soon it will be all over. I want you to know that I die free from Fear or Hatred. De C. will be with me, but I carry L. in my Heart. I go proudly, my regret only for my Dearest of Friends and Cousins. Remember me sometimes, without Sadness, and know that you came to mean more to me than anyone else. It will be your Face with Louis' that I carry on the Ride that awaits.

I owe Three Livres to the gardener at Neuilly and certain other Sums to the servants of the House. I charge you to see to these, on their Discharge my Honour rests. I know You will not Fail me. I will ask for this to be sent to England.

Your Friend and Cousin, Héloïse
September 27th, 1793

Her next letter was for Louis. It was infinitely harder and more painful to write.

Mon cher ami

I die Loving you more than Life. You are the one who gave it Meaning and Reason. For that I Thank You. De C. will be with me, but I shall watch for you until the very last Second. If you receive this Letter, keep it for me. I shall enclose

with this a Lock of my Hair, and I shall ask for Them to be
sent to Neuilly. My debts will be attended to by Sophie.

Louis, my hand trembles a little, but it is not entirely Fear.
It is so Dark and Close in here and there is so much Sorrow,
but rest assured I shall be True to us when the Time comes. It
approaches. I understand pain, and I know this instrument is
swift, and Death is ever present, so why should mine be
difficult?

Nevertheless, my Beloved, it hurts to say Goodbye. And I
must. Live Long and Happily. My tenderest Feelings and
Passion have been given only to you. I am sorry our Child
died.

Your Héloïse
September 27th, 1793

Héloïse folded the papers and tucked them into her bosom. She
raised her hands and slowly removed the combs from her hair
which tumbled down over her shoulders. Marie-Victoire rose
from the stool. They had made her dress in the red shirt of the
parricide and her face, shorn of its curls, was suddenly elfin but
for the violet shadows under her eyes. She touched Héloïse'
hair.

'Madame's beautiful hair,' she said wistfully.

Héloïse's face contracted. 'I am sorry, Marie-Victoire,' she
replied. 'It is I who have brought you to this. If only I had not
taken you to Paris.'

Marie-Victoire understood what Héloïse was trying to say. She
bent and touched her fingers to Héloïse's mouth.

'Please,' she said. 'There is no need. I am glad to die, for I
have nothing and I feel so tired.'

'The three of us, you, Sophie and I, have made our journey,'
said Héloïse wonderingly, 'and now it is the end.'

The assistant grasped her hair and twisted it down her back.
The scissors clicked and snapped, sawing at the thick rope and
pulling unmercifully at her scalp. Released from its customary
weight, her head fell forward on to her breast and it took her a
moment to raise it again, so unfamiliar was the sensation.

She stooped to the floor and, gathering up a fistful of her hair,
held it for a moment before extracting some strands. The assistant
snatched the hair back and tossed it into an overflowing canvas-
lined basket where it lay in a pile of gold, white and brown locks.
Héloïse took the letters from her breast and sealed her hair into
the one for Louis. Then she turned to the assistant.

'Monsieur, if I pay you, will you see that these are delivered?'

The assistant had heard this request many times before, and

e had grown used to the extra source of income. Without a
ord he proffered his hand, grabbed at Héloïse's last louis and
ocketed the letters and the money. It cost Héloïse her greatest
ang so far to see them disappear. She held out her hands to be
ed.

'It is on your honour, monsieur,' she said, 'to see that they are
elivered.'

The assistant nodded indifferently and continued with his
ork, without replying.

The odours of the little room grew stronger and the scent of
ar sharper. The walls seemed to bear down on its victims,
enying them even a glimpse of the life-giving light. But some-
ow a laugh rang out. It was Athenée de Thierry. She came over
Héloïse.

'I am sorry I did not know you better,' she said. 'But perhaps
e will share the same cart. I had expected a little more for my
neral, but one must be philosophical.'

She laughed again, and to her surprise Héloïse found herself
ining in. It pleased her to do so – a small gesture in the face of
eath.

The guardsmen had arrived to check over the names. They
ok some time because the lists contained errors, but at last they
ere ready.

'Forward,' shouted their sergeant, and the women began to file
ut of the room, through the *guichet* and out into the courtyard.

A storm of cat-calls, jeers and whistles greeted them where
ey stood, blinded by the clear afternoon light, and the rotten
egetables that rained down from the *tricoteuses* above burst with
latters on to the ground. Marie-Victoire had the impression of
monstrous confusion of colour and light, of noise and turmoil,
d she turned giddy from the suddenness of it. Her stomach
ntracted, for she had seen the waiting carts.

'The *griache*,' she murmured to the guard.

'Help her,' begged Héloïse beside her, and the guard,
rompted by some humane impulse, untied Marie-Victoire's
ands and led her to the wall. Héloïse stood over her, shielding
er from the stares of the crowd, as Marie-Victoire made use of
e bucket.

'Thank you,' she said. 'I will be all right now.'

The women were helped into the tumbrils and made to stand
ith their backs to the horses. Héloïse and Marie-Victoire
epped in turn on to the uneven planks and stood pressed
gether.

De Choissy was the first to appear of the men. He walked
uickly towards the cart and climbed in beside the two women.

395

Héloïse regarded him in some surprise, for his shorn head gav
him a very different appearance, throwing his features into
cast that she did not recognise. He was still handsome in h
way, superbly so, but younger-looking, and the dissipated lin
that customarily marred his face had smoothed away. He looke
down at his wife.

'I would hold your hand, Héloïse, if I could. Just as I wou
hold your heart if I could.'

Her raw and heightened emotions did nothing to help h
when she raised her face to meet his gaze. But for the first tim
there was an understanding between them, and she did not loo
away.

'Is your lover here?'

'Somewhere. I know it,' she replied. There was no longer an
need for deceit.

'Well, then, so be it. But he cannot share this with you. I sh
do that. It is how I predicted. You shall not, nor can you, den
me that.'

'No, I shall not,' Héloïse replied quietly. 'I owe it to yo
Hervé, for all that is past. We did not deal very well together
life, but perhaps we shall in death.'

He smiled at her words and appeared to be satisfied.

'Well, then, *ma femme*, we shall show the *canaille* how
die.'

De Choissy said no more. The carts were now full and t
order was given to move. The whips cracked over the horse
backs, and with a growling shriek the rough wooden whee
of the tumbrils ground over the stones. Héloïse fell back agai
the rail and strove to stay upright, her eyes searching the sea
faces. The carts paused at the gates while the guards endea
oured to manoeuvre outside. But it was impossible. For fifte
minutes they hung suspended between movement and stillnes
and the baying of the crowd ebbed and flowed like a sea in th
ears. The faces came and went – angry, menacing, awe-struc
dirty, red, disease-ridden, young and old. A panorama of h
manity, roaring for death.

He was there! She could see him to her left.

'Héloïse,' he cried, to the figure dressed in her white dres
'Héloïse,' he said, to the fragile, flawless head and swan ne
now exposed to every onlooker.

Louis forced his way through the packed bodies and reach
out a hand towards her. But he was too far away.

'At the corner of the Rue de la Monnaie,' he shouted. 'A
promised.'

'A letter, to Neuilly. Send for it there,' she cried back an

396

ith a jerk, the cart rolled forward out of the gates and turned
the left.

Louis waited to see which route they would take. The first cart
lled towards the Pont au Change, so he sprinted towards the
nt Neuf, over the bridge and down a small street that ran
arallel with the Rue de la Monnaie, emerging at the corner
at turned left into the Rue St Honoré. Once there, he stood
atching, and his eyes lit on the figure of the priest, who was
aiting patiently by a stone set into the street. They acknowl-
ged one another with a nod and Louis went to stand behind
m.

Are you there, Pierre? asked Marie-Victoire to herself, gazing
ghtlessly over the faces, her face lifted to the sky. It is strange,
at I really don't mind this at all because I know I am coming to
in you. Perhaps, after all, God is merciful and he will grant me
me time with you and our daughter. I have one more thing to
ce, Pierre, so be patient.

The slanting sun kissed Marie-Victoire's face through the heat
d rankness. She sensed the fresh, wild scents at La Joyeuse
d saw again the calm green of the fields that enfolded the
use. There was the orchard, the splashes of field flowers and
e magic of a summer evening deepening into dusk.

'These I knew and understood,' said her heart, 'and they were
ue, just as my feelings for you, Pierre, and my child are deep
d true.'

Héloïse pressed up against her, cold even in the warm after-
on, and very pale, like the other faces in the cart.

To die like this is not so very terrible, Héloïse thought. I am
ved. I have loved. I reached reconciliation with the man I
ought I hated and he travels with me in strange partnership.
ave tasted of life. She moved back to avoid being jolted by the
oman in front of her. I have been muddled and wrong, but
mehow it does not matter, just as all of this noise and hatred
es not matter. I feel only pity for them, because they do
t understand what they are doing. She felt the shape of de
hoissy's body against hers. But I shall be free, she thought
ain. I love you, Louis, and to love you brings me so much
ppiness that I can hardly bear it. Into her face crept a soft flush
hich stained the high cheekbones so that her face glowed with
beauty that many remarked on.

In the Rue de la Monnaie a horseguard joined the procession
d tried to clear a path, but the tumbrils' progress was still
tifully slow. One of the women was close to fainting, but
r companions laughed and joked with admirable composure,
nong them Athenée de Thierry. A small boy ran alongside the

397

leading cart, beating a drum in a parody of a soldier's march. Rattle, boom, went his drumsticks, rattle, boom.

Héloïse felt the unaccustomed air ruffle the shorn hair on the nape of her neck.

'Patience, *ma femme*,' said de Choissy, but the sweat stood out on his forehead.

Héloïse pulled her thoughts back from Louis and glanced at her husband.

'Are you frightened?' she asked.

De Choissy swallowed. 'Of dying, a little,' he said, the confession costing some pride.

'It will be over soon,' she said, offering the only comfort possible.

De Choissy laughed harshly, but his eyes told her he appreciated her effort, and they remained fixed on her as if drawing solace from her face.

At the corner of the Rue de la Monnaie, the carts prepared to turn into the Rue St Honoré. Héloïse looked around her; there was so little time. Was he? Yes, he was there, and she understood at once the significance of the man standing beside him.

'Marie-Victoire, look up,' she said very softly. 'He has brought the priest.'

The two of them watched as the little man raised his hand in a silent gesture of benediction, and they bowed their heads.

'I am free now, madame,' Marie-Victoire said, 'I can die shriven.'

Héloïse felt a peace steal over her, flowing gently through her veins and stilling the pumping of her heart.

'*Merci, mon père*,' she whispered to herself, and then looked in the other direction. She was afraid her gaze might expose the brave little priest. The curé lowered his arm, wrapped his cloak around him, and melted away.

Louis began running once more towards the Tuileries Gardens and the guillotine, where he forced his way through the rows of spectators who were ensconced on the terraces situated at the end of the gardens overlooking the Place de la Révolution, and headed for the area to the south of the scaffold.

The carts went on. Here the crowd, drawn from the nearby market, were free with their insults. Héloïse noticed a wrought iron balcony on a fine Louis Quatorze house and pointed it out to de Choissy. A little later the procession ground again to a halt by the Arbre Sec fountain and yet again by the Oratory. The tall ancient houses in the narrow street seemed to enclose the prisoners, denying them even the pleasure of the open sky.

he crowd had massed in rows on the steps of the Church of St
oche, and as they passed a woman held up a fair-haired baby.
larie-Victoire's heart contracted with pain. She determined to
ok no more.

In the third cart a prisoner began to sing. He was young and
andsome, and his rich tenor voice floated effortlessly above the
aring noise.

Pour nous quel triomphe éclatant
Martyrs de la liberté saintée
L'immortalité nous attend . . .

e sang, and there was something in the words full of courage
nd regret that shamed the onlookers into silence and wrenched
t the hearts of the prisoners who listened. The tears flowed on
any of their faces now, even the strongest, and ran unchecked
own their cheeks. Héloïse met de Choissy's eyes, and into hers
orang forgiveness, pity and farewell.

An hour had passed since they had left the Conciergerie. The
umbrils turned left and lumbered down the Rue Royale and the
un, lower now in the sky, flooded the open space that lay in
ont and etched the outline of the waiting guillotine into sharp
elief. A sigh greeted the sight and one of the women cried out.
he rail bit once more into Héloïse's bruised arms and she
ruggled to remain upright. At last, the carts drew up in front
f the scaffold and a shout went up from the watchers.

'A good batch.'

'Look at the women.'

'To your work, Sansfarin.'

There was no time any more to think. The assistants worked
uickly and efficiently, lining up the pale and shivering prisoners
ith their backs to the guillotine. Marie-Victoire stood quiet and
osorbed, driven deep into herself. De Choissy was placed next
her. Beside him, Héloïse searched for the face that she wanted
see. Louis made one last gigantic effort and reached the front
ows behind a gaggle of women who had come to eat, gossip
nd knit. He dared not push past them and risk these last
oments. Drawn like a magnet to her white dress, he locked his
aze with hers.

Remember, said her eyes. You were the only one I loved. You
ave my life meaning and shape. You have given me courage,
o, for I die loving you.

Go in peace, his answered. I shall live with the memory and
othing shall take it away or spoil it. It will be with me always.

De Choissy saw their interchange and understood. Making a
upreme gesture, he turned his head away to allow her the

privacy of that look, and in doing so gave Héloïse the gift of unselfish love which he had so unaccountably denied her in life.

It was beginning. The crowd swayed and muttered its excitement. Sanson consulted his list for the last time. The assistant helped the first victim up the wooden steps. Thud. The sound of a body thrown on to the platform. Thud. The sound of the neckpiece being swung into place. Thud. The sound of the huge knife swishing down. The crowd moaned. The assistant threw the head and body into the waiting basket and a second victim was led towards the steps.

Marie-Victoire stirred.

'*Adieu*,' she said, and smiled at Héloïse so sweetly and confidently that Héloïse could not prevent her tears.

'Goodbye, Marie-Victoire,' she whispered.

They came for Marie-Victoire next. Cold hands helped her up and steadied her on the dizzily high platform. Already the floor was slippery with blood. Someone took her by the right hand, another by the left and threw Marie-Victoire down. The wooden neck piece clanged over her, shutting her out from the world.

'Pierre,' she cried. 'It is over.'

The knife came down with a crash. The blood ran in pulsing streams on to the ground. Marie-Victoire was dead.

'We will meet soon,' said de Choissy, smiling his familiar smile, but this time something deeper was hidden in the curve of the lips. 'I won as I promised, but it is not entirely my victory, is it, *ma femme*?'

'*Adieu*,' Héloïse said for a second time. 'God go with you.'

'Can you not give me something more, my dear? I think I have need of it.'

'I can give you something of myself,' she said. 'Is that enough?'

'It is enough,' he said, and bent to kiss her on the forehead before he was taken away.

Louis remembered afterwards the look that de Choissy threw the crowd and the outline of his figure on the platform, framed against the houses lying to the north of the square. De Choissy remained motionless for a moment and shook off the hands that made to throw him down. He gazed back at his wife. Then he allowed himself to be taken, and died without a sound.

The crowd were inflamed by de Choissy's obvious contempt and they bayed like so many animals for more.

'Give her peace,' Louis prayed.

Héloïse's feet slid on the steps and she stumbled. An assistant helped her. Anguish tore through him when he saw how her poor pinioned hands shook, and the weary gesture with which she straightened her shoulders once she had gained the platform.

here are so many of them, Héloïse thought, the faces blurring
before her dazzled eyes. But, as if in answer to Louis' prayer,
the watchers nearest to her quietened, shamed into silence by
her youth and beauty.

In the seconds Héloïse had left, she saw rows of houses and
trees and the sky arching above. She felt the pain of her bound
hands and the air prickling at her neck. Her stomach lurched
with a terror that went as quickly as it came. A drum beat into
the silence. She took one last deep breath. Her arms were seized.
The wooden platform rose up to meet her and she smelt the
acrid odour of blood. She shut her eyes, and the memory of
Louis kissing her at Neuilly one wine-flushed night mingled
achingly with the scent of roses – and vanished as the knife
carved into the darkness that enfolded her for ever.

All afternoon the dull thuds of the guillotine at work echoed out
into the square, until at last it lay silent and the crowds went
away. The executioner removed the knife from the guillotine and
packed up his things. His assistants sluiced down the platform.
The carts containing the bodies lumbered their gore-stained way
to the cemetery up at the Madeleine, where they disgorged
their burden and the bodies were stripped and thrown into the
trenches. As luck would have it, the three who had been linked
in life were entwined in death. Marie-Victoire, Héloïse and de
Choissy lay sprawled together in the final embrace of the grave.

The shadows lengthened, throwing dark patches over the
silent square. A child appeared and skipped up to the scaffold
where he danced around it, humming a tuneless song. After a
while, he grew bored with his game and ran for home, his feet
leaving bright, red footprints wherever he trod. The smell of
blood lay over the city. In the evening the mist came, stealing
white and heavy up from the river, silently cloaking the shadowy
square. Tall, fearful and ugly, the guillotine loomed out of it,
spending its shadow over the land.

A figure got up from where he had been sitting on the terraces
of the Tuileries. He moved slowly, dragging his feet as though
the exhaustion had bitten deep into his bones. Louis turned once
to look again at the guillotine, and then he gestured in a hopeless,
defeated way, before melting into the shadows to be seen no
more.

AFTERWORD

Sophie and William Jones reached England after a storm-tosse
crossing when Sophie feared for the life of her babies. Th
Luttrells welcomed her warmly, though they never quite forgav
her for her defection to France and for marrying William.

Six months later, the Joneses left for America, leaving Ne
ruling High Mullions and the Luttrells in possession of the dowe
house. It took some time for Sophie to settle in her adopte
country and to recover from her experiences, but in the end sh
grew to love America and the life that she made there. Despit
William's encouragement, she never tried to write about th
Revolution, although she was the author of a popular boo
on practical housekeeping. William became a successful an
progressive farmer and Senator for Virginia and was a membe
of Jefferson's government which bought Louisiana fro
Napoleon in 1803. He and Sophie had six children in all an
their descendants may be found in Virginia today.

Louis d'Épinon left Paris the night of Héloïse's death and took
the country, where he lived rough for many months befor
rejoining a royalist force in Germany. He lived in exile throughou
the Napoleonic era and returned to France after the restoratio
of the Bourbon Louis XVIII. He retired to one of his family'
smaller estates where he lived quietly for the rest of his life. H
never married, and when he died a letter, brittle and yellow wit
age, containing a lock of dark hair, was found in a casket by hi
bed.

Adèle de Fleury escaped in a laundry basket to Brussels just befor
the Terror reached its height. Her husband was not so fortunat
and lost his head early in 1794. Adèle soon found cor
solation and married an immensely rich Belgian aristocrat. Sh
spent the rest of her life quarrelling with her embittered siste
who lived in extreme poverty in England, over the de Choiss

estates. Adèle's son, born of her second marriage, eventually succeeded to what remained.

The Marquise de Guinot died of a prison fever in the Abbaye not long after the marquis' murder.

Miss Edgeworth sailed to America with the Joneses, and after helping her ex-pupil to settle into her new life astonished everybody by marrying a rich widower. She lived, happy and respectable, into a ripe old age.

Sir Robert Brandon survived the Revolution and Napoleon's empire. When the French monarchy was restored in 1815 he was decorated by the king. He lived in Paris until he died.

Jeanne, Marie-Victoire's friend, died of syphilis at the age of thirty-five. Her body was flung into a pauper's grave.

Many of the figures who dominated the French Revolution met violent ends. Both *Marie-Antoinette* and *Danton* were guillotined. Most of the Girondins were hunted down and brought to the scaffold, and on July 28th, 1794, *Robespierre* and his fellow Jacobins met the same fate. By the time the Terror was over 3,000 executions had taken place in Paris and 14,000 in the provinces.

THE UNFORGETTABLE NOVELS
by
CELESTE DE BLASIS

*From the superstition-bound peasant villages
to the perfumed decadence of the mysterious
Forbidden City, comes a tale in which two
people must seek within their hearts and find
themselves in the*

EMPIRE OF HEAVEN

Linda Ching Sledge has crafted in EMPIRE OF HEAVEN an incredible sweeping saga of nineteenth-century China and one of the most remarkable heroines of recent historical fiction. A tale of depth and emotion set against the unrest and turmoil of China during the Taiping Rebellion, it is the story of Rulan, daughter of a village spirit woman and a healer in her own right. Thrust by events beyond her control into the center of the rebellion, she is torn between her own desires to control her fate and those of the rebel leader Hung. A charismatic stranger who claims to be the younger brother of Jesus, Hung leads a band of rebels from villages across the countryside in a quest for freedom. He has promised to free the oppressed and raise on Earth an Empire of Heaven. But nearly as strong as his wish for liberation is his obsession with Rulan, an obsession that endangers both them and the entire revolution.

From the tiny villages where life is a futile struggle bogged in the morass of gambling and opium addiction to the society of the Golden Orchids, a group of women who shelter Rulan and battle ferociously to protect their way of life, EMPIRE OF HEAVEN is rich in historical detail and the product of years of research. A grand tale of love, it is the triumphant odyssey of a woman who is transformed by destiny into the symbol of revolution, and of a mysterious and endlessly fascinating land.

**On sale in hardcover in March,
wherever Bantam Books are sold.**

THE LATEST IN BOOKS
AND AUDIO CASSETTES

Paperbacks

- ☐ 27032 **FIRST BORN** Doris Mortman $4.95
- ☐ 27283 **BRAZEN VIRTUE** Nora Roberts $3.95
- ☐ 25891 **THE TWO MRS. GRENVILLES**
  Dominick Dunne $4.95
- ☐ 27891 **PEOPLE LIKE US** Dominick Dunne $4.95
- ☐ 27260 **WILD SWAN** Celeste De Blasis $4.95
- ☐ 25692 **SWAN'S CHANCE** Celeste De Blasis $4.50
- ☐ 26543 **ACT OF WILL**
  Barbara Taylor Bradford $5.95
- ☐ 27790 **A WOMAN OF SUBSTANCE**
  Barbara Taylor Bradford $5.95

Audio

- ☐ **THE SHELL SEEKERS** by Rosamunde Pilcher
  Performance by Lynn Redgrave
  180 Mins. Double Cassette 48183-9 $14.95
- ☐ **COLD SASSY TREE** by Olive Ann Burns
  Performance by Richard Thomas
  180 Mins. Double Cassette 45166-9 $14.95
- ☐ **PEOPLE LIKE US** by Dominick Dunne
  Performance by Len Cariou
  180 Mins. Double Cassette 45164-2 $14.95
- ☐ **CAT'S EYE** by Margaret Atwood
  Performance by Kate Nelligan
  180 Mins. Double Cassette 45203-7 $14.95

Bantam Books, Dept. FBS, 414 East Golf Road, Des Plaines, IL 60016

Please send me the items I have checked above. I am enclosing $_____
(please add $2.00 to cover postage and handling). Send check or money
order, no cash or C.O.D.s please. (Tape offer good in USA only.)

Mr/Ms _____

Address _____

City/State _____ Zip_____

FBS-4/90

Please allow four to six weeks for delivery.
Prices and availability subject to change without notice.